Rebel Dragon

Aloha Shifters: Pearls of Desire

Book 1

by Anna Lowe

Twin Moon Press

Contents

Other books in this series

Aloha Shifters - Pearls of Desire

Rebel Dragon (Book 1)

Rebel Bear (Book 2)

Rebel Lion (Book 3)

Rebel Wolf (Book 4)

Rebel Alpha (Book 5)

visit www.annalowebooks.com

Chapter One

Jenna's fingers were shaking so hard, it took her three tries to buckle her seat belt. Then she peered out the airplane window, watching the last streaks of sunset paint the sky the color of blood. A red light flashed at the next gate, dragging her gaze to the right. Beyond it, shadows danced over unlit areas of the terminal, and she squinted at every one.

On instinct, she reached down as if to scratch her ankle, then stopped. Shit. The knife wasn't there. Of course, it wouldn't be. She'd had to pack it in her luggage for the flight.

She took three deep breaths and glanced around the plane, counting rows to the next exit. Then she watched baggage handlers thump the last suitcases onto the cargo belt. Which was fine, right? The likelihood of her needing that knife in the next six hours was close to zero — or so she hoped.

You'll probably never need it, her sister Jody had said when she'd handed over that frighteningly sharp blade. *It's just in case. You know how it is.*

Jenna fidgeted with the bangles on her wrist. Up to a few weeks ago, the *you know* part would have made her draw a blank. Like most people, she'd grown up believing vampires and other supernatural creatures were only legends. Her sister Jody had too. But after Jody's fateful trip to Maui, everything changed.

You need to be careful. The monsters who attacked me might come after you, Jody had said when she'd last visited California. She'd taken Jenna over to a quiet corner of Old Town Park and explained.

Werewolves. . . tigers. . . vampires. . .

1

Apparently, those weren't just a bunch of harmless legends. They were real — and any one of them might come after Jenna for a taste of her blood.

Jenna shivered and hugged herself.

Yes, there really are vampires, her sister had said in a hushed and scratchy voice. *And other evil creatures. You need to keep your eyes open, okay? Not that I'm aware of a specific threat. It will probably be all right.*

At first, Jenna had thought it was all an elaborate joke, but the fear in her sister's eyes was real, and it had jumped over to her. Especially when the stalking began.

It started with one text — then another and another.

Dear Jenna. I know we are meant for each other. I am your destiny, and you are mine.

The mystery texter would ask her to meet, and he'd follow up afterward, sounding hurt that she hadn't come. At first, she'd ignored the messages, but the tone had gone from relatively harmless to dark and threatening.

My dearest Jenna. We're meant for each other. Don't you see, my pet?

She held her head in her hands, desperately wishing she could go back to her old life. Helping her dad at home and in his shop, surfing or beachcombing in her free time, and generally putting off the serious stuff in life. And why the heck not? She'd felt a decade older than her true age for a long time now, so she'd given herself license to live a simple, carefree life for a while.

But here she was, jumping at shadows, suspicious of everyone.

The texts were followed by little gifts and trinkets. Flowers delivered with unsigned notes. Seashells with little hearts scratched into them left on her locker near the beach. An antique music box — all of which meant the stalker knew where she lived, where she worked, and where she surfed.

Did you like my gift? I thought you would.

No, she didn't. Not one bit.

She sat back, forcing herself to take a deep breath. There was no reason to be paranoid. Everything was going according to plan. She'd taken a circuitous route to the airport, and only her closest family members knew where she was headed. Now that she was on her way to Maui, she could finally relax.

Or try to, at least.

She kept perfectly still, tuning into the hairs on the back of her neck. They weren't registering the slightest hint of *I'm being watched* — not the way they often had over the past few weeks, so that was promising. She'd never seen her stalker — well, not that she knew of — and frankly, she never wanted to. She just wanted him gone. Forever. She wanted her freedom back, her innocence. The ability to wake up and enjoy a day without the feeling of impending doom hanging over her head.

Except she couldn't, not with the specter of some creep sneaking up on her from behind and—

She cut the thought off and fidgeted with her bangles — a gift from her mother, who'd died a long time ago. So long that Jenna had more memories of memories than direct recollections of her mom. But deep in her heart, she held on to the lessons her mother had taught her and her dad had reinforced. Life was for living. Enjoying. Making the most of each and every day.

So, no, damn it. She wasn't going to let her imagination run away from her. Especially not when she was traveling to beautiful Maui, where she'd be able to talk to her sister and figure things out. Not only that, but she would make the most of an incredible opportunity to apprentice with a master surfboard shaper for a few weeks.

A phone pinged — not hers, but with a tone just like hers — and her eyes snapped open again.

"Welcome aboard," the flight attendant said as each new passenger filed by. "Welcome aboard."

Jenna scrutinized each and every one. Even if they appeared normal, you never knew. Her eyes darted from the near to the far aisle, checking every man against a mental lineup of shadowy faces provided by her imagination. There was a tall, pale guy who looked a hell of a lot like a vampire — up until the moment the woman behind him handed him a baby and rooted around in a diaper bag. Okay, so maybe he wasn't a vampire, just a really overworked dad. But what about that fiftysomething woman with long, unkempt hair who scowled as she shuffled down the aisle? Was she a witch, maybe? According to Jody, there were all kinds of supernatural beings living secretly among humans.

Jenna closed her eyes. She would drive herself crazy if she kept this up. Any minute now, a perfectly normal human would take the seat next to her, and the worst that would happen would be a conversation that dragged on for too long.

Still, her heart beat faster as witch lady approached. But the woman passed without so much as blinking in Jenna's direction. An older woman in a flowery Hawaiian dress moved past next, flowing more than walking, almost like the fairy godmother Jenna had always wished for. Then came a scary-looking bald guy in a rumpled suit and a too-wide tie, and Jenna's nails dug into the armrest. Was he a vampire?

She inhaled and wrinkled her nose at his body odor. That meant she could strike him off the lists of suspects. According to her sister, vampires had no smell. So as long as Tie Guy didn't sit next to her, she was okay.

"Twenty-six D, right over there," the flight attendant said, making Jenna gulp. A moment of truth, because that was the seat next to hers. But she couldn't see past the next couple in the aisle — a happy twosome who looked like they'd come straight from a wedding chapel. It was only when the groom turned his head to kiss the giggling bride that the view behind them finally opened, and Jenna's mouth cracked open at the sight of the next man in line.

Not the man of her nightmares. More like the man of her dreams.

He had dark, piercing eyes — an intense green with a hint of brown. Below them were thickly muscled shoulders and a chest a mile wide, construction-worker style. His gray T-shirt couldn't quite contain his bulging biceps, and his jeans were just snug enough to show off a tapered waist.

Jenna's eyes went wide. Even a woman on the run from supernatural beings could stop to admire a good-looking man, right?

4

His short brown hair was spiky and a little mussed, but he didn't seem to give a damn. Another passenger stood for a last stretch — a big islander — then hastily sidestepped at a single, expressionless look from that man. Then he strode right up to her row, checking his boarding pass, and even that little motion made his chiseled forearms bulge.

"Hi," he murmured, towering over her.

"Hi," she said, playing it cool.

He put his khaki-colored duffel bag in the overhead compartment and closed it with a decisive thump, then sat down beside her with a faint jingle of the dog tags around his neck. Jenna inhaled a lungful of his scent. It was pure, airy, and fresh, like he'd spent the past hour flying an open biplane and had only now switched over to a regular commercial flight.

No way was he a vampire. But, damn. For all she knew, the flight attendant was a witch and the pilot a warlock. Now that a terrifying new world had been revealed to her, she didn't know who to trust or what to believe.

Except every vibe in her body told her this man was honorable, through and through.

I'm Jenna, she wanted to say. *Nice to meet you.*

Her pulse quickened. Maybe he was one of those air marshals placed randomly on flights. That would explain his size, his black belt aura, and his vigilant eyes. And that meant she could relax, right? Or at least try to, because the second he slid into the seat next to her, her pulse skipped.

Definitely not the stalker type. If that man wanted a woman, he'd come straight to the point and ask her out.

So she was strangely deflated when, ten minutes later, he hadn't uttered so much as a word. Up to that moment, she'd been hoping for a not-too-talkative human to sit beside, but she started wishing for the opposite. Who was he? Was he working or vacationing in Maui? How long was he going to stay?

Get his number, a giggly inner voice told her. *You know, just in case.*

Yeah, just in case her vampire stalker showed up? Jenna kept her mouth shut and spied on him from the corner of her eye. No book, no music player. Not even a phone. Nothing to keep him busy on the six-hour flight. His lips were pulled in a firm, straight line, his hands quiet on his thighs. He hardly moved, but she had the distinct sense of some slumbering giant inside.

And the good news? Anyone who wanted to get to her had to get past G.I. McStud first.

Ha. She'd like to see her cowardly text stalker try that.

But that was the problem. Her stalker wasn't man enough to approach her in the open. He'd sneak up when she least suspected and—

A shiver went through her, and she went back to gripping the armrest hard enough for her fingers to turn white.

"You okay?" her neighbor rumbled in a deep, resonant voice.

She looked left, meeting his hazel eyes. The mottled greenish-brown formed twin pools that seemed to connect to a soul with fathomless depths. An impenetrable soul, too, one that had seen much more than a guy in his early thirties ought to have seen.

She slapped on a chipper smile. "I'm fine, thanks."

"It'll be all right, you know." He nodded to where her hands were twisting her seat belt. "I'm sure we'll have a smooth flight."

She laughed. He thought she was scared of flying? How cute.

If only she could say, *I'm terrified of the stalker who's turned my life into a nightmare for the past few weeks. A stalker who might be a vampire. Any way you could help me with that?*

"I'm sure we will," she said, releasing her death grip on the armrest.

His eyes dipped, catching that detail, and she wondered what else he noticed. The nibbled fingernails? The shadows under her eyes? Or did he stick to the superficial like most guys did — her blond hair, blue eyes, deep tan.

The phone of another passenger pinged, and when her head jerked up, Good Guy looked up too. His eyes scanned the width of the plane — really scanned it the way Secret Service guys did on TV — then landed back on Jenna. She could feel the weight of them on her, sense the unspoken question.

No, I'm not terrified of anything right now, she'd say innocently. *Why do you ask?*

God, he'd think she was a total pushover — not a girl who paddled into the teeth of the gnarliest waves, claiming her spot alongside the most accomplished guys, nor the girl who'd given the star quarterback the shiner of his life when he'd tried to grab her ass in her junior year of high school. She was a woman who could hold her own against any man, damn it.

Well, any man brave enough to actually face her, at least. A cowardly stalker, on the other hand...

"Boarding completed. Doors to automatic and cross-check," the captain announced.

She swallowed away the *Thank God* on the tip of her tongue and smiled at her neighbor. "Sorry. I'm fine. Really. Just a little preoccupied with something at home. Good time for a trip, huh?" She tried joking it off.

"Good time for a trip," he echoed, studying her face.

Any normal person would have smiled, opened a book, or commented on the weather. But Jenna found herself speechless, motionless, and staring into those bottomless eyes. Wondering why it felt like a momentous occasion and not just another passing encounter. For every second she stared, the man's eyes shone brighter, like he'd stumbled across something he'd never seen before.

Then he jolted a little and swung his jaw from side to side as if holding a private conversation with himself. When he turned back to her a moment later, she half expected a probing, insightful question or some deep truth. His mouth opened and closed a few times before he finally spoke.

"First time to Maui?"

She blinked and shook her head a little. So much for deep truths.

"Second time. My sister lives there."

Her sister, who'd gone to Maui, met the man of her dreams, and settled down, talking about love and destiny and forever. Jenna's chest rose and fell with a sigh.

Of course, her new neighbor wouldn't have much interest in that. Guys like him knew about sweat and clocking in on the job — and possibly killing people with his bare hands — but not about mushy things like love.

"How about you? First time to Maui?" she asked.

"Yeah. First time."

She looked him over, searching for a clue of some kind. He didn't seem like the type to lie around on the beach or to hit the waves. Was he visiting a relative? Embarking on a top secret underwater salvage operation?

"Work or pleasure?" she asked. And damn it, her voice went up on *pleasure*, implying all kinds of intimate things.

The right side of his chin twitched — a chin covered with the kind of light stubble a girl could drag her cheek across a few times — and his eyes shone with a suppressed smile. "Work."

Which was a good thing, because hearing that deep, gravelly voice utter a word like *pleasure* would probably make every woman in a ten-row radius orgasm.

"New job," he added.

Just enough of her old, unfettered self snuck back in to make her hazard a guess. "Fireman? Lifeguard? Construction?"

He smiled, and she checked his teeth as he weighed up his answer. No pointy fangs, which was a plus. Her eyes wandered to the swirling edge of a tattoo barely poking out from under his short sleeve.

Nice tattoo, she burned to say. *Is it a dragon?*

She imagined him flashing a huge, perfect smile and pulling the sleeve up to show it off. Then she would turn to show him the leaping dolphin tattooed on the small of her back, and before long, they'd be chatting like old friends. Maybe even trading phone numbers, arranging to meet up someplace.

But then she remembered her stalker and went stiff all over. She wasn't giving her number to anyone. Not even this man.

The plane lurched away from the gate, getting ready to taxi down the runway. The man's eyes flicked to the window, and a ripple of foreboding traveled through him, as if he, too, had just remembered the importance of protecting some deep, dark secret he could never reveal.

"Security," he said in a clipped, no-bullshit tone that made it clear he wasn't going to volunteer much more.

"Security, huh?"

He nodded curtly then rolled his neck absently as if limbering up for a fight.

"Nice," she murmured.

And damn — it *was* nice just having him there, shrinking her world down to a protected, manageable space.

Within minutes, the engines were straining, the plane rattling, and gravity pressing Jenna into her seat. The plane took off, rose sharply, and banked in a big curve over the Pacific. A totally normal takeoff, but somehow, Good Guy didn't seem impressed.

"Do you know much about flying?" she asked.

His nostrils flared as if he were the one watching out for a vampire. But then he cracked into a grin, amused. "Yeah. I do."

His tone had a note of finality to it, and he looked away. Okay, so he didn't want to talk. So she gave up on conversation and looked down at the lights of LA. Somewhere down there was her stalker. And, ha — she was getting away! But the elation was followed by a riptide of exhaustion, and she blinked as the stress of the past weeks slowly steamrolled over her eyelids. She rested her head against the wall. Maybe her neighbor wasn't going to provide sparkling conversation for the next six hours. But as long as he was there, protecting her like a castle boxing in the king on a chessboard, she might as well get some sleep.

Just as she was bundling her sweatshirt into a makeshift pillow, though, a hand appeared beside her head, and she nearly jumped out of her skin.

"Sorry," the man in the seat behind her murmured, releasing her seat once he turned on his overhead light.

Jenna tried to slow her speeding pulse by taking a couple of deep breaths and closing her eyes. When she opened them again, Good Guy was studying her.

"Did you say something was bothering you — or someone?" His voice was a low rumble, his eyes fierce.

She froze, not sure what to say. Could she even come out with it? *Yes. I'm afraid I have a stalker, and he might be a vampire.*

"Maybe I can help," he said, very quietly.

He put his left hand on the seat in front of him, blocking off any dangers that lurked in the aisle or beyond. That revealed another tattoo on the inside of his forearm — a sword crossed by lightning strikes.

Special Forces. A friend of Jenna's had once crushed on a soldier, going on and on about every little detail of the man and those elite fighting corps.

Her heart thumped with new hope, and *yes, please* jumped to the tip of her tongue. But she bit her lip before the words slipped out, because the answer had to be no. She already had help — or rather, she would as soon as she got to Maui.

"Thanks," she said, shaking her head. "I think I have it under control."

His eyebrows went up a little, catching her lie.

"Well, if you change your mind, you let me know." After another long minute of studying her, he nodded slowly and extended a hand. "I'm Connor."

The moment her hand slipped into his, her whole body tingled, right down to her toes.

"Jenna," she said a little breathlessly.

It was a good thing her sister wasn't there to tease her about going all dreamy-eyed over a man, and Jenna couldn't understand it herself. No one had ever affected her that way.

Her pulse skipped in a burst of anxiety. What if no one ever did again?

"Jenna," he whispered, trying her name out like the first notes of a song.

She didn't realize they were still holding hands until the plane shook with a little turbulence, making her grip her armrest. The second she did, something in her wept. Why couldn't she have gone on holding his hand?

"So. Jenna," Good Guy said in a low, secret voice that vowed never to expose her fears to anyone. "It's a long flight. Too bad I'm not tired. But you could get a little shut-eye."

Jenna smiled. Connor was definitely a nice guy, subtly promising to watch out for her. Not assuming or posturing, just suggesting. She bit her lip. How often did a guy like that come along?

"That would be nice. Thank you," she whispered, hoping her tone said more than those overused words did.

"Sure."

He looked down the way men uncomfortable with praise did, and her heart thumped a little harder.

His words — and body language — didn't leave much room for a response, so she closed her eyes and leaned against the window. Even if she couldn't actually sleep, she could rest a little. Sleep had been tricky to find lately, and when it came, it brought dark, twisted nightmares.

But when she inhaled deeply, catching Connor's scent, her mind went blissfully blank. Her shoulders slowly unwound, and instead of anticipating nightmares, she imagined guardian angels fluttering down around her. Angels with fluffy white wings sent by her mother to assure her a good night's sleep.

Everything will be okay, the angels sang, lulling her to sleep. *Everything will be all right.*

The airplane's engines hummed, and the cabin was quiet. And instead of vampires, her mind filled with serene images of sea life. Turtles grazing on sea grass. Fish flitting around in silvery schools. Coral bursting with color and life. Her favorite dreamscape — one she'd had since she was a little kid.

And slowly, gradually, she drifted off into a blissfully peaceful sleep.

Chapter Two

Connor spent the entire flight testing the stale air of the cabin with his keen dragon nose, studying the passengers with cool, darting eyes. Otherwise, he kept perfectly still so as not to disturb the sleeping beauty at his side.

Someone had threatened her. Spooked her enough to flee LA. He could see it in her restless, haunted eyes. Incredible blue eyes — blue like the purest part of the sky. The part straight overhead he loved to fly toward on sunny fall days, climbing until the air grew too thin to support his wings.

But someone had pulled a cloud of anxiety over her, and he strained for any hint of who or what that might be.

How he sat so still for so long, he had no clue, because his dragon was raging inside.

Find him. Kill him. Whoever it is who scared her.

He balled his fists against his thighs. What the hell was it about this woman that had such an effect on him?

Her name is Jenna, his dragon grumbled.

The beast said her name like it was pure poetry. Like he'd missed her for years even though they'd never met before.

That doesn't matter, his dragon insisted. *Not if she's my mate.*

Connor chewed the word over a couple of times. Frankly, he was a little hazy on the whole destined mate thing. His father was a notorious womanizer who never bothered to stick around for any of the children he'd sired around the world. Connor had only ever heard his mother cursing the fact that she'd fallen for that no-good son of a bitch. And when she finally did settle down with a man, it was a lackluster relationship in which her primary source of happiness stemmed from not being alone rather than being with exactly that person.

So — a destined mate? Who was he to judge?

Trust me. I know, his dragon insisted.

That made him snort aloud. His dragon had gotten him into hot water more times than he could count. A harmless prank here, a hot-headed reaction there...

His dragon grinned. *That fireworks show we put on was worth it, man.*

Connor sighed. Duct-taping grenades to footballs and launching them in the air might not be the usual way to celebrate the Fourth of July, but hell, they had just been working with what they had in Iraq. They'd made sure to do it far from any civilians, and a whole company of weary soldiers had been entertained. And if he'd aimed a little dragon fire at the footballs to add some sparkle to the show — so what? No one had seen him do it, so no harm done, right?

Of course, that little stunt had nearly earned him disciplinary action and a permanent mark on his record.

He frowned at the memory. That was just one little prank. When he'd eventually filed for discharge — honorable, he hoped — his commanding officer had sighed and flipped through a thick file of incident reports first.

Failure to obey orders...

He'd rolled this eyes at that one. Like he would obey an order if it meant leaving a fellow soldier behind. He'd saved three guys that day — men everyone else had given up on.

Conduct prejudicial to good order and discipline...

Another bullshit rule. The lieutenant who'd filed that complaint didn't know his ass from a hole in the ground. He'd made a mess of assigning duties, so Connor had quietly reassigned them. Everyone was happy — except the lieutenant when he found out.

Delays in returning from field assignments...

Connor scowled. So he occasionally had to take off and let his dragon out. That wasn't a crime, and he'd made damn sure never to cross the line into Unauthorized Absence territory. Of course, he couldn't explain where he'd been. None of his commanding officers knew about shifters — except the few who were shifters too. And it was an unwritten rule of the shifter world to never, ever allow humans to discover their existence.

Connor huffed quietly. Written rules were hard enough to obey sometimes. Unwritten ones were damn nigh impossible to follow — but the one about keeping shifters secret, he knew.

The officer had wrapped up with a list of descriptors in his file. *Loose cannon... temperamental... impulsive. And that's from the men recommending you, son.*

The officer had finally handed over his discharge — honorable, no less — along with a stern look in the eye.

Make something of yourself, Hoving. And help your brothers do the same. They look up to you, you know.

Connor sucked in a long breath. His mother had uttered almost those exact words when he'd first left home. But, hey — he was doing his best. And with this new job, he might actually reach his long-term goal: proving himself in the shifter world. Rising to a position he deserved.

But what about Jenna? his dragon muttered.

He curled his hands into fists. No matter how much the woman called to him, he had to resist.

Cannot fuck this up. Cannot fuck this up.

He'd been offered a dream job — one that would bring in much-needed cash as well as helping him climb a rung or two in the dragon world.

Goddamn snobs, all of them, his dragon huffed.

He held his breath lest it escape as a whiff of sulfurous ash.

Sometimes, he wished he were a regular human. No hiding his second soul, no trying to follow unwritten rules. In the human world, he was a battle-hardened soldier returning from successive tours of duty in the world's most dangerous combat zones. A guy getting ready to transition to a new life. But in the dragon world, he was a rookie. A nobody without the benefit of a noble bloodline.

Well, he had his chance to make up for that now, and he couldn't allow anything to foil that new mission.

Not even her? His inner dragon lashed its tail so furiously, Connor kicked the seat in front of him.

Definitely not her, he shot back, because a sunny California girl was bound to lead him astray. Sure, she had a problem of some kind. And yes, he'd love to solve it for her. But now was not the time to get involved. He had to focus on his mission. It wasn't just his chance, it was a chance for his brothers too.

So he sat still as a statue across a stretch of ocean even the greatest dragon would be hard pressed to cross on his own, giving the mystery woman the only gift he could — six solid hours of rest. No one was going to bother her, not even the flight attendant. Sleeping Beauty looked like she needed every second of being blissfully checked out of her world. A couple of hours wasn't enough, but it was a start. Maybe it would help Jenna clear her mind and shake whatever worry had chased her onto the plane.

Every now and then, he glanced over and watched her sleep. Her facial muscles had finally relaxed, and a faint smile played over her lips. Was she dreaming? Wishing? Yearning? Her chest rose and fell peacefully, and she tucked her hands up by her chin.

Then he'd yank his gaze away before his dragon got carried away with anything. Like imagining there might be space for him to fit into her embrace.

His joints grew stiff and his back ached in the too-small space of the economy seat, until finally, the cabin lights flicked back on.

"Ladies and gentlemen, we are preparing for our descent to Kahului. Please ensure you return your seat to an upright position..."

The announcement started the countdown to the end of his time with Sleeping Beauty, but it was almost worth it for the adorable way Jenna woke up. Her nose wiggled a little, and she blinked like a sleepy kitten — another image he banked away. Then she smiled, stretched, and—

He could see the exact second her troubles caught up with her again because she frowned, and the lines on her brow reappeared.

"All good?" he murmured, hoping that might help.

She smiled — a smile tinged with worry, but genuine all the same. "All good," she whispered, looking out the window into the inky night. "Wow. Are we already there?"

His heart swelled at the *we* even as he mourned the idea of *goodbye.*

She didn't say much while the plane landed or taxied, but when they finally had the chance to disembark, they both turned to each other.

"Connor," she started.

"Jenna," he said at the exact same time.

Then they both broke into grins that said so much more than *nice to have met you* or *have a good trip.* But Jenna did get one more word in when he finally dragged himself into the aisle and stood there, making space for her to exit first.

"Thanks."

One little word, a big smile, and a hint of regret. Yeah, he knew just how she felt.

"Take care," he managed, and when she slid past him, he inhaled one parting taste of her saltwater-and-sunshine scent.

After that, he kept his mouth shut and his eyes straight ahead. No use letting his dragon get tempted.

Already tempted, the inner beast grumbled.

Not going there, he ordered the beast.

The second they were outside, the humid scent of rainforest hit him, but that just seemed to complement the lingering goodness of Jenna's scent. Maui smelled of sweet tropical flowers and lush mountain valleys. Of surf, ginger, and a little bit of brine. Like someone had taken everything alluring about Jenna and amped it up a hundred times.

He stayed two steps behind her all the way to baggage claim and waited, taut as a spring. Watching everyone, noting the way Jenna's face darkened when she turned on her phone for new messages — and the way she brightened a moment later before turning it off. Apparently, no news was good news.

Another guy tried helping her haul her bag off the carousel — clearly out to impress a pretty girl, now that Connor had taken a few steps back. But Jenna took firm hold of her bag and swung it out of the man's grasp.

17

"No problem. I got it. But thanks," she said, rolling it away from that man.

Connor grinned — at the woman and at the bag. It was a big rolling duffle covered in a pink flower print, all cute and peppy. A lot like Jenna, especially now that whatever had bothered her was starting to ease up.

Then she looked back and gave him one last, hopeful smile. "Maybe we'll see each other around."

God, he hoped so, but it was probably better if they didn't. Something about her made his mind want to switch off and float around a dreamy place, and he couldn't afford that right now.

Still, he couldn't resist a grin. "Maybe we will."

She stood looking at him for a few seconds as if she might add more, then finally blinked a little and stepped away. "Bye."

"Bye," he whispered, watching her go.

Meeting a woman had never felt so much like a revelation, and saying goodbye had never felt so wrong.

Stay with her. Follow her. Protect her, his inner beast cried.

He was tempted, awfully tempted. But he couldn't fall for his dragon's pleas this time.

Want her. Need her, the beast clamored.

Right. Sure. His inner beast was his own worst enemy at times.

Luckily, his bag came out next, which let him keep her in sight all the way out to the sidewalk. Jenna waved and rushed toward a woman — her sister, judging by the way they squeaked and hugged. His eyes got stuck on Jenna's legs — long, sculpted legs, like she spent half the day doing leg lifts — before he managed to drag his gaze away.

He gave himself a little shake. Mission accomplished. Sleeping Beauty was safe and sound. It was time to get started with his new life.

Funny, though, how it felt like a bitter end, especially when Jenna drove off into the night.

Chapter Three

Hey, Connor, a low grunt sounded in Connor's mind.

He spun around and broke into a grin despite his grim mood, setting a new course for the far end of the sidewalk.

"Hey, Timber," he rumbled, giving his brother a one-armed man-hug.

They smacked each other on the back a few times then stood grinning like a couple of fools. A guy didn't spend most of his life with a big lug of a bear shifter and not learn to love the guy, even if Tim had been a pain in the ass younger brother at times.

But man, they had come a long way since then. They'd grown up fast and learned a lot — mostly the hard way. And yes, they'd done their fair share of messing up too. The important thing was that they had both sworn to follow a new path, and that path started here. Now.

It starts with her, his dragon cried, pulling him back toward Jenna. *Destiny.*

He snorted. Destiny? Was any of that even true?

"Right over here," Tim murmured, motioning toward a dusty white pickup at the curb.

Right over there, his dragon insisted, glancing in the direction Jenna had driven off. But all he caught was a glimpse of the Land Rover she'd gotten into, and then that, too, was gone.

Connor threw his bag in the back and slid into the passenger side of the pickup. Then he tipped his head and looked up at the stars, wondering what adventures — or misadventures — they would lead him to next.

"Some vehicle," he murmured, eyeing the torn upholstery.

"Hey, man, it's a start."

Connor looked around. All of this was a start — a new start on a new life. His last chance.

"Oh, and by the way, it's a quarter yours," Tim announced. "We all agreed to split it evenly."

Connor sighed. That was exactly how he'd ended up in trouble a couple of times — one of the guys coming up with a great idea and dragging the others along for the ride. Though, to be fair, he'd been the one to initiate a few misguided missions in his time.

He fingered a tear in the dashboard. Maybe it was time to shake that habit for good.

"What time is it here?"

"Twenty-two thirty," Tim said as he pulled onto the road.

Connor blinked a few times, trying to stay alert. His trip had started several time zones away, making this one of those stretched-out days that spanned more hours than he wanted to count.

"I got this, man," Tim murmured, reading his mind.

Connor let his eyes shut for just a little bit, not seeking sleep so much as visions of Jenna. But sleep found him, and he drifted off into dreams before too long. Dreams of him and Sleeping Beauty back on the plane. Replaying it in a way he liked better, with her putting her head on his shoulder before falling asleep.

This okay with you? she asked in that sweet siren-call voice of hers. At least, she did in the dream.

It was plenty okay with him, and apparently, putting his arm around her was okay too, because they ended up snuggled together like two halves of a happy clam. No more alarms in his mind, no state of alert.

It was a great dream until the mood slowly shifted to something more sinister. He dreamed the plane hit turbulence. Passengers started to scream, snapping him and Sleeping Beauty wide awake. The plane spun out of control, and all he could do was clutch Jenna as the plane barreled toward the ground. Down and down it went, whistling through the sky like the piece of hulking metal it was, doomed from the start.

Help, Jenna screamed, clutching his hand. *Help.*

Then the dream skipped a beat, and he and Jenna were hurtling through the air on their own — no plane, no other passengers, just hurricane force winds that whipped them around, trying to yank her out of his determined grip.

Hang on, he yelled, ready to shift.

For all the terror of the dream, it still felt good to sense her nervous nod, her trust.

The wind tore at his hair and screamed in his ears as he shifted into dragon form, but something was wrong. He couldn't get his wings open, and a deep voice laughed at him from some unidentified place over on the far side of his dream.

She's mine, the voice taunted, while the wind tried to pry her from his arms.

She's mine, he roared back, desperate to keep her safe.

"Uh... Connor?"

He jerked his head up, startled and sweaty. Wondering why his brother was looking at him that way. Then he ruffled a hand through his hair. Jesus, what a dream.

Tim handed him a bottle of lukewarm water, and he took a long swig.

"How far to go?"

"Not long now. Ten minutes, maybe."

Connor nodded, trying to anchor himself in time and place. Maui. Coming up on eleven p.m. New job.

"How's the place?"

Tim grinned and motioned to the ocean on the left. "Those guys from Silas's unit really lucked out."

Connor had heard about that. Silas Llewellyn, the dragon alpha of another shifter unit, had inherited an oceanfront estate and settled down there with his entire unit. They were all there — Kai, Hunter, Boone, and Cruz — and each had found a mate.

"It will be good to see them all again," Connor murmured. They'd worked closely with Silas's unit on several missions, and he'd grown close to his fellow shifters in that time. Of course, now that those men were all mated, maybe things had changed.

Tim laughed, reading his mind. "They're still the same at heart. Really easy to talk to." His voice grew hushed. "They understand, you know?"

Oh, Connor knew, all right. It was hard enough to relate to someone who hadn't lived the military life, and even harder to find someone who understood shifter issues too.

He snorted at the word. Issues? Yeah, maybe he had a few. But, hell. Who didn't?

"Their mates are great too," Tim added. "And the estate we're protecting — Koa Point — is out of this world. They've got everything you can imagine. Helicopter, fancy cars, private beach." Then he laughed. "Just don't get your hopes up. We get the run-down plantation next door. But we've survived worse, and there's plenty of space for everyone to spread out once we settle in."

Connor looked around, wondering if he had it in him to settle in anywhere. But maybe someday—

His dragon sighed, filling his mind with visions of a nice little seaside home, high on a cliff. A place where he could spend his days with steady work, open views. Dark nights in which to spread his wings. Maybe even someone to share it all with—

Like Jenna, his dragon said, fantasizing about the way the light had glinted off her hair. *Imagine how shiny it would be in daylight.*

Dazzling came to mind, but Connor frowned, remembering the dream. He cracked his neck from side to side. God, was he stiff.

"Is everyone here?" he asked.

Tim nodded. "Yep. You, me, Chase. . . "

Chase — their younger half brother, a wolf shifter. A guy who took *reserved and quiet* to a whole new level, unlike any wolf shifter Connor had ever met.

"How's he doing?"

Tim tilted his head left and right. "Not bad, considering."

Connor made a face. Wolves like Chase didn't take well to change, and he'd had change forced on to him too many times in his life. Which only served to remind Connor how important it was not to mess up this new assignment.

"Dell got in earlier today," Tim continued.

Connor relaxed a little bit more. Dell was a lion shifter they'd served with, a good guy to have around — and a near-brother to them all by now. Gregarious and funny, Dell was an expert in all kinds of skills that seemed pretty dubious until they saved a man's ass.

How the hell can you three be brothers? he remembered Dell cackling the first time they'd met. *A dragon, a bear, and a wolf?*

Connor made a face, thinking of his deadbeat dad — a rare myriad shifter who could shift into a variety of forms. Each of his father's offspring had taken a single animal form — at least, of the kids Connor had met. Who knew how many other Hoving half-siblings there were out in the world and what shifter forms they took? For him, Timber and Chase were enough.

"And then there's that widow we have to share the place with," Tim finished.

He said *that widow* in a carefully even voice Connor couldn't decipher.

"So what's the plan?" Connor asked, trying to focus on the big picture.

"We're all meeting tonight, as soon as we get there."

Good. A meeting would help get his mind off Jenna. He checked his watch and jerked his thumb up. "Why not drive a little faster?"

Tim shook his head firmly, and Connor stared. "Since when do you obey the speed limit?"

"Since this," Tim grumbled, reaching over to pop open the glove compartment.

The pickup zipped under a streetlight, and Connor saw a sheaf of papers. "Speeding tickets?"

Tim sighed. "There's this cop who's always patrolling and never cuts anyone any slack. Not even for a fellow bear."

Connor stared at the tickets. "A bear shifter cop? Who is he?"

"Who is she, you mean. A cop not to be messed with, I can tell you that. Officer Meli. Hunter's new mate. Believe me, you don't want to get on her bad side. Her and some other women around here."

Connor tilted his head at his brother. What was that supposed to mean?

Tim waved a hand. "When we took the job, we knew we would have to share the place with someone else, right? Someone the owners put in charge."

Connor scowled. Every instinct screamed for him to be in charge. But it didn't work that way, not until he made a name for himself. He had to count himself lucky that Silas Llewellyn had hired him and his buddies as security for the sprawling estate. They would earn solid salaries along with free housing on the neighboring property. All in all, a pretty sweet deal, except it came with two stipulations.

First, the Hoving brothers had to clean up their act — no unassigned missions, no shenanigans, and no pranks, in Silas's words.

Which was pretty unjust, since Connor and his brothers had never really meant to cause trouble. It was just that trouble found them.

Second, they had to accept whatever authority Silas — or Kai, his cousin and second-in-command — saw fit to put in charge.

That clause had made Connor rankle at first, but he'd signed on anyway, figuring they'd work out their own hierarchy as time went by. Silas could call anyone he wanted the boss, but the man truly in charge would be the one who earned that right.

He frowned at the sugar cane stalks that spiked up along the road. "Whoever Silas puts in charge will be keeping an eye on us, you know."

Tim flashed a wicked grin. "Seriously, wouldn't you keep an eye on us? Anyway, it's not a guy. It's a girl. A woman, I mean."

Connor frowned. Silas had put a woman in charge of the place? Not that he had a problem with women in command

— it just didn't fit Silas's brief description of the woman they would share the plantation with.

It will be you, your brothers, Dell, and a woman I know. A dragon shifter widow who's been through some hard times. I expect you to treat her well.

Connor scratched his head. Silas hadn't said anything about the widow being in charge. "Didn't he say something about her being fragile?

Tim snorted. "Either he meant someone else, or he hadn't met her when he said that. I swear that woman is tougher than half the guys we know. You've got your job cut out for you, bro."

Connor bit back a sigh and stared at the moonlit sky. He'd had his work cut out for him from the day he was born. That was just the way it was. At least he got to live in a nice place like this, with a fresh breeze whipping his hair and the scent of the ocean tickling his nose. The hulking form of another island slumbered on the horizon in an additional reminder of where he was. Maui. No one out there aiming their cross hairs at him, no scheming enemies on the prowl.

Just a mate to track down, his dragon murmured.

He shoved the thought aside and went back to the business at hand. It wouldn't take long for him and his brothers to sort out a new hierarchy, the shifter way.

Just don't mess up, a familiar voice of warning whispered from the back of his mind.

"Anyway, you'll meet her soon enough," Tim said.

Connor made a face, trying to focus instead of making that *her* into Jenna.

Tim drove on until a long line of hotels and condos gave way to a quieter stretch of coastline with fewer homes. He made a left onto an unmarked road and continued at a slow pace.

"Over there's Koa Point." Tim pointed at a carved wooden gate that hinted at the understated wealth of the place. Then his finger swung forward and drooped a little bit. "This is us. Koakea Plantation."

"Koakea?"

Tim shrugged. "It means white tree. Something like that anyway."

They rattled past a plain metal gate that had been pushed aside and left open, hanging askew on rusty hinges.

"Used to be a coffee plantation," Tim murmured. "But it went bust, and nobody has lived here for years."

Connor sniffed, catching a dry, flowery scent that didn't relate to coffee — not the brewed kind, at least. A tangle of low, scrubby bushes lined both sides of the driveway, and they drove past several sheds and barns.

"This is the best part." Tim grinned as they turned a corner.

The bushes had been cut back there, opening up an incredible view. The property occupied a long incline that sloped downward toward the Pacific. The whole ocean lay glittering under the moonlight, as far as he could see. It was as if he'd shifted to dragon form, spread his stiff wings, and taken to the air to enjoy the view.

"That's the main house." Tim pointed to a long, low building set at a slight angle to the hillside.

The only sources of light came from there, though those only lit two or three rooms, giving it a haunted look. The porch had to have an incredible vista, though Connor doubted he'd have much time to enjoy it.

A faint network of trails crisscrossed the huge property, and a little stream bisected the hillside. The whole sweeping landscape ended abruptly at a cliff on the south end of the property, while the north side sloped gradually to what looked like a small beach.

"Not bad," Connor said.

Spectacular might have been the word a few decades ago, but he couldn't overlook the creeping weeds or the crooked slant of most of the structures in view. One section of the western slope had burned out not too long ago, and several tractors lay rusting to one side.

But, okay. The main thing was, the property had space. Lots of it. The perfect place for a group of shifters to protect their privacy from the human world.

"It needs some fixing up," Tim deadpanned as they cruised down a bumpy dirt road and stopped in front of the main house. Even in the moonlight, Connor could see the sagging porch and peeling paint of the once-grand place.

"So, we'll fix it up," he said, gearing himself up for a challenge as he slid out of the pickup. That's what life was — a series of challenges. Tests. Life was one endless proving ground, and this was his big chance.

"Anyway, here we go," Tim grinned. "Ready to meet the gang?"

Chapter Four

Connor steeled his shoulders and ascended the porch stairs. The first one creaked under his right foot. The second step gave a sharp groan, and the third he skipped entirely, just in case.

"Connor!" a cheery voice called from among the figures waiting to greet him. "The man is back!"

Connor grinned. Leave it to Dell, the lion shifter, to give him a grand entrance.

"Hey," he said, shaking hands with Dell. In the few weeks they'd spent apart, Dell had grown a thick mane of a beard — golden blond, like his hair.

Chase greeted him next, wearing his version of a smile. The guy had grown up with a wolf mother — an all-wolf mother, not a shifter. Their dad had met her when he'd tried out wolf form for a while — just long enough to knock up the she-wolf and disappear again, in other words. Chase had only come in from the wild in his late teens. Even after a decade of practice, Chase was still pretty clunky when it came to human behavior. But, hell. Family was family, and Chase was a great man to have on a team.

He drew his hands out of his pockets to shake, but Connor pulled him in for a brief hug. "Good to see you, man."

Chase nodded by way of reply. Then a tall, willowy figure emerged from the shadows of the house, and Connor straightened quickly. That had to be her. The widow. Or was it?

The other guys watched closely as Connor and the woman approached each other. He sniffed covertly, as did she. She took a half step to the left, and he did the same to the right, circling the way two wild animals might. Finally, the mystery

29

woman stepped into the arc of light cast by the open bulb on the porch and gave a curt nod.

It was the nod of royalty to a commoner, and the woman's regal bearing reinforced the impression of privilege and wealth.

She was tall and athletic, with long black hair that fell over her shoulders in loose waves, contrasting with the pure white of her pearl necklace. All of which made the gears of his mind reverse back to *widow* and *fragile* then grind awkwardly over them a few times. Weren't widows supposed to be old and gray and fragile? This woman had *warrior princess* stamped all over her.

"Connor Hoving," he said, extending his hand, telling himself not to grip as hard as his alpha instincts told him to.

Her grip was steely, her nod curt. "Cynthia."

She didn't supply a last name, and he wondered why. Dragons placed ridiculous emphasis on family bloodlines, and he'd been sure she would come out with *Llewellyn* or *Baird* or one of the other famous clans on the opposite end of the shifter scale from the lowly Hovings. But nope — nothing. Just a first name.

"Kai will be here soon," Cynthia said. No *nice to meet you* or *how was your trip.*

"Can't wait." Dell flopped down on one of the porch chairs and propped his feet on the barrel that served as a table. He leaned back like a man ready to watch a football game, only his grin was aimed squarely at Connor and Cynthia as if that was where the competition might be.

Cynthia swept past Connor and snapped her fingers. "Feet. Down. I just cleaned this place."

The easygoing lion shifter cracked a huge grin and retracted his feet. "Yes, sir. I mean, yes, ma'am."

Cynthia stepped around him, rearranging the chairs, fussing over candles set in glass jars. Then she snatched up old magazines and empty glasses from the table and did an about-face into the house.

Connor stared after her. The woman wasn't fragile. She was a goddamn hurricane.

Dell grinned and spoke into his mind as all closely bonded shifters could. *Brilliant mind. Great body. She and I would be a match made in heaven if she didn't have such a chip on her shoulder.*

Tim snorted. *As if she'd be interested in you.*

Dell's smile stretched. *All women are interested in me. She's just good at hiding it.*

Cynthia strode out of the house and tossed a sponge to Dell. "Wipe the tables. Please."

"Yes, ma'am," Dell said in his easy drawl.

Whatever attraction she's hiding, Connor said, *she's hiding in the center of the earth. You have no chance, man.*

Tim cleared his throat, speaking softly, as most bear shifters did. *I suggest you don't piss her off. She's in charge, remember? Plus, she's a widow.*

Black widow, Dell chuckled.

"Can you light the torches?" Cynthia tossed Chase a box of matches. "Please."

Please always seemed to be an afterthought with her. But, hell. Connor supposed she was trying.

Trying to take my job, his dragon grumbled as Chase lit two rows of tiki torches set into the yard leading up to the porch. Cynthia was giving Kai Llewellyn the kind of reception afforded a high-ranking shifter, which Connor had no problem with. The fact that he hadn't been afforded the same courtesy didn't bother him either. He was used to working his way up from the bottom.

Tim looked at him in surprise, as if waiting for him to protest or fight. Cynthia stood at the entrance to the house with her arms firmly crossed, waiting for the same reaction. But Connor kept a neutral expression and his mouth shut. He'd learned a thing or two about patience lately. He could handle this.

Tim hid a tiny smile and shot a thought to Dell, letting just enough of it slip out for Connor to hear.

Oh, yes. This will be interesting, all right.

Dell winked. *My money's on the widow.*

Mine is on Connor. Tim laughed. *I think.*

Footsteps crunched over gravel, signaling the approach of their boss.

"Connor, good to see you," Kai Llewellyn called with a genuine smile.

That broke the ice, because Connor's unit and Kai's had cooperated on several missions, and there was that instant feeling of a common bond and mutual respect. Of course, Kai was one of his bosses now. The big kahuna of Koa Point was Kai's cousin, Silas, but he was overseas taking care of business interests, which put Kai in command.

"Thanks for bringing us in," Connor said as Kai came up the porch.

The dragon shifter was about his size, but wow. His entire demeanor was quieter and more relaxed than Connor remembered. Kai's smile was deep and steady, as if life was treating him well. Was that a positive side effect of living on Maui, or the fact that Kai had found a mate not too long ago?

Perspective, Connor remembered being told. Apparently, life looked different to mated shifters, though he couldn't imagine how.

He and Kai shook hands heartily, and Connor felt himself relax as Kai made his rounds, giving every man a slap on the shoulder. Just like old times, in other words. Cynthia got one of those European-style, left side-right side pecks on the cheek that old dragon families liked to use.

Dell gave Connor a pointed look. *Now, if you were classy, you would do that too.*

Connor rolled his eyes. He wasn't classy. Never had been, never would be.

"Well, let's get to business," Kai said, motioning everyone to take a seat.

Everyone sat except Chase, who remained standing in the shadows to one side — a wary wolf habit he'd never been able to shake.

"You've met, I assume?" Kai asked. "Well, just in case — Connor, Timber, and Chase Hoving." He pointed at each of the brothers then at Dell. "Wendell O'Roarke."

"Dell," the lion shifter corrected with a pained look.

Connor grinned. It seemed more and more like old times —
the good-natured digs at each other, the subtle reestablishment
of pack hierarchy.

Then Kai tilted his head. "And I see you've met Cynthia
Brown."

He left just enough of a pause between *Cynthia* and *Brown*
to convince Connor that wasn't her real name. No self-
respecting dragon had a name like Brown. Most of the leading
families had ancient Welsh names, and Lord knew they loved
showing them off. Cynthia was one of those, for sure. He could
see it in her regal bearing, her slightly upturned chin. What
made her assume a name like Brown?

He caught Tim's eye and shot a thought over to all his
brothers, careful to veil it from Cynthia and Kai.

Apparently, the black widow has something to hide.

Or hide from, Dell mused, stroking his golden beard.

Kai cleared his throat and went on. "As you know, Silas
and I have called you in as backup. We need extra security to
keep watch over Koa Point. Our clan has grown a lot lately,
with mates and babies and such—"

Kai tried to sound like a gruff army commander at that
part, but his eyes went all warm and mushy.

You think Kai and the others are going soft? Dell asked in
a private aside.

Connor hid a grin. Maybe that was that *perspective* thing.
In any case, he'd never call Kai or any of the others *soft*, even
if the love bug had infiltrated Kai's elite military team. They
were all hitched and breeding like bunnies from what Connor
had heard. Boone and Nina, the wolf pair, had baby twins,
and word had it that Kai and his partner, Tessa, were working
on some baby dragons of their own. So, yeah, it made sense
to bring in outside help — top military guys who wouldn't be
distracted by that kind of thing.

Except, damn it, Connor was drifting off already.

I wonder what Jenna is doing now, his dragon sighed, flood-
ing his mind with all kinds of fantasies he couldn't entertain.
Like spending a pleasant evening under the stars with her, or

taking her on a walk down the moonlit beach. Maybe even kissing her and—

"—which means we'll be relying on you to keep a constant lookout," Kai said, nailing each of them with a firm look.

Connor blinked and focused on Kai a split second before the dragon shifter caught his eye.

Cut that out, he barked at his inner beast.

Cut what out? it murmured dreamily, still imagining impossible things. Like wading into the ocean with Jenna and maybe even going for a midnight swim.

Which was nuts. He hated open water. Looking at it was nice from shore, and flying over it was great. But splashing in the water? No way.

Connor rolled his head from shoulder to shoulder, trying to remain focused.

"We've been subjected to a number of attacks over the past months, so security is our top priority," Kai said with gravity. "Part of our plan is to use you as extra eyes and ears — not just on your security rounds, but also on the side. Connor will pilot the occasional helicopter charter for us, and we'll help the rest of you find part-time work in the community — jobs that will help you keep your feelers out for trouble we might miss otherwise."

Connor nodded. He'd been warned about that, and it made sense.

"Of course," Kai said, "that can wait until you've settled in and fixed this place up. Everything other than security is secondary, but we expect steady progress all the same. Any extra time you have, you're free to use to fix up your own places. How you work out the details is up to you, but we've decided on two lines of command for now."

Dell winked at Connor. *For now* proved that Kai was thinking what Connor was thinking. Once he, the guys, and Cynthia had worked out their own hierarchy, a real alpha would be named, not just a temporary one.

"So," Kai continued, "Cynthia is in charge of the plantation." She sat a little straighter as Kai ticked various points off his fingers. "Renovations, budgeting, duty roster — that's all her domain. Connor, you're heading up the security detail, and the other guys report to you."

That meant it was Connor's turn to sit straighter and return Cynthia's cool look.

"So that's the chain of command. You guys answer to Connor, who coordinates with Cynthia, who answers to me. Got it?" Kai finished. His voice took on an edgy, alpha growl.

Cynthia gave a firm nod, while Connor replied with a curt "Roger."

The security job was perfect. Having Cynthia whoever-she-was keeping an eye on him like an underage den mother was not. Still, he kept his best poker face on as he shot her a look — a look she returned, totally cool and poised.

So, yes, he'd have his work cut out for him with the Ice Queen there. But it was just a question of time before he proved himself top dog — er, dragon — here.

I wish we could trade her for Jenna, his dragon hummed absently.

Connor nearly snorted out loud. That would be nice, but not exactly a formula for success in this job.

Kai nodded and went on. "Like I said, the details are up to you..."

That was code for *May the best dragon win.* Connor grinned at Cynthia, who glared at him.

"The main thing is for you to keep a tight watch on things and be ready for action whenever the need arises," Kai said. Then his harsh eyes softened, and he broke into a friendly smile. "But tonight is a night off for you guys. Hunter and Dawn are patrolling tonight. Tomorrow, we'll show you around and really get started."

Connor nodded, and the rest of the guys looked to him to reply as the leader of their little band. But before he could so much as clear his throat, Cynthia jumped to her feet.

"Thank you, Kai," she said the way a keynote speaker might after a glowing introduction. "Since there's so much to do, I've taken the liberty of making a duty schedule to get us off to a good start. Any objections?"

Connor opened his mouth. Dell raised his hand. Chase stopped pacing, and Tim's thick eyebrows shot up. But Cynthia plunged ahead as if the nanosecond she'd given them was plenty.

"Perfect. As you can see here, I've color-coded the schedule by person and task."

Everyone squinted as she produced a whiteboard out of nowhere, propped it on a spare chair, and tapped along the neat columns and rows. "Connor can fill in the security rotations here. I have rotations for cooking, cleaning, and grounds work. But our priority — besides security, of course — needs to be setting up some kind of common space."

Connor felt obligated to object, except he'd come to that conclusion himself. Damn.

Tim caught his eye. *Are you good with this, man?*

Connor wasn't good with Cynthia snatching power, but no big deal. She could be as organized as she wanted. In the end, an alpha was an alpha, and that would be him.

Now about Jenna, his dragon murmured, drifting off again.

Cynthia went on without skipping a beat. "And in this column, you'll see—"

"Pink," Tim growled, stopping her short.

"I beg your pardon?"

"Why do I get pink?" Tim pointed at the whiteboard.

Dell cackled and smacked Tim on the back. "You get first cleanup duty too. Enjoy."

Cynthia frowned. "Does color matter?"

"It does when it's pink," Tim grumbled.

Normally, bears were among the most amiable of shifters, but once something rubbed them the wrong way...

"Real men don't mind pink. I'll take it." Dell grinned, reaching for the board.

Cynthia looked on, aghast, as Dell licked his thumb, smudged out Tim's name, and filled his own, then swapped their other duties around. His crooked print stood out beside Cynthia's neat letters.

"Problem solved."

Cynthia stared at the desolation of her tidy plan.

Why can't she be more like Jenna? Connor's dragon sighed. Jenna was fun. Sparkly, even when she was worried about something.

He considered the schedule and shook his head. "Nope. Big problem."

"What problem?" Cynthia asked.

Kai stood with a sigh and turned to go. "Ah, the Hovings at their best. I'll leave this to you, Cynthia. Goodnight, gentlemen, ladies."

Connor swore Kai grinned as he disappeared into the night.

"Big problem," Dell agreed, pointing at the whiteboard.

"Huge problem," Tim said with a grave nod.

They all leaned closer and tut-tutted in unison.

Cynthia jammed her hands on her hips. "What problem?"

Connor pointed. "You've got Chase on kitchen duty this week. Not a good thing."

Dell shook his head. "*Never* a good thing, Cynth."

"Cynthia," she insisted.

Dell went on as if he hadn't heard. "The only thing Chase can cook is spaghetti."

Chase shrugged at Cynthia. "Sorry."

"Seriously, for our own preservation, we want Dell in the kitchen," Tim said.

Dell blessed Cynthia with his cheekiest grin. "Well, I hate to boast, but I am a good cook. Steaks, burgers, you name it." He kissed his fingertips and flicked them outward like a prize chef.

"Burgers?" Cynthia frowned.

Out of nowhere, a thin voice cried out and frantic steps pitter-pattered down the hall.

"Mommy! Mommy!"

Connor turned as a little kid in dinosaur pajamas ran out of the house and threw himself into Cynthia's arms. "The witch came back!"

Connor spun in a quick circle, on high alert. What witch? Where?

Cynthia pulled the boy into a tight hug, and just like that, the warrior princess morphed into a doting mom. All the guys leaned away, exchanging looks of surprise.

"The witch and the monsters!" the little redhead cried.

"No, sweetie," Cynthia cooed in a totally different voice. A warm, calming voice that promised a world full of law and order. A world in which everything would somehow turn out all right. "No witches here. We came to a nice place."

"But I saw them," the little guy cried. "And Daddy..."

Connor's chest tightened as he recalled Kai's words. *Widow... hard times... fragile...*

Connor looked on as Cynthia rocked the boy the way his mom used to hug him after a bad dream. Then he cleared his throat and looked away. That mother-kid bond was sacred, and he wasn't about to mess with it. He and Cynthia could subtly wrestle for leadership of this little pack some other time. Tonight, he'd give her a break.

"No monsters here, Joey," Cynthia murmured in a voice that cracked a tiny bit. "Daddy fought bravely so they'll never come again. They can't follow us here."

Jesus. Now the widow *part is making sense,* Tim said in a hushed tone.

Okay, maybe we should give her a break, Dell said.

I guess I could live with pink, Tim muttered.

Cynthia stroked the child's rumpled hair. "No monsters any more. We'll never see them again."

She sounded pretty convincing, but the tremble of her hand said she wasn't so sure.

Connor took a deep breath as he turned to look out over the gently sloping grounds and out to the moonlight rippling over the ocean. Jenna had been scared too. On the run from something — or someone. Why was the world full of shitheads who wouldn't leave innocent people alone?

Maybe we can fly tonight and find Jenna, his dragon said. *To check on her, I mean.*

He took a deep breath. He hoped to hell Jenna didn't have the kind of trouble Cynthia had. As a human, that was unlikely, so he had to keep his focus here. A good leader protected his pack — and that meant Cynthia and her son.

"Hey there, little guy," Dell said, turning on his best big-brother voice. He sank down to his haunches as the boy peeked out from his mother's arms. Dell opened his eyes wide, pretending to be impressed. "Wow. Are you a real dragon?"

The boy nodded silently.

"That's so cool. Your mom is too?"

Joey nodded solemnly.

"That's amazing. You know what I am?"

Joey shook his head.

"I mean, other than being your new friend." Dell winked and poked his thumb at his own chest. "Lion shifter here. That guy over there is a grizzly," he pointed to Tim. "And Connor is a badass dragon."

Connor straightened. *Badass* might be overdoing it, especially since he was supposed to be turning over a new leaf. But, yeah. No one messed with him.

"And Chase over there is a wolf. You know how he got his name?"

Joey shook his head again, watching Dell uncertainly.

Cynthia did too, but Connor knew where Dell was taking this. The guy had the ability to make shell-shocked kids in the world's meanest war zones smile.

"He used to chase his tail." Dell turned his finger in a circle to mime the action, and Joey broke into a faint smile.

Chase grinned and turned slowly, faking surprise as he looked behind him. "Hey, what happened to it?"

The little boy giggled. "You don't have one."

"Not when he's human, he doesn't," Dell said. "But when he turns into a wolf, it's there. And you know what? He's a really ferocious wolf. All of us get that way when we shift, and we beat the bad guys every time."

"Every time?" The little boy's eyes went wide.

"Every time," Dell said solemnly. "So, since you have your mom here — and she's scary as anything..."

Cynthia shot Dell a look that was equal parts *watch it, buster* and grateful mom.

"...I can promise you no monsters are going to come along. Not with all of us here to protect you. From now on, your greatest danger is Chase's cooking."

The little boy giggled and looked up at his mom.

Cynthia hugged him and nodded. "He's right. So how about we get to bed? It's late."

"Is your meeting finished?" the little boy peeped, rubbing his hands in nervous circles.

Connor's heart melted all over again. The poor little guy had probably been given a stern warning not to disturb his mom at work, or else.

Remind you of anyone? Tim murmured into Connor's mind.

He closed his eyes. *Yep.*

He and Tim knew a thing or two about single moms and absent fathers. Their mother had done her best, working two jobs to keep them afloat. It was a wonder he and Tim hadn't gotten into more trouble, considering all the times they'd had to fend for themselves while their mom was at work.

"I just need to finish the schedule," Cynthia said, reaching for her whiteboard again.

Dell hooked his foot around the chair it was propped on and slid it out of reach. Then he faked a huge, slow yawn, letting just enough of his lion fangs show to impress the kid. "Nah, it's definitely bedtime. And you know what, boss?"

Cynthia raised one thin eyebrow.

"I'm sure we can take the rest as it comes."

She stared at Dell like he was speaking a foreign language. One after another, Cynthia looked at each of them until her gaze rested on Connor. Other than the chirp of crickets and the quick whoosh of a swooping bat, the place was totally silent, the air charged.

Connor stared back at her, quietly resisting the urge to take command. Yes, there was a hierarchy to be sorted out. And, yes, he wanted to be the one who came out on top. But he wasn't going to use Cynthia's moment of vulnerability to assert his power.

"Bedtime," he agreed quietly. "Chase and Dell can take the first watch tonight, with me and Tim taking over after that. Okay with you?"

Cynthia gave him a long, hard look like he was trying to trick her instead of offering a peace pipe. What kind of world did she come from? Some fucked-up world, for sure.

And just like that, he thought of Jenna's sunny smile and the way she'd bounced into her sister's arms. Maybe what his mom used to say was true — that common shifters had it better than the upper classes, what with all their backstabbing and archaic laws.

"Kai said it was a night off," Dell protested.

Connor shook his head. It was never a night off. Not in his world.

Cynthia nodded at last. "Okay with me." She took Joey's hand and headed inside, then paused at the doorway.

"Oh, wait. I have to show everyone their rooms—"

Tim shot Connor a look. *God, she's already assigned us barracks. Act quick.*

"I'm sure we'll figure it out," Connor said as gently as he could. "Goodnight." He waggled his fingers at Joey, who waved back.

Cynthia fingered the string of white pearls around her neck, then went inside after uttering two quiet words.

"Thank you."

Her words hung in the air, fluttering there like a pair of doves, and eventually wafted away with the sea breeze.

No one said anything after that, not for a long time, at least. Every man sank into his own thoughts while the stars slowly arced overhead. At some point, Chase and Dell lumbered off to start their patrol, and Tim headed for one wing of the big plantation house. Connor had gotten a second wind and wasn't ready to sleep. Instead, he stood on the porch and gazed out at the sea, wondering if he'd ever find the inner peace to enjoy the view that stretched all the way over the plantation to the sea. For now, all he could do was mull over everything he'd seen and heard that day.

Starting with Jenna. Where was she? What had brought her to Maui? But his thoughts wandered over to Cynthia too. On the surface, the two women had nothing in common, yet both appeared to be on the run.

He dug his nails into the porch railing. Damn it. Both those women had gotten under his skin, if in totally different ways. Cynthia was like a long-lost sister appearing out of nowhere, the way Chase had a decade ago when he'd had nowhere else to turn. Jenna, on the other hand, knew all about trust and support. What she needed was protection, and beyond that — well, what did she need?

A mate. A powerful, loving one, his inner beast growled.

Did she? Or was his dragon projecting his own needs onto Jenna? And if so, then, shit. What did that say about him?

We definitely need her, his dragon insisted. *And she needs us.*

A voice chuckled faintly in the back of his mind. That no-good, gossipy voice of fate.

Both those women have to do with your destiny, dragon. Both of them will help you prove yourself.

Connor frowned. He didn't want or need help to get ahead.

The voice grew blustery then dropped off again, like a boxer past his prime. *You do not get to choose the path to your destiny. Only the choices you make once the journey begins.*

He snorted. Right. Choosing paths. Making decisions. Some shifters had an unshakeable faith in fate, but not him. Fate had fucked with him from the day he'd been born, and it was messing with him now. Trying to distract him from his true course.

Whatever that may be, his dragon sighed.

He frowned at the deepest, darkest part of the sky. *Whatever that may be.*

Tim ambled out of the adjoining room, scratching his chest. "What are you thinking about, man?"

Sleeping Beauty. Destined mates. A peaceful existence in a quiet corner of the world.

"Work," Connor lied, then slowly stood. "Good night."

Chapter Five

Jenna woke, stretched, and yawned a mile wide. She'd slept like a baby—

She giggled. Maybe *baby* wasn't a good word for a woman who'd fantasized about sex all night. She turned over in the big bed, wishing her fantasies could fill the extra space with the real thing.

Namely, Connor.

Somehow, her mind had turned every one of his chaste gestures and careful words into an entire raging lineup of a girl's hottest dreams. They'd started with kisses in their airplane seats, and the deeper those became, the more her libido stirred. Soon, she'd needed more — desperately — and she dreamed of sneaking to the airplane restroom with Connor and doing it perched on the sink. Then her mind had turned the back half of the plane into a private jet with a huge, heart-shaped bed and silk sheets where Connor had laid her out like a feast.

Special Forces. Gorgeous eyes. A hint of mystery. What girl wouldn't dream of a night with him?

She rolled onto her stomach and propped her head in her hands, looking out the door to the beach. Yes, the beach, not ten steps away. Her sister had set her up in the estate's guesthouse, an adorable hobbit hole of a cottage built right at the edge of the beach.

So — wow. Her sister hadn't been kidding about living the good life.

Jenna watched the surf break on an offshore reef. Given a view like that, she figured her mind would be filled with images of riding those waves or exploring the depths with a couple of long free dives. But all she could think of was the man from the plane. Preferably naked and dripping with water.

She glanced around. What she wouldn't give for him to stroll by now. Or better yet, to knock at the door and come in with a tray of her favorite pancakes. Hell, she'd be content to have his number to be able to call.

Hi, Connor. It's me — Jenna, from the flight. I was thinking we might be able to meet.

She kicked the sheets, wishing she'd asked for his number. She'd probably never see him again.

She thumped the mattress and stood, determined to stay positive. The plane ride — and Connor — had helped her relax, and Maui was doing its part too. California and the notion of vampires seemed far, far away from this well-protected private estate. She stepped outside, breathing deeply while finger-combing her hair. Maybe there really was magic here on Maui. She could feel it in the sweet scent of roses arranged along the porch of the tiny cottage and in the never-ending pulse of the sea.

She'd agreed to find Jody by breakfast time, so she ducked back inside to pull on her favorite cutoff jean shorts and a blue tank top, and—

"Ugh."

She stared at the knife she'd left on the bedside table — a reminder of everything that had driven her here.

"Fine," she muttered, strapping it to her calf before heading out to explore. It looked a lot like a diving knife, so she wouldn't appear too loony to anyone who noticed it. Anyway, she'd promised herself not to think about bad things in her first day in paradise. She had exactly one free day before starting work, and she was going to squeeze in all the carefree living she'd missed over the past weeks.

So she dug her toes into the sand with gusto and gazed out over the endless blue sea. She listened to palms dancing in the breeze and inhaled blissfully clean air. Then she splashed through the shallows, pausing here or there to pick up a shell or interesting rock. According to her dad, she'd been a beachcomber from the time she could walk.

Just like me, he often said with a proud grin.

She smiled and pocketed a shell. Later on, she'd send a picture of it to him. In the meantime, she really had to get to breakfast. So she walked to the end of the beach where a couple was spreading out a blanket in the shade. Jody had introduced Jenna to her new friends when she'd arrived, and that was Nina and Boone, if she remembered correctly.

It had to be, because each of them held a baby as they arranged the blanket and settled down. Nina waved with a hearty, "Aloha!"

"Hi," Jenna called.

"Say Aloha, sweetie," Boone murmured to the baby he held. He propped one tiny arm up and made the baby wave, and then rewarded the child with a huge smooch. "That's my girl."

"You'll have to excuse Boone," Nina said. "He's still living on proud daddy cloud nine."

"Not my fault I have the two best kids in the world." He shrugged and started tickling the other child's foot. It gurgled and kicked with glee.

Jenna grinned. "I know the type. My dad is like that with my niece."

Her stomach rumbled, and Nina laughed. "Let me guess. Time for breakfast." She motioned toward a path that led between the palm trees. "Just keep to the main trail, and you'll find the meeting house."

"How about you?" Jenna asked.

Boone laughed. "We're on the babies' schedule now. I'm pretty sure we had breakfast at about five, but it's all a blur. I'm practically ready for lunch." Then he cuddled the baby right up to his face and switched to baby talk. "How about you, Luna? All nice and full?"

Nina rolled her eyes as if the sight of a big, muscled man holding a tiny baby wasn't the cutest thing ever, and Jenna excused herself with a smile. She turned up the path with a light step. If those two could hang out on the beach with their babies, she could feel safe too.

The path meandered this way and that. While Nina had made it sound easy, Jenna couldn't always tell which branch of the trail to follow. But surely, the estate wasn't so big that she could lose her way.

"Wow," she murmured five minutes later. Maybe it was big enough. She'd wandered under enough palm trees to line most of the boardwalk back home and startled more skittering crabs that she could count — and she still hadn't found the estate's meeting house. Her stomach was rumbling, and she was starting to wish she'd slipped on her flip-flops, after all.

"First world problems," she muttered to herself, picking up her pace as she turned around the next bend.

It was a really tight bend, and the foliage was extra thick, so she had no forewarning of the solid slab of rock she ran into a second later.

"Sorry," the rock said as she stumbled back. Two thick arms steadied her, and a deep voice sounded in her ears.

"Jenna?"

She blinked. "Connor?" Because, wow. That hadn't been solid rock. It was him.

A smile flashed over his face — a from-the-heart smile that told her he was as happy to see her as she was to see him. He still had that fresh, outdoorsy scent, but he looked tired from too little sleep.

She blushed. Was it possible that he'd been kept up by the same hot fantasies she'd had, or was she flattering herself? After all, she'd slept through the flight, and he hadn't.

His eyes sparkled, and a vein pulsed at his neck. Maybe it was the former, after all.

"Hi," she managed.

He grinned. "Hi."

She fished for something to do or say that wouldn't make her come off like a love-struck teen, but nothing came out. After another few seconds of staring at each other, they both spoke at the same time.

"What are you doing here?"

She laughed, and he did too.

"I'm trying to find my way to breakfast," she said.

His hazel eyes looked more green than brown in the morning light, and they swept up and down her body — not ogling her the way some men did, just warming her up. Warming himself up too, judging by the pink flush that spread over his cheeks.

Jenna bit her lip. Her skin tingled all over, and she leaned closer. It was crazy, the pull she felt toward him. Like a fever had struck both of them at the same time. Of course, there were people she had hit it off with right away. But this was different. This was the thrill of a chance meeting combined with the warm goodness of a reunion with an old friend.

She blinked, trying to snap out of it. Maybe there really was something magical about Maui. Or maybe it was just the romance of a tropical island combined with that burst of freedom she'd started the day with.

"No, I mean, what are you really doing here?" Connor asked.

"Visiting my sister, like I said."

His eyes went wide — really wide, like a guy who'd just discovered a girl's father owned a very big shotgun. "Your sister lives here? At Koa Point?"

She turned away from Connor long enough to wave at the path she'd come down, about to explain. By the time she turned back, he'd inched closer to peer over her shoulder, and they bumped again. He caught her arms and held her a little closer. A little tighter, like a treasured possession he didn't dare release.

Her breath caught as she gazed up into his eyes. Back on the plane, they'd been almost eye-to-eye. Now, his height showed, and she had to look up. And not just look up but look *deep* because his eyes were doing that trick of theirs again. Swirling. Glowing, almost. Or was she seeing things?

She dropped her gaze to his lips, watching them form soundless syllables. Maybe she wasn't the only one drunk on a mysterious elixir of love.

A bird zoomed by overhead, breaking the spell just long enough for her to pull away an inch. "Wait. What are *you* doing here?"

He didn't answer right away, still looking stunned. When he did speak, it was a single, quiet word. "Destiny."

She wondered if she'd heard right. "What was that?"

He gave himself a little shake and cleared his throat. "I mean...er, duty. I work here. Well, I do now."

"I thought you said you worked in security."

"I do." He waved around. "For Koa Point estate. I'm staying at the plantation house."

Her jaw hung open in one of those *holy crap* moments. "So you're...you're..."

"Your new neighbor," Connor rumbled in that low, growly tone she already loved. And damn if the man didn't lick his lips.

Her cheeks flushed. Connor McStud was her neighbor, and he was on foot, which meant they were only separated by a short walk. So technically, she could sneak over to his place whenever she wanted, or he could sneak over to hers. Which meant...

She gulped. Her interlude on Maui had just gotten a lot more interesting.

"Neighbor, huh?"

He grinned. "Maybe I'll get to see more of you, after all."

Maybe we can do more than see each other, her girl parts giggled.

"That would be nice," she said, trying to keep a straight face as her imagination ran away with visions of barefoot walks on a moonlit beach.

His smile was mesmerizing, his eyes twin pools of hope, and she found herself leaning closer. The sea breeze whispered between the trees, playing with her hair, and the warmth of the rising sun kissed her skin. The air began to crackle with energy that swirled around her fingers, tempting her to reach out toward Connor.

Connor's mouth cracked open, and he stood there, staring.

"Do you feel that too?" she whispered.

If he said, *Feel what?* she would have struggled to explain. It was as if the world was falling away until everything funneled down to just him and her. It was one thing to have that happen in a plane when the lights dimmed and rows of seats formed a barrier to the outside world. But out here amid the grandeur of Maui? Surf crashed. Craggy mountain peaks reared up to the sky. Flowers exploded from every bush, and umbrella-sized leaves opened beneath them, ready to catch sparkling dewdrops. But all she could really focus on was Connor.

His lips moved, and he whispered so low, she barely caught what he said.

"Destiny..."

She took a deep breath. Could it really be?

Of course there's love at first sight, her dad used to say. *For the luckiest guys on earth, at least.*

Without thinking, she slid her hands up Connor's arms, all the way to his shoulders and back down. She waited for the mirage to shimmer and vanish, but Connor was still there, brushing his thumbs over her skin.

"Yeah." His whisper was hoarse. "I feel that."

Her lips trembled, and she tilted her head to match the angle of his. He dipped his chin, coming closer, and she rose to meet him, steered by that same mischievous force.

Kiss him, a voice whispered in the back of her mind.

How could she kiss him? She barely knew him.

Not a stranger. A friend, the voice assured her.

She wondered what the voice was and where it came from. But she got distracted by calculating the distance to his lips, which seemed much more important just then. They weren't far, but even that was too far. She rose to her toes, suddenly desperate for a taste of his lips because she already knew how perfect it would be.

But something rustled on the path behind her. Something determined to rip that kiss away from them before it was too late.

Too late for what? her muddled mind asked.

Quick as lightning, Connor pushed her behind him. He stepped forward, sticking his chest out, doing that human barrier thing he'd done on the plane. Then he froze, alert as a dog sniffing the breeze.

Jenna stared. Wait a second. He actually was sniffing the breeze.

"Jenna?" a familiar voice called.

She stepped forward and touched Connor's arm. "That's my sister." In a louder voice, she called out to Jody, "Coming."

Her voice was light, but her heart sank. She didn't want to go anywhere, and she didn't want anyone butting in.

That didn't stop Jody from walking up, followed by her boyfriend, Cruz, who glared the second he spotted Connor. Around Jody, Cruz was a sweetheart — well, a gruff sweetheart — but sweet, indeed. Around other men, though...

Jenna backed up to give them space and bumped into Connor, who was glaring right back at Cruz. His face stiffened, and she swore his stubble thickened as his laser gaze warned Cruz away. Cruz's eyes were screaming all kinds of deadly warnings too, and neither man showed the slightest sign of backing down.

Help Connor. Touch him, the little voice said. *Calm him.*

She fought away the urge to place a hand on his chest, but she did hum under her breath, telling him it was okay.

"Hey, Jenna. Did you sleep well?" her sister asked as if she was used to men growling at each other like a couple of angry Rottweilers.

The second Jenna placed a hand over Connor's forearm, heat rushed through her veins. His hand brushed her lower back, out of sight of the others. Was that just an innocent bump, or did he relish the contact too?

"Great. Super. I slept really well," she stammered, trying not to blush.

"Hi," Jody chirped at Connor, offering her hand. "You must be one of the new guys. I'm Jody, and this is Cruz."

Cruz bristled as Jody and Connor shook hands, but he didn't say a word.

Connor forced a polite smile. "Connor Hoving. Nice to meet you."

Hoving. Connor Hoving. Jenna parked that little tidbit of information away in her mind.

"Great that you're here," Jody said, then waved Jenna in the direction she'd come from. "Breakfast is that way, little sis. After that, we really need to talk. Remember?"

Of course, Jenna remembered. Jody had hinted at some big secret the night before, and she wondered what it was. Was Jody pregnant? Planning to marry Cruz? It sounded like something big, that was for sure.

"Would you like to join us for breakfast, Connor?" Jody asked.

Cruz's glare said, *Who said we have to invite him?*

Connor shook his head. "I have to meet Kai, but thanks." His eyes dropped to Jenna's and hung on. "See you later?"

Was it just her, or were his words loaded with subtext?

Before she could so much as smile an enthusiastic reply, Cruz's mouth opened a tiny bit, and Jenna swore she heard a muffled growl.

"See you later, Connor," Jody said, quickly leading Jenna away.

"See you later," Jenna called, looking back.

But Cruz had already positioned himself between her and Connor, making a wall with his body the way Connor had done on the plane.

Jenna shook her head and whispered to her sister as they walked away. "Man, oh man. What is it with these überterritorial guys?"

Jody glanced at her, looking uncharacteristically serious. When she whispered back, it was in a strangely scratchy voice. "I'm about to explain."

Chapter Six

Jenna clutched a pillow to her stomach and sat very, very still. Only half an hour had passed, but the yearning sense of possibility she had felt around Connor was replaced by cold fear.

She was on her sister's couch, face-to-face with a Bengal tiger. A huge tiger with big whiskers and a ridiculously long tail that swiped left and right in an *I want to eat you* kind of way.

Jenna's heart raced, and she wished Connor were there. He seemed capable of wrestling a tiger with his bare hands, didn't he?

"Jody?" she whispered, hoping that really was her sister.

The giant cat's whiskers twitched, and the beast showed its fangs.

Jenna pulled her feet up and backed as far into the couch as she could. "Holy shit, Jody. Is that really you?"

The tiger nodded and butted Jenna's knee with her head until she had no choice but to pet it.

Right, sure. Okay. The last time they had met, Jody had told her about shifters, but she hadn't admitted to being one. Her sister, whom she'd known her whole life, could turn into a wild animal?

Jenna stared, and the evidence stared back — evidence in the form of an orange-and-black-striped cat that extended at least eight feet from nose to tail, not to mention a set of startlingly long teeth.

"A tail, Jody? Seriously?" Not that the tail was the biggest surprise, but she had to focus somewhere.

The tiger winked while it paced, followed by a calico kitten that mimicked its every move. Then the tiger backed away and stretched. The light filtering through the trees shimmered, and a second later, the animal was her sister again, curled up in what looked like a graceful yoga position before she stood with a wry grin.

"See?" Jody said, all matter-of-fact.

Jenna yanked the pillow from her belly and threw it at her sister. "Yes, I did see. Did you have to come so close?"

Jody just laughed and threw the pillow back. "I had to make sure you knew it was me."

The kitten pounced on the pillow, not the least surprised at what had just happened.

"Yeah, I saw, all right. But — wow, Jody. How? No, wait. Put some clothes on first. Please. It's like looking at your modeling pictures, but worse."

Jody made a face and pulled her shirt back on. "Don't remind me. Thank goodness my one and only modeling gig is over."

"I still don't get how modeling made you a tiger."

Jody laughed. "Modeling didn't. Cruz did." She pointed overhead.

Jenna followed Jody's finger up into the shadows of the luxury treehouse her sister lived in with Cruz. Platforms had been built into the branches of an ancient monkeypod tree, some covered, others open to the sky. A series of rope bridges curved here and there, connecting them. The shadows stirred, and an even bigger tiger peered down at her, looking bored. Was that Cruz? Jenna had gotten to know her sister's new flame on her last visit to Maui, and yes, *tiger* fit him to a T. But still — a real tiger? Holy crap.

"Right. A mating bite," Jenna said, staring into her mug. Maybe her drink had been spiked.

"Yep. See right here?" Jody tipped her head back and pointed to the pair of tiny scars on her neck. "It's called a mating bite. You do it in the middle of sex and—"

Jenna slammed her hands over her ears. "Too much information."

Normally, she didn't mind giggling over the particulars of a steamy encounter. But right now, she could be spared the details supplied by the satisfied look on her sister's face. Jody had let Cruz bite her in the middle of wild, raging sex? And that had made her into a tiger shifter?

Not that Jenna wasn't a fan of wild, raging sex. It was just a little too much to process right now.

"And you're saying everyone here is a shifter? Everyone?" Jenna demanded. She stared at the kitten. "Wait — what does he change into?"

"She," Jody said. "Nothing — Keiki is just a kitten. A really sweet one," Jody hastened to add, petting it. "But, yes — everyone on the estate and next door at Koakea is a shifter. Cruz and I are the only tigers here. The others are wolves, bears, and...well, other things."

Other things? Jenna wasn't sure she wanted those details either.

Then it hit her. "Whoa. What about Connor?" God, could he turn into an animal too?

"Who? Oh, the new guy?" Jody looked at her closely. Too closely.

Jenna waved her hands, changing the subject. "Hang on. Do you all end up naked after you change?" She cast a wary glance at Cruz. "By the way, I believe it now. No need for you to demonstrate too."

Cruz grinned and flicked his tail.

"We don't change bodies," Jody said. "We shift. The animal side is always there, inside."

A voice echoed through Jenna's mind, and she thought about the whispers that had urged her to kiss Connor. But that was different, right?

"So... Tigers. Wolves. Bears. And you're one of them. Does Dad know?"

Jody shook her head. "I haven't told him yet. But here's the thing." She tugged on Jenna's hands until they were sitting face-to-face. "It isn't just shifters most people don't know about. There are other beings as well."

Jenna's jaw dropped, and in the ominous silence that followed, a raven cawed in the distance. Cruz, she saw, was glowering into the shadows, and even Keiki looked somber.

"Others? What others?" she demanded, even though she already knew.

Her sister took a deep breath and held her hands tighter. "Like I told you. A vampire came after me here on Maui."

Jenna nodded slowly, trying to digest it all. Yes, Jody had already warned her of that. But still — seeing her sister transform made the notion of other supernatural creatures that much more real.

She shivered. "You said he wanted your blood."

Jody looked down, avoiding her eyes. "He wanted *your* blood."

"What?"

Jody glanced up, her eyes filled with dark memories. "The vampire wanted me because he thought Dad was my biological father. But you're the only one with Dad's genes."

Jenna shrugged. Technically, Jody was her half sister. Same mother, different fathers. So Jenna was the only one with Monroe genes.

"When did that ever matter?" she protested.

"It doesn't matter to us. Sisters are sisters, and Dad is the best dad ever to all of us. But the vampire was after what's in dad's blood, and you're the only person that was passed on to."

Jenna blinked. "The only person *what* passed on to?"

"Mermaid blood, Jenna. Dad's family has some mermaid ancestry. That means you have it too."

Jenna blinked, about to protest. Tigers, vampires, and now mermaids?

But before she could open her mouth, a slew of watery images filled her mind. Visions of light filtering through the ocean, seen from deep below. The streamlined keels of boats zipping by overhead, the peaceful sway of kelp below. Jenna held her breath. When her sister spoke, her voice seemed far away.

"Jenna? What is it? What do you see?"

The same thing she'd seen in her childhood dreams — and on quiet nights when the sound of the surf reached all the way to her bedroom back at home. Schools of tiny fish glittering like thousands of diamonds, turning in uncanny harmony. Frolicking dolphins, squeaking with glee, surrounded by the beautiful green froth of a wave as seen from underneath.

Mermaid, a voice whispered in her mind, all hushed and mumbly as if awakening from a deep sleep.

Sometimes, when a big wave kicked her off her surfboard, she would stay under an extra minute or two just to watch the waves roll and foam. As a child, she'd terrified her parents when she'd remained underwater longer than any child ought to be able to.

Jody gripped her shoulders. "There's no mermaid in my blood, Jenna, but there is in yours."

"Mermaid?" she asked, still trying to digest it all.

"Apparently, the last full-blooded mermaids died out generations ago, but there's a little left in Dad's family."

Jenna looked toward the ocean. It was out of sight, behind the trees, but she could hear the surf roll in. She could practically feel it, in fact. As a kid, she'd dreamed of living under the sea — *Yellow Submarine* and all that — but she'd never related it to having mermaid blood.

She shook her head as if coming out of a spell. "Why didn't Dad ever say anything if there are vampires around?"

"I don't think he knows, and when I asked Aunt Frida, she didn't know what parts of the old family stories were myths and what parts might be true."

"Wait." Jenna grabbed her sister's arm. "Does that mean a vampire could be after Dad?"

Jody shook her head. "Apparently, it's mermaid blood that has a special taste, not merman."

Keiki, the kitten, shoved herself between them, demanding to be petted. Jenna reached out absently, but even the soft feel of the cat's fur didn't help as Jody went on.

"It's you I'm worried about. And when you mentioned a stalker... That started after your picture made the newspaper, right?"

Jenna gulped, and the peace brought on by the watery images vanished. A few weeks earlier, a freelance photographer had snapped a picture of her coming out of the water at Seal

Beach as a couple of young girls looked on in open wonder. One of the kids had a *Little Mermaid* bucket in her hand, and the shot had made the LA Times weekend edition with a huge caption. *Modern-day mermaid?* Jenna's blond hair was slicked back, and water trickled over the aquamarine sun shirt she'd worn that day. Aside from the goofy caption, she'd been amused to make the paper, and her dad had framed a copy in the window of his shop with his own caption.

No mermaids. Just the best boards in town. Come on in.

But, shit. Jody was right — the stalker had started texting her not long after that.

"Are you still getting those creepy messages?" Jody asked, looking more concerned than ever.

Jenna's mouth went dry and took on a bitter taste.

Dear Jenna, I know we are meant for each other. Can we meet on the pier at one?

That had been the first one, and she'd hit delete without a second thought — until the next one came in.

Dear Jenna, So sorry you didn't make it. I know you'll make our next meeting, however. Let's meet at...

The sender tried at least three more of those, and at one point, she'd been foolish enough to text back.

Who the hell are you?

I am yours, and you are mine, my pet.

Pet? She wasn't anyone's pet. Who was that creep?

She'd punched *Leave me alone* into the keyboard and blocked the number. But soon after, more messages from a new number came through and continued even after she changed her number.

You cannot avoid me forever. I am your destiny, and you are mine.

"Destiny," she whispered. "Who the hell talks like that?"

Jody's eyes filled with fear, and the tiger overhead started pacing in unease.

"Shifters do," Jody said. "Shifters and other monsters you never want to see."

Jenna watched Cruz striding back and forth. God, it would be handy to have a guy like him around. Then her brain sidestepped to the image of Connor. He would do nicely, too. But — whoa. Was he a shifter? If so, what kind?

Her mind ran away with a thousand crazy ideas. He was as big as a bear, but quick too. A mountain lion, maybe?

Then she caught herself. What exactly did she expect Connor — or anyone — to do against a vampire?

Do not be afraid. I will bestow countless riches upon you, and you shall be my queen.

The outdated language, the sense of entitlement, the veiled threats... Were they the hallmarks of a vampire or just the words of a crazy human?

She'd started finding little trinkets too — things she wouldn't have thought much of if they hadn't been followed up by more texts.

Did you get my gift, my sweet thing?

Once, it was a dried-up starfish. Another time, a sand dollar. Then a conch shell. All bleached and bone-dry, void of all life.

Those are nothing compared to the treasures I will gather for you, my queen.

It was creepy as hell. Had the guy actually bought into the mermaid thing?

And then came the message that finally pushed her over the edge.

Dear Jenna, I've waited a long time for you. A lifetime, you might say. But my patience wears thin. Don't disappoint me, my pet. It would pain me to have to take matters into my own hands.

That had freaked her out, and she'd come close to asking her dad what to do. But just when she'd run to see him, he'd told her about Jody's latest news.

"Listen to this, Jenna. Jody has an amazing offer for you." Her dad's eyes had been shining with excitement.

Teddy Akoa, who ran the surf shop where Jody apprenticed, was a living legend, and he'd invited Jenna to help out during an especially busy month.

"It's a great opportunity," her dad had said, as excited as if he'd been the one offered the job.

"What about you?" she'd protested at first. "What about the shop?"

Her dad smiled that bittersweet *my girls are all grown-up* smile of his. "Aw, don't worry about me, sweetheart. Your uncle Barry is coming out next week, so I'll be fine."

She'd nearly exhaled in sweet relief. Her dad and his brother had talked about working together for years, but now that it was finally happening — well, she really could leave with a clear conscience.

"And seriously, honey," her father had added. "It's time you spread your wings."

That was pretty much the clincher. She'd been yearning to do that for a while, but she hadn't had the heart to leave her dad alone. But now, with a baby granddaughter to dote on and his brother for company, her dad would be okay.

Teddy Akoa's surf "factory" on Maui was a shed right on the water, run by one of the legends of the sport. Even if she'd only be helping out with small tasks, it was too good an offer to resist — especially since she had a stalker on her hands. So she hadn't said anything to her dad other than, *Great!* and booked her ticket on the spot.

"Jenna," her sister said, pulling her attention back to the present. "Tell me. Have you heard more from that stalker?"

Jenna looked at Jody, then at the tiger pacing overhead. Her older sister had always been protective — too protective, sometimes. And nice as Cruz seemed, he didn't let Jody out of his sight. If Jenna told them about the newest messages, those two would cage her on this gated estate. Worse, Jody would probably tell her dad and their sister Eileen, who'd recently given birth to a baby girl. They were all over the moon about that little miracle. Why ruin their joy on the basis of a few text messages that might not mean anything? And she hadn't received a single one since leaving California, which was good, right?

On the other hand, she had never lied to her sister, and she didn't want to start now.

"There were a few more," she said, trying to make it sound trivial.

"What did he say?"

Jenna shrugged, but her feet tapped nervously, and her mouth went dry.

My patience wears thin...

"I deleted them. The same old shit, though."

Okay, that was kind of a fib, because *My patience wears thin* and *It would pain me to have to take matters into my own hands* had scared her on a totally new level.

"I haven't heard anything since," she hurried to add.

Jody exchanged hard looks with Cruz, who gave a curt, mysterious nod and padded off.

"What?" Jenna demanded, looking between them.

Now it was Jody shrugging to hide something. "Cruz has some friends in California. They're looking into it."

Looking into it could mean all kinds of things, but considering Cruz's Special Forces background, Jenna gulped. Did she dare ask?

Jody went on. "Now just in case — not that I ever think you'll really need it — there's that knife. Do you keep it with you at all times like I said?"

Keep it with you at all times didn't exactly go with *Not that I think you'll need it,* and Jenna's fingers trembled as she pulled the weapon from the scabbard on her calf. She raised it slowly, watching sunlight glint off the blade.

Jody nodded in approval. "Good. Like I said, it's not a regular knife. It's coated with pure silver and spelled to work on vampires."

That part was new, and Jenna balked. "Spelled — by a witch?"

The blade glinted wickedly, sending a ray of light over her face. Jenna winced. Could she really bring herself to stab anyone?

Then she thought of the creepy texts and decided, well, maybe she could.

"Just hang on to it," Jody said. "It will make me feel better."

Jenna bit her tongue. It sure didn't make her feel better. But the second she slid the blade back into the scabbard, a shot of warmth spread up her leg. Comforting, protecting, a little like Connor.

"You'll be safe here," Jody assured her. "But seriously — no more messages from that creep?"

Jenna's mind whirled as she considered the flowers and gifts, but she really didn't want to bring those up. She'd come to Hawaii to avoid the guy, and so far, it seemed to be working. If a new text came in, she could still ask Jody for help. There was no use in worrying everyone... yet.

She pulled out her phone to reinforce her point. "No new messages. But I do have this awesome picture of baby Wendy and Dad. Isn't that the cutest ever?"

Jody's face broke back into a smile, and a minute later, they were both cooing over pictures of their adorable niece.

Well, Jody cooed. Cruz paced back into view, refusing to let down his guard, and Jenna's mind kept wandering to vampires. Theoretically, baby Wendy was safe since she didn't have mermaid blood. Jenna's dad had adopted both her older sisters when they were little; Jenna was his only biological child, and therefore the only one at risk.

"Oh my gosh, I love these." Jody smiled as she flipped through the images.

Jenna barely heard. Her eyes darted around, exploring the shadows, studying every flicker of light. The estate had the security of Fort Knox, and if it really was crawling with shifters, then she was safe.

Safe, the way she'd felt next to Connor? Or was that all wishful thinking, along with the feeling of some deep connection to him?

Jenna shook her head a little, trying to focus on one thing at a time. Shifters. Mermaids. Vampires.

She took a couple of deep breaths just like her father always said. The best course of action was to stick with her original plan — lying low, helping out at the surf shop, and making the most of her month on Maui. Four weeks was a long time. Enough to shake a stalker. And if he reappeared?

Jenna suppressed a shiver, telling herself that wouldn't — couldn't — be the case.

Chapter Seven

Connor shifted his weight from foot to foot and sniffed the breeze. His eyes kept darting to one corner of the estate, but he hauled them back each time. That was where Jenna had disappeared to with her sister for whatever talk they had to have.

He wished he and she could have a talk too. Just the two of them sitting down and figuring a few things out. Like why he could barely see straight, let alone think straight, around her. Like what she was doing visiting this estate. Did she know about shifters? Had he somehow missed the fact that she might be one herself?

The wind stirred the palm trees that circled the estate's helicopter pad, and Connor bounced impatiently on the balls of his feet. So many questions. More questions than answers.

"Quit fidgeting," Tim hissed.

"I'm not fidgeting."

Tim gave him a look.

Okay, okay. Maybe he was fidgeting. That was his dragon, insisting he go after Jenna and haul her away like some kind of prize.

Good plan, the beast noted.

Connor snorted. Not a good plan. Especially not when so much was at stake.

"Focus, already," Tim muttered as Kai strode toward them from the edge of the clearing.

Connor scowled. He was focused. Well, he had been a little while ago when he checked the chopper over for the upcoming flight. His first mission, as it were, in his new job at Koa Point.

But Kai had taken forever to show up, and the wait was killing him. Too much time to think, no opportunity to act.

Exactly what he had to practice, in other words. He could practically feel his mother and every commanding officer he'd ever served under scrutinizing him. A good thing Kai finally showed up and the action could begin.

"Ready to go?" Kai asked as his mate, Tessa, joined them.

Connor and Tim replied with two thumbs up and boarded the helicopter — Connor piloting, Tim beside him, and the finely groomed Kai and Tessa in the back. Once they were all strapped in, Kai nodded for him to take off. "I'll explain once we're underway."

It was a rare occasion, indeed, when Connor flew by the books. He was a dragon, and flying was second nature to him, whether under his own power or in a machine. But with Kai there — a dragon and an accomplished pilot — Connor did a strict preflight check. Twice. He could feel Kai's eyes on him, almost waiting for him to mess up.

"No unnecessary stunts, hotshot. Just fly," Kai murmured.

Connor nodded tersely and swore to fly in a straight, boring line.

Tim grinned. *I guess he heard about the time you—*

Connor glared him into silence. Okay, so he'd earned a reputation for the occasional wild ride, like flying upside down under bridges — backward. Barrel rolls were fun too, but maybe it hadn't been the best idea to do one with a commanding officer on board. But really — what fun was flying without trying out something new?

Back then, though, the worst consequence he had to fear was being grounded for a while, in which case he could sneak off in dragon form and fly under cover of darkness, any way he damn well pleased. Now, his chance to make something of himself in the shifter world was at stake. So he eased the chopper off the ground, got a feel for the weight distribution, and climbed higher, watching the estate shrink below.

Jenna must be somewhere over there. His dragon looked toward a thick stand of trees on the north side of the property.

"Aw, come on, Kai. Let him have a little fun." Tessa grinned.

Connor hid a faint nod. He liked that she-dragon already.

Kai shook his head in a strict no and pointed south. "Just follow the coast for now."

Connor sighed and forced himself to look forward, not back. Ribbons of greens, blues, and indigo divided the ocean into ever-deeper sections the farther he looked offshore. Flying over Maui beat flying over featureless deserts and inhospitable mountains, that was for sure.

"All right, here's the deal," Kai said, speaking through the headset. "I'm representing Silas. We're going to pay a visit to an esteemed guest, and you two are my backup. Tessa is backup, too, but she also helps to make this look like a social call and not a reconnaissance mission. Got it?"

Connor glanced back. Backup? Reconnaissance? What did that have to do with meeting a guest?

"Not just any guest," Kai explained, catching his expression. "Randolph Draig — a high-ranking dragon shifter from out of town. An associate of my late uncle's."

He said the name *Draig* in a way that suggested Connor ought to recognize it, but all he did was roll his eyes. Dragons and their family bloodlines. How could anyone keep track?

"He's asked permission to visit the island," Kai continued. "Normally, we don't tolerate any outside shifters here, but seeing as he's a friend of the family..."

Connor nodded the way he did when dragons talked about treasure, properties, or inheritances, pretending he knew all about that kind of thing when he actually had no clue. Basically, he was an accidental dragon. With a myriad shifter for a father, he could have turned out to be anything.

Think of the bright side, Tim used to joke whenever they got down about their deadbeat dad. *We could have turned out to be reindeer. Or worse, skunk shifters.*

So Connor supposed he ought to be satisfied with being a dragon, even if he didn't fit into the dragon world.

"That means we have to show respect, but make it clear who's boss. You copy?" Kai asked.

Connor gave a curt nod as he flew south, keeping a good distance away from the condos and beaches of the coastline.

"You two keep your eyes open for anything suspicious. Not that I expect trouble." Kai pointed ahead. "That's Lahaina, and at the back of the anchorage..."

Connor searched the horizon, following Kai's finger. The visiting dragon was on a boat?

A minute later, Tim whistled.

"Yeah. Nice sea toy, huh?" Tessa said.

Connor sized up the three-story motoryacht. The vessel had to be at least two hundred feet long, complete with a helicopter pad, a pool, and a jacuzzi on the aft deck.

"Circle it once," Kai ordered. "Not too close, not too far. Let him know we're checking him out without being obnoxious about it."

As Connor guided the chopper in a slow circle, a man appeared on the helicopter pad, making hand signals to warn him of a crosswind. Connor snorted. Having landed in far trickier places — and under enemy fire — this was a walk in the park. A minute later, they touched down, and the rotors gradually slowed.

"Like I said," Kai murmured before opening his door. "Don't do anything. Don't say anything. Just follow me."

"Yes, sir." Tim nodded.

"Yes, sir." Connor nicked his head, making sure to dim the resentment out of his eyes. Kai was a good man, giving him a second chance. It was up to Connor to prove he wasn't the loose cannon they thought he was.

Two men in crisp white polo shirts and blue shorts quickly secured the helicopter while a hostess in a snug-fitting dress that showed off every curve of her figure led them down an exterior stairwell. Connor sniffed as he went. So far, all the crew were humans, as were the next staff members they were handed off to. None carried the signature scent of a shifter, but one thing was quickly apparent.

Whoever owns this yacht likes redheads, huh? Tim muttered into Connor's mind.

He gave a curt nod. Yeah, that was obvious. Every female member of the crew had red hair — everything from strawberry blond to rich auburn. They came in all shapes and sizes too, from the petite purser who met them at the second level to the buxom hostess who led them down a long, lavishly decorated hallway, but every single one was a redhead.

Like Tessa, Connor couldn't help noting. Somehow, he was glad Jenna was a blonde.

No shifters yet, Tim murmured. It was only when they were ushered into a huge stateroom on the second level that his nose caught the scent of a fellow shifter.

Tim took up position half a step to the right of Kai and Tessa. Connor took the left, facing two burly security guards — one wolf and one bear shifter, if his nose was right. An aquarium at least fifteen feet long was built into the wall behind the men, and a puffer fish drifted lazily back and forth. For the next, long, quiet minute, the only sound in the room was the bubbling of the aquarium and the quiet hum of the air conditioner.

Connor glared. Neither of the guards actually took a step back, but he did catch them blinking. He hid a smile. He and Tim could put on pretty fierce expressions when they wanted to, and it worked every time. Those two guards wouldn't go stepping on his toes anytime soon.

And for a long time, that was it. Nothing happened. No one appeared. Connor found himself studying the aquarium just to have something to do. Fish of all colors flitted around, some ponderously, others rushing as if to find a way out. One ducked into a tiny model — the wreck of a galleon — and another disappeared into a miniature treasure chest.

Treasure. Dragons. He nearly snorted out loud. Well, that fit.

Are those things real? Tim asked, subtly angling his head toward the aquarium.

Connor tried to figure out what Tim meant. *What things?*

Those pearls.

Connor looked closer. Wow. The pearls scattered around the treasure chest did look like the real thing.

Jesus, how rich is this guy? Tim muttered.

Connor looked around. Plenty rich, judging by the yacht.

Then a door opened to the right, and Connor's head snapped around. The door fit so seamlessly into the woodwork he hadn't spotted it before. A gray-haired man stepped out with a sly grin that said sneaking up on people was a specialty of his.

"Kai Llewellyn. My, my," the older man said, coming straight for Kai. "Jack and Cornelia's little boy."

Connor held back a snort. Dragons loved playing the game of who outranked whom. But he had to give the guy credit for making a pretty formidable impression himself. Tall and not the least bit stooped in spite of his age. Long, wavy hair. A thick, chest-long beard. If the guy had a trident in one hand instead of a cigar, he'd make a perfect Neptune.

"Mr. Draig," Kai said in a perfectly even voice.

"Please, call me Randolph. And you must be Tessa," Draig said, holding her hand a little too long.

"Nice to meet you," Tessa said, extracting herself after an awkward pause only Draig seemed to miss.

"My, she's lovely," Draig said to Kai as if Tessa were a painting or a vase.

Connor leaned forward, watching the old man's eyes gleam. *What an asshole,* he muttered to Tim.

Pure asshole, Tim agreed.

Kai bristled but didn't act other than subtly stepping forward while Tessa stepped back.

"This is my nephew, Anton," Draig said, motioning to the young man who'd followed him in. A twentysomething-year old with carefully styled hair and an upturned nose, wearing a polo shirt embroidered with some kind of sailing emblem. The guy exuded *private school snob* and *big money.*

I hate him already, Connor couldn't help muttering into his brother's mind.

"Come, have a seat." Draig motioned to the leather couch while reaching for a decanter. "Can I get you a drink?"

A striped angelfish drifted past the glass wall behind Draig, looking every bit as self-important as its owner.

"No, thank you," Kai said, sitting down in a way that protected Tessa from Draig.

Draig didn't acknowledge Tim — lowly bear shifter and all that — but when he caught a whiff of Connor's dragon scent, he did a subtle double take. A second later, he exhaled a thin plume of smoke in Connor's direction — cigar smoke mixed with a disdainful puff of dragon's breath — and turned his full attention to Kai. And a good thing, too, because Connor could just imagine how that introduction would go.

You're Mister Who? Hoving? Funny, I'm not aware of that clan.

Connor had received the same dismissive response from dragons for most of his life. Kai and Silas were among the few dragon shifters who judged a man by his merits rather than his pedigree, but most dragons tended to sniff and turn their noses up — like Draig and his even less subtle nephew, Anton, who yawned.

Connor ignored them — on the outside, at least. When Draig's security guards fanned out to opposite corners of the room, Connor and Tim did the same, staying on high alert. Draig might have been a friend of Kai's extended family, but he sure smelled like an enemy to Connor.

"So good of you to indulge my wish to visit this beautiful island one more time," Draig said, getting all chummy with Kai. "May I offer you a cigar?" Kai turned it down with a polite shake of his head, and Draig went on. "Your uncle was a great host in his time. I was so saddened to hear of his death."

That part sounded genuine enough, but Connor kept a close eye on the guy for any sign of deceit. Kai's uncle had been poisoned by a rival dragon — just more evidence of how fucked up the dragon world was. It was practically medieval at times — shiny megayachts aside.

Nothing like Jenna, his dragon sighed.

That was for sure. She was genuine, down-to-earth. The antithesis to all this bullshit he couldn't stand. He could picture her there, wearing cutoff jean shorts, popping gum, refusing to play by the rules. A little like him.

Anton dropped three ice cubes into a glass and poured himself a drink, wearing a *don't you wish you were me* expression the whole time.

Right. As if Connor ever wanted to be anything like that. Pampered. Privileged.

"May I ask how long you'd like to stay?" Kai asked, sticking to business.

Draig gave the ice cubes in his glass a little shake. His eyes strayed over to Tessa — or rather, the hem of her skirt — then jumped back to Kai's face. Connor could see Kai fighting to keep cool. No self-respecting shifter put up with another man eyeing his woman, but this was one of those delicate situations even Connor could recognize. The old geezer was checking out Tessa, but — well, she *was* beautiful. As long as Draig didn't go any further — and judging by his old-time manners, he wasn't likely to — Kai had no grounds to react.

"Our departure is weather dependent, I'm afraid. And regrettably, my captain has informed me that he is having trouble locating a replacement engine part." Draig frowned and waved a hand as if to say, *It's so bothersome to have to deal with staff. Don't you agree?*

Not just an asshole. A snobby asshole, Tim muttered into Connor's mind.

Snobby, womanizing asshole, Connor agreed, watching Draig eye the hostess, who moved silently around the room, setting down macadamia nuts and crackers. Anton ogled her even more openly, turning Connor's stomach.

"I hope not to remain for more than a week or two," Draig said, sounding bored already. "I so wanted to visit the island, but not quite for so long."

"I'm sure we could arrange for a private jet," Kai said in a thinly veiled hint. *I can get you away from this island anytime I want.*

Draig puffed out three perfect smoke rings. "I'd appreciate that, my boy, if it comes to that."

Boy? Connor would have socked him for that. Which was why he supposed Kai did the talking. Maybe Connor could learn a thing or two from him.

"And how exactly do you plan to spend your time on Maui?" Kai asked, making it clear he intended to establish strict limits when it came to anyone visiting his turf.

Draig grinned and held a hand to his back. "I'm not quite up to my old carousing these days. Just a little golf. A little wine sampling. Old man activities. Someday, you'll understand."

The man was a master of subtly reminding his audience that he was the elder and better dragon.

Kai sat straight, his shoulders wide, reminding Draig — and Anton — who ran this place. Finally, he nodded slowly. "We'd be happy to accommodate your request. With one stipulation — one we insist on for the few dragons we allow on our territory. No shifting and exploring in dragon form. You will remain in human form at all times."

Anton opened his mouth to protest, but Draig laughed first. "Oh, that won't be an issue, my boy. I like the occasional swim when the water is warm enough, but sadly, these old bones are not up to flying any more."

Kai glanced at Anton in warning, then looked over at Tessa, who gave him a quick nod of approval. Connor had to agree. The old dragon might be an ass, but what harm could he be as long as he stuck to golf carts and wine bars? Anton, he wasn't so sure about, but it was up to Draig to keep an eye on him.

Kai stood briskly and shook Draig's hand. "Good. We have an agreement." *And I expect you to abide by it,* his stern eyes said.

Anton stuck out his hand, but Kai ignored it, as did Draig.

"Enjoy your time on the island," Kai said. "We'll check on you from time to time."

In other words, *We'll be keeping an eye on you.*

Connor liked that part, because it assured him his new job wouldn't only consist of routine patrols around the estate.

"And remember," Kai finished. "We're happy to arrange for a jet for you anytime."

That was polite dragon code for *We can boot you off this island whenever we want.* That much, even an uninitiated dragon like Connor knew.

He hid a grin. Kai was one smooth operator when he had to be, toeing a thin line between etiquette and threat.

"We'll be sure not to impose. Now, I couldn't persuade you to stay for a round of bridge, could I?" Draig asked. His eyes slid over to Tessa.

She barely wrinkled her nose, but the message was clear. *No way.*

Kai deftly translated that to, "So sorry, but we have pressing business to attend to. Thank you for your time." Then he took Tessa's hand and turned to go. Connor and Tim closed ranks behind them, following the hostess who escorted them to the helicopter.

Goodbye, assholes, Tim muttered as he glanced down at the lower deck where Draig and Anton remained.

Connor gave a tiny nod. Assholes he'd be watching closely, just in case.

Chapter Eight

"I figure it's perfect for you."

Connor looked around, trying to focus on what his brother was saying. The cliffside location was perfect for a dragon, what with its rocky ledge for takeoff and landing plus the small house with an expansive view over the Pacific.

It was perfect, but something about the night was not. He peered out into the darkness, wondering what was making him uneasy.

"There are just the two rooms up here, but wait till you see what's down there." Tim motioned toward a natural tunnel in the adjoining rock. "...or not," he muttered a moment later.

Connor gave himself a shake and turned to his brother. "Sorry. It is perfect." He clapped Tim's shoulder to make sure his brother knew he meant it. The bear shifter had taken the time to check every corner of the plantation for places the others could eventually call their own. He'd found a big, creaky barn that Chase could convert into a wolf den, and a nice, creekside location for Dell, who already had grand plans for the place. Tim had also scoped out this cliffside for Connor and found a split-level coffee shed he could convert for himself. Someday.

Connor hid a sigh. It would be nice to fast-forward to *someday*, but life didn't work that way. They would all have to earn their futures, one hardscrabble day at a time.

"It will be great to get this all set up once the plantation house is done," he added. "Thanks, man."

Bears weren't big on showing emotion, but Tim's lips curled up at the corners, which told Connor all he had to know.

"Yeah," Tim added. "It will be good. Someday."

They both looked out over the Pacific, alive with the moon's silvery reflection. Then Tim gave a little nod and turned to go. "I have a patrol. See you, man."

"See you," Connor murmured. "And thanks again."

The land leading up to that clifftop was dry and scrubby, but Tim walked off, hardly making a sound. Connor would have liked to spend a little longer talking about everything he'd absorbed in his first full day on Maui. But that uneasy feeling of *something* kept itching at his mind, and he couldn't settle down. Was it just the bad taste he'd been left with after meeting Draig, or was there really something out there he had to watch out for?

One way to find out, his dragon grumbled.

That was true. And hell, this new job, unlike his old one, actually called for shifting into dragon form from time to time.

Stripping quickly, he left his clothes bundled in the lee of a rock. Then he stepped up to the very edge of the cliff and closed his eyes.

All yours, buddy, he told his dragon. *Come on out.*

The shift came so fast, he winced as his body elongated and reformed. But a second later, he spread his wings and cracked into a huge dragon grin.

Feels good, his dragon hummed.

It did feel good to be able to shift anytime. Okay, he still had to take the usual precautions not to be seen by any human. But the plantation offered acres of privacy, and once he flew out over the sea, he'd have even more space to roam. Kai had been right when he'd described Maui. It was the perfect place for a dragon to settle down.

Perfect, his dragon agreed. *Win over my mate. Settle down.*

Connor frowned. Who said anything about a mate?

Quickly, before his dragon got sidetracked with those dangerous thoughts, he shuffled forward until his claws were scraping the edge of the cliff. The wind bounced up the sheer rock face, cooling his outstretched wings.

Yes. His dragon peered into the night. The word came out as a throaty grumble, and a second later, he jumped.

Taking off was always a thrill, no matter how often he did it. But taking off from a great height came with its own high, and he reveled in the sensation. The brief free fall. The crash of waves far below. The whoosh of air over his wings.

He dipped his right wing and made a long, sweeping curve over Koakea, taking in the grounds. The plantation house was three-quarters of the way up a rise, lit by a handful of lights. The barn was next to that, and several decrepit coffee process-ing sheds a little farther to the south. The creek ran down the center of the property, and thick stands of trees guarded their privacy from all sides.

Connor squinted into the night. It wasn't home yet, but it could be.

His dragon swung its head toward the manicured grounds of Koa Point and growled. *Jenna...*

Yeah, he'd love Jenna to be part of that equation. But that wasn't his mission tonight. So he rolled to the left, initiating a long turn out to sea. Night flying was the best, because the world was quieter. Colors more muted, and darkness lent everything a hint a mystery.

He beat his wings a few times then glided on the light breeze. Horses had different paces, and dragons did too, each with certain ratios of wingbeats to glide. This was his most relaxed pace, all the way at one end of the spectrum. Over at the *speed* extreme lay a full-out, teeth-grinding, eye-squinting sprint in which he flapped his wings twice for every beat of his heart — the kind of warp speed he'd only needed to whip himself into a few times in his life. But this was his cruising speed, his walk in the park.

Could do this for hours. His dragon stretched out each glide phase, then powered forward again. As he flew, his eyes narrowed on dots of lights clustered in the south — the an-chorage where Draig's yacht lay. Was that the source of his restlessness?

Just as he was about to fly over to inspect it, something caught his eye. With a quick snap of his tail, he whirled toward the west. What was that?

His nostrils flared, emitting tiny twin flames, each barely bigger than a candle. The first few times he'd changed into dragon form as an adolescent, he'd nearly torched half of northern Utah to the ground. Since then, he'd learned to curb his fire-breathing instincts to go unnoticed and leave the landscape unscathed.

Enemy, his dragon snarled.

He stretched his neck forward to pick up speed and sniffed the air. His eyes focused on a *now-it's-there, now-it-isn't* movement way out by one of the neighboring islands — Molokai. Something just like a bird rising and dipping in an unsteady wind. But he wouldn't have been able to see a bird from this distance, which meant whatever was flying out there was big.

Dragon-big.

Another little puff of fire escaped his mouth, and his chest burned the way it always did when anger set in. What dragon dared come so close to his new territory?

He sped onward, keeping low to the water, stalking the mystery dragon. Had Draig already broken his word and taken off for a flight? Connor doubted it was any of the dragons of Koa Point. Silas and Cassandra were away on business, and Connor had seen Kai and Tessa fly into the craggy mountains of West Maui earlier that evening. So, who the hell was that?

Wind whistled in his ears as he raced along, his heart pounding faster all the time. The dragon wasn't flying directly off Molokai, he realized. It was swooping around a rocky islet off the island's east coast. One of those sheer, craggy islets where birds liked to roost and boats came to tragic ends. There wasn't a light on that spit of land, nor a boat anchored nearby, which was good. If it did come to some kind of fight, they were unlikely to be detected by humans.

Or so he hoped.

In any case, that was definitely a dragon. And damn, if that was Draig, the old dragon was spry as hell. The beast hovered over a spot in the sea then abruptly climbed higher — not nose first, the easy way, but rather, with huge scooping motions of its wings while its head stayed firmly oriented toward the sea. The dragon made the move look easy, but Connor knew how energy-sapping that maneuver could be. A heartbeat later, the dragon flipped around and dove.

He stared. Dragons soared, glided, or hovered. But going for a dip?

I like the occasional swim when the water is warm enough, Draig had said.

Connor diverted eastward, giving the area a wide berth until he located the dragon. So far, he hadn't been noticed, and he wanted to keep it that way.

There! He whipped around as plumes of water exploded and the dragon shot upward just as gracefully as it had dived.

Connor went from wait-and-see to full speed ahead, recognizing his moment to catch the enemy off guard. He sped straight for the unsuspecting dragon until he was close enough to see water dripping off its yellow-brown wings. Then he opened his mouth and bellowed in his deepest dragon voice.

"Who the hell are you?"

To human ears, his words would have been a garbled, ear-splitting roar. But any fellow dragon could understand him perfectly.

The other dragon whirled as Connor zoomed past, waiting for the last possible second to angle away from a bone-breaking crash. For a split second, he saw the whites of the unknown dragon's eyes, spread wide in terror and surprise.

He chuckled and gave himself a mental point for the element of surprise.

"Who the hell are you?" the other dragon spat a moment later.

Connor circled it in the air, letting his teeth glint in the moonlight. "I'm the one who asks questions here."

His next sentence would have been *So who the hell are you?* but the other dragon turned, and the answer popped into his mind.

"Anton," he growled. Draig's nephew, the entitled little punk.

Humans stuck their palms up to show innocence; dragons showed the undersides of their wings.

"Um..." Anton stammered, backing away.

"What part of *no shifting and exploring in dragon form* do you not get?" Connor growled.

"I thought you meant my uncle," Anton tried.

Connor couldn't tell if the young dragon was stupid enough to mean that or assumed Connor was dumb enough to buy that crap. He roared, letting a six-foot flame slice into the night. "Try again, asshole."

"Honestly, I didn't know," Anton insisted, skittering away.

"Then what are you up to out here?" Connor demanded.

Anton grinned. He actually grinned. "Pearl diving."

What the hell? Connor was just trying to puzzle that out when Anton lunged at him. Dagger-like teeth clacked an inch away from Connor's wings, and the dragon's eyes glowed a fiery yellow.

"Doing whatever the hell I want," the punk sneered.

Connor spun away, then roared. The kid wanted a fight? He'd get one. "Not on my turf, you're not."

Anton laughed as he darted to the left, avoiding Connor's next blast of fire. A short, thin blast, because even way out at an uninhabited island, a dragon had to be cautious about being discovered.

"Ha. It's not even your turf," Anton sneered. "It's the Llewellyns'. For now."

Connor wasn't sure what pissed him off more — the personal insult or the veiled threat. "You're messing with the wrong dragon," he warned, moving in.

Anton's eyes narrowed to slits. "No, you are. Do you even know who my uncle is? Do you know who my father is?"

Connor scowled. The only thing he hated more than rich, entitled, and self-absorbed dragons was their offspring.

"Someday, I'll inherit everything they have. I'm the only heir."

"Lucky you," Connor muttered.

Anton laughed. "You can't touch me, asshole."

Connor was so, so tempted to shoot back a reply. But this was one of those *actions speak louder than words* moments, and he knew it. So he feinted left as if to bite Anton's tail, then spun to the right and raked his claws across Anton's chest.

The kid was fast — Connor had to give him that, because he dodged the move by a hair. A split second later, the bastard was on counterattack, swooping low to attack the softer flesh of Connor's belly. Connor rolled into a quick turn, then flipped back, spitting fire. The kid had better moves than he expected — good enough to drag this out longer than Connor would have liked. Anton was also angry as hell, like all those snobby types got when they had to face up to facts, like maybe they weren't God's gift to the world. But that was dangerous, because Anton was likely to pull out all the stops — roaring, breathing fire, the works — without considering the consequences. All that increased their chances of being spotted, and Connor couldn't afford that.

He reached for Anton's tail, but the sly bastard saw that coming and smacked it away. Then Connor rose, ready to wrestle Anton to a lower elevation where they were less likely to be seen.

"Try me," Anton hissed as he twisted and escaped. He climbed higher and breathed fire, just as Connor had feared.

"Cut that out," he yelled, powering forward and snapping at Anton's tail. His teeth sank in deep, and Anton screamed in pain.

But damn it, the kid was quick as anything. He spun on the spot and shot a broad volley of fire at Connor, forcing him to deflect to the left. A second too late, as it turned out, because the fire caught him on the wing, and the acrid scent of burned leather filled the air.

Anton roared in triumph, and Connor's vision went red.

Time to teach that punk a lesson, his dragon growled.

Ignoring the pain in his wing, Connor barrel-rolled straight back and chomped down on Anton's wing. The young dragon's scream echoed off the sheer cliff on the islet, and a hundred birds took off in panic.

With a flick of his tail, Connor smacked Anton's back, and followed that up with a head butt. A full-force, dragon head butt, not one of those *now we're both dizzy* human moves. Anton wobbled off, barely avoiding the snaps Connor followed up with. Then Connor hung back, breathing deeply, getting himself back under control.

A few months ago, he would have continued the onslaught without thinking about the consequences. But he was supposed to be turning over a new leaf, so he forced himself to slow down and consider his options.

Like killing the little shit? his dragon grumbled.

Yeah, he'd love to do that. But he knew the way the dragon world worked. If an ass like Anton killed a nobody like Connor for trespassing, no one would think twice. But if the reverse were true, Connor would be accused of overreacting, and there'd be hell to pay. Draig would have it out with Kai about hiring hotheaded half bloods, and Connor's ass would be toast.

And Anton, it seemed, knew that. The young dragon spun and fired his own blast of fire at Connor, not holding back in the least.

"Jesus, cut that out," Connor hissed as he pivoted out of the way. That amount of fire could be seen from as far as Maui. Did Anton think the time-honored rule of never drawing the attention of humans didn't apply to him?

Apparently not, because Anton snorted another long flame. The stupid kid didn't know when to quit.

Connor lunged again, aiming a thin stream of fire directly at Anton's throat. The younger dragon screamed and fell away, but Connor didn't relent. Following up with raking claws, pounding wings, and bites, he drove Anton lower and lower until he was hurtling toward the rocks.

"Stop! Wait!" Anton screamed, finally giving up.

Connor scowled. *He* never gave up, not even in the face of defeat.

"I'll stop long enough to see your ass back to Maui," he said, starting to drive Anton across the channel. The island was miles away, but damn it, he'd drag the kid in if he had to. Then he'd kick the kid's sorry ass over Kai's threshold and leave his boss to deal with the rest in a more diplomatic way than he ever could.

"You can't do this," Anton cried, trying to keep one length ahead.

"Watch me," Connor growled, nipping Anton's right wing.

Anton screamed again, but Connor just snorted. The only reason he didn't shred that wing was to save himself from having to haul Anton all the way back to Maui himself.

"My uncle will get you for this," Anton muttered, turning to resist once more. He flailed, kicked, and clawed. Then, with one spiraling flick of the tail, he whipped Connor on the same wing that had been burned.

Connor hissed and drew a deep breath. He was that furious. Close to not giving a damn whether he brought Anton back dead or alive. Mad enough to—

"Stop. Now," a deep voice boomed through the night.

Connor snapped his head up. Shit. Was that Kai?

Worse, it was Kai and Tessa, and Kai was frowning — deeply.

"What exactly is going on here?"

Anton opened his mouth as if to defend himself, and Connor could just imagine how that might go. *Help! I was innocently minding my business when this violent half-breed came along and attacked me.*

Hopefully, Kai wouldn't fall for that, but Connor decided not to test his new boss. Instead, he jerked his head at Anton and growled.

"Junior here decided the no-fly rule didn't apply to him."

Kai's eyes glowed a fiery red. "Oh, he did, did he?"

Anton sputtered and stammered before trying his best line of defense. "My uncle—"

Kai cut him off with a low, dangerous growl. "Your uncle will be as furious as I am, you little shit."

Connor squinted through his rapidly swelling eye. Kai sounded mad, but just at the kid. Maybe there wouldn't be hell to pay for this latest caper, after all.

A dragon could hope, at least.

Chapter Nine

Jenna lay on her stomach, listening to waves roll over the beach a few steps away. It was late — too late to be up, really. The sun had long since set on her first full day on Maui, and what a day it had been. Enough that she couldn't get to sleep. The thrill of bumping into Connor had quickly given way to the shock of Jody's news, and she'd spent most of the afternoon in a daze. Jody had insisted on spending a couple of hours surfing a break a little way up the coast, which was better than sitting around fretting, and being in the water had always given her a sense of peace. But now, her mind spun.

Jenna Monroe, surfer girl, or Jenna Monroe, part mermaid?

She'd spent most of her time in the water overanalyzing every sensation and memory. Did she love diving under oncoming waves just for the fun of it, or was that a hallmark of her mermaid ancestry? Did the thunder of an oncoming wave thrill her because her dad had passed on his love of surfing or because of his genes? Most surfers kicked for the surface the second they got bowled over by an errant wave, but Jenna had always stayed underwater for as long as she could, watching the foam-green water froth and turn. It was magic, the way the color of the water changed as it went from dark ocean swell to building blue breaker to turquoise and finally white foam. But she didn't have to be a mermaid to appreciate the beauty of that, did she?

But beauty was only part of it. There was horror, as well. Was her stalker an ordinary human or a vampire?

She turned back to the book that lay open before her on the bed and muttered, "*Vampires: Volume One?*"

Whatever was in Volume Two, she wasn't sure she wanted to know. Volume One was scary enough. It was an ancient, dusty volume with a cracked leather cover and hand-decorated pages. One illustration was a Michelangelo-type sketch of a man with his arms and legs extended — but that "man" was a vampire with monstrous fangs. Another sketch showed a close-up of a terrifying face with teeth bared wide. Little lines pointed out various features captioned on the sides. The fiery red eyes. The fangs that connected to ducts called...

She squinted at the tiny print. "Blood conduits?"

She slammed the book shut, pushed it aside, and looked out the open door of the guest cottage. A sea breeze made the palms sway, and crickets chirped in a steady chorus all around. She was reading by candlelight so as not to dim her view of the stars, and that only added to the mystery in her mind.

Vampires. Tiger shifters. Mermaids. Could it really be true?

She pulled over another book Jody had lent her — *Weres, Wolves, and Whims* — and leafed through the pages.

Are you serious? Jenna had protested when Jody had first dropped the books off at the guesthouse.

I'm serious. Silas has a whole library of this stuff, Jody had said. *Who knows what you might find out?*

Frankly, Jenna wasn't sure she was ready for more. She was still in shock from that morning.

Everyone here is a shifter. Cruz and I are the only tigers. The others are wolves, bears...

Jenna turned a few pages and stopped in the *Ursines and Werebears* section. What about Connor — what would he be? He was big, but not as bulky as a bear. A wolf, maybe? She flipped to the front of the book and checked the *Wolf shifters and related canines* section. Connor did have that canine protectiveness, that constant state of alert. She read a few lines, then stopped short.

Wolf shifters, like all shifters, feel an intense pull toward their destined mates...

Little alarms went off in the back of her mind. Mates?

...and once fully mated, they share a lifelong bond.

Mated? She frowned and flipped back to the introductory section of the book, which had an entire subsection on the theme.

Placement and depth of the mating bite may differ, but each species and subspecies completes a mating rite at the height of copulation...

Her eyebrows jumped up. It all sounded so primitive. So crude. And yet, her body heated at the thought, and she couldn't help picturing wild, instinctive sex with Connor.

Most fated mates recognize each other on first sight, the book went on to say.

Jenna sucked in a slow breath, going back to the first time she'd met Connor. She'd stopped breathing for a minute or two.

Your mother and I, we just knew, her dad often said in a dreamy voice.

Her eyes drifted over the text in the book. *Mates are true to each other for a lifetime and never go astray.*

That fit too. Her dad hadn't so much as dated another woman after her mom died fifteen years ago.

Don't need anyone else. Besides, she's still here, he'd say, tapping his heart with a misty-eyed smile.

Jenna stared off into the distance. Some people believed in soul mates. Maybe mates were like that. Then she frowned. What about mermaids? Did they bite too?

She checked the glossary and skipped to the mermaid section, which was all the way at the back of the book along with unicorns and pegasi, all marked *Believed Extinct.*

Little is known about mermaids, with the last confirmed report coming from 1736...

She blinked a couple of times. 1736?

...but rumors of small communities persist even to this day.

Somehow, that made her brighten again.

Mermaids had some of the greatest variation among shifters in terms of time spent in human and shifted form. Some spent entire lifetimes underwater, while others lived predominantly among humans, indulging in the occasional deep dive...

A rush of watery images flooded her mind along with muted underwater sounds. The churn of distant surf, the squeak of a dolphin. Rays of sunshine stabbing into the water the way beams of light flooded a cathedral. Swirling bubbles, paddling turtles. Some of those images were memories of sights she'd actually experienced. But others had an ethereal quality, like visions from a collective memory that came from somewhere beyond.

Jenna thrust the book aside, rolled to her back, and stared at the ceiling. Mates. Shifters. Mermaids.

Slowly, she slid the knife under her pillow and blew out the candle. A thin wisp of smoke danced in the breeze until it faded into the night. She tapped her fingers against her stomach. *Sleep. Sleep, Jenna. Sleep.*

Images of shapeshifters danced through her mind, keeping her wide awake. A lumbering bear. A snarling tiger. A howling wolf, followed by Connor, looking perfectly human. What was he?

Ordering herself to sleep didn't help, and neither did picturing her bed at home.

Shifters. . . mating rites. . . Forever. . .

As letters on a printed page, those words were pretty hard to digest. But when they came with the image of Connor. . .

Her hands went from hugging herself to sliding over her body. Slowly at first, then more sensuously, and finally, she gave in to the urge. She let her hands slide a little lower, imagining Connor was touching her. His hands would be big but gentle, not teasing so much as warming her up. He'd kiss her, long and deep, and cup her breast at the same time. Her breath quickened as she imagined Connor rolling his fingers around her nipple until it was hard and high, ready for him to kiss.

Slowly, she let her knees fall apart and slid one hand down. She closed her eyes, making that Connor's hand. Letting him touch deeper and faster until she was panting out loud.

"Yes. . ." she murmured, feeling the need grow.

The touch became a pumping motion, and she started to gasp as Connor — even pretend-Connor — brought her higher and higher.

"Oh..." She tipped her head back and rocked her hips, it was that real. That satisfying. Her muscles coiled. Her pants became gasps, and finally—

She groaned, hanging on to the high that swept through her blood.

Jenna, she pictured Connor murmuring as he stiffened over her.

A minute later, she rolled to her side, imagining Connor doing the same. Spooning her from behind, sliding a hand around her waist. Kissing her neck softly, keeping the world at bay.

Go to sleep, Jenna, he'd say.

Funny how much easier those words were to obey when Connor said them.

She closed her eyes and repeated them a few more times. *Sleep, Jenna. Sleep.

∞∞∞∞

*

And she did sleep — really well. At least, for the first part of the night. Quiet, pleasant dreams that befitted a place like Maui. But at some point, when the moonlight was at its brightest, she woke and couldn't get back to sleep. She lay staring at the ceiling, listening to the swell roll over the sand. Calling to her?

She stood and went to the door, looking out. The view was breathtaking, all sparkling water and twinkling stars. Almost as if she were a sailor, out in the middle of the sea.

Come and look, the silvery moonlight seemed to say. *Come and play.*

It wasn't the first time she'd heard that whisper, but now, she wondered where it stemmed from. Did it come from a healthy imagination, or was it the sea calling to her mermaid blood?

She ran her hands over her arms, thinking it over for a long time. Then she pulled on some clothes, strapped on her knife, and strode out to the center of the beach. Why not make the most of a beautiful night?

An owl hooted, and a wave tickled her toes.

She smiled and took off down the beach, splashing through the shallows. The sand was soft on her bare feet, and bioluminescence whirled around her ankles. Like fireflies for mermaids, she told herself, then laughed.

She stopped for a shell and threw a piece of driftwood out into the waves. Everyone was asleep on the estate, and she felt like she had the whole world to herself. A big, beautiful world made of wind, waves, earth, and sky.

By the time she reached the end of the beach, she felt no desire to go back yet. How often did a girl get a chance to enjoy a night like this? She walked on, picking her way around a rocky bend. Jody had assured her Koa Point was perfectly safe, as was the well-protected property next door. Connor was there, and he and *well-protected* went hand in hand. So she kept right on walking, relishing the feeling of freedom. At home, she rarely walked alone at night. But here, on a private estate...

She sighed a little. Maybe she could follow in Jody's footsteps by finding herself a job on Maui and staying. Even better, she'd find herself a job *and* a man.

"Yeah, that would be nice," she snorted, walking on.

But, heck. Even just walking was nice. The salt air scrubbed her skin, and the breeze ruffled her hair. Maui's rich natural fragrance seemed twice as sweet with night-blossoming flowers adding to the potpourri. The ocean was quieter here, with a rock wall forming a calm pool on the section of coast she'd reached. The remnants of an ancient Hawaiian fish pond, perhaps? Something splashed gently, and she stopped to gaze out over the water.

"So beautiful," she whispered.

Moonlight shimmered over the surface of the ocean, creating a long, pale line of sparkling light that wiggled with each tiny wave. She hopped up on a foot-high rock for a better view.

She'd always loved California, but... wow. Maui was amazing. Especially this extra-quiet, extra-private version of Maui, when everything was slumbering and serene.

Her eye caught on a glint in the water — really in the water, not a reflection from above. If it hadn't been such a pristine area, she would have called that a discarded bottle and forgotten about it. But she doubted there was any trash in this water, so what was it? A fishing lure? An especially shiny shell? Something with a golden tint — one minute there, the other, hidden again.

She waded in as far as her knees, tempted to dive to see what it was. And why not? Water was her element, and that section of beach was perfectly safe. So she dipped in once, clothes and all, and stroked a few times. Her hair streamed out behind her, tugged by the water, as was the fabric of her clothes. When she came up for breath, she was all smiles. It felt deliciously naughty to be out there alone, so she did it again.

Over here, the shiny thing called, and she dove to search for it. But the moonlight teased her, mixing with that underwater shine, and her groping fingers didn't close on anything other than rock or shells. Something splashed out in the darkness, and she looked up, feeling vulnerable for the first time.

"Okay, enough playing mermaid," she told herself and retreated to the shore.

She stood there for a few minutes, dripping salt water, watching the stars. Feeling silly, because what if she was taking the mermaid thing too far?

She shook the water out of her ears and crinkled her nose, trying to decide. Well, if there really was something to be found out there, she could try at daylight. For now, she'd head back to the cottage and get some shut-eye.

She set off, following a path she'd missed before. It started in open grasslands, but soon, rough bushes and trees closed in from both sides. A leaf dragged along her calf, and a vine scratched her shin. The crickets sang louder, and a bird — or a bat? — fluttered overhead, making her jump.

She froze, looking up. Bats. Vampires. Were they really linked, or was that just another movie myth?

Either way, her serene night had suddenly taken a turn toward *creepy*, and she turned around. Maybe it was better to stick close to the water, just in case. Her pace quickened, and her eyes started darting about. A twig snapped behind her. Not too near, not too far. A big enough twig to have been broken by a fairly big *something*, judging by the sound.

And just like that, a solo stroll at midnight *really* seemed like a bad idea.

She hurried back the way she'd come, telling herself she was just imagining that feeling of being watched. It was probably just a bird guarding its nest, right?

She power-walked onward, trying to judge how far she'd come. The next time she glanced over her shoulder, the bushes behind her were swaying. Was that from her movement or something else? And, shit. Had she just seen a flicker of red — twin flickers, like a pair of menacing eyes — or was that a trick of the light?

She reached down and pulled the knife out of the scabbard strapped to her calf. The blade glinted as she broke into a jog, hurrying back to the beach. A moment later, she pulled up short again. Something was moving in front of her — unless that was the motion of the swell. God, which way should she go — forward or back? What was out there?

She stood perfectly still, growing more anxious with every too-quiet second that ticked by. Then something really did move behind her — not a figment of her imagination this time — and she spun.

Too late, because two hands were reaching toward her, and her feet refused to budge.

"No!" she screamed, slashing out with the knife.

"Whoa," her attacker said, catching her wrists before the blade met its mark. He squeezed, and she dropped the knife.

Frantically, she combed her mind for a trick from her last self-defense class. What was it again? A vague memory flashed, and she snapped back and jerked her wrists. An instant later, her hands popped free and, *smack!* She slapped her attacker on both sides of the face.

"Hey," he muttered, grabbing her before she could flee.

"Leave me alone!" she yelled, trying to wrench away.

But this time, those hands cuffed hers like rings of steel, and all she could do was wiggle in place.

She raised a knee, because even vampires had to have balls to crush, right? But the dark figure just sidestepped and cursed. She opened her mouth to scream — *really* scream so help might reach her in time.

In time for what? a vague corner of her mind wondered.

In time to do more than find her body sucked dry of all its blood, she hoped.

"Wait a second," her attacker muttered, loosening his grip a tiny bit.

Her heart hammered as she stared. They'd wrestled into a half turn, and with the moonlight shining from the side—

Green eyes. Brown hair. Wide shoulders. Dragon tattoo.

"Connor?"

"Jenna?" He dropped her hands, and she jumped back.

"Damn it! You scared the crap out of me!"

He rubbed his cheek, looking her up and down as if seeing her in a whole new light. When he knelt for the knife, her heart jumped to her throat in a new wave of panic. But Connor just rotated it smoothly and handed it to her, grip-first.

"So," he rumbled. "Out for a midnight stroll?"

The anger and surprise that had fueled Jenna suddenly seeped away, and she let out a slightly hysterical chuckle. "Yeah. I do this every day."

Chapter Ten

Connor did his best not to stare. The first time he'd seen Jenna, he'd sensed she was special. But, wow. When was the last time someone caught him off guard long enough to smack him that hard? And what was up with that knife? The second he'd touched the grip, his hand had tingled with a faint trace of energy that had to indicate some kind of spell.

"Seriously. Are you okay?" he asked.

She took a deep breath. "Now that I survived my heart attack."

His gut flipped at the thought of how badly he'd scared her. Her pulse was racing, her eyes wide, her scent laced with fear — and now, relief.

"Sorry. I didn't realize it was you."

It had been an hour since he'd escorted Anton back to Draig's yacht with Kai, and he had just started to wind down. But then he'd picked up on a movement in the darkness and had to investigate. With the wind at his back, he couldn't catch the scent. At first, he'd worried it might be Joey sleep-walking. Timber used to do that, driving their mom wild with worry that he'd fall into the rushing creek behind the house.

But it wasn't Joey. It was Jenna, and man, had she turned the tables on him.

She pursed her lips and motioned to his cheek. "Same here. Sorry."

He laughed, and she did too, breaking the ice. "That was a pretty good move."

She grinned. "Gotcha, didn't I? Well, almost." Then her smile faded, and her eyes darted around. "Shit. *Almost* isn't good enough, is it?"

He wanted to touch her. Hug her. Tell her she'd done good.

"Hey, that was a great start. But, well..." His eyes drifted to her six-inch blade. "Do you know how to use that?"

Her shoulders slumped. "Not really." She waved around weakly. "This is all a little new to me."

Get her out into the open where she'll feel better, his dragon hissed. *And don't you dare scare her again.*

So he took her elbow — very slowly — and led her back to the beach. Her hair was slicked back, her clothes wet. Had she been swimming or something?

He backed up, trying to stay on topic. "What's all new to you?"

She stood staring at the moon before answering, hugging herself, her face hidden by the shadows of night.

"This." She waved around again. "I mean, shifters. Vampires. All that scary shit."

His eyes narrowed as his dragon went on high alert. *Who said anything about vampires?*

Shifters and vampires rarely crossed paths, harboring mutual disdain along with a healthy respect for each other's powers. For the most part, vampires stuck to cities, while shifters preferred open country where they could change to animal form and roam. Just about the only thing they had in common was an interest in keeping humans ignorant of their existence. Connor had met two vampires in his life and hated both on sight. But there weren't any vampires on Maui, were there?

He sniffed the breeze, not so much to search for a scent but the lack of one — the hallmark of a vampire. But all that reached him was the faint whiff of exotic flowers.

"Sorry," Jenna murmured. "I hope I didn't wake you. Or were you already up?"

Connor sighed and muttered under his breath, looking up at the sky he'd been swooping through not too long ago. "Yeah, I've been up, all right."

Jenna tilted her head at him, trying to figure that out. Did she even know about dragons?

"What about you?" He motioned to her wet, clinging clothes.

"I, uh...took a quick dip," she said, a little sheepishly. Then her eyes narrowed. "Oh!" She touched his elbow then turned his chin into the moonlight. "What happened?"

He followed her eyes to his arm. Oops. The burn still showed, and his black eye probably did too. By morning, both injuries would have healed, but for the moment...

He put his hand over hers with the intention of moving it away, but once they touched, he forgot all about that and stared into her eyes.

Destiny, his dragon murmured.

A second later, he gave himself a little shake and glanced around. Oops. He'd better get Jenna back to the estate before anyone came across them and got the wrong idea.

He sucked in a low breath. It would be pretty disastrous for Cruz to find him out alone at night with Jenna and assume he was not only slacking off from the job, but messing around with Jody's kid sister.

"How about I walk you home?" he said, trying to make it sound like an offer instead of an order.

She stared down at the knife in her hands then stuck it back in its scabbard. Then she nodded and stepped close to his side — nice and close, making his dragon preen.

I swear I'll keep you safe, the beast murmured inside. *Forever.*

He tried to wipe *forever* out of his mind, because he wasn't even allowed one night with this woman. But, damn. Her blue tank top brought out the color of her eyes, even in the moonlight. Her khaki shorts managed to make her look cute and rugged at the same time.

"Jody is your sister, right?" he asked, hoping he'd somehow gotten that part wrong.

She nodded.

He sniffed. "You don't smell like tiger, though."

She snorted. "I'll take that as a compliment."

"I mean, not like a tiger shifter."

"What exactly does a tiger shifter smell like?"

He chewed on that one for a while. "Like the jungle. Like fresh rainfall. Like lilies floating on a pond."

She stared. "They do?"

He shrugged. How much did she know about shifters? Why hadn't her sister explained?

"Anyway, I wouldn't know," she said, kicking the sand as she walked. "I guess Cruz is a tiger, and now my sister is, too."

Connor sucked in a slow breath. Cruz was one badass soldier — definitely not to be messed around with, even if he'd supposedly mellowed as of late. Tigers were ridiculously protective of their mates — and that would extend to younger sisters, for sure.

He peered around. The problem wasn't that he was intimidated by Cruz. It was just that he couldn't afford to mess up this job. Where he went, his brothers and Dell followed, and they needed this chance, bad.

"So you didn't know about shifters until now," he murmured as they edged around the promontory that marked the property line between Koa Point estate and the plantation grounds.

Finding out that shifters existed had to be a shock, but that wasn't what had scared her that night or what had made her so nervous on the plane. It also didn't explain a spelled knife.

She shook her head emphatically. "No clue, until I found out they're all around me." Her voice wavered, and she edged away. "You're one too?"

That stung even more than all the combined rejection of the dragon establishment ever had, and Connor stiffened. He'd learned not to care about what other dragons thought of him. But to have Jenna reject him...

He took her elbow gently, though his jaw was clenched hard. "Listen, I—"

She turned to face him, and the pure blue of her eyes made him forget what he wanted to say.

Mate, his dragon whispered. *I swear, she is mine.*

He'd felt a pull toward her all along but resisted the idea. But now, in the moonlight, it was all unmistakably clear — to his human side as well as his dragon.

She is your mate, a deep, distant voice whispered in the depths of his soul.

God, she really was. He'd yearned for a lot of things in his life — opportunity, acceptance — but he'd never, ever felt a need this strong or this sure.

"You what?" she demanded, balling her fists.

His inner beast cooed. *She'd make a great dragon.*

That, she would. But *smart* and *feisty* was the hardest kind of woman to convince of such things.

"I'd never hurt you," he said, and it came out all rumbly. "We're not so different from humans, you know."

She made a face. "Humans can suck, in case you don't read the papers."

His cheeks heated, and his voice took on a hard edge. "Oh, I've noticed, all right."

Her eyes dropped to the dog tags hanging around his neck, and she covered her mouth with her hand. "Sorry. Stupid comment."

She took his hand, and as quickly as he'd taken offense, he calmed down again. Really calmed, as if the tornado that always seemed to be spinning around inside him had whirled off to bother someone else for a change. Without thinking, he took her other hand and rubbed his thumb over her skin.

"There are good people too, you know. And good shifters. The ones who know right from wrong. Who'll never, ever let you down." His voice went fierce as he thought of Tim, Chase, and others, like Kai and even ornery Cruz.

I will never, ever let you down, his dragon whispered, even though she couldn't hear.

His pulse quickened because, shit. What if he did let her down someday? He'd messed up often enough, and half the time, he'd never seen it coming. Like fitting in to the dragon world with all its unwritten laws. Love had to be a hundred times more complicated than that, and neither came with a book of rules.

She looked down, biting her lip. Then she straightened and faked a lighter tone. "And what are you? Bear shifter? Tiger? Armadillo?"

Arma-what? his dragon protested.

"Armadillo?"

She smiled ever so slightly, and the harsh shadows of the moon showed a faint hint of a dimple.

"Sorry," she murmured. "This shifter stuff is all new to me."

This falling in love stuff is all new to me, he might as well have replied.

"So which is it?" she demanded.

I think you really are my mate, his dragon whispered.

But she'd only just found out about shifters. He couldn't exactly hit her with that right now, right? Instead, he bluffed, blurting out the first thing that came to his mind.

"Armadillo."

She burst out laughing, and a second later, he did too.

Since when are you the class clown? his inner beast demanded. *That's Dell's job.*

He had no idea. Only that this woman could knock him sideways just by looking at him.

"Aha." Jenna grinned. "You roll up in a ball whenever danger calls?"

He made a face. "No rolling up in a ball."

"Not an armadillo, then."

He shook his head, wondering how it could be so much fun to do something as simple as amble alongside a woman and talk.

"A merman?" she tried next.

He laughed outright. That was an easy no. He hated open water, even though he barely remembered the time he'd been swept away by the undertow on the first — and last — beach trip his poor mother had taken him and Tim on.

"Merfolk are extinct, I'm sorry to say."

She dragged her foot through the shallows and mumbled something like, "Are they?"

"Yeah. Kind of a shame, huh?"

The outline of the guest cottage came into view, and his gut tightened. Soon, it would be time to say goodbye.

"What about vampires?" Jenna asked in a much tighter voice.

It seemed better not to reply, the same way he had the sneaking suspicion this might not be the best moment to tell her he was a dragon shifter. But it seemed like she already knew about vampires, so he nodded toward the porch, only a few steps away. "Unfortunately, they do exist. But there aren't any around here."

She hmpfed and strode on with her slim shoulders thrown back, telling the world how tough she was. He studied her perfect silhouette, then frowned at the bump along her leg — the knife.

"Hang on," he called out.

She stopped on the second stair of the porch, thrusting her hands to her hips.

"What? Hey!" she protested a second later when he kneeled at her feet. "What are you doing?"

He worked the strap of the knife loose to switch it to the other side. "Wrong leg. You're right-handed."

He could feel her stare on his back. Yes, he'd noticed. When she'd smacked him, that palm had hit first and hit hard.

"It needs to go about an inch higher," he said, making sure his hands touched nothing but the knife. As much as he'd love to feel the smooth skin of her calf, that was off-limits.

For now, his dragon muttered.

"Do you know how to use this?" he asked, looking up.

Her eyes met his, and his breath caught as his entire body fired up again.

Mate, his dragon murmured dreamily. *Mine.*

"Might be that I need lessons," she whispered.

His heart thumped in hope at the same time as his mood sank in despair.

This is our chance, Tim had said when they'd first been offered the job at Koakea. *But damn it, we have to focus this time. No messing up.*

Connor frowned. If there was a fast track to messing up, getting involved with Jenna was it.

"Maybe you can help me," Jenna murmured, leaning closer to him. Her flowery scent teased his nostrils and tickled his skin.

She knows it too, his dragon cried. *Deep inside, she knows she's ours.*

"Not sure that would be a good idea," he managed.

Her eyes flashed. "Why not?"

An entire catalog of compelling reasons thumped open in his mind. *Bad timing. Big trouble. For you and for me.*

He forced himself to lean away. Following his heart had always gotten him in hot water. Maybe he ought to try a new tack and think things through for a change.

"You don't want to teach me?" Hurt flashed in her eyes.

He let out a bitter chuckle. "I want it too much."

Her mouth dropped open.

"You want—" she started, but something cut her off. Namely, him pinning her against the roof post and covering her mouth with an out-of-nowhere kiss he didn't see coming either.

So much for trying a new tack.

His dragon hummed, insisting it was all right. *She wants this. We need this. Just one kiss. Not leaving without a kiss.*

For the first instant, Jenna tensed, but then she melted against him. Her hands fluttered over his back, and her mouth opened to his, letting him taste.

Their tongues touched. Her legs bracketed his, and her body pressed close in all the right places. His mind exploded with warmth and light, like a love bomb had been detonated in there rather than a grenade.

Tastes so good, his dragon groaned.

Her skin was salty, but that was only one ingredient in her delicious *Jenna* flavor. All in all, she tasted like his and, damn. It was possible that he was gripping her shoulders too hard. But his dragon had seized control—

That's not me, the beast protested.

If that was true, then he was a goddamn marionette to fate. Hell, he could practically hear the cackling laugh now.

But he pushed the thought away. Shoved it away, in fact, hanging on to this kiss in case it was his last. Losing himself in it entirely.

The bed's right there, the palms overhead whispered over the thatched roof.

Two steps and we could be in it, Jenna's body all but cried to his.

So tempting. So easy to imagine her beneath him, hugging him with her legs, welcoming him in.

A year ago — even a month ago — he wouldn't have had the willpower to break away. Hell, he could barely pull himself together now. But after a last, *imprint-this-memory-in-your-mind-while-you-can* tug on her lips, he forced himself back. Not too far back, because if Jenna decided to slap him for kissing her out of the blue, he deserved it.

He sucked in a deep breath, watching her eyes come out of their haze. When Jenna reached for him, her face was flushed and her chest rose and fell with each heavy breath.

"No," she mumbled.

He blinked. "No, what?"

She licked her lips and slowly shook her head. "You're definitely not an armadillo. I doubt they could kiss that well."

He risked a cheeky grin.

"Didn't know humans kissed that well," he murmured.

"Maybe I'm not all human," she purred.

And damn — the bed looked closer and more enticing than ever before. But it was definitely time to go and think things through — once he got his shit together enough to see straight.

"Gotta go," he said, stepping back to ground level but still gazing at her. Practically stuck there. "You gonna be okay?"

She moved a little, tantalizing him with her long legs and lean curves. "For tonight, maybe."

The owl hooted, making her expression darken.

Maybe we should stay, his dragon wavered as her eyes wandered to the moon.

But Jenna cleared her throat and gave a determined nod. "I'll be okay. Thanks."

He knew she would be, because he'd be out there, keeping her safe.

"See you soon?" he couldn't help asking.

She brightened a little, giving him enough willpower to step away for good. "See you soon."

Chapter Eleven

Days passed, and it took all Connor's willpower not to spend every waking minute thinking about, seeking out, or trying to engineer ways to bump into Jenna in better circumstances than last time.

It's not like that ended badly, his dragon said smugly.

No, it hadn't, and he'd relived that kiss every night since. So much that he could barely keep his head on straight when it came to other things. But he'd come to Maui to prove himself a worthy dragon, not prove himself a fool.

So instead of hunting down Jenna, he spent long, tedious mornings tailing Draig to various corners of Maui, making sure the old dragon was behaving himself. Anton was gone, sent back to Miami in disgrace, which left just the old man to keep an eye on. According to Kai, Draig had been all in with disciplining Anton, so everything had settled down again.

So far, Draig played by the rules, which meant Connor had to endure hours of watching golf — or even worse, hanging around wine tasting places way up on the slopes of Haleakala where Draig demonstrated just how much of a wealthy snob he was.

"Dry but fruity, don't you think?" Draig said to one of the half-his-age redheads he always kept close by his side.

Connor scowled. Could it really be worth it to have a sugar daddy like Draig?

The old dragon swished the wine around his glass and sniffed. "A floral bouquet..."

Connor hid a snort. What the hell did that mean?

At least the old dragon posed no danger, and with his hotheaded nephew safely off Maui, Connor found his mind constantly drifting to Jenna. Where was she? What was she doing just then?

Sanding. No, wait. She's sweeping the shop, his dragon said.

Which blew him away completely. How did the beast know that?

He closed his eyes, pictured her face, and — bang, there it was. Exactly that image of her at work. The more time passed, the better he became at sensing where she was. He pictured her hunched over a surfboard, pushing a stray lock of hair behind her ear. Another time, he'd sensed her driving along the road to work with the wind in her hair. And then there were the times he pictured her at night, touching herself on the bed...

He'd gotten so swept away with those images that he nearly lost track of Draig — an error that could have cost him his job if he hadn't snapped to his senses in time.

"Hand me that hammer, will you?" Tim called.

Connor blinked a few times. Damn it, he'd just tuned out again, this time, on the roof of the plantation house. That was the other part of his job — fixing the place up. Kai hadn't set a deadline, but the plantation house had to be renovated before anyone could work on their individual homes. So far, Cynthia and Joey lived upstairs, while the guys shared two bedrooms in the wings of the house. They were used to barracks living after years in the military, but the prospect of setting up their own places — not to mention the incentive of moving out from under Cynthia's watchful eye — made everyone work double time.

The jury was still on out on whether Cynthia belonged in the *unbearable bitch* category or *pretty okay*, but two things were for sure. Cynthia knew all about pulling long hours, and second, she knew how to get things done. Even Tim had whistled as another perfectly timed delivery rolled in.

"She's better than the best supply sergeant I've ever seen."

And he wasn't kidding. In the military, there was always a point when something ran out. Caulking. Elbow joints.

Cables of a certain diameter. Sooner or later, construction works always ground to a halt.

Not with Cynthia in charge. Less than a minute after Connor and the others had descended from a full day of repairing the roof, a truck had rolled in with stacks of siding.

Cynthia had nodded, pointed, and said, "Good. Now you can start on the walls."

The thing was, no one could complain, not when she was the first one up and the last to turn in. Even Joey pitched in, and it was amazing to observe Cynthia go from alpha boss lady to warm, cuddly mom.

"Wow! Sweetie, what a great job!" she cooed when Joey pulled protruding nails out of the floorboards on the porch.

Connor, on the other hand, got a stern, "You're finished? Good. That means you can start on the kitchen."

The woman was a dynamo, he had to give her that. Beyond being bossy, she was a good mom. Protective. Nurturing. Even tender, which pretty much blew Dell's Ice Queen theory away.

"Oh, honey. You hurt your finger? Here, let me kiss it."

That was just about the only thing Cynthia took a break for — cuddling little Joey and rocking him from time to time.

Which made her hard to hate, and frankly, hard to beat, too. Who better to run things than a woman ready to sacrifice herself for another member of their fledging clan?

Dell shook his head, reading Connor's mind. *You never know. If the shit ever hit the fan, she could get too emotional and distracted to make a strong leader. Not chopping on women,* he added quickly. *I'd be the same if it were my kid.*

Connor considered. Maybe that was one of those *perspective* things.

Your advantage, bro, Dell pointed out.

Connor hid his inner snort. Like he wasn't getting all emotional or distracted with Jenna constantly on his mind. All he could think about was protecting her. Getting to know her. Making her happy.

So he couldn't exactly claim to be better suited as leader of the Koakea shifters, not unless he got his head back in the game.

"Me and Chase are ahead of you slackers," Dell taunted from the porch. "Right, Chase?"

Chase didn't say anything — nothing new there — but he did flash a grin before disappearing into the house with a roll of cable. And that grin reminded Connor of what else was at stake here. Namely, the other guys. If he screwed up here, they'd all be out of a job. Word would get around, and then what would they do? Most of their skills had a military slant, which meant their only other option would be hiring out as mercenaries.

Fighting for a cause was all right. But fighting for money? Every one of them hated the idea.

Otherwise, their only real option was taking regular security jobs, but that wouldn't provide the focus and challenge they needed. Before long, they'd be bored — and in trouble all over again. Worst case, they would have to break up and go their separate ways. Shifters didn't need much company, but they needed each other. A clan, a pack, a pride — it didn't matter what you called it. They needed each other to stay sane in a fucked-up, human-dominated world.

Connor ran a hand through his sweaty hair. Everything depended on this job. Which meant everything depended on him.

Jenna depends on us too, his dragon insisted.

So what the hell was he supposed to do?

An hour later, he puffed out a long breath. Work was winding down, and the sun was setting. The afternoon breeze was dwindling, and the sky was turning a golden color. The only thing he needed to make this a perfect evening—

You mean, other than Jenna? his dragon butted in.

—was the scent of steaks sizzling over a fire. But Chase was on kitchen duty that evening, which meant...

"Spaghetti! Yay!" Joey cried, racing by.

Connor headed over to the solar shower set up around the back of the barn. Cynthia's bathroom on the upper floor of the plantation house was finished, but the guys were still showering outside.

Jenna, his dragon whispered over and over, driving him nuts.

At least dinner wasn't far off, as he discovered by the time he wandered back to the house. Joey was on the porch, setting the table as Cynthia lit candles around the big table where they'd eaten together, family style, for the past week.

"Am I doing a good job, Mommy?" Joey asked so earnestly, Connor's heart ached.

"You're doing a great job, honey," she said, kissing him on the head.

"But there's no tablecloth," Joey said with a frown. "And the wrong kind of serviettes." He held up a paper napkin.

Connor thought that over as he edged around them to distribute glasses. Tablecloths. Serviettes? Between those comments and the shiny string of pearls Cynthia always wore, Connor was sure she came from some highfalutin dragon family. The question was, what had happened to change her fortunes? His guess was some kind of dragon battle — one that had killed her mate.

"As long as we have each other, sweetie, we have everything we need," she said to Joey.

Damn it. The woman was getting harder to resent every day.

Then all hell broke out as Dell roared from the porch stairs. "Watch out. Incoming lion!"

Joey squealed in delight and ran. He didn't get more than three steps before Dell tackled him in a carefully timed roll that made sure Joey got all the thrill of a play-fight without the bruises.

"Gotcha!" Dell declared, loosening the loop of his arms just enough to let Joey escape. "Wait a second..."

"I got away, I got away!" Joey laughed, scurrying ahead to grab the cardboard sword Tim had made for him. "You can't get me."

Dell pounced slowly enough to let Joey hit him with the sword, at which point Dell collapsed in an exaggerated death scene.

"Oh, he got me! He got me..."

Joey bounced down to declare victory, but Dell rolled and snatched him up, sweeping him over his shoulder. "Snag! Now I really have you."

Joey squealed. "Look, Mommy! I'm upside down!"

Cynthia's mouth was set in a thin line. "Yes, I see that."

Tim lumbered up the stairs with a quick wave. "I see Dell finally found someone at his maturity level."

"Yeah," Connor added. "He'd be a great dad if we could find him the right woman."

"No way, man," Dell said, swinging Joey around. "I'm strictly uncle material. You have to be responsible to have kids."

"You don't say," Cynthia murmured. "Joey, sweetie, time to get down."

But Dell was tickling Joey, who didn't hear.

"Do they have to play so rough?" she sniffed, fingering the middle pearl of her necklace.

Tim shrugged. "Connor and I were that rough as kids, and look at how we came out."

"Exactly my point," Cynthia said dryly.

Connor hid a grin and headed back to the kitchen to check with Chase. "You nearly done?"

The wolf shifter was bent over a steaming pot, his mouth pulled in a tight frown of concentration as if he were preparing a five-course feast and not spaghetti Bolognese.

"Almost," Chase growled.

Almost meant *Let me concentrate,* so Connor went outside — just in time to whip his head around at a shadow coming around the side of the porch.

"Hello there," a woman called from the dimming yard.

Connor stopped short.

"Hey," Tim called back like that was just anyone. But it wasn't anyone. It was Jenna.

She strode up just like she did in his fantasies, with her hair bouncing around her shoulders and her long, bronzed legs sticking a long way out from her cutoff jeans. Her white blouse was like the rest of her — fresh, pure, and bright. She held out a tray and smiled her perfect smile to everyone, making his heart thump.

"Special delivery from next door. I'm Jenna, by the way." She waved to everyone on the porch.

We've met, his dragon rumbled inside. *Boy, have we met.*

Their kiss replayed in his mind in torturously slow motion, and he gulped, hoping she could read the emotions in his eyes.

I want a thousand more kisses like that one, but I can't. We can't. Would she understand why?

She looked him straight in the eye and smiled in a way that said yes, she wanted more kisses, but no, she wasn't about to let *can't* get in the way.

"Tessa asked me to bring this over," Jenna said to Cynthia. "She heard spaghetti was on the menu, so she sent over a batch of garlic bread."

She pranced over with a wink in his direction, telling him she'd engineered the whole delivery thing. Smart girl. Maybe he should find something to bring over to the estate sometime.

"Perfect. We'll have something to eat if Chase messes up the spaghetti." Dell grinned, setting Joey back on the floor.

"Got the takeout menu right here," Tim added.

They were just kidding, but both paled a second later when Connor pinned them with a killer glare. Nobody knocked his younger brother. It didn't matter that military guys were used to poking fun at each other. Connor made damn sure no one did it to Chase. The wolf shifter had spent too long in the wild to understand sarcasm or good-natured jokes. How the hell was Connor going to keep his brother on the human side of the shifter line if the other guys messed with his head?

"Dinner's ready," Chase called from the kitchen.

Tim hurried inside to help, while Dell hoisted Joey to his shoulders.

"See? Now you're as high as a dragon."

Joey waved his sword around. "I am a dragon."

Everyone laughed except Jenna, who paled and shrank back.

Connor winced, remembering the conversation they'd had that night on the beach. Had no one told Jenna about dragons since then?

Sorry. This shifter stuff is all new to me.

Her eyes swept over everyone on the porch then landed squarely on him and went wide. Shit. He hadn't actually gotten around to telling her what kind of shifter he was, had he?

I'm a good dragon, he wanted to say. *You can trust me.*

"Maybe someday I'll be a mighty dragon," Joey went on.

Dell grinned. "If you're anything like your mother, everyone will be terrified."

Cynthia didn't bat an eye. "I'll take that as a compliment."

"I knew you would," Dell sighed.

"You're Jody's sister, aren't you?" Cynthia asked Jenna. "How are you enjoying Maui so far?"

Jenna's eyes jumped to Connor and heated, showing mixed emotions. *The kiss was great,* they might as well have said. *Finding out about dragons, not so much.*

She whipped her gaze away from him and stammered to Cynthia. "Yes... Uh, absolutely."

Besides finding out about shifters and dealing with a stalker, Connor figured she would have filled that blank spot with.

"Having a great time," Jenna finished, looking stiffer than ever.

"Want to stay for dinner?" Dell asked.

When she'd first come up the stairs, she'd looked so relaxed and eager. But ever since Joey mentioned dragons, her eyes were worried and her face drawn. "Well, I'd love to, but—"

"Yay!" Joey said before she could protest. "I'll get an extra plate. I'll get it!"

Jenna stared as the boy ran into the kitchen, and without thinking, Connor pulled a chair up next to his. "You can sit here."

"I... uh... Sure," Jenna said as Joey came running back out.

"Perfect. Here you go," Tim said, scooping a giant helping of spaghetti onto her plate.

Connor held up two bottles. "Wine or beer?"

Jenna stared.

Yes, we're more human than animal, he wanted to say. *And yes, my mother managed to teach us some manners along the way.* Maybe not enough for the highest echelons of dragon society, but not too shabby when he was motivated enough.

And boy was he motivated. That was Jenna, after all.

"Beer," she murmured.

He nodded in satisfaction. He was a beer guy himself.

Cynthia took wine — of course — plus the second scoop of spaghetti Tim served in a *ladies first* kind of thing. He served Connor next in accordance with the rules of shifter hierarchy, followed by everyone else.

"Saved the best for last." Tim winked, setting a plate down in front of Joey.

"So, Jenna. I hear you've been working with your sister," Cynthia said.

"Yes. She's apprenticing with a master board shaper, and—"

"A master what?" Cynthia tilted her head.

"A guy who makes surfboards," Dell said as he wolfed down a huge forkful of spaghetti.

"Or a woman who makes surfboards," Jenna pointed out.

Connor grinned. Jenna might have been thrown by the *dragon* thing, but not for long.

"You two ought to go into business," Dell said, ripping off a giant chunk of garlic bread. "You know, like boards made by women for women or something like that."

"We've thought of that. We even have a name for it. Surf Chique." Jenna's eyes shone. "We could partner with my dad's business — Wild Side Surf Shop." Without skipping a beat, she rattled off dozens of ideas. "Custom-made boards... peppy colors... lighter materials..."

Connor listened in, as fascinated by the answers as by the differences between the two women. Jenna was alive, exuberant. Cynthia was stiff as a board. Had she had as strict an upbringing as poor Joey? And man, had she gone to business school or something? Cynthia asked questions about all the boring, practical stuff — Had they identified their target market? How much capital would they require? — but Jenna countered each like she'd done her homework and then some.

Connor found himself hanging on her every word and gesture until Tim kicked him under the table.

Stop drooling, bro. The spaghetti's not that good.

Connor straightened quickly and tried to find something else to pay attention to. The light flickering from the candle? The crickets chirping outside? The sweet, nighttime air of Maui? But all that just seemed like background filler; Jenna was the star of the scene.

Still, he forced himself to look past her. Joey was forking through his spaghetti, looking disappointed.

"Here. Put some ketchup on it," Dell whispered, handing Joey the bottle the moment Chase stepped into the kitchen.

Cynthia stopped talking to Jenna long enough to poke through her dish. "Isn't there a single vegetable in this?"

A good thing Connor wasn't sitting closer to Cynthia. She might have heard his growl.

Jenna heard it, though, and she turned to him with wide eyes.

"Spaghetti Bolognese doesn't need vegetables," Dell pointed out.

"It could, though," Cynthia said, not getting the point. Connor would have to have a word with her, for sure.

Jenna looked between him, Cynthia, and the kitchen, slowly catching on.

Dell nodded. "It could have vegetables when it's your turn to cook. Oh, wait, I have a different idea. Chase and I can swap. He does my chores, I take his turn to cook."

"I don't know," Jenna said as Chase came out from the kitchen. "This spaghetti is delicious."

Connor could have hugged her right then. And really, the spaghetti wasn't bad. It just wasn't great.

"The garlic bread is good too," Connor murmured, using the cheap excuse to look in Jenna's eyes. They were shining again, and the hesitation had faded all the way to the back.

"It is good," Dell agreed. Then he pointed his fork at Cynthia. "But I can make spaghetti with vegetables. In fact, I can make a lot more. Like steak. Meatloaf. *Coq au vin.*"

Cynthia's jaw dropped. "You know what *coq au vin* is?"

Dell smiled. "Of course. French for fancy chicken." He kissed his fingers and flicked them outward. "Old family recipe. I only use genuine Burgundy, of course."

He was working Cynthia hard, that was for sure.

"I can make lobster," Dell went on casually. "Grilled swordfish. Sushi. Pizza..."

"Pizza!" Joey bounced up and down.

"Or are you more of a seared *foie gras* kind of girl?" Dell asked Cynthia.

Seared what? Tim asked in a quiet aside.

Shut up. It's working, Dell shot back.

Cynthia's mouth hung open. "You know how to make seared *foie gras*?"

"Lady, I can make anything you want." Dell leaned forward, going into full seduction mode.

Connor thought Cynthia was going to drool, but she caught herself and took a hasty swig of wine. Then she pressed her napkin delicately to her lips and said, "I suppose we could make one change to the schedule."

Dell gave Joey a high five and reached for the whiteboard.

"I'll do that," Cynthia said quickly, grabbing it out of his hand.

Way to go, man, Tim chuckled.

Cynthia, meanwhile, took her napkin, neatly wiped Chase's name off the cooking roster, and substituted Dell's in her perfect script.

"Where did you learn to cook?" Jenna asked.

Dell yawned. "The army."

"What?" Cynthia screeched.

Dell grinned a mile wide. "Ha. Gotcha, Cynth."

Cynthia scowled and opened her mouth to protest, but Dell didn't give her a chance.

"I come from a family of chefs. You can say I'm the black sheep of the family."

"Do lions come in black?" Joey asked.

Connor tensed the second Jenna did. "Lion, huh?" she murmured.

Dell looked at her, then Connor, then back to Jenna, and spoke carefully, like he knew he'd messed up.

"Yes, ma'am. A very nice lion shifter."

Jenna made a *hmpf* sound and pointed at Tim. "And you are. . . ?"

Connor blinked. Wow. Jenna could be as bossy as Cynthia sometimes. Only Jenna being bossy was cute, not grating.

"Um. . . a very nice bear?" he managed.

Connor exhaled. *Bear* sounded better than *grizzly*, for sure.

Jenna's finger jerked one spot over to Chase.

"Wolf," he growled.

Connor kicked him under the table.

"Very nice wolf," he added.

Jenna rolled her eyes then smiled at Joey. "Obviously, you're a mighty dragon. Which means your mom is a dragon too. Right?"

Cynthia nodded, and everyone went quiet as Jenna turned to Connor. "And you?"

His throat had gone all dry, so he took a sip of water before answering. "Dragon, of course." He tried to make it sound as natural as possible, though every nerve in his body was tight.

"A very nice dragon," Dell added with a sly look.

Jenna swung her jaw from side to side, and Connor drew back, anticipating the worst. But all she did was scan all the faces at the table and mutter, "Of course." Then she took a quick swig of beer and stared into her glass.

Who knew what she might have said next if Dell hadn't saved the day. He stood, making his chair screech, and reached for the serving bowl with a look that said he was having way too much fun.

"Seconds, anyone?" Dell grinned.

Chapter Twelve

"Holy shit, Jody." Jenna pushed her sister when they met outside the garage to drive to work the next morning. "How could you not tell me about dragons?"

It was time to head over to Teddy Akoa's surf shop for another day of work, but she was still reeling from the previous night. Up to then, she'd been gradually getting used to the idea of shifters — as long as they were nice, furry shifters that resembled the stuffed animals she'd covered her bed with as a kid. Bears, wolves, and tigers could be nice and cuddly, right?

Dragons, on the other hand...

She might have jumped away from the dinner table last night if it hadn't been for little Joey. If a cute kid could be a dragon shifter, then maybe she could learn to deal. Maybe. But the fact that Connor was a dragon shifter still blew her away. She'd kissed him, for goodness' sake!

Her blood heated, thinking of how Connor had walked her home after dinner. Keeping his distance yet wrapping her in his body heat at the same time. Every time he looked at her, his eyes were ablaze with desire, and when he'd leaned against the doorframe of the cottage to say goodnight...

I know you might not agree, but I think that was the best dinner I ever had.

Oh, yes? she'd managed. *Was the spaghetti that good?*

He'd smiled that half smile of his and cupped her face. *Not the spaghetti. The company. Everyone who means anything to me was there — okay, except my mother — and everyone was all right.*

His eyes flared on *everyone who means anything to me,* telling her just whom he meant.

115

She ran a hand down his arm, looking at his dog tags, taking a deep breath. Peace, food, and good company. A reminder of the things that really mattered in life.

That deep breath turned out to be a good thing, because a second later, she was kissing him long and deep. Deep enough to close her eyes and imagine scenarios that had seemed a lot less crazy in the heat of the moment than they did now. Like hooking up with Connor and staying in Maui a little longer. Maybe even a lot longer. Like trusting the little voice that told her he was the one.

It was Connor, not her, who'd broken off the kiss, and even that was a close call, because their lips stayed stuck together a little longer than their bodies did. Then they, too, gave up, and all she could do was stare into Connor's bottomless eyes.

Goodnight, he'd whispered, stroking one thick thumb against her cheek.

Goodnight, she'd replied, clinging to the doorframe, lest she cling to him instead.

So, yes. The previous night had been equal parts *crazy* and *magical,* and her mind still spun with it all. Was the man she'd fallen for really a dragon?

Jody just opened the door to the Land Rover and motioned her in with a casual, "Dragons aren't what you have to worry about. Vampires are."

Jenna slid into the back seat and buckled in — as ever, the baby of the family — with Jody and Cruz taking the front seats.

"Don't worry about dragons?" Jenna protested, thinking along the lines of *big, hunky ones who steal my heart?* But she couldn't exactly say that, so she came up with something else instead. "Big, fire-breathing dragons who sneak up on you in the middle of the night?"

And just like that, her body heated, replaying the way their first nighttime encounter had turned into a kiss.

Jody whipped her head around. "Who snuck up on you in the middle of the night?"

Cruz frowned in the rearview mirror, looking ready to murder someone. "Yeah, who?"

Jenna waved her hands. That was not what she'd meant.

"Dragons don't hunt down mermaids," Jody assured her as they zoomed along the coastal road. "It's vampires you have to watch out for."

"And how exactly am I supposed to do that?"

Jody and Cruz exchanged looks, and finally, Cruz gave a curt nod. "We called in a couple of experts. Vampire hunters. They're in LA now looking into it. Intensively. In the meantime, you'll be safe here."

Her jaw dropped open. "You have... What?"

Cruz just shrugged, like everyone had a network of supernatural buddies to call on for help.

"Anyway—" Jody motioned around "—we're not worried about vampires coming here. They wouldn't dare."

Jenna wanted to snort. Of course not. Cruz stood guard over Teddy Akoa's surf shop all day, every day, as long as Jody was there.

"Anyway, I'm sure you're safe on Maui," Jody said. "It's when you go home that I worry about."

Jenna sat back and stared at the ocean as the car rushed along the road. Did that mean she could never go home? On Maui, she was surrounded by elite military men and tough shifter women day and night, but it wasn't as if she could take them with her when she went home.

And just like that, her mind skipped back to Connor. So tough and hard on the outside — but damn, were those lips soft.

A frigate bird swooped high above the coastline, and she followed it with her eyes. Now, that would be useful — flying like a bird. Better yet, like a dragon. Let a vampire try to get her then.

She closed her eyes, imagining what it would feel like to spread her arms, change them to wings, and take off into the air. Within a few wingbeats, she'd be high in the sky — or turning to dive-bomb her vampire attacker with a long plume of fire.

Ha! Take that! She pictured herself roaring as the vampire turned to a pile of ash. Then she'd do an aerial victory lap and—

In her mind's eye, that sweeping arc turned into a daring dive into the sea. Deep, deep down, where the sunlight started to thin out and the pressure increased. And when she imagined surfacing, she saw herself in human form, sweeping her hair back as if she'd just been out surfing.

She found herself smiling. Maybe you couldn't take the *mer* out of a mermaid, even in a watered-down mermaid like her.

Mermaids — and dragons — occupied her mind for the rest of the day. Well, at least in the quieter parts of her workday. She thought she'd learned everything there was to know about shaping surfboards from her dad, but Teddy Akoa really was a master, and even sweeping up the sawdust in his workshop would have taught her new things. Teddy was quiet, calm, and unpretentious — the very image of a Zen master, especially with his wizened islander looks and long, skinny beard. He treated Jody and Jenna like the daughters he'd never had and even joked at turning the shop over to them one day. Which got Jenna thinking. Maybe Surf Chique didn't have to remain a pipe dream. Maybe she and Jody really could start their own line of custom boards...

...if she ever solved her stalker problem, that is.

The second she returned to the estate that afternoon, she pored over the shifter book Jody had loaned her for anything on dragons.

Among the most magnificent of shifter species, dragons are also those whose behavior is most difficult to categorize or predict.

She snorted. Great.

Great dragon lords were legendary for their steadfast commitment to duty, honor, and clan.

Well, that didn't sound so bad.

However, jealousy, inbreeding, and a hunger for power led to infighting and feuds among the leading dragon clans, and certain individuals earned bloodthirsty reputations. They stopped at nothing in their quests to amass great treasures, power, harems—

"Harems?" Jenna yelped. Her eyes bounced up to the illustrations at the top of the page. In one corner was what appeared to be a good dragon protecting other creatures under his outstretched wings. In the other, a dragon with an evil grin torched a medieval village to bits.

So — were dragons good or bad? Which was it?

There are good shifters too, you know, Connor had said. *The ones who know right from wrong. Who'll never, ever let you down.*

She chewed that one over as she turned a page in the book.

Among the most legendary of this species were the mighty dragon queens. Though few in number and rare in modern times, such queens were credited with having changed the course of shifter history. Some for the better, ushering in periods of peace and prosperity. Others brought about dark eras in the entire shifter world due to their treachery, deception, and unparalleled greed.

"Moira," Jenna muttered. She didn't know much about dragons, but Jody had given her a crash course on the drive home. The shifters of Koa Point had recently vanquished an evil dragon lord named Drax. But his mistress, Moira, was still at large, and no one knew whether to fear her next move or write Moira off as defeated for good.

Jenna slammed the book shut. None of that helped solve her current dilemma. Connor had scared her shitless that night she'd been out wandering. If he had been a vampire, she would be dead.

She pulled the knife out of its scabbard and turned the blade in the afternoon light. At one angle, the steel shone with a hint of gold, and at another, red. Could it really kill a vampire? Did she want to find out?

She picked up her phone, suddenly intent on calling her dad and asking for the number of her aunt — the one who everyone had always thought crazy because she believed in supernatural beings. Jody had said she'd failed to get any useful information out of Aunt Frida, but it was worth a second try, right?

But the moment Jenna turned on the screen, she stopped cold at the incoming message it displayed. Her thumb shook over it for a full minute before she finally worked up the nerve to read.

Enjoying your sunsets, my pet? So am I. And soon, we will enjoy them together. Forever.

She jerked her head up to look out the open door of the guesthouse. Shit. Her stalker was back. Was he out there somewhere, watching her?

The hair on the back of her neck stood as she forced herself to study the message, searching for hidden clues. Sunsets implied Maui, but the sun wasn't setting yet, and the text was two hours old. So maybe he wasn't actually spying on her at that moment. But, shit. Just the fact that he was texting gave her the creeps. Was he a human stalker? A vampire?

She would have loved to run to Jody with the phone, but she had already taken enough of her sister's private time. Besides, Jody and Cruz were like a couple of happy honeymooners, and for all she knew, they were lounging around naked in the rock pool near that treehouse of theirs. The other shifters who lived on the estate were the same way. Hunter, the bear, was so in love with Dawn that he practically bumped into things. Boone and Nina never stopped cooing at their babies — and each other. Did she really want to burst everyone's happy bubble with a text that could have been sent from the other side of the world?

Besides, she'd reported the older texts. What clues could this new one possibly contain? Not only that, but Cruz had called out a team of vampire hunters. What else could she ask anyone to do?

Nothing. But that didn't mean there wasn't anything she could do.

She threw the phone down, picked up the knife she'd left on the bed, and stared at the razor-sharp edge. God, could she even bring herself to slash at someone with that thing?

A second later, she nodded firmly. Hell yes. She could if someone threatened her.

But how exactly did one use a knife in self-defense? She turned it this way and that. Would she use a stabbing action or a slashing motion? Should she target the heart?

Slowly, she slid the knife back into its scabbard, strapped it into the position Connor had shown her, and stood in the wide-legged stance she'd learned in self-defense class. Then she pulled out the weapon as quickly as she could. But, damn. Was she supposed to hold the knife out in front of her or back with her weight on her right foot? And which way was the blade supposed to face? She tried it one way, then the other, then started all over again out on the beach where she had more space. If the stalker was out there watching, fine. Let the creep be warned he'd picked the wrong chick to mess with.

"One. Two. Three." She counted under her breath, trying to break things down. A lightning move to pull the knife out of its sheath, a tight grip, and a quick swipe at an imaginary enemy.

A dozen tries later, she kicked the sand. "Damn it." Her *lightning* wasn't all that fast, and her swipe traveled at a different angle every time. Either it was time to give up or time to find help.

She stood there for a minute, undecided. A crab scuttled over the sand. A gull cawed. A coconut fell from a palm tree with a dull thump. Every scratch in the bushes made her flinch.

"Find help," she muttered, raising her chin as she strode toward the path to the center of the estate. But a few steps later, her determined stride fizzled out. Who exactly could she ask for help? Cruz?

God, no. Cruz was great, but he had to be the world's most growly, overprotective tiger shifter. Not that she knew many, but even so. She couldn't picture him as a patient, encouraging coach.

Who else, then?

Her body leaned right, where the path to the adjoining plantation lay, and a little voice cheered inside. *Connor! Connor!*

She sure wouldn't mind a lesson or two from him. But would he be game?

You don't want to teach me?

I want it too much.

Could it be that she wanted him a little too much, too? Maybe she ought to ask one of the other guys of Koa Point to help her. Kai. Boone. Cruz...

Connor, the chorus in her mind insisted as her feet started leading her down the path to his place.

Chapter Thirteen

"Like I said, not a good idea."

Jenna figured Connor might say that. She took a deep breath and stared him down, having decided on the way over she wasn't taking no for an answer. So she widened her stance and scowled at him. *We can do this the hard way or the easy way, mister. I need you to teach me, and you will.*

But the little line of sweat sliding down his bare chest screwed with her mind, and she could barely get a single sentence out right.

Hard way, his firm eyes said.

When she'd first found him working on the plantation house — halfway up a ladder, shirtless, and glistening with sweat — she'd whispered a little *Lord have mercy* to herself. Maybe getting up close and personal for private lessons with Connor wasn't such a good idea. She might learn about all those amazing muscle groups and fascinating scars, but she'd be too flustered to remember anything about defending herself.

He crossed his arms, making his dog tags jingle in an unnecessary reminder of his credentials. "A knife like that is not something to mess with."

Her cheeks heated, and she saw red. Did he think she was messing around?

"Are you saying a woman can't fight for herself?" She stuck an accusing finger at his chest.

"No, but—"

"Are you saying I should sit back and let someone else protect me?"

"Listen, Jenna—"

"Are you saying I should let this stalker come at me when I have no means of self-defense?"

Connor went totally stiff and growled. "Stalker? What stalker?"

Oops. She hadn't intended to mention that, except maybe as a last resort. She turned on her heel and marched away. "Forget it. I'll just figure this out for myself."

She'd half expected him to follow, but wow. Before she had even shifted her weight, Connor had caught her hand and turned her around to face him.

"What stalker?"

She was about an inch away from his bare chest by then. Heart thumping. Face flushed. Girl parts way too excited for a woman who was supposed to be scared.

"A stalker who may or may not be a vampire. Who I may or may not be able to use this knife on." Her voice rose with all the anger and frustration she hadn't been able to release before. "A stalker who makes me feel like I have no control of my life. So, damn it, I really need help, all right?"

She was puffing by then and glaring, too. Connor stuck his hands up and tilted his head as if to say, *She really is a new species. I've never met someone like her before.*

Finally, his mouth opened, and he grunted one word. So quietly, she barely heard it over the sound of pumping blood in her ears.

"Okay."

"Okay, what?"

"Okay, I'll teach you. Just calm down."

"I am calm," she growled, gesturing with the knife.

Conner's eyebrows knotted as he replied. "Yeah, I can see that." Then he cleared his throat and looked her over again. Differently this time, like a man sizing up a used car, judging just how functional it might — or might not — be. Then he cupped a hand and called up toward the roof. "Hey, Tim."

"Yeah?" an equally gruff voice called, and Tim popped into view. "Oh. Hiya, Jenna." His eyes widened at the knife in her hands.

"Hi," she said, still a little curt from her outburst.

"It's time to wrap up for the day," Connor said.

"But—"

"I said, time to wrap up," Connor barked.

Which is when it dawned on Jenna that she'd pretty much barged in on him.

"Right. No problem," Tim murmured, disappearing from view.

"Sorry," Jenna said, suddenly flustered. Maybe her problems didn't have to be other people's problems. Maybe Connor had enough of his own. Everyone had been so friendly at dinner the previous night, but they'd been weary, too. There were tools all over the place and a dozen projects progressing at once. Clearly, everyone at Koakea was hustling to get a big job done.

"Sorry." She sheathed the knife. "Not so important. Maybe some other time."

"Nope," Connor said, taking her by the arm. "Give me two minutes, and we're on."

And just like that, he was in charge. *Really* in charge, like he had a whole platoon of recruits to whip into shape and a battle to march into at dawn.

"If it's not a good time. . ." she mumbled.

"Never a good time to fight vampires," he muttered, leading her off toward the barn. "Or a stalker. You want to tell me about that?"

She frowned. "Not really, no."

He stared at her, and she stuck her hands on her hips.

"Look, Cruz is on it. Jody gave me this knife, and I doubt I'll ever have to use it. But I sure would sleep better if I knew how to use it."

"I would sleep better if you told me."

She laughed bitterly. "I doubt that. Just thinking about it makes me. . ." She trailed off there, because she hadn't come to show weakness or doubt. She'd come to prepare herself for the worst, which she hoped would never come.

Connor bristled for a long minute then finally nodded. "Okay."

She stared, and one whispered word slipped past her lips. "Finally."

He tilted his head. "Finally?"

She gave herself a little shake. "Not you. It's just good to have someone not treat me like a little kid."

The right side of his mouth crooked up. "Of all the things you make me think of, Jenna, *little kid* is not one." His eyes drifted up and down her body then locked on hers, telling her *woman* was more like it. A woman he respected to make her own decisions and to choose how much she wanted to divulge.

Wow. She nearly pinched him to check if he was real or a dream.

"So," Connor's tone went from resigned to calculating, and he looked around. "First, we need a training knife..."

She glowed a little at the *we*, like suddenly, they were a team.

"Some water..."

He muttered as he went, leading her to a clearing behind the barn. He disappeared then returned moments later with a few things. He guzzled down an entire bottle of water then wiped his glistening lips.

"This is for you." He tossed something at her.

She yelped when she realized it was a knife, and it landed on the ground with a dull thump. "Oh. Training weapon, huh?" She picked up the dull resin knife, turning pink.

"Yep. So no one gets killed. No one we don't want dead, at least."

Connor managed to say that in a way that bolstered her instead of terrifying her, but still, she shook a little. Was she really prepared to use a knife?

Enjoying your sunsets, my pet?

She tightened her grip on the knife and gave herself a quick nod. She could do this.

"So, I guess I'm sneaking up on you, right?" Connor asked, all businesslike.

She nodded curtly. Yes, sneaking up sounded about right for a cowardly stalker.

Connor circled behind her, and the hair on the back of her neck tingled in anticipation. She knew he was back there, but she couldn't see what he was doing. Couldn't judge how near or far he was.

"So we'll play it out slowly," Connor murmured from right behind her ear.

A shiver went through her body — the good kind, because she'd fantasized about him whispering from about there many times. Every one of her fantasies of wild, raging sex ended that way — with warm whispers and soul-nurturing cuddles, all skin-to-skin.

"Okay," she croaked, piquing her senses, hoping he'd touch her soon.

Slowly, gently, he put his hand on her shoulder in a way no stalker would ever do. A way that made her feel safe and protected instead of scared for her life. Then he turned her and looked into her eyes.

Her mouth fell open, because his eyes were glowing like brilliant jade lights. The way Cruz's eyes sometimes glowed when he looked at Jody, his mate.

Connor reached for her neck so slowly, she almost leaned in for a caress. But when his hand closed around her neck — tenderly, yet firmly — she remembered what the lesson was about.

"So now I think I have you. But you've got a knife..."

His deep voice worked its way into her bones and wandered around there for a little while, like a cat rubbing up against all the furniture it could find, marking everything as his.

Her heart thumped. Her blood rushed. Her cheeks went all warm.

Another quiet second ticked by, and Connor finally whispered. "Jenna."

She snapped out of her reverie and ducked to reach her calf. "Right. Knife."

But she couldn't get anywhere, not with that huge hand wrapped around her neck like a yoke.

"Nope." He shook his head. "Gotta get free first."

"Right. So... uh..." She wracked her head for something from self-defense class and came up with that move where she was supposed to sweep her hands around and chop down to get free. It didn't work, and Connor shook his head.

"Again."

She tried it again, growing angry at herself, and this time, he grinned. "Better. You can use that or a head butt. Or you can knee the guy in the balls." Then he held out a hand and added quickly, "But please don't go for my balls."

That grin of his did all kinds of dangerous things to her body, and she nearly licked her lips. But Connor grew serious and nodded curtly. "Now try it again, and once you're free, go for your knife."

He hid behind her and started the whole process again. Over and over until *useless* became *clunky* and *clunky* eventually became *passable.*

"Not bad. Now your grip," he ordered, taking her hand in his.

Jenna had never imagined fighting could be so wickedly arousing, but damn. With a teacher like Connor standing over her shoulder, nice and close, guiding her through every move...

"Outward grip. Thumb there, index finger there..."

His callused fingers guided hers into position, and his body boxed her in.

"Okay, index finger to the front, flip it, and grab," he murmured, showing her how to position the grip in her palm. "Index finger, flip, grab."

A bead of sweat built on her brow as she concentrated on the feel of his body and the angle of the knife. The position of his elbow as he demonstrated the move, and the way the blade turned in her hand. Somehow, sensual and practical became one, and it didn't matter which was which anymore.

"Now push my arm away, and aim here..." he murmured, pointing at a dip in his collarbone.

She was tempted to aim her lips there instead, but okay. As long as she got to stay this close to him...

Even cold and calculating terms like *dig for the clavicular artery* or *go for the soft tissue of the neck* wafted like clouds across the sky of her mind. All hovering at a safe distance from the thinking part of her brain. It was all action, all instinct.

Connor started changing up his moves, catching her off guard, making the exercise more realistic. Then he pinned her arms behind her back. She wiggled and grunted, struggling to get free.

"So, are you ready to give up?" he asked, an inch from her ear.

Her blood rushed. "Hell no."

He chuckled. "Good."

He showed her how to break out of that hold, too, which was her favorite move yet. She got to go from having her back held firmly against Connor's chest to turning to face him from an inch away.

"Now, let's suppose he pushes you to the ground..." Connor said, hooking his foot around hers.

She didn't fall because he lowered her gently and followed her down, pinning her knife hand above her head. His knees came down on either side of her hips, and his bare chest came parallel to hers.

Not a single alarm went off in Jenna's mind, because it wasn't intimidating at all. Just...good. Solid. Snug and secure. Her body was all achy, though, and her lips yearned for his.

"So you need to consider your options," he said in a slightly hoarse voice.

Oh, she was considering her options, all right. Like using her free hand to guide his head down and get those hungry lips within reach.

His mouth opened and closed. A bead of sweat slid down his brow. That tic started up in his right cheek exactly as it had the night they'd kissed.

"Am I doing this right?" she mumbled, running her free hand along his ribs.

Connor closed his eyes and held perfectly still. "Too right," he rasped.

Good. Then she'd do it a little more.

"I found a problem," she whispered, tilting her head so that her hair swung away from her eyes.

"What problem?" His gaze dropped to her lips.

"What if I don't want to get free?"

His nostrils flared, and he lowered his body until his chest rested on hers. Most of the weight was on his arms, making his biceps bulge.

"That is a problem," he rumbled. "Especially since I don't want to let you go."

A hundred sparkly firecrackers went off in her soul, stoking the fire within. Her eyelids drooped, and her chest rose in a deep breath — the kind she would take before going for an especially deep dive. And a good thing, too, because she arched up to kiss him at the same time he leaned down to kiss her, and when their lips met. . .

She sighed, because Connor kissed the way he touched. Expertly. Firmly. Uncompromising yet gentle, all at the same time.

Her kiss, on the other hand, was sloppy. Deep. Eager as a puppy yet sensual as a woman who knew just what she wanted, and that she wanted it right now.

Connor cupped her jaw while he kissed her, telling her that kiss was his. She dropped the knife and threaded both hands through his thick hair. He could take charge of all the kisses he wanted as long as they were that good.

"Jenna," he whispered, coming up for air.

She tilted her head back, offering him her neck, and he groaned, coming down over her again. Suckling and nipping her skin, stroking her sides. Finding her breast and cupping it as he mumbled into his next kiss. A low, throaty moan like a man in terrible need.

The sand was soft behind her back, the afternoon sky a pure blue overhead, but all she caught were quick glimpses through hazy eyes. She pulled at Connor's shoulders and wound a leg around his, letting their hips bump until she could feel his body respond.

Oh, yes. He wanted her as badly as she wanted him. Or maybe *need* was a better word, because she'd never felt as possessed by sheer, unwavering desire.

He smelled good — fresh and airy, yet woodsy at the same time. And he tasted even better, from the hint of salt around his lips to the maltier taste deeper down that she could reach if she kissed hard enough. The energy in the air intensified like a brewing storm. Connor was just sliding his hand toward the waistband of her shorts when—

"Connor? Connor?" someone called.

They shot apart, caught like a couple of deer in headlights. Well, not quite caught, thank goodness, because Jenna had just enough time to yank her shirt down, and Connor pulled her up a split second before little Joey came around the corner, calling, "Connor. Connor!"

Jenna wanted to groan, but Connor kept his voice even and warm. "Heya, buddy. What's up?"

When Joey stared, Jenna's stomach sank at what they must look like to him. But all his excitement was focused on the knife.

"Wow. Can I touch it?"

Jenna exhaled and handed Connor the training knife, giving it a little flick to hand it over grip-first.

He grinned, and she did, too. Maybe she had learned something, after all.

"Yeah, but just touch it."

Jenna fanned herself a little, trying to cool down. How had they managed to get so hot and heavy so quickly? Maybe Koa Point was rubbing off on her. The place was a hotbed of sexual activity. She could see it in the glowing faces and the sly, loving looks each couple exchanged.

But that didn't explain the intense attraction she'd felt toward Connor the second they'd met. Connor had just enough *good guy* in him to melt a girl's heart, with just enough *bad boy* to make her pulse skip.

Maybe it's destiny, a little voice whispered in her head.

Joey's eyes shone as he touched the training knife Connor held out. "Can you teach me how to fight, too?"

Jenna's heart had felt too big to fit in her chest a second earlier, but now it felt all bunched up. She knew that wistful, *I want to be grown up* feeling all too well.

"I'm not sure your mom would approve," Connor murmured. Joey's face fell, but he pepped up the second Connor added, "But I could teach you some dragon stuff."

The kid jumped clear off the ground in his excitement. "You will?"

"You will not." Cynthia's voice sliced through the air as she stalked around the corner to take her son's hand.

"But, Mommy," Joey protested, crestfallen.

Cynthia glared at Connor, and a whole conversation seemed to zip between them without either uttering a word.

I will not risk any harm to my son, her blazing eyes said,

No harm done, and he needs to be a kid, Connor's eyes said, now glowing red.

I decide what's best for my son. Fear showed in the lines of Cynthia's face — fear and the utter determination to protect her son.

Give the kid a break, the hard lines of Connor's face said.

He'd never looked as mature and weather-beaten as just then, and Jenna touched his arm, trying to help him regain his inner balance. Most of the time, he was as solid as any man she'd known, but every once in a while, she caught him tipping wildly to one side or another. Sometimes toward the side of lust, other times toward anger, and sometimes toward what seemed like a chasm of determination to prove himself to something or someone.

When Connor glanced her way, Jenna nearly gasped. His gaze was that angry, his soul blazing with the pain of barely healed scars. But a moment later, the red fire became a softer, marigold hue, and she smiled. Really smiled, because it had worked. Her sister could do that with Cruz, too — loosen up the pent-up tension whenever her mate got riled up.

Jenna froze. Mate?

She blinked at Connor, suddenly shaky again.

"We'll be going now," Cynthia said, guiding Joey away. "You know what Chase found in the attic, sweetie? Legos. A whole box."

And just like that, the boy pepped up again. "Can I play with Dell?"

Cynthia heaved the kind of sigh only an overworked mother could. "Sure. Why not."

Jenna watched them disappear around the corner. "At least there's that."

Connor nodded, though he still looked glum. "Maybe Dell will build him a castle and play knights against dragons. Cynthia would love that."

With a sigh, he leaned over for a water bottle, giving her a perfect view of all the chiseled muscles that rippled as he moved. When he turned back, he handed her the bottle he'd drunk from. A tiny gesture of intimacy, a smoothing over of the way they'd been torn apart. She drank, keeping her eyes on him.

His gaze dropped to her knife, then wandered out to the horizon, where the sky was gearing up for its evening show of color. She braced herself, ready for him to lecture her on what a bad idea all this had been.

But Connor didn't lecture. He just studied her, head to toe, and spoke in a perfectly even voice.

"Tomorrow. Same time. Bring a water bottle. Okay with you?"

She rolled to the balls of her feet, tempted to throw her arms around him. In the end, she held that back, but not her smile.

"Okay with me if it's okay with you."

His smile went up on one side and down on the other, like he knew the answer should be no. But his eyes sparkled, and he nodded. "Okay with me."

Jenna was badly tempted to kiss him to demonstrate just how okay that was with her, but she recognized the chance to make a smooth exit while she could.

"All right, then. Thanks," she said, as casually as possible. "See you soon."

Chapter Fourteen

Connor stood at the edge of the cliff, looking up at the night sky. The moon was a little past full, with the right edge fading, but as bright and brilliant as the last few days. Days he'd spent thinking, wanting, and wishing for Jenna. Desperately.

They'd made the lessons a regular thing, with him carving a little time out of Cynthia's strict plan. Nothing was as important as Jenna's safety. The problem was, he was having trouble keeping it all business, and every lesson was a mix of heaven and hell. Heaven because he got to touch her, talk to her, look her in the eyes. Hell because being that close for so long drove him absolutely wild. They'd strayed over into the no-go zone on more than one occasion since that first lesson, and breaking out of those passionate kisses was agony every time. Jenna managed to combine the innocence of a virgin with the hands of a woman who knew just what she wanted and how to get it. The little sounds she made when they kissed made his inner dragon roar. Every instinct told him to make her his. But Joey had taken to sneaking over to watch from time to time, and a good thing too. Joey was the reminder of everything Connor had to protect — his brothers, this clan, the future. A future he would completely fuck up if he didn't resist Jenna.

So he'd taken to flying every night, long and hard, trying to work off the aching need in the few precious hours he had between a day of work and patrols.

Trying. Not always succeeding. But what else could he do?

He curled his toes over the edge of the cliff, raised his arms, and jumped.

There was a high to shifting in midair, a thrill to that last hint of recklessness he allowed himself these days. Surf crashed into sheer rock at the base of the cliff. *His* cliff, because he and the guys had finally made enough progress on the main house to move in to their own homes. His place needed a lot of work, but it was his.

Like Jenna is, his dragon growled.

Wind screamed through his ears, whipping his hair as he shifted in midair. His fingers stretched impossibly wide, and the little folds of skin between them became huge, leathery wings. He stretched his chin forward, farther and farther until his dragon neck extended to full length. His pectoral muscles went broad and tight, becoming his chest armor, and the ridgeline of his back stood out.

Sometimes, shifting was agony. Other times, when his dragon was most desperate to fly free, it felt good. A brief flash of white-hot pain that bordered on pleasure, and that was it.

Tonight was the latter kind. It felt so good, the only thing he could equate it to was the feeling of burying himself deep inside Jenna, if he ever got the chance.

I swear, if we do, we'll make her cry with pleasure and lose all self-control, his dragon growled.

With a sharp flick of the tail, he shot upward along the face of the cliff and roared. That was another thing his cliff was good for — muffling sounds, so no human would hear and wonder what the hell that was.

A second later, he shot over the lip of the cliff, reaching for the stars. Every muscle strained as he powered upward and executed a tight barrel roll to the right. The earth sped by under his wings, tilted with his angle of flight.

That way, he urged his dragon.

The beast grinned and obeyed, not because it was any good at following instructions but because it happened to agree with him. *That way* was where Jenna was, just around the corner and up the coast. He straightened out to skim the treetops, letting the tallest tickle his belly.

The guest cottage where Jenna was staying lay tucked so tightly among the palms, catching sight of it was a blink-and-you'll-miss-it kind of thing, so Connor kept his eyes wide. And *zing!* There it was, the thatched roof flashing below. Of course, it wasn't the roof that made his blood rush. It was the knowledge that Jenna was sleeping in there, and he was protecting her. He craned his long neck to extend the thrill, then sent a tiny puff of fire into the night.

Watch it, show-off, he told his dragon. *She's still wary of dragons.*

His beast side snorted. *Right. That's why she kissed me.*

No, she kissed me, he insisted.

He allowed himself one more sweep over her rooftop — *whoosh!* — then made a lap over the estate. He caught sight of two lumbering shadows — Hunter and Dawn, the bear shifters of Koa Point, out on a patrol, judging by the purposeful way they moved. Their sides brushed as they paced side by side, disappearing quietly into the woods. Kai gave a lazy wave from where he sat on the balcony of his cliffside house, looking out at the view. Tessa came out and waved, too, then hugged Kai from behind and drew him into the house with a sly smile. A moment later, the lights went out, and Connor looked away.

Apart from the cry of a baby that was quickly soothed, all was quiet on the estate. And not just quiet but satisfied. All those shifters, happily settled down with their mates. Moving ahead with their lives and enjoying every minute of every day.

He turned out to sea, wondering if he and his brothers would ever reach that state. Sometimes, it seemed impossible. Other times, he thought of Jenna, and his hopes rose.

He followed the main avenue of moonlight, rising and dipping with every undulation of the swell. Then he flicked the corner of his right wing up to turn south, paralleling the coast from a mile out. A safe enough distance not to be seen by any honeymooners who might be stargazing from the beaches of Kaanapali. He squinted at a field of wavering dots ahead — the mooring field off Lahaina. Draig's megayacht was still anchored there, and it was high time to pay a visit, dragon style.

Sure. A visit. Shall we have some tea? his dragon growled.

He snorted. Draig would only roll out a red carpet for pedigreed guests like Kai, but it was good to swing past, just in case. The old coot had just about reached the time limit Kai had put on his stay on Maui. Draig had dined, sipped, and teed off to his heart's delight, so any day now, he ought to be off.

Or so Connor thought, but there was the megayacht, lit up like a Christmas tree at the outer edge of the anchorage, looking like it wasn't going anywhere soon.

Connor snorted as he raced over the water, belly to the waves. What was it about rich people that compelled them to show off their wealth? The luxury yacht wasn't just lit up from bow to stern; floodlights illuminated the helicopter from four directions, and underwater lights shone all around the vessel's waterline. Even in his wildest fantasies, Connor never dreamed himself into that kind of wealth. Simplicity seemed so much better.

Simplicity and Jenna, his dragon threw in.

He smiled back in the direction of Koa Point then frowned, remembering Draig's predilection for pretty girls and Anton's pompous rants.

This isn't even your turf, he remembered the little shit saying. *It's the Llewellyns'. For now.*

Connor frowned at the yacht. Anton had been sent packing, but the words stuck with him. Could Draig be up to something, or had that arrogant young dragon been talking big?

A second later, he dismissed the thought the same way Kai had when they'd had a follow-up briefing after that encounter with Anton. Draig was an old dragon nearing the end of a long and illustrious career. He was already as rich as sin, and there was no way he'd risk his reputation by stirring up trouble in Maui.

Besides, Kai had said. *He's an old family friend. He used to visit my uncle here.*

Connor knotted his brows as he circled the motor yacht once more. Okay, so Draig was just an arrogant old bastard. That wasn't exactly a crime.

Let's buzz him. Connor's dragon grinned. *Zoom right over that upper deck and rattle all those bottles of gin in the bar.*

For a second, Connor grinned too. But he caught himself at the last minute and circled the yacht instead.

No pranks. No messing around. No trouble, he barked at his other half.

No fun, his dragon muttered.

Still, he tilted all the way over on his right wing, nearly perpendicular to the sea, and did a full lap of the megayacht. Not near enough to give Draig grounds to complain, but close enough to make his message clear.

We've got an eye on you, dear guest.

There was no reason to make a secret of his surveillance. The more obvious, the better. Draig would realize the shifters of Koa Point were serious about keeping a close eye on their turf. Even better, Draig would let the shifter grapevine know that Maui was not a place to drop in to unannounced.

Connor completed his first loop, pulled a tight turn, and repeated the maneuver on his left wingtip. Showboating a little, because gliding for so long at such a tight angle wasn't a trick many dragons could pull off. He held his breath, straining to complete the full loop without a single beat of his wings. Then he exhaled and powered up to higher altitude, letting his backwash ruffle the flag hanging off the stern pole.

He almost wished Draig would rush out and shake a fist, or better yet, shift into dragon form and fight. But no lights clicked on, and no one stirred on board. Connor glided quietly, tuning in. Normally, he could sense another dragon shifter nearby, and an older, powerful dragon like Draig would make his presence felt from miles away. But it was almost as if no one were around.

Connor peered through the darkness, studying the yacht from above. The afternoon winds had long since given way to the faint breeze of night, and the yacht drifted in peaceful circles around its anchor. The helicopter was powered down, and the twenty-foot tender Draig's crew used to shuttle him to shore was tied up securely for the night. So far, the elder dragon had been punctual about returning to his yacht every afternoon. No carousing in Lahaina bars, no late nights out.

Which was all good. But the yacht was almost *too* quiet tonight.

Connor circled, trying to figure it out. Could Draig be asleep? Did he have some kind of dragon-proofed walls?

He folded his wings and spiraled downward in long, slow loops, studying the ship from all sides. The lights were on in the salon Draig had received Kai in, and another few lights dotted the hull. But the windows were all tinted, and he sensed no movement aboard.

Then something flashed off the stern. Something big. Connor twisted to see, too late to catch sight of whatever it had been, but in time to see the long line of phosphorescence that had been stirred up.

Dolphins? A whale? He swooped down for a closer look. Like most dragons, he knew all about the air: crosswinds, thermal updrafts, drag, and glide slopes. But water? Not his specialty.

Could Draig have his own submarine? his dragon asked.

Connor nearly snorted, but then again, who knew? A guy as rich as Draig could have any number of toys.

The water around the vessel's bow erupted upward. Connor whirled, just catching sight of a long, sleek shape before it disappeared into the depths. Sparks of phosphorescence lit a flurry of bubbles as something corkscrewed around the anchor line and vanished out of sight.

Connor dive-bombed to the surface, fighting the urge to spit fire all the way down. But there was no target, no bad guy. Not a hint of the creature that had teased him a moment ago.

He circled another few times, watching the surface of the sparkling sea. The shallow water fringing Maui might be clear as glass during the day but it was inky at night, and other than another few flashes — some long as a snake, others small as a turtle — Connor couldn't see a thing. Even those flashes didn't reveal much, because phosphorescence could be set off by anything — even a school of fish.

But whatever had made that splash was a hell of a lot bigger than a school of fish. More sinister. He made another tight loop of the megayacht then rose higher and spent a good fifteen minutes scrutinizing the area. What had that been?

We're in Hawaii, his dragon noted. *That could have been anything. A shark. Dolphin. Maybe even a whale.*

He considered that one. Didn't whales breed off Maui or something like that?

Anyway, what is the old coot going to be up to? He's probably asleep or down in the hold counting his cash.

Connor made a face. He'd like to know exactly what Draig was up to, but his dragon was probably right. The old guy hadn't caused any trouble in the past ten days. Was he really going to do so now?

Slowly, Connor glided out to sea before circling back and studying the area one more time. Then he flew away uneasily.

Anyway, we have to check on Jenna, his dragon said, stretching his neck an extra inch and picking up the pace.

Connor groaned. When was his dragon going to get things straight? He had an estate to check on, not Jenna.

Jenna, his dragon spat back. *Only Jenna.*

Can't have Jenna, he tried.

It's destiny, his dragon growled.

Destiny? Connor scowled at the moon as he flew. Who knew what tricks destiny had up its sleeve?

He crooked his neck and glanced back at Draig's yacht, then flew on toward his new home. Toward Jenna.

And that time, it was the moon, not his dragon, that murmured to him.

Toward destiny.

Chapter Fifteen

"No!" Jenna struck out at her attacker and jumped back. A face like that from the vampire book reared out of the night, fangs flashing white in the darkness. Strong hands held her down and forced her head back.

Ah, my pet. Let me taste you. Let me drink your blood.

She struggled and screamed, pushing the vampire away. But somehow, she couldn't move. Her body was frozen, her voice cut off.

No! No!

No matter how she thrashed or yelled, her body wouldn't obey. The vampire laughed and licked his lips.

Mermaid blood. I might have to keep you alive if it tastes as good as they say. Then he cracked his mouth open, revealing huge white fangs.

"No!"

She blinked, suddenly awake. Sweaty. Terrified. She scooted back in the bed, threw the pillow aside, and grabbed her knife.

Get away from me, she wanted to yell, but there was no one there. Just the shadow of her dream, chuckling at her, and the outline of the shells she'd placed on the dresser. She sat there for a full minute, heaving for breath, trying to calm down.

"Damn it." Never again would she read books about vampires before going to bed.

She went to the door and looked out at the beach. No one there either, and nothing awry. All of the bad images had been in her head. She grimaced in the direction of her phone, still lying on the bedside table. Some of the blame lay there, because another text had appeared the previous night.

My patience wears thin, my pet. Will you come to me, or shall I come for you?

She'd shivered just reading it.

Dinner, Thursday night, a second text had said, as if the lunatic had answered his own question. *As a sign of my generous nature, I will allow you to name the time and place we meet. Pack light, my pet, for your new life. I will provide everything your heart desires, just as you shall give me everything I desire.*

Jenna glared at her phone as if it had composed that crazy message itself, and then looked out over the sea. The faintest hint of pink creeped over the dawn sky, spreading slowly.

"Damn it." There was no way she'd get back to sleep after that nightmare, so she yanked on a bikini and cover-up, strapped her knife to her lower leg, and set off along the beach. Furiously at first, then a little more calmly as she tuned in to the sights and smells of an awakening island. The surf set a steady rhythm on her right, while light and warmth built on her left, the direction of the sunrise. Dewdrops sparkled like diamonds on giant leaves, and birds started chirping their morning songs. Koa Point was a Garden of Eden, and she was the sole inhabitant. So why did she feel as if a serpent was hiding out there, ready to bite?

She forced herself to swing her arms instead of hugging herself tightly while she paced.

Everything is okay, the universe seemed to sing. *Everything will be all right. See how beautiful the sunrise is?*

Every breath of fresh air and every extra beam of sunlight helped her internalize those words. She paused, trying to think rationally.

The stalker's messages were getting scarier, though no more specific. Was the man bluffing, or was he really closing in? She didn't relish the idea of showing the texts to Jody and Cruz, but what choice did she have? On the other hand, she hadn't received any little gifts, not at the guest cottage, nor at Teddy Akoa's surf shed. Maybe that meant the stalker didn't know where she was.

Still, the message was creepy enough. She turned one way then another, undecided. Jody and Cruz would probably flip out if she told them. She stared at the dawn-lit sky, trying not to peek southward, where a second option lay. Connor. She could ask Connor. Maybe he knew how seriously to take anonymous texts.

Then again, her stalker wasn't Connor's problem, and he seemed to have enough issues of his own. Did she really want to burden him with another one?

She looked up at the last, faint stars, wanting to scream, *What do I do?*

But there was no advice, just a twinkle that reminded her the stars were millions of light-years away. Connor, on the other hand, was just a short stroll along the coast.

She thought it over a minute longer before telling herself she would decide what to do along the way. With slow, ponderous steps, she picked her way over the rocky point that marked the boundary of both properties. A few minutes later, she emerged on the tiny patch of sand that made up Koakea's beach and perched on a boulder there, still undecided. The ocean remained a sparkling blue expanse, void of answers, and her wish for an easy solution came to a crashing halt against the sharp cliffs that rose up on the next stretch of the shoreline.

A sea gull cried and disappeared over the cliffs. Connor lived up there somewhere; he'd recently moved from the plantation house to his own place. A place he hadn't invited her to visit, so...

Her chin dropped to her chest, and she looked at her feet. Maybe she had been imagining there was more between them than really existed. And the texts — could the danger be a product of her imagination too?

She pulled off her cover-up and walked to the edge of the water, squeaking at the first chilly touch.

"Weenie," she muttered, forcing herself knee-deep. The water wasn't cold. That was just fear, making everything seem worse.

She stood quietly, letting her hands play over the water, thinking. Wondering what to do.

"Oh!" she squeaked as a fish splashed the surface a few yards away.

One silver flash and it was gone, leaving a circle of ripples in its wake. Ripples that spread wider and wider while her gaze stayed in the center, because a shining *something* remained. Was that what she had noticed before?

From one angle, she saw a glint of gold. From another, it was a shimmer of alabaster, barely peeking out from a clump of seaweed. But if she angled her head even more, it disappeared altogether.

In a series of halting steps, she waded a little deeper, trying to keep the shiny spot in view. But it teased her, playing hide-and-seek under the shimmering waterline, just as it had done before.

Jenna cupped her hands around her eyes and held her face so low, a ripple of water splashed her nose.

"I see you," she whispered at the shimmering something.

But what was *you*? Was it the same thing that had caught her eye a few days earlier, or something else?

"Easy to find out," she murmured. All she had to do was dive in.

Water had always been her escape, her private place. A quieter netherworld where her thoughts and imagination could roam. And having a strip of water to herself as the sun rose was a rare treat. She waded one step farther, took a deep breath, and dove, happy to leave her worries behind. That mysterious *something* glinted again, and she started stroking toward it. But diving changed the angle of the light, and she lost sight of her goal. Every time she popped to the surface, the shiny object seemed a mere arm's length away. Once she ducked under, it hid among the rocks and pebbles of the ancient fish pond.

Well, fine. What did she care anyway? A sea turtle was peeking around the collapsed corner of the rocky wall, so she swam over, following it out into open water. Several more turtles were feeding out there, and she watched them, finally feeling like the miserable night was finished and a good day had begun. The turtles were slow and ponderous but majestic at the same time, and she nearly forgot to come up for air from time to time. Then she treaded water, paddling in a slow circle to absorb the beauty of the scene. The rising sun. The emerald mountains of West Maui. The golden splash of beach. The pure blue sky.

She stopped when her gaze turned to Connor's cliff. Was he still in bed? Had he been up all night?

Her body warmed as she remembered the last time they'd touched. But those thoughts would make her hungry for him, so she turned and dove once more, putting the outside world on mute and immersing herself in the quieter, underwater realm. The nearest of the turtles was a few yards away, gliding along with lazy movements of its feet.

For another few seconds, the scene remained bucolic and serene. But then the turtle whirled and shot off to one side, sprinting for its life. The other turtles zipped out of sight too, going into hiding. An entire school of tiny silver fish changed direction and zoomed away. A parrotfish rushed by, its bulging eyes telling her to get to safety too.

Jenna paddled backward, searching the water for some sign of what had scared them off. Then she surfaced and looked around.

A gull was wheeling lazily over the water nearby, but a second later, it, too, hurried away.

"What the..."

There was no reason to panic, just an inexplicable urge to flee. When the theme music from *Jaws* started running through her mind, she turned back toward shore. It took everything she had to take slow, even strokes. If that was a lurking shark, moving quickly would only draw it in.

On the next stroke, she peered over her shoulder but saw nothing. Not on the surface anyway. But the sense of unease built, and red alarms flashed in her mind, ordering her to get out of the water, fast.

Her flutter kick grew faster as she imagined a high seas predator biting her from behind. A shark? An orca? She didn't want to picture what it might be. Following the turtles had taken her a few yards out, and the distance stretched to a mile in her mind.

Smooth strokes, she ordered herself. *Take it easy.*

But instinct hollered even louder. *Get the hell out of here! Now!*

Rounding the corner of the rocky enclosure didn't make her panic dissipate. If anything, it increased until she was in a full-out sprint for shore.

"Jenna!"

Even with her arms whirling at full speed, she caught a glimpse of Connor rushing down the beach. Her imagination got to work, picturing the scene from his point of view. Was he seeing her barely ahead of a giant fin? Were the colossal jaws already opening, ready to drag her under as a meal?

The next time she glanced up, the shore was only a few yards away. Her panic must have showed, because Connor started splashing into the water, calling to her.

"Jenna!"

Was it the water in her ears, or was his voice muffled? The outline of his body was distorted as well. Was Connor really that long? That big? He lifted his arms, and his steps grew short. His neck stretched and stretched, and—

Jenna pulled up in mid-stroke, because that wasn't just Connor running at her any more. It was a greenish-brown dragon, launching itself over the water, coming straight for her with a wide-open mouth.

She dove, ducking under the grasp of his outstretched claws, and drove herself toward the beach. The air pressure over her back rose, and a muffled *whoosh* sounded overhead. Jenna lost all sense of direction until her palms skidded against pebbles. When her feet hit the ground, she scrambled through the shallows and threw herself on shore. Even there, she scuttled backward, looking at the water in fear.

"Connor?" she whispered, watching the massive dragon hurtle out to sea, barely a foot above the waterline.

Was that really him? What was he doing?

The blue-on-blue scene of sea and sky was broken by a roar and a churning ball of fire.

Jenna fell back on her ass, unable to string together any thought more coherent than *Connor... dragon... fire...*

She squinted at the water but couldn't see a thing. The dragon circled, looking down. Angry sparks erupted from the creature's mouth as it turned in one direction after another in pursuit of... what? Shadows or a genuine foe?

Jenna held her breath, half expecting a massive squid to erupt out of the depths, wrap its tentacles around the dragon, and drag it underwater. But the surface was unbroken except for tiny wind-driven waves, giving no hint at the secrets that lay beneath.

Her chest heaved as she tried to catch her breath, but a second later, she yelped. "No!"

The dragon was coming straight for her. She ducked, covering her head. Even if it did pass a good fifteen feet above, that still felt too close.

She watched, dumbstruck, as the dragon touched down on the scrubby tongue of land that led to the beach. It folded its wings neatly, flicked its tail, and shook its head much like a dog would. When it turned and looked at her, she nearly ran. But then she saw its eyes — brilliant eyes the color of jade — and her pulse skipped to an entirely different beat.

Slowly, she got to her feet and wobbled a little. That was still Connor in there, right? Or did he forget who he was — and who his friends were — when he gave way to his dragon side?

"Connor...?" She meant to call out, but her voice was a mere whisper in the silence that ensued.

His eyes never left her as he shifted back to human form, and she was so mesmerized by them, the rest was a blur.

"Jenna." His voice was all growly as he ran to her. The second he came close, he took her by the shoulders and hurried her away from the water. "Are you all right?"

"Yeah." Her hands fluttered over his arms, shoulders, and chest, making sure it was really him. The armored plates of the dragon's front were now the broad panels of his chest. The muscles of his arms — sinewy in some places, bulky in others — all had their counterparts in his dragon wings. And his eyes

149

were exactly the same. Breathtaking. Fascinating. A deep, soulful green.

"Um..." She started, then gave up and hugged him fiercely. Closing her eyes, because comfort came from his warm touch. His arms closed around her just as tightly, like she wasn't the only one who never, ever wanted to let go.

How long they stood there hugging, she had no clue. Only that at some point, her chest rose with a shaky sigh. She rested her cheek on his chest, staying close as she looked out at the water.

"Did you see what it was?"

Connor shook his head slowly. "I didn't see a thing."

She frowned. "I didn't see it either, but..."

"But you sensed something," Connor said.

She nodded. "Yeah. I just felt it. Something coming at me."

They both turned and looked over the water, but no matter how hard she looked, she couldn't find a hint of anything awry.

"Maybe a shark?" Her voice shook a little.

"Didn't see a fin." His voice was tight, and the glow of his eyes changed back and forth from comforting malachite to furiously cool green depending on whether he looked at her or the water. His brow knotted with concern as he patted her down. "Are you sure you're okay?"

Every limb was shaking. Her heart was pounding. Her eyes were so wide, they hurt. But aside from a few coral scratches, she was all right.

"I'm okay."

Which was an understatement because, wow. Connor had been a dragon just a minute before. All that remained of his secret was the long, swirling dragon inked into his right arm.

A drop of water trickled from her dripping hair to him and slid slowly down his chest. She swallowed hard, trying not to picture him wet all over like a... a...

She blanked on the word for a moment, but then it came to her. *Like a merman.*

Without thinking, she pressed her hand against his chest, feeling his heart pound as hard as hers. Her eyes couldn't help but wander up and down his frame, and—

"Oh." She blushed and looked up quickly. Definitely not a merman. Just one-hundred percent, rock-hard, naked man.

He grinned. "Side effect of shifting. Sorry."

Her cheeks had to be a blazing red, judging by the heat. Not that she took a shy step back or turned away. She stayed right where she was and let her hand wander to his hip.

"Nothing to be sorry about, except maybe buzzing right over my head. A little warning next time, okay?"

His smile was the most beautiful thing she'd seen all morning, putting the sea, the craggy mountains, and even that perfect Maui sky to shame.

"I'll do my best." His voice was all husky, and after a minute, his grin turned into an intense look aimed squarely at her lips.

Her chest rose on the next couple of breaths, and she leaned closer, tilting her head. Her eyelids dropped to half-mast, and her breath caught.

Kiss me, she wanted to beg. *Kiss me.*

Connor's eyes were begging too. Which was unusual, because everything he did, he did decisively, taking the lead. But there seemed to be some invisible sign over her head, proclaiming her taboo.

"If I want you, and you want me . . . " She trailed off there, suddenly second-guessing herself.

"I want you, believe me."

"Then what's the problem?"

He snorted and shot a cryptic look over his shoulder. "With shifters, there's always a problem. Unwritten rules."

She cupped his face and turned it back to hers. "Well, guess what?"

A tiny grin spread over his scowl of frustration. "What?"

"I'm rewriting them."

She kissed him, just as deep and hard as he'd first kissed her that night at her cottage. Within seconds, her body was on fire with an intense craving that went far beyond normal human arousal. Did all shifters have that effect, or was that destiny? She struggled to kiss and think at the same time. Moments ago, she'd been terrified. Now, raw, sensual energy flowed through her veins. His lips claimed hers, and his taste took over her mouth as if marking her with a firm *Mine!*

Her mind spun. *Mates... Shifters have mates.*

Connor pulled her closer, deepening his kiss.

Dragons have mates...

Her hands slid from his hips to his firm ass, barely controlled.

I just knew, her dad always said about her mom.

Connor's chest heaved as he gulped a breath of air. He dove into the next kiss, consuming her. She whimpered and pressed closer, mashing her breasts against his chest, aching for him to touch her everywhere.

We just knew, Jody had said, going all dreamy-eyed when she talked about Cruz.

Jenna let her hands rove lower, one around the back, the other around the front, driven by a desperate need to touch him. To love him. To possess him the way she wanted him to possess her.

Did mermaids have mates too?

His hands slid along her sides, teasing her breasts. When one thick thumb nudged a nipple, she arched. Nearly gasping, she was that wound up. Was it morning? Noon? Night? She'd lost track. All she knew was that she wanted him.

The side of her palm came into contact with his thick shaft, and she just about dropped to her knees for a taste. But before she could, Connor growled and gripped her hand.

"Hang on," he rasped, guiding her hands back to his face.

Jenna opened her mouth to protest, but he covered it with one more burning kiss. When he broke it off, he held her hands tightly against his chest. "We can't do this. Not now. Not here."

She wanted to scream. "I'm rewriting the rules. Remember?"

He smiled and shuffled back an inch, tipping his head toward the path to the plantation house. "Any second now, Joey is going to come running along, and..."

She groaned and drooped against his chest.

"...but later..."

She popped up again, bright with hope. "Later?"

Connor nodded. "Tonight."

She shook her head. "Tonight is too many hours away."

He liked that and showed it with another wide grin. A childish grin, full of innocence and delight. "You have work, and so do I."

"I'm in grave danger," she tried. Maybe that would work.

He snorted. "The person in grave danger is the guy who tries to pull any shit on you." Then he took a deep breath — deep enough for both of them — and rested his forehead against hers. "And possibly me."

"You're in grave danger?" She shook her head. "What could possibly pose a danger to a big, bad dragon?"

Connor looked at her, giving nothing away. But then he took her hand and held it against his heart.

"You," he said in a shaky voice. "You."

Her jaw hung open, and she watched with misty eyes as he kissed the knuckles of each hand in turn. Finally, he nodded and let her go with a deep breath.

"Promise me you'll stay out of the water today."

She made a face. That would be easy. "And you promise about tonight. No excuses. No second thoughts."

"Tonight. I promise."

She held his gaze, making sure he meant it. "Okay, then. See you tonight."

Neither of them budged after that, though. So she went for a lighter note and let her eyes travel down the length of his body. "You might want to dress up a little, though."

He laughed out loud and pulled her into a parting hug. "I promise that too."

Chapter Sixteen

Connor stood perfectly still on the beach, watching Jenna go. That took all his willpower, because his dragon was raging inside.

What the hell are you doing? Never let her go!

He didn't want to, but it was the right thing to do.

So wrong, his dragon insisted. *We belong together.*

Yes, they did. Every time they came together, his soul sang, and every time they parted, he mourned. They were destined for each other, all right. But he had to think this through.

What's to think about? his dragon demanded.

He rolled his eyes. First, he had to figure out what the hell had been in the water. Second, was that connected to Jenna's fear of vampires? He couldn't see how, though. And third, how could he possibly win over his mate without losing his job?

"Tonight," Jenna called, pausing right before she stepped out of view.

He waved and whispered, "Tonight."

Those two little syllables were a pair of solemnly tolling bells, at least in his mind. Were they heralding a new era — or utter doom?

He stared out over the water before heading back to his house. First things first.

Jenna, his dragon barked.

Clothes, he ordered himself. What he'd been wearing had been shredded in his sudden shift.

Jenna!

Connor shook his head. Clothes, breakfast, and work. Then he'd try to figure something out.

He tried all day, as it turned out, to no avail. No matter how often he pored over possibilities in his mind, he couldn't tease apart the riddles facing him.

"What's with you, man?" Tim asked.

Connor shook himself and looked around. "Huh?"

That had been sometime during the interminable morning, when they put the finishing touches on the porch of the main house.

"Another drink, sir?" a waiter asked, startling him. "Compliments of your friend?"

Connor had to blink three or four times to figure out where the guy had come from.

"Friend?" he bluffed, buying time. He wasn't at Koakea any more, but somewhere else, and a little later in the day. Everything blurred in his mind but Jenna.

"From the gentleman on the green," the waiter explained, pointing as Draig went by in a golf cart.

Then it clicked. He was at the golf club at midday, making sure old Draig was playing the goodbye round of golf he'd announced. It was the old man's last day on the island, which meant some of the slowest surveillance work Connor had ever done was about to come to an end.

"No drink, thanks," he murmured, watching Draig go past.

Another couple of hours dragged by, then a few more.

"Earth to Hoving. Earth to Hoving, come in."

That sounded vaguely like Dell, but Connor didn't care any more. He tuned in enough to recall he was back on the plantation, helping paint the interior of the house, thinking lots but not able to conclude too much.

"Either he's sick or in love," Dell laughed.

"He'd better be sick," Tim growled, looking none too pleased.

His words hit Connor like a well-aimed brick, and the impossibility of his situation closed in all over again. He spent the rest of the afternoon trying to talk some sense into himself with little success. Now that he'd gone and promised Jenna to meet, he couldn't stand her up.

In the end, help came from where he least expected it.

"Don't mind him," Dell said, nodding in the direction Tim had gone off in once they had put their tools away at the end of the afternoon. "Mr. Logic doesn't get matters of the heart."

Connor stared, because what did Dell — aka Casanova — know about matters of the heart? And, whoa — did those words really apply to a messed-up dragon like himself?

"Trust me." Dell grinned. "I got this."

Connor frowned. Those were exactly the words that had gotten his gang into hot water in the first place. It had been Dell's bright idea to duct tape grenades to footballs. Of course, it had been Connor's bright idea to go along with that crazy plan.

Still, he found himself nodding along.

"Well, we'd better get cleaned up," Dell announced once Tim came back. "Chase and I have our first shift on the new job tonight."

That part was true. Kai had encouraged everyone to find local part-time jobs as a way of keeping their ears to the ground, and Dell had found a perfect solution.

"Can I just say what a genius I am?" Dell grinned. "I mean, where better to hear gossip than as a bartender in a popular local bar?"

Tim gave him a thumbs up. Cynthia shot him a look of disapproval. Chase just looked resigned as Dell smacked him on the shoulder.

"Come on, man. Being a bouncer is awesome. And you'll get all that fresh air, working the door."

That, Connor had to give to Dell. It was a pretty perfect setup for each of them. And it only got better from there.

"So, Connor. You're coming, right?"

At first, Connor had no idea what Dell was talking about. Why would he go visit his friend on the job when he could spend time with Jenna?

"Come on, man." Dell hid a wink from Cynthia. "I need you to help us get a good start. You know, like ordering a drink and telling everyone how good it is. Tipping high. That kind of thing."

Connor frowned, still not following.

Run with it, you stupid dragon, Dell whispered into his mind. *Do you want the perfect excuse to get out tonight or what?*

Connor warmed immediately. Yes, a good excuse would come in handy around now. And he did have the night off from security, with Tim scheduled to cover that tonight.

"Are you coming, Cynth?" Dell asked, sweet as pie.

"Cynthia," she corrected in a dry voice.

Dell ignored that, as he always did. "Tim here can babysit."

Connor nearly snorted. Cynthia really didn't seem like the bar-hopping type, and he doubted she'd leave her son alone.

The corners of her mouth turned down even more sharply, but her tone was — wow, wistful? — when she replied, "I'm afraid not."

Connor studied her for a moment. Could it be that Cynthia had actually had a wild side, once upon a time?

"Pity," Dell said almost before she spoke. "Who else can we ask? Oh, I know." He jerked his thumb in the direction of Koa Point estate. "Jenna. I'm sure she'd enjoy a night out."

Cynthia's frown grew, but Connor beamed. "Good idea."

Great idea, his dragon agreed.

"Perfect." Dell grinned. "Well, I have to get ready. Gotta make a good impression on my first night. Can you go ask Jenna?"

Dragons didn't wag tails, but Connor's inner beast did a few ecstatic backflips. "Uh, sure," he said, trying hard to sound bored while he shot Dell a sincere *I owe you, man.*

You do, Dell hummed slyly, and Connor knew damn well the lion shifter would call him on that someday.

"Can I go?" Joey asked.

"Sorry, buddy, not tonight." Dell tousled his hair. "But you get to stay in with Tim, and I know he tells really good bedtime stories. Right, Tim?"

Tim looked up, startled, then nodded quickly when he saw Joey's hopes rise. "Uh, sure. That would be fun. Right, Joey?"

Cynthia looked fifty-fifty on that one, but Connor had to give it to Dell. For every dumb idea the lion shifter had ever come up with, he managed to pull off two or three good deeds.

Dell grinned at Joey. "But because Tim is completely incompetent when it comes to giving rides — and who'd want to ride a bear when they could ride a lion? — you get one extra ride before I go tonight."

Before Cynthia could protest, Joey hooted and launched himself from the couch onto Dell's back. Dell made a roaring sound and took off at full speed across the porch, heading for the stairs. "Hang on, bud! We're going airborne!"

"Be caref—" Cynthia blurted, her eyes wide as Dell took the six steps in one jump. But he landed just as smoothly and sprinted across the lawn with Joey squealing in glee. At which point Cynthia clutched her pearls and murmured, "Oh, dear."

Amazing, Tim murmured for Connor's ears only. *Cynthia is the only woman I know who looks — well, cover-girl gorgeous — but acts like an old aunt.*

Connor wasn't sure about the *cover-girl* part, because Jenna would get that title, for sure. *I don't know. I guess she's not my type.*

Well, make sure you don't have too much fun with your type tonight. Tim shot him a look of warning.

Connor didn't bother replying. He had a chance to beat Dell to the shower, so he'd better use it while he could.

And so it was that an hour later, he found himself purring down the highway to Lahaina in a red Ferrari driven by Jenna, who'd jumped right on board with the plan to help Dell and Chase get a good start at the bar.

"Cool car, huh?" She patted the dashboard.

The wind coming in the convertible tousled her blond hair. Between that and the peacock blue blouse that brought out the intense color of her eyes, Connor couldn't stop looking at her. Jenna was always beautiful. But Jenna ready for a night out on the town was downright stunning. Her swishy skirt had made it hard not to stare at her legs on the short walk to the car, and her dangly gold earrings mesmerized his dragon. Connor had never really felt the need to hoard treasure, but

Jenna gave him all kinds of bad ideas, like spiriting her over to his place and keeping her there forever.

He leaned over to see the speedometer, sneaking in a deep whiff of her heavenly scent while he could. "Cool car and... forty miles per hour don't really go together."

Jenna gave him a stern look. "Hey, the speed limit is forty-five."

"Exactly. Forty-five," he said, stressing the *five*. Though, truthfully, he didn't care how fast or slow they went. Being this close to Jenna suited him just fine.

"It's Boone's, and I have to take care of it," she insisted.

Connor nearly laughed aloud. Should he tell Jenna how reckless and wild the wolf shifter had been before he'd settled down on Koa Point and become the proud dad to twins? But, whatever. Fast or slow — Connor had one night off. One night with Jenna, and a perfectly feasible excuse for spending time with her.

It was nice, seeing her so happy. Relaxed, for a change. Excited about a night out with him.

"Right turn here?" She pointed.

Connor had done enough tailing of Draig by then to have a pretty good sense of the local roads, and he nodded. "About a mile... Now left..."

She arched an eyebrow at the supermarket parking lot he waved toward. "Are we picking up some mustard or something?"

He laughed. "Nope. But the five-dollar parking is hard to beat, and they'll keep a good eye on the car."

Also, that gave them a nice, long walk down Lahaina's Front Street, though he didn't mention that. His dragon might be yearning to fly wingtip-to-wingtip with Jenna, but this was the next best thing. And when she casually took his hand and swung it while they walked — well, dang. Maybe walking was even better than flying.

The sun had set an hour before, and the cool night air made everything seem fresh and energized. The town was alive with pedestrians, party lights, and the sounds of street musicians playing soulful island tunes on ukuleles and slack-key guitars.

Connor slipped his arm over Jenna's shoulders, and she snuggled in good and tight. All that hand-to-hand combat training had made them comfortable together — too comfortable?

He decided to park that thought and the worries that accompanied it for the time being. Well, he tried. His gut flipped when it hit him that tonight might be his first and only chance to spend time with Jenna in a normal setting. A *safe*, normal setting, because he would have Dell and Chase nearby for backup if any fool dared to come too close to Jenna. But apart from that, who knew? Jenna wasn't staying on Maui forever, and he had too many good reasons to let her go.

"Oh, that's gorgeous," Jenna breathed, stopping to admire a photograph of a whale hanging in the window of an art gallery.

The photographer had managed to capture the scene above and below the waterline, with the whale swimming in a graceful arc and the emerald mountains of West Maui filling the upper half of the shot.

"Gorgeous," he agreed, touching her soft, flowing hair. With the gesture, he made a silent vow to push thoughts of tomorrow far, far away. Tonight was their evening to enjoy.

So, he did — every step and every stop Jenna made along the way.

"Oh, look at those," she murmured, leaning over a jewelry store display.

Connor glanced at the pearls she indicated then let his eyes stray back over to Jenna. That was way more interesting — watching her expression, the curve of her back, the playful sway of her skirt in the wind. He did regular sweeps of the area as well, keeping alert, just in case. The fact that he kept a hand on Jenna's back the whole time served both purposes — enjoying being with her and keeping her safe.

"Made right here in Hawaii," an older islander in a pink, flowery dress said from behind the counter.

Jenna looked out at the sliver of ocean visible between two buildings. "Really?"

"In the old days, pearls were harvested from the wild. Nowadays, most of the world's pearls come from cultivated oysters, like ours."

"Oh. Nice." Jenna looked out at the ocean with dreamy eyes.

Connor rubbed her back a little. Jenna had some serious water-baby genes, for sure.

The saleswoman leaned closer and spoke in a conspiratorial voice. "There are still some of the old-time pearls around, from a long time back."

Jenna perked up immediately, hanging on every hushed word.

"Some that belonged to royalty, and some that belonged to..." The woman looked around before whispering the rest. "...to others."

"What others?" Jenna asked.

"Witches... Warlocks... Sharks."

Jenna's eyes went wide. "Sharks?"

Connor frowned at the woman. Jenna didn't need a reminder of her scare in the water that morning. But the saleswoman rambled on, happy for an audience for her outlandish tales.

"Like Kamohoalii, the shark king, who could change shapes and walk the earth as a man."

Connor whipped around and exchanged uneasy glances with Jenna. Shapeshifters?

"He had a son, Nanaue. Sad story," the woman said, as if some tragedy had befallen the boy next door instead of a figure from legends. "But not many folks know that Kamohoalii had a daughter too, and she collected the most precious pearls of all. Precious pearls. Magical pearls. Pearls that could—"

A second saleswoman came closer, making the older woman break off sharply and clear her throat. "Anyway, those were the old days. You should read the stories, honey." She winked.

Jenna took another look at the pearls while Connor studied the woman. Were there really old legends about shark shifters, or was she just playing up the story? He'd have to ask Kai and the others about it later on.

A young couple in matching Hawaiian tops — newlyweds, no doubt — came up to the counter, and Jenna edged away with a polite, "Thank you." Then she sighed and continued walking down the street. "Not that I'd ever have the money to get one." Then she brightened and wrapped her arm around his. "But you know what?"

Her smile was pure sunshine, her side warm against his.

"What?"

"There's some super rich, super unhappy woman out there right now with all the pearls in the world, and she doesn't get a night like this."

He grinned. "A night like...?"

Jenna motioned up and around. "The stars. The music." She gave him a coy look. "The company."

He pulled her into a hug and looked into her eyes. Big mistake, because every time he did that, his dragon rose to the surface, demanding to make her his. He could feel the beast getting ready to rumble about destiny, need, and forever, and he could feel his body warm with the intense need to kiss her again. To him, those kisses were pure pleasure. To his dragon, they were a means of marking Jenna as his.

Jenna's eyes dropped to his lips, and her hands touched his sides. Yep, she wanted it, too.

"I'd love to kiss you," he whispered, running his hands over her shoulders.

She looked up, catching the warning in his tone. "But...?"

He took a deep breath and turned sideways to steer her down the sidewalk again. "But once we start..."

"Stopping is impossible," Jenna finished.

He wondered for the hundredth time if she had shapeshifter blood. How else could she feel what he felt and with the same intensity?

"Exactly. So we save the kiss for later. Okay with you?"

She slipped her arms around his waist and tucked her hand into the rear pocket of his pants. "Nope."

He did a double take at the mismatch between her gestures and words. "Nope?"

"I want more than one kiss later. Lots, in fact. Only that is okay with me."

Her hip bumped his, hinting at what else she wanted. What she needed, he guessed, if she was as full of pent-up desire as he.

"Got it, boss," he said, trying to keep his voice light rather than growly with need.

"Promise?"

He nodded firmly. "Promise."

"Well then. Where's this bar?"

He laughed. "All business tonight?"

She shook her head. "All pleasure."

And damned if she didn't purr the word, making his cock twitch.

Chapter Seventeen

Connor kept Jenna nice and close as they continued down the street. "There it is," he said, pointing at the old-fashioned swinging sign above the sidewalk ahead.

"The Lucky Devil?" Jenna laughed.

"Yep. That's Dell to a T."

Connor could see Chase and another guy at the door, checking IDs. Light and music poured out from the second-floor bar above, attracting a crowd.

"It looks great," Jenna exclaimed, making a beeline for the door. "Hi!" She gave Chase a bright smile.

Connor expected his half brother to do that robotic, nod-and-curve-his-mouth-upward thing he'd learned over the years, but Chase flashed a quick, genuine smile. Wow. That was new. Connor watched his brother closely while he checked Jenna's ID. Maybe leaving the military was good for Chase. In the civilian world, smiling came more easily to everyone. And while working the crowded, noisy bar upstairs would be a nightmare for Chase, being down at street level seemed to suit him just fine. The fresh air and open sky would keep his wild wolf side at peace.

"You're checking my ID?" Connor protested when Chase held a hand out.

His brother snapped his fingers. "I check everyone."

Which, Connor supposed, was the point of that job. And Chase did have to make a good impression on his first night. So Connor flashed his ID, clapped his brother on the shoulder, and followed Jenna up the rickety stairs. The Lucky Devil took up the upper floor of one of the historic buildings on Front Street, and the ocean view was great.

"I got this." Connor whipped out his wallet to pay the cover charge before Jenna could protest.

"I owe you," she insisted over the classic rock tune playing in the background.

"No, you don't."

"Yes, I do."

Connor couldn't help smiling. Who knew he liked stubborn, independent types? Or that he liked fun, flouncy types? Jenna was both. Of course, he'd never had a type until meeting her.

"Like I said, I owe you. And also, this place is awesome," Jenna chirped, motioning around.

The bar managed to combine pirate and devil themes without being too kitsch, even with the waitstaff sporting Hawaiian shirts and the occasional pair of fake devil horns. Fishnets and tattered signal flags hung in the rafters, and black-and-white photos of old Lahaina in dusty black frames decorated the walls. A pair of silver swords hung above the bar, along with a couple of antique glass fishing floats.

"Not bad," Connor murmured, impressed. The crowd was a cut above what he'd pictured. A few grizzled locals clustered around the bar, while the tables were mostly occupied by sunburned tourists. Dell had a way of pulling off small miracles like landing a job at a decent place instead of a dive on his first try.

"Wow. He's good." Jenna pointed behind the bar to Dell.

Connor had seen his friend in action before, but, man. Dell was pulling out all the stops tonight, flashing his winning smile and making a show of mixing drinks. Two men leaned their chins on their hands, studying his technique. A gaggle of young women in a bachelorette party squeaked, clapped, and fluttered their eyelids. Dell tossed one bottle behind his back while flipping a tumbler in one hand, then poured the drink in midair and cut off the last drop with a flourish.

A round of applause broke out from the bachelorette party, and Dell winked.

"I don't think he needs our help," Jenna declared.

"Not a bad start," Connor agreed.

Dell would pour the local guys extra big shots, making sure he turned his best sources of local knowledge into repeat customers. Meanwhile, the tourists would keep coming thanks to Dell's showmanship and good looks.

Which meant all Connor had to do was find a table and enjoy his night out. A waitress led them to a table on the open patio facing the sea, and Jenna sighed as she slid into a chair.

"Wow. This is perfect."

Connor tried counting back to the last time he'd gone out for a nice, normal, civilian night on the town and came up blank. He tipped his head up to the stars and took a deep breath. This was a whole new life. A whole new planet, in a way. Not only did he get a night out with Jenna, he got it in a place like this. Sun. Surf. Laid-back attitudes. No mortars whizzing overhead, no land mines to avoid. No *we might get shipped out tomorrow, or we might wait another six weeks*. No wonder he'd goofed around and avoided thinking about the future in his former career. But now...

He looked at Jenna, and it hit him all over again — how amazing the future could be. Even better than the present, because in one version of the future, he got nights like this, knowing Jenna was his. Forever.

He swallowed the bubble in his throat and took his seat.

"I'll take a Big Swell IPA," Jenna said, beaming at the waitress then at him. "What about you?"

Even the simple task of ordering a drink was a little beyond him just then, so he nodded to the card on the table. "You choose."

"Southern Cross?"

He nodded. Whatever it was, Jenna had picked it, so it had to be good.

The waitress whirled away, leaving them alone. Jenna's incredible blue eyes locked on his, and he never wanted to pull away.

"What are you thinking?" she asked.

Connor couldn't exactly say, *How to make you my mate without fucking up everything else*, so he settled for "You."

Her cheeks turned pink, and her eyes shone. "Me, huh?"

He nodded.

"Seriously," she said when he didn't reply. "Why me?"

Destiny, he nearly said. Instead, he turned the question around.

"I was kind of thinking the same thing." He pointed at his chest. "I mean, why me?"

She grinned and leaned in to whisper. "Maybe I have a thing for mysterious dragon types."

He studied her, wondering if he dared come clean. Jenna was new to the dragon world. Did she understand what an outcast he really was?

"You know how I told you there are dragons and there are *dragons*? I was talking about good guys and bad guys. But there are other kinds too."

He expected his words to scare her, but Jenna nodded, showing utter confidence in whatever type he revealed himself to be. Which scared the bejesus out of him, because what if he ever let her down?

He took a deep breath and went on. "Mostly, there are the old clans, like the one Kai and Silas come from."

"Llewellyn." She nodded, listening closely.

"Exactly. Baird is another, and Draig is another." He nodded out in the direction of the megayacht.

Jenna's eyes wandered out then back, looking blank. Totally unaware of what he was about to tell her.

I'm a nothing, Jenna. A dragon, but not one of those classy ones.

"Those are all old, purebred lines with lots of class and incredible wealth. They're born with it." Connor tried to keep the bitterness out of his voice but didn't really succeed. "They run their world with a thousand unwritten, archaic rules that don't make any sense."

He stalled out there, and eventually, Jenna tapped his hand. "And the other kind?"

He snorted. "That would be me. No family name, no inheritance. Not even real dragon lineage. My father was a myriad shifter."

She tilted her head.

"He could change into different forms. That's why Timber is a bear and Chase is a wolf," he whispered. Given the noise level of the bar, he had no fear of anyone listening in.

"Cool," she said. "Kind of like me. I'm part mermaid."

He did a double take. "Part what?"

She shrugged. "Not like that part does me much good. Well, I can hold my breath for a really long time. Go, me." She gave herself an unenthusiastic cheer. "Other than that, I'm just the little sister of the Monroe gang." She put air quotes around *little*.

He studied her. So that explained the surfing and the wistful way she looked out at the ocean. Maybe it explained those amazingly clear eyes and the determination to prove herself, too.

"Anyway," she went on, all breezy as if his big revelation meant nothing to her at all. "Who cares about part this or that? We are who we are, right?"

He stared at her for a second, fishing for words. But, hell. What if she was right?

Her foot brushed his, reminding him of her knife, and suddenly, his thoughts took a sharp turn, making everything click into place. Her questions about vampires, the way she'd been spooked on the plane. He stiffened and scanned the room one more time.

"Nope, none of that," Jenna said, taking his hand. "I'm having a very nice night out with a very nice guy, and no one is going to ruin it. Plus, Dell and Chase are here, right?"

He nodded but kept his senses on high alert.

"Jenna, there are lots of people who wouldn't consider me a very nice anything. I'm kind of a mutt. A mongrel. The illegitimate cousin no one wants to know about."

Jenna shrugged. "Their loss."

He stared at her. "You don't understand. The dragon world is all based on who's who."

She shrugged. "Fine. Let them stick their noses up their asses. You know who you are and what you can do. Why does it matter?"

It shouldn't, but it did. From the time he'd been old enough to understand what being an outsider meant, it had eaten away at him. No matter how much he tried or how hard he fought, he'd never belong. Which still rubbed him the wrong way. Not around guys like Kai, who were okay, but around Draig and, to an extent, Cynthia not-Brown. Maybe that was why he'd never bothered to prove himself a good man.

Until now. Suddenly, he wanted to prove that more than anything. But how?

Jenna's hand tightened around his, speaking volumes without uttering a word. The soft rub of her thumb over his hand made his muscles go loose, and her unwavering gaze said she believed in him — *him*, not the rest of the dragon world. The leg she'd left wedged comfortably against his said she trusted him, and her eyes—

He held his breath. Those eyes were thinking *love*.

Connor blinked a couple of times. Damn it, if he weren't careful, his eyes would fill with the telltale glow of shifter attraction.

"One IPA, one Southern Cross." The waitress thumped two frothy glasses down, making them jump apart. "What can I get you to eat?"

Connor squinted at the glasses. Where was he again?

Jenna, of course, had herself together enough to order a burger. Connor jabbed blindly at the menu, willing the waitress to disappear. The second she did, Jenna raised her glass.

"To rebel dragons." She grinned. "Let 'em prove the assholes wrong."

Connor broke into a smile and tapped his glass against hers. "To the little sisters, all grown-up. Watch out, world."

The clink of their glasses was like a bell heralding some significant event. Which was funny, because people toasted all the time, so it didn't have to mean anything, right?

The shine in Jenna's eye said, *Maybe so. Maybe not.*

They drank, never breaking their gaze. The cool beer slid down his throat, and the froth tickled his lip.

A second later, Jenna licked the foam off her lips, waking up a whole new part of his body. And then she was off, talking in that singsong tone of hers — another mermaid holdover, he figured. He talked too. Lots more than he usually did. Asking questions. Answering others. Dodging a few, taking others full on. Innocent topics like pets and flowers and high school teams. Heavy stuff like family troubles and making ends meet. All kinds of stuff he'd never really tried putting into words before. Like how getting sent to the principal's office turned into getting sent to the commanding officer's desk. How he'd saved his ass with a couple of well-timed accomplishments then set himself back all over again. Why it felt so important to stick together with Tim, Chase, and Dell.

His whole life story, narrated for the very first time, because someone cared. Someone believed.

Jenna covered his hands with hers, hanging on every word.

"So," she chuckled, going for a lighter tone. "Now I know why Kai and Cruz are keeping an eye on you."

Only Jenna could say that and make it sound really grave and really funny at the same time.

He sighed. "What about you?"

She paused as if wondering where to start. Then she held up her wrists, showing him her bangles. "These were my mom's..."

Her voice was hushed for some parts of her story, bold at others, laughing outright at times. She talked about her parents taking her surfing before she was old enough to walk or talk. Then she moved on to losing her mom to cancer and how everyone had pulled together to get through that. How she'd stepped up to help her dad when her two older sisters moved out, even though they always stayed close. Why she'd put off college and decided against giving the pro surf circuit a try.

"You know." She shrugged. "All those snobs. Who needs them?"

He laughed outright, then nodded slowly. "So that's why your sister and Cruz are keeping an eye on you."

She raised what was left of her drink. "See? We're birds of a feather, you and I."

The crowd roared at Dell's latest, greatest trick, but Connor barely heard. Forget the busy bar and the breathtaking view

— all he saw was Jenna's bright blue eyes. All he registered was her voice, despite the hubbub in the background. All he smelled was her flowery scent, filled with hope and tinged with arousal.

And all I want, his dragon growled inside, *is her.*

Chapter Eighteen

Jenna forced herself to take long, steady breaths. Everything about Connor fascinated and enticed her. His low, growly voice. The glow in his eyes that waxed and waned with his moods. The hidden wounds he'd revealed when he'd talked about the past.

"Do dragons know magic?" she asked out of the blue.

His eyes went wide. "Magic? No."

Then what was this mysterious force acting on her? *Love* seemed too simple for something that powerful. She nearly asked, too, but just as she opened her mouth, the waitress whirled by with their meals.

"One hula burger, one falafel salad."

Connor stared. "Falafel what?"

"It's what you ordered." The waitress leaned over to treat him to a view down her low-cut blouse. Connor didn't appear to notice. He'd barely looked the woman's way all night.

Just in case, Jenna took a page from Connor's playbook and cleared her throat in a growl. No woman was poaching on her turf tonight. The waitress glanced at her, then backed away quickly.

Ha. Maybe you didn't have to be a dragon to give off dragon vibes.

When another customer waved for the waitress's attention, she scurried off. Jenna hid a triumphant smile and picked up her burger. But Connor was still staring at his meal, so she paused.

"Something wrong?" she asked.

He poked at his plate, and she laughed. "Want to trade?"

Connor happily accepted and wolfed down the burger in about three bites. She asked about how he'd come to Maui and ended up in his new job, and conversation started flowing again. But, damn it, every time she got to the brink of another huge question or revelation, the waitress would interrupt.

"Everything okay here? More ketchup?"

"We're fine," Jenna said, trying not to scream.

Some of the attention, Jenna suspected, stemmed from her broad-shouldered date. The waitress definitely had the hots for him — poor girl, because Connor didn't seem to notice her at all.

"Can I get you another drink?" the waitress tried.

"We're fine," Jenna finally barked.

A fatal error, because when they both finished and Jenna was dying to leave, the waitress was nowhere to be found. It was only when Connor signaled that the waitress cantered over.

"Check, please."

The waitress's face fell. "Sure."

Connor insisted on paying, but Jenna insisted on leaving the tip and even found it in herself to round way up.

"Was she that good?" Connor looked on dubiously.

No, and the woman had made eyes at Jenna's man all night. But still, she was trying to be gracious. "Have you ever worked as a waiter?"

Connor shook his head.

"Well, I've waitressed. And believe me, it's a lot of work."

She waved goodbye to Dell as she and Connor left, barely catching his eye in the midst of some kind of intricate setup of drink dominoes that took up the entire length of the bar. When Dell did spot them leaving, he gave a naughty wink.

"Have fun, kids."

Oh, Jenna was ready to have some fun, all right. However, she did stop to fill out a customer satisfaction slip with *The bouncers are awesome. Especially the cute new guy.*

Connor looked at it and laughed.

"Well, we have to support Chase and Dell, right? Plus, he is cute."

"Hey. That's my kid brother."

She smacked his shoulder. A good thing her feet were braced, because Connor didn't budge, but she nearly had to take a step back.

"You know how much it sucks to be the baby of the family?"

"Uh. . . no. I guess not," he said. Then he scratched his chin and took his own feedback form. She peeked as he wrote in slanted block letters. *Security appeared fully alert and checked IDs carefully.*

She laughed. Leave it to a security guy to comment on that. She took the pen back and added another note to her card. *Bartender (Dale?) was awesome. Mixes the best drinks in Hawaii.*

"Which you would know because. . . ?" Connor murmured.

She elbowed him in the ribs.

Connor took the pen from her and appended his card. *Excellent drinks delivered quickly. Suggest the bartender gets a better haircut.*

Jenna chortled, pointing at the appreciative flock of females crowded around one end of the bar. "Oh, I think the ladies would disagree."

Connor gave her a sharp look and stuck out his elbow. She looped her arm through it and nestled close to his side as they descended the creaky steps back to the street. She'd never felt taller, more beautiful, or freer in her life than just then.

Except when they stepped onto the street, waved goodbye to Chase, and turned — running smack into Jody and Cruz.

Jody was her usual easygoing self, but Cruz looked furious. In other words, his usual grumpy-except-for-loving-Jody self.

"Hi," Jody said, chipper as can be.

"Hi," Jenna said, trying not to look at Cruz nervously. He was a tiger shifter, and tigers could pick up on fear, right?

It was only when Jody nudged Cruz that he growled, "Hi."

After ten wordless seconds of glancing back and forth between Jenna and Connor, Cruz crossed his arms and frowned. The air pressure rose by a factor of a hundred, like a thundercloud was about to erupt.

"How did you like the place?" Jody asked, taking no notice.

"It was nice," Jenna murmured, putting a hand on Connor's arm. He was doing that stiff, hackles-rising thing, staring Cruz down.

The tiger shifter didn't relent. Finally, he grabbed Connor and dragged him to the street corner. "Need to talk to you, man."

Jenna nearly went after them, but Jody held her back with a low, "Uh-oh."

Uh-oh was right. "What is Cruz doing?" Jenna demanded.

Jody weighed her words carefully before replying. "Look, it's obvious what's going on between you two. And Connor seems like a really nice guy..."

"But?" Jenna demanded, slamming her hands on her hips.

"But he's new, okay?"

He's misunderstood, Jenna wanted to shout. *He's trying so hard. And all he needs to rise above all the crap in his life is one person giving him a chance.*

Jody blazed right on without giving Jenna a chance to pipe up. "From what I hear, he's been something of a loose cannon. Cruz is just watching out for you, all right?"

Jenna's cheeks heated, and her hands chopped the air. "Listen to yourself! People talked about us when we were growing up, but they didn't understand, did they? Remember that? How they said we needed more supervision, and that Dad needed to find a new partner to bring us up properly. Thank goodness Dad didn't listen to that crap. What right did they have to judge?"

For a second, they both stopped, thinking back on all they'd overcome as a family. And again, Jenna felt overwhelmingly indebted to her father for all he'd done.

A lump rose in her throat as she looked at her bangles and the matching pair on Jody's wrists. They'd been through so much together, come so far. Jody only meant well.

When her older sister spoke, it was in her gentlest tone. "Jenna, I know you mean it. But you're new to all this. Hell, I still feel new to all this. Every shifter species has a different code, and between shifters, it's even more complicated. So, really — how much can you judge?"

Jenna looked at her feet. Jody wasn't being condescending. She was pointing out the painful truth. Was Jenna really in a position to revolutionize the hierarchies of a totally foreign world?

If it hadn't been for Cruz's comment, carried to her in a brief lull of pedestrian traffic, Jenna might have tucked her tail and admitted defeat. Instead, her head snapped up, and she stomped over to the two men.

"What was that?" she demanded, because she'd heard Cruz drill into Connor, clear as day. *Isn't she a little young for you?*

Connor looked about to blow his top, but she put an arm out, keeping him back. This wasn't his battle to fight. It was hers.

"What did you say?" she demanded a second time.

Cruz looked from Jenna to Connor and back. Then he crossed his arms firmly. "I was saying you're a little young for a guy like him."

Something in Jenna snapped, and before she knew it, she was shaking a finger in Cruz's face and letting the speech of her life fly.

"Too young? You know when I was too young? When my mom died."

Cruz glanced at Jody with a *Help me, baby* look, but Jenna didn't relent.

"And you know when else I was too young? When my sisters grew up and moved out. I was too goddamned young to be the one to take care of my dad and everything at home. But, now?" She shoved Cruz hard enough for him to topple back. "I'm an adult, and I will decide what I will and will not do. Do you understand?"

Her vision was red, her blood racing through her veins, making her hands shake. Fury hurt, she decided. Fury was scary. What if it swallowed her up and stole away the sunshine in her life?

Then the thunderclouds in her mind parted, and a ray of light broke through. She glanced down and found Connor touching her arm. The lightest, least intrusive touch ever, yet one with a power its own.

Love. She could feel it coursing through her arm. Like the antidote to a deadly poison, it combined with the fury and cleaned it all away.

She stared at the point of contact — Connor's massive hand dwarfing hers. Is that what he felt when she'd touched him all those times he'd gotten worked up?

When she finally looked up, Connor's eyes had that reassuring glow. Cruz had gone very quiet, and Jody was studying her and Connor with a totally different kind of concern.

"If you so much as—" Cruz started, giving Connor one last, unrelenting look.

Jenna whipped a hand out and caught Cruz by the chin, shocking herself as much as him. Shit. She might not know much about shifters, but you didn't mess with an angry tiger shifter, especially when that tiger was Cruz. But she'd acted without thinking and spoke just as rashly.

"I'm the one you're talking to, not him. You got that?" Then she caught herself and let go, giving him a little pat instead. "Look, I appreciate you looking out for me. I really do." She softened her touch and her voice. "You, along with Jody, my dad, my sister, my brother-in-law, and just about everyone else. But I've had it with being a little sister. I've had it with being treated like a kid. I grew up a long time ago, and I can make my own decisions. Okay?"

Cruz didn't look convinced, but Jody broke in with a hug. "I know you can," she murmured. Then she wrapped her arm around Cruz and kissed his cheek. "Now, back to what we came for. A nice night out." She winked at Jenna. "What do you recommend?"

Jenna's arms and legs went a little rubbery with relief. In a way, Jody had just saved her ass — again — by defusing the tension. But somehow, it felt more like a favor between equals than the usual big-sister thing.

"Stay away from the falafel salad," Connor grunted, offering his own olive branch. "But the Big Swell IPA looked pretty good to me."

"Perfect," Jody announced, guiding Cruz along. "I can't wait. Oh, hi, Chase!" Then Jody turned to look over her shoulder one more time. "Have fun, you two."

Cruz stiffened, but to his credit, didn't turn back.

"Thanks. We will," Jenna said, pulling Connor down the sidewalk. "Right?"

He let out a forced chuckle. "Sure. But you see what I mean?"

"Yeah, I see what you mean," she sighed. Then she ran her hand down the alley of thick muscles that lined each side of his back and borrowed a line from her father. "But like water off a duck's back..."

Connor laughed. And he laughed even harder when she tacked a question on to that.

"Do dragon's backs work that way?"

"You're something, you know that?" he chuckled, stopping for a huge hug. The kind where his arms went all the way around her — and then some — and rocked her from side to side. She buried her face in his shoulder and inhaled, pushing the last wisps of the thundercloud away.

Her own words echoed in her mind — *All he needs to rise above all the crap in his life is one person giving him a chance* — and she chewed on them for a while. Did she have to wait for Cruz, Kai, or someone else to give Connor a chance, or could she be the one?

With the world closed away in the safety of his embrace, she felt invincible. But as desperately as she wanted to be the one to help him, she wondered if she really was. Jody was right — she was a novice in the shifter world. And worse still, she had no particular powers of her own. What could she possibly do to help Connor?

Just trust, a little voice told her. A voice that could have come from deep in Connor's soul or the center of the Earth for all she knew. *Trust.*

Trust him, she wondered, or trust herself?

Connor let her out of the hug slowly and gifted her with one of his rare smiles. "I'll have to show you someday."

She tilted her head, confused.

"A dragon's back. So you can check for yourself, I mean."

She laughed. "How about I check something else out first?"

His eyebrows jumped up, and his eyes took on a possessive glow. "What would that be?"

Your naked body, she wanted to say, *Your human, naked body, but with the chance to enjoy it this time.*

She cleared her throat. "How well you dance." She nodded ahead to a band playing under a huge tree, where several couples were swaying to the music.

Connor gave her a wry grin. "Just a dance, huh?"

She gave him her best sultry look. "And maybe some other things."

A little pink showed in his cheeks. Had he read her mind?

"Well, I can pretty much guarantee being a terrible dancer."

"Oh? And how are you at...other things?" She let her voice drop.

"Oh, you know." He socked her with a cocky grin. "You'll have to judge for yourself."

Which made her want to forget about dancing and find the nearest bed, deserted stretch of beach, or back seat of a car.

"Don't mind if I do," she said, as demurely as possible.

Now Connor was the tease. "Dance, you mean? Or...other things?"

She did a brief estimate of the distance to the car and back to the estate, then gave up. She'd never make it that far without dying of lust. Maybe dancing would take the edge off that need.

Then again, it could only make things worse.

Connor's eyes sparkled, daring her. But, hell. She was game for a little torture if he was.

"Dance," she said. "For starters."

Which was how she found herself in one of the most magical settings ever. Her sister's treehouse at Koa Point was in that category, as was the thatch-roofed guesthouse she got to stay in. But dancing with Connor under a banyan tree on that particular night... That was the greatest magic of all.

She didn't need to stop and read the historical marker to know that banyan had to be one of the oldest trees in the state.

A massive central trunk shot branches out toward every point on the compass, and when those grew too heavy to support themselves, they simply sprouted vine-like roots which gradually anchored them with a whole new trunk — and another and another until that single tree had created an entire forest of interlocking trunks. A latticework on which birds chattered, and a canopy to catch the notes of the band. Voices floated along with laughs and the faint scuff of dancers' shoes.

"So, you put your hand here." She touched her shoulder and took a deep breath.

"That much, I know." Connor frowned in concentration.

"Hey," she said as he cupped her waist. "You can step on my feet all you want."

"Just keep in mind I'm better at other things," he muttered.

For a second or two, he looked around, watching the other couples, nodding with the beat. Then he swung into his first step... and swept her breath away. Not with polished movements or expertise, but with the dormant power and innate confidence of his frame. His eyes locked on hers, and all she had to do was focus there to fall into perfect harmony with him.

She watched the stars — er, the sparkles in his eyes. He turned, carefully at first, then more smoothly, and she laughed at the joy of the movement. It was a little like surfing, but slowed down, all the better to relish it with. The magic of momentum, the feeling of floating along. The total muffling of every thought except those related to the here and now.

Their chests squeezed together then slowly separated with every simultaneous breath. Her legs bracketed his, close enough to trip up entirely, except she never did.

Nice and close, the naughty girl in her giggled.

"Hmm?" he murmured.

She sucked in her lips. Had she said that aloud?

"Nice," she said very innocently. "It's just so... nice."

"Not just nice," he mumbled, sniffing her hair. "It's destiny."

His words were so low, they slid smoothly between the notes of each refrain.

She nodded slowly. Of course, it was destiny, bringing them together. What else could it be?

One song ended and another started, but Connor danced right through the brief breaks.

"Blue moon..." The rich-toned singer held each note perfectly, and Connor pulled Jenna a little closer on the lines about seeing her standing alone.

She hummed against his chest, listening to the singer go on. No love of his own? Funny how she'd never considered how hard that might be.

Her heartbeat slowed, but each thump had twice its usual power, and her whole body went warm. She dreaded the moment when the song would end. But after a last, long note, Connor made it even more perfect by turning the song into a kiss. A kiss with the same slow, lingering movements of their dance.

His arms slid over her shoulders, and she arched into him as the mood slowly tipped from *ballad* to *dirty dance*. And when that broke off — the world's most perfect kiss — the rest of the evening played out in Jenna's mind.

"Take me home, dragon," she whispered.

He kissed her one more time, then rested his forehead on hers and nodded. "I can do that."

His voice was still a whisper and his hand firm in hers, but his Adam's apple bobbed — twice. Then he looped his arm over her shoulder and walked her back to the car. A long way back, but every step felt right.

Jenna shivered in anticipation. If Connor was that good at dancing, how good would he be in bed? Every nerve in her body tingled, and the heat pooling in her body swirled around in sweet anticipation.

"Hang on," she whispered, pulling him over for one more kiss. A thank-you kiss, telling him just how perfect the evening was.

He grinned then turned back to continue walking, and—

Connor's face fell, and his whole body went stiff.

"Mr. Hoving," the man in front of them said. More an accusation than a greeting.

"Draig," Connor muttered, pulling Jenna back.

It was a tiny, unobtrusive movement, yet a thousand alarms clanged in her mind.

Llewellyn. Baird. Draig. Connor had mentioned those names before. The oldest, richest dragon clans.

Jenna glared. Draig was an older man, more silver-haired than gray, but his eyes were sharp as an eagle's searching for prey. He held his chin and nose high, exuding privilege. Or maybe arrogance was a better word.

Jenna tried not to scowl, but she hated the man already.

"Enjoying a night out, I see," Draig said, obviously finding pleasure in agitating Connor with his words.

And agitate he did, judging by the way Connor's jaw clenched. Because there was an entire subtext coded into the man's words. A haughty attitude fit for an emperor who occasionally amused himself by observing the behavior of the lower classes.

The rabble, Draig's unturned nose said.

Those clans run their world with a thousand unwritten, archaic rules, Connor had said.

Two beefy, expressionless men — bodyguards, no doubt — flanked Draig and his too-young, too-beautiful, and all-too-quiet companion who kept her eyes firmly on the ground. One of those trophy girls who gave herself over to a rich, older man. Would she SOS her misery to the outside world if she looked up?

"Enjoying your last night in Maui?" Connor all but spat back, emphasizing the *last* part. Obviously, Connor wouldn't shed tears when the man left.

Jenna gripped Connor's hand tightly. They'd been having such a nice night, and she didn't want anything to ruin it. She nudged him forward, but he stood as still as a brick wall, blocking her. So she stepped out and around, really to drag him away if she had to.

The movement brought her out of Connor's shadow, and she froze the second Draig focused on her. His eyes flared red, just like those of the stalker in her nightmares, and instinct told her to flee, far and fast. But she was rooted to the spot.

Horribly, helplessly rooted, unable to move for all the panicked messages crisscrossing her mind.

There are dragons, and there are dragons. She'd only had the vaguest sense of what Connor had meant before, but now it was perfectly clear.

"My, isn't she lovely," Draig said slowly, raking his hot-coal eyes over her body.

A chill ran down her spine as the full force of his gaze violated her personal space. Draig wasn't just a rich, conceited snob she could ignore. He was a dragon. A beast who could claw her in two. A beast who could roast her alive — slowly — and enjoy every minute of it.

Draig's eyes glinted, and Jenna glimpsed even worse tortures in those fiery orbs. Like being carried away and locked up by him. Being touched by him, knowing no matter how much she screamed, no one would hear her cries.

She'd never felt that terrified in her life. Connor was coiling for an outburst behind her, and that scared her almost as much. The last thing she wanted to witness was a full-blown dragon fight. But Connor was at the breaking point, a volcano about to blow.

It was all too easy to imagine what would happen next. Connor would jump Draig. Draig's bodyguards — whatever type of shifters they were — would jump Connor. Even if Connor fought them off and got to Draig, the blame would be pinned on Connor as the aggressor. The loose cannon, as Jody had put it. A rebel who had to be stopped. And if Connor went as far as showing his dragon in public — even in her defense — the shifter world would come down on him with full force.

Within the space of a heartbeat, Jenna dragged her last scrap of willpower out of hiding and scowled at Draig.

"And aren't you rude," she snipped.

The redhead at Draig's side looked up in shock. Draig's eyes narrowed. Connor growled, a prelude to imminent attack.

"Goodbye," Jenna barked, dragging Connor forward, praying he wouldn't snap. She hated walking away from a challenge, but someone had to defuse this simmering confrontation — or else.

Miraculously, Connor followed. Mostly to cover her back, she sensed, but that was fine too. She forced herself to stride along at a normal pace instead of running as Draig's eyes bored into her back. She felt the heat of them — the brand, almost — every time she got out of step with Connor. It was only when she'd put three blocks between her and that beast with the piercing gaze that the feeling eased.

"Jenna," Connor murmured.

She plowed right along, looking forward to getting into the Ferrari, slamming the door, and racing away.

"Jenna," Connor insisted, slowing her down.

She stopped and faced him, angry that her fury turned on Connor instead of Draig, but angry nonetheless. "Yeah?"

He took both her hands in his and pressed them to her cheeks, shrinking the world down to just him and her.

"You're amazing, and I love you for that." He shook his head and went a step further, blowing her away. "No — I love you for a lot of things. But you have to be careful around dragons like Draig."

Yeah, she got that now. "Assholes like Draig," she muttered. His type was bad enough as plain old humans. But a dragon that arrogant was truly bad news.

Then she caught herself. Whoa. Wait. What else had Connor said? "You love me for...?"

He covered her lips with a touch so gentle, it melted her. "Just that part. I love you. I tried really hard not to, but I can't help it."

She stared. "Why would you try not to?" A dozen ugly thoughts ran through her mind. Was there someone else? Had all her idiosyncrasies and shortcomings annoyed him? Worse still... "Am I not good enough?"

Connor's eyes bugged out, and he clutched her shoulders. "I'm the one who's not good enough. Can't you see that?"

She blinked wordlessly for a while. "No, I do not see that. Are you nuts?"

The lottery bowl of emotions roiling inside her spun a few more times, and pity popped out next. God, what struggles had Connor been through as a kid?

Sorrow was next, and she cupped his cheeks the way he had with her. "I know who you are. And if anyone, I'm the one who's not good enough. A part-blood mermaid. What good is that?"

"Don't you knock it," he said fiercely.

She looked him straight in the eye. "Then don't knock who you are."

He stared at her for a good long while. Long enough for a group of partygoers to crowd past on the sidewalk and bump them a few times.

"Whatever she's saying, listen to her, *brah*," a young man called out with a laugh. "The woman is always right."

And *zip* — somehow, those casual words transported Jenna from the terrifying world of shifters back into the realm of humor, heart, and hope. The world she knew and loved.

"Yeah. Listen to me, mister," she said, shaking her finger at Connor like a child.

The faintest possible smile ghosted across his face. "Yes, ma'am."

"Good. The car's not far now, and when we get there, all of this will disappear. I mean, the bad parts. I'm throwing those out and keeping the rest. Like dancing." She started walking again, piecing together her confidence with every step. "And dinner. Dinner was great. And walking. And, oh, kissing."

Connor made a soft sound. "I liked that part too."

She nodded like that was a given, even though her soul swelled. "Perfect, because I have a few more planned."

He raised her hand and kissed her knuckles. "Like here?"

She snorted. "Okay for when I'm driving, but once we get home, no."

"No?"

She shook her head firmly. "You promised, mister. Lots of other things. And I intend to hold you to that."

He stopped her — for a nice little hug, she assumed. But man, was she was wrong. Connor took her by the shoulders and claimed her mouth in a searing kiss that had every nerve in her body panting, *Yes! Yes! More!*

Then he slowly released her, making sure she was steady on her feet before letting her go.

"Wow. What was that?" she mumbled.

His eyes went through every possible shade of green like blinkers going on and off. Angry jade. Determined, forest green. Aroused emerald. All that was in this man, and it was up to her to bring out the best parts.

"A promise," he growled, making her toes curl.

Chapter Nineteen

For the first part of the drive, Connor sat quietly, ordering his raging dragon to calm the hell down. But the beast was spitting fire and roaring, intent on setting off on a rampage. His dragon didn't even specify what it wanted to destroy — Draig? His deadbeat father? The entire dragon world?

Anger was nothing new, and neither was frustration. Yearning was often part of that testy cocktail too. But having them mixed with hope and desire — that was totally new. New and dangerous, because he could not — would not — get any closer to Jenna without getting himself under control.

If only it were as easy as she had said. To make the bad parts disappear and hang on to the rest.

"Not far now," Jenna murmured, shifting into fourth gear.

Connor put his hand over hers on the gearshift and closed his eyes, focusing on her smooth, warm skin, trying to calm down.

"Hang on," Jenna said, slipping her hand out from under his and placing it on top. "How about this?" She massaged his fingers with her thumb.

"Nice," Connor whispered.

Her contact had a way of pulling the plug on his dragon's rage. Instead of vowing death and destruction to all the evil in the world, his dragon slowly shifted its focus to positive thoughts. *Jenna... love... kiss...*

"Driveway coming up," she said quietly, as if to check whether he needed more time.

He took a deep breath. How was it possible to be that tuned in to someone in such a short time?

Destiny, an earthy voice rumbled in the back of his mind.

Which was all well and good, but did destiny have something good in store for him, or just a miserable, crashing end?

Good or bad is for you to decide, the voice rumbled. *For you to deserve.*

He scowled. What was the point of destiny, then?

The voice growled ominously. *Destiny steered your mate onto your life's path. Shall I take her away again?*

Connor just about thrust his hands up in surrender. God, no. He didn't want that. *I just have no clue how this works,* he wanted to plead. *No one ever explained.*

The voice laughed remorselessly. *All the better. You can learn for yourself.*

The hard way, he figured. But okay. He was a master at that.

Just don't let her get hurt, he pleaded. *Please.*

The deep voice snorted. *She must do her part as well. Perhaps even more than you.*

Connor raked his fingers through his hair at the warning in those words. No, no, no! He was supposed to keep Jenna out of danger, not drag her down.

He waited for an answer. Even a cryptic hint would do. But destiny had wandered away again, off to torture some other soul.

"Koa Point," Jenna said softly, tapping his hand as she waited for the gate to open. "Hey. Time to reboot."

Connor blinked a couple of times. "Reboot?"

"Yep." She motioned around. "A clear, starry night. Peace and quiet. And just smell those flowers."

He sniffed, tentatively at first, then more deeply. He didn't care about the flowers, but Jenna's sweet fragrance brought the last bit of calm to his soul.

She shifted into first gear, moving his hand with hers, and rolled down the drive. "Yep. You and I are coming back from our very nice night out. We're in a very nice car." She patted the sleek dashboard. "In a very nice place."

The woman was a master of shedding the bad and hoarding the good.

And a master of distraction, his dragon cooed in its first intelligible words of the evening when she moved her hand to his thigh. Not too high, not too low. Just right. When she parked the car in a bay of the estate's long garage, she set the hand brake and leaned over for a kiss, all in the same move. As if they had a weekly evening out that always ended in a kiss.

Not ending yet, his dragon rumbled. *And not just with a kiss.*

Her tongue swept over his, assuring him it wouldn't end there. Then she pulled back, smiled, and nodded to the door. "It is a nice car, but considering our options..."

He broke into a smile and followed her out, then met her at the threshold to the garage, where he backed her gently against the wall. Her arms slid right into place around his waist, and she raised her chin for a kiss. He squeezed closer, pressing every inch of his body against her.

"And what exactly are our options?" he growled between kisses. The good kind of growl for a change.

She tipped her head up, cooing while he kissed his way down her neck.

"Lots of options..." Her voice was light and dreamy, like she wasn't in a hurry to go anywhere fast. "There's the guesthouse... the beach... and your place."

He worked his way back up to her mouth, delving deeper, holding her tighter. "My place."

His dragon gave a firm nod, like he wouldn't have it any other way.

Jenna smiled into his kiss, then slowly pushed him away and took his hand. "Then show me the way, mister, before I strip you naked right here." She giggled, and the sound was as soothing as that of the ocean in the distance. "Not sure I can wait that long."

Connor didn't think he could wait either, and he nearly detoured to the guesthouse. But the long walk along the beach worked wonders for clearing the last clouds from his mind. It was only when they walked past the fish pond where Jenna had been spooked earlier that his muscles tensed.

"Up there, right?" Jenna whispered, a woman on a mission.

He nodded, leading the way, sniffing as he went. His brother Timber had been by recently, patrolling the grounds. Cynthia had done a quick flyover too, it seemed, before settling down to watch over the area from the top floor of the plantation house. He could tell as much from the tiny zephyrs of lavender scent she left in the air. But Jenna's saltwater-and-sunshine scent filled his senses and emptied his mind. The closer they got to his clifftop house, the harder his heart beat. Would she like the place?

"It's kind of a work in progress," he warned. *Like me,* he nearly sighed.

"I can't wait to see it," she said, swinging his hand as they went.

The sea breeze increased as they climbed, tossing her hair with each light step she took. When they crested the hill, Jenna stopped in her tracks.

"Wow."

Connor looked out too. The view was amazing, encompassing everything from the dark silhouettes of neighboring islands to the lights of the West Maui coast. The ocean sparkled with moonlight, and the swell dashed against rocks far, far below.

"Perfect place for a dragon," she whispered.

Connor nodded and gulped. That Timber had suggested the location to him made sense because his brother knew him better than anyone else. But Jenna immediately understood too. His need for a high lookout, a place to perch after a long night flight.

It was perfect, but he was painfully aware of how rough the actual living quarters were. All fine for a bachelor to make do with, but for Jenna?

But her hands waved in excitement, and her voice rose high. "Oh my gosh, this is amazing. You get to live here?"

He grinned and pushed open the unlocked door. "It needs a lot of work, but..."

His eyes jumped from the unfinished cabinets and the tattered couch to Jenna, who went right to the wooden table he'd rescued from the barn the day before. She ran her hand over the surface, following the grain of the wood. "This is gorgeous."

He exhaled a little. Maybe she wouldn't mind the rough edges of his place, after all.

"This part of the house only has two rooms. The kitchen and a living room." Both were laid out in a straight line, one after the other, with a roof that slanted upward toward the sea. He rolled open the patio doors, hoping she'd focus on the ocean view instead of the lack of curtains or the fact that one of the doors needed a good shove to move. The house opened onto a natural stone patio that hugged the edge of the cliff.

"Oh my God. You could dive right in from here," Jenna said, stepping straight to the edge.

He snorted. "Not sure I'd recommend that."

Jenna pointed out a spot amidst the frothy surf below. "I think if you hit that spot just right..."

He gaped, because she meant it. Maybe her mermaid side was closer to the surface than she knew.

"You mean, if you were nuts."

"The old Hawaiian kings jumped off cliffs, you know. To prove themselves." Her eyes sparkled.

"I'll make a mental note of that for the next time I have to prove myself."

It was a joke, but his soul grabbed hold of the idea and stored it in his personal library of just-in-case files. A big, messy place all the way in the back of his mind, because a guy like him had learned over time that *just in case* happened more often than he wished.

Jenna breezed back inside and flopped down on the couch. "Wow. Inside is like being outside." A second later, she bounced up and explored the kitchen. "Amazing."

"Well, it would be amazing if the cabinets were all in."

"It will be amazing." She nodded firmly, looking around.

He couldn't tell what she was picturing, but clearly, she saw the promise of the place. The way she saw the promise in him — or so he hoped.

"Does the couch pull out?" she asked, looking around.

He laughed, loving that she seemed to have no problem with that at all. Maybe destiny knew what it was doing in bringing them together, after all.

"I think if you pulled on it, it would fall apart." He motioned to the far side of the room. The roof extended a little farther, sheltering a set of outdoor stairs. "Keep going. We're getting to the best part."

"This isn't the best part?" Jenna squeaked.

He hit a light and descended the set of spiral stairs. "This cliff was created by an ancient lava flow, and whoever set up this place used the old lava tubes for a series of cellars. This is the first one." He motioned around the small space the stairs opened on to, then to a tunnel branching off to one side. "Check this out..."

Jenna followed right on his heels, not the least bit fazed by wandering through a low, narrow cave. The footing was good, with a smooth layer of cement laid over the raw rock underfoot, while the tunnel walls were rough.

"Watch your head," he murmured, tapping an outcrop.

"You mean I can't watch your ass?"

He laughed, and it echoed through the room they stepped into next.

"Oh...my...God..." Jenna stammered, looking up and around.

"It was a lava bubble, but it makes a pretty cool room, don't you think? Skylight and everything." He pointed up.

The room was perfectly round, and enough of the rocky roof and one wall had collapsed to create two openings — a wide skylight and a window to the ocean, filling the space with fresh air and light.

"Right now, it's just shelves around the edges..." he started.

"But you could build a circular couch to fit right in. Put a table there... Use it at the hottest parts of the day..." Jenna filled in, describing exactly what he had pictured creating someday.

Hope welled up in him. Hope he didn't dare hold on to too tightly, because who knew what the future could bring?

"What's through there?" she asked, indicating the next tunnel.

"Have a look," he said, hanging back to watch her discover it for herself. His heart thumped even harder than when he'd first explored the place for himself and saw how perfect it could be. If Jenna liked it then maybe...

"Holy shit," she said, stepping out into the open.

"Cool, huh?" He grinned.

"This is beyond cool." She turned in a slow circle.

They'd stepped out onto a scooped-out step in the cliff — a huge, open area with a natural ceiling that ranged halfway out to the ledge, offering shelter from the elements as well as an open space.

"Oh my gosh. You can barbecue here. You could throw a massive party here. God, you could just about run laps here," Jenna gushed.

I can take off and land here too, his dragon rumbled, showing off.

The space was that big — big enough for him to spread his wings. Big enough for two dragons to spread their wings, in fact, which only got his heart beating faster.

She motioned to an alcove off to one side. "Let me guess. That's your lair."

He laughed. "That's the bathroom."

"Ha. So, no treasure?" Her voice was a tease.

Just one, his dragon murmured, looking straight at her.

He shook his head. "No gold or silver, if that's what you mean."

Jenna looked around, not showing the slightest disappointment. On the contrary, her eyes shone with wonder. "So in the mornings, you can sit up in the kitchen and enjoy the light..."

He could picture it exactly. Her sipping coffee from a mug on the couch, her hair mussed from sleep, wearing nothing but one of his shirts.

"... and in the middle of the day, you can cool off on the couch there..." Jenna pointed to the lava bubble living room he had planned.

He instantly imagined Jenna calling him over and patting the spot next to her. She'd hand him a lemonade with a swirly straw and smile the way only she could.

That couch that hadn't even been built yet, but what the heck. Just dreaming about it felt good.

"...And you could finish up with the sunset here," Jenna concluded, spreading her arms wide as wings.

We could teach her to fly, you know, his dragon said.

He held back a snort. That meant mating with Jenna, and he had no idea if she wanted that.

But if we did mate...

No matter how he tried to reel in such thoughts, they ran away from him. If Jenna did let him claim her with a mating bite, she would become a dragon shifter too. They could fly into the sunset together, swoop around a few times, and land back right here. They could start and end every day together and settle into the kind of easy rhythm his soul yearned for.

Home, his dragon whispered. *We could finally feel at home.*

Jenna took his hand and looked out over the sparkling sea. Was she thinking the same thing? She took a deep breath, not giving away a thing. But when she turned to him, her eyes were as sparkly as the sea.

They both moved at the same time — her looping her arms around his neck, him taking firm hold of her waist. When their lips met, his pulse skipped and warmed.

"Only one thing missing from this tour," Jenna whispered between kisses.

"What's that?" he whispered, tilting her head to one side to kiss deeper.

Her lips danced over his, going from playful to hungry in the space of a few heartbeats.

"A bed. Or don't dragons need those?"

He slid his hands over her rear, pressing her hips against his. "Dragons, no," he whispered, pushing back a stray lock of hair, then covering her mouth with his before forcing himself to finish the sentence. "Humans, yes. Right over there."

"Over where?" Her voice was husky, though her eyes didn't leave his.

His dragon side was ready to pick her up and carry her to that section of the patio, but he forced himself to release her and lead the way.

"There — the bed."

He motioned to a platform built above the natural stone, curtained off on three sides like a room. Well, it was, in his imagination. Right now, it was just a big four-poster bed set in the middle of an open platform, sheltered by the natural roof. "Give me one second. I'll be right there."

"You need a second? For what?"

"It'll be worth it. I promise."

She folded her arms and tapped her foot impatiently. "Let me guess. Mood music? Lava lamps?"

He chuckled and stepped to a dim corner where the cliff wall sloped down. "Better than that."

There'd been a lot of junk around the place when he discovered it, and he'd stacked the old boxes and pallets to one side. Not the nicest kind of wood for a fire, but somehow, it seemed important to light one just now. Jenna would think him crazy, so he did his best to explain as he set it up in a circle of rocks.

"My grandmother — my mother's mother — was born in Switzerland," he said in response to Jenna's unspoken question. "Yeah, there used to be bears and bear shifters there."

"Wait — bears?" Jenna asked as she slipped off her shoes.

He did his best to keep his eyes on the wood and not on those amazing legs. "Yeah, bears. My mother's side of the family is all bear shifters. But my father was a myriad shifter who could change into different forms..."

"Neat," Jenna murmured, looking at him with dreamy eyes.

If only she knew about not fitting in. "Anyway, my grandmother used to tell us all kinds of stories about old times back there."

"What kinds of stories?" Jenna asked, leaning back on the bed.

He stacked the wood in a teepee shape, setting smaller bits of kindling between the bigger pieces. "They had all kinds of old customs, and the one she kept up had something to do with an end-of-winter ritual."

Jenna, to her credit, didn't bolt at the word *ritual*. On the contrary, she seemed to hang on every word. Of course, the starry backdrop and grayscale palette of night over the ocean helped set the mood.

"They would build big bonfires, and some people would dress up in ugly masks. Then they'd go around and make a ruckus, scaring the bad spirits away."

"Bad spirits, huh?"

He almost didn't dare look at her, but he had to check if she understood. He didn't want to dwell on Draig, vampires, or any other form of evil tonight. But he sure as hell wasn't going to spend a night with Jenna without a few precautions, even if they were the superstitious kind.

"Yeah. Scare them all away," he murmured into the wind. "Make sure they left everyone alone."

Jenna didn't say anything for a second, but then she nodded. "So, light that sucker up and come to bed."

How she managed to mix sweet, sultry, and innocent together, he had no clue. Only that he'd never met a woman anything like her before.

"Need a match?" she asked when he hesitated.

"Match is the slow way."

"What's the fast way?"

He motioned to his chest and gave a little cough, wondering how she would react. "Dragon, remember?"

Her eyebrows shot up. "Holy crap. You must have the best party tricks."

His laugh echoed into the night. "I can use a match if you want."

She shook her head and leaned forward, resting her chin on her elbows. "This, I have to see."

His nostrils flared as he considered. Maybe this wasn't the best idea. Stunts like this got him in trouble every time.

"What are you waiting for?"

"Trying to think before I act," he admitted.

Jenna waved the notion away. "Now what fun is that?"

He grinned then leaned back, huffed a few times, and released just enough of his dragon side to spit fire. Just a small, foot-long flame, enough to get the bonfire crackling. But for a brief instant, his teeth extended and his jaw hung wide, giving Jenna a glimpse of the first stage of a shift.

That part, he hadn't been counting on, and he looked up, worried at how she would react.

Her eyes were wide, and her hands clutched the sheets. Her mouth popped open, but she didn't say a word — at first. Then she pushed her lower lip out, exhaled, and murmured, "Cool."

He stared. Was she really okay with the dragon part?

She crooked a finger, beckoning him closer. "You know, that is a dangerous move."

He stepped away from the fire, closing the distance between them fast. "In what way?"

She leaned back on her elbows, leaving just enough space between her knees for him to step into. "That's a hard act to follow. What if you don't live up to expectations?"

He leaned over her, feeling every inch a powerful dragon, even though he kept that body safely locked away. Behind them, the bonfire crackled higher, egging him on.

He came down on his elbows, making her sink back into the mattress. "I promise not to let you down."

He meant it in more ways than one, and his dragon quietly made a vow. To pleasure her. To protect her. To make her proud.

She grinned and scooted back, reaching for his shirt at the same time. The second she got it over his head, he came down with a hard, open kiss that made her whimper. Within seconds, she was writhing and panting for more.

"Yes," she moaned as his hands swept over her glorious body. "Yes..."

Chapter Twenty

Jenna's mind filled with a thousand lights, and her body surged with need. Connor hadn't just lit a bonfire on the rock ledge. He'd kindled one inside her too, and she couldn't get enough of him. Her hands were everywhere at once, touching all the muscles that had been taboo. His thick shoulders, his iron-hard chest. The dragon tattoo inked into his upper arm, and the Special Forces one hidden beneath. The checkerboard of his stomach made a maze for her fingers to trace. His ass was all coiled power, too, and she yearned to feel him moving inside her.

"Connor...never..." she mumbled in desperate pants.

He stopped instantly and held himself an inch above her, rock hard. "Never?"

She shook her head, because that sounded all wrong, but she couldn't get her tongue in the right place to speak. "I've never wanted anyone as much as I want you. Never needed it this bad," she panted.

His eyes burned into hers. "Neither have I. Neither have I."

Which said a lot, because he certainly had more experience than her. Not that it was her first time, but somehow, it felt like a first all the same. A first. A last. An only, or so her soul hoped — that she'd get to stay with this remarkable man for a long, long time. Living. Learning. Loving.

"Oh," she gasped as his right hand swept along her ribs and cupped her breast. He dipped lower and kissed her there, too, first through her shirt and bra, and then—

With one quick rip, those barriers were gone, and he dove back down on bare skin. Scooping her soft flesh with one hand

and kissing at the same time. Kneading, pinching, and sucking until she couldn't see straight.

She plowed her hands through his thick hair, arching her back. And when he switched from one side to the other, she cried out again.

"So good..."

Which had to be obvious, but she couldn't help it. She couldn't help winding her leg around his either, or grinding her hips against his thick, hard cock. When Connor broke away and sat up, his eyes glowed.

"Not too fast?" he asked in a low rumble that made her blood surge. She'd barely shaken her head when he grunted, "Good," and moved her up the bed in one smooth move.

Apparently, dragons liked it fast and hard. Which proved once again what a perfect match they were. She wiggled and lifted her hips, helping him strip her to the skin.

"And now this," he murmured, reaching for the knife she still had strapped to her calf.

It was fun, holding her leg out and letting him take it off. But the best part was lying back once she was totally naked to bask under his gaze. Connor sat back on his heels, poised over her, his mouth open, his eyes glowing.

"So beautiful..." His chest heaved up and down.

Her chest was heaving too, and she couldn't help but circle her own breasts while he watched. She bent her knees outward, and when Connor looked down, she felt the heat of his gaze on her, as hot and insistent as a hand.

"All yours, my love," she murmured, unabashed. The words came from out of nowhere, yet felt natural on her tongue. Like she hadn't just found her true love but rediscovered him.

Connor trailed a line of burning kisses over her abdomen, then pushed both hands under her ass like a shovel, raising her off the bed. When he dipped out of sight to kiss her, every nerve in her body exploded at once, and she arched back.

"Yes..."

His tongue was hot and insistent, and what it didn't reach, his fingers did. She clutched the sheets and dug her heels into the mattress, opening every inch of herself to him. His stubble scratched her inner thighs, and his fingers gripped her like a vise. He made pleased little muttering sounds as he explored, and she pictured a dragon admiring his treasure. Stroking gold coins, fingering long, silver chains. Holding precious goblets up to the sun. But it was even better than that, because *she* was that treasure, that precious possession. That home he'd come back to again and again.

Her body shuddered when she came for the first — and second — time, but Connor didn't let up one bit. The few times she peeked, the glow of the bonfire reflected off his glistening shoulders, giving his skin an orange glow. She turned her head just far enough to train her unfocused eyes on the fire, watching the crackling flames spin into the night.

Then she cried out and came for a third time. For a long minute, the only sensation that registered was that of intense heat reaching into every corner of her body, and she sighed. When she blinked and opened her eyes, her hips were back on the mattress. Connor was cradling her body, stroking her breasts, murmuring something in low, sweet tones.

She tipped her head back and let out a crazy laugh that made him look up.

"You don't have to worry about not living up to expectations," she explained, patting him with the little coordination she had.

He kissed her belly. "Good thing."

She panted for another long minute, feeling like jelly. Almost purring like a cat cuddled in its master's lap.

Which was a little scary, because as much as she trusted Connor, she didn't want a master. She wanted a partner. The real thing. So after a few controlled breaths, she sat up under him and nudged him back. Which was a tricky operation, because you didn't move a body like Connor's unless he decided to comply.

"My turn," she whispered, motioning for him to lie down.

He tilted his head, and his eyes sparked enough to make her hold her breath. That was his dragon, staring back out at her, and she could practically hear the beast growl.

You want me to what?

Maybe dragons preferred maidens who lay back and let themselves be ravaged. And on many levels, that worked for her. But somehow, she knew it wasn't enough. Connor, she figured, would agree to just about any ground rules. But the dragon peeking out from his eyes — he would take some taming, for sure.

"Lie back." She patted the bed, practically cooing. *You can trust me.*

His eyes flared. *I trust no one,* she imagined the dragon grumbling.

That message rang all too true. Did his dragon even trust itself?

"Trust me," she murmured. "I'll make this good."

Slowly, gradually, Connor leaned back. For a while, his abs bunched at his centerline, refusing to relax. But eventually, his lower back settled on the mattress, followed by his shoulders. He held his head up, though, watching her.

"Seems only fair, you know." She trailed a hand across his stomach. "You taste me..."

His eyes were twin flames.

"...I taste you."

She popped the button of his pants and slid the zipper down slowly. Then she stopped and palmed every long, hot inch of him through the material.

"Need a little help, though," she admitted once she got down to ridding him of those clothes.

Connor looked serious — dead serious — and she wondered if he'd ever let a woman call the shots before.

"Trust me," she whispered one more time.

He nodded slowly and helped her get his pants and boxers off. Then he settled back, watching her like a tiger. Or a dragon, she supposed. A vigilant dragon, ready to jump in and wrestle back control.

She cleared her throat. Yeah, well. Even a mere human could teach a dragon a thing or two.

She straddled him and dragged her body up and down his until his eyes glassed over. Then she covered his mouth with slobbery kisses that hinted at what she had in store. Her hips started rocking, and with his hands nudging, it would have been so, so easy to discard her plan and sink down on his cock there and then. To roll over and hand the reins to him, letting their bodies connect at last. But she fought off the urge and followed the thin line of hair down his centerline instead. Down his chest, down his belly. She circled his navel a few times while shifting her legs into the right place. Then she reared up on her knees and swept her hair back.

Connor's eyes blazed. He didn't move a muscle, though a tic started up in his cheek. His dragon was close to its limits, she sensed. So she rubbed her lips together and leaned down before the beast could seize control. She didn't want him pushing her head down or guiding her in. She wanted to show him exactly what she could do.

So she did, starting with a long, lollipop lick that started at the base of his thick shaft and traveled slowly to the straining tip. She fluttered a few kisses over him there and blew lightly, making him shake. Then she went back to licking, up, down, and around. Again and again, until she couldn't tell whether the hungry moans in her ears were his or hers.

Connor sank back into the mattress, weaving his fingers through her hair, letting her set the pace. A pace that grew faster and hungrier with every second that ticked by, because he tasted that good. Her senses filled with him — sight, smell, taste, touch — until she was bobbing up and down, taking him deeper every time.

When she gulped a quick breath of air, she caught the haggard sound of Connor's breath. He was close to coming, and part of her wanted to take him that far. But another part wanted him to come inside her — deep inside her — their first time.

So after two more mind-blowing sucks, she released him with an audible pop. Connor moaned, every muscle coiled tight. In an instant, she crawled up his body and plunged her tongue into his mouth, sharing the taste with him. Their tongues tangled, and his hands gripped her ass.

She pulled back to look into his eyes, and for the space of three hammering heartbeats, they paused.

"Jenna," he growled, reaching for her.

They rolled, and he thrust inside her with one smooth, hard stroke.

No condom. No barriers. Which was reckless, but at that moment, she couldn't think straight. She moaned, arching her body. Connor withdrew and immediately thrust deeper. He repeated the action again and again, moving her body up the mattress in strong, deliberate strokes. His face was a mask of concentration, and he didn't utter a word. He didn't have to because his hands said it all, stroking hers softly while keeping them pinned over her head. She tightened her legs around his waist, urging him deeper. Arching higher and higher while he delivered everything she'd ever wanted and more.

"Yes. . ."

Her body wound painfully tight, and his next hard thrust pushed her over the edge. She cried out, exploding with pleasure, seeing only a blur.

With another hard pump of the hips, Connor bottomed out and groaned. He threw his head back, showing his teeth, and exploded inside her.

Flying. She was flying. Her eyelids fluttered. Was this what a dragon felt when it launched off a cliff? This sweet rush, the thrill?

Connor held her tightly, and she imagined swooping through time and space. Eventually, his grip softened as if he were lowering her to the ground. Cushioning her head with one hand, touching her hands with the other. The glow of his eyes was softer but just as intense. She studied him, watching his lips move without forming words.

"So good." She sighed.

His jaw clenched, and he covered her mouth in a deep, searing kiss. Her legs tightened around his waist as an aftershock of pleasure hit, and Connor started moving inside her again. One thrust, then another, answering her cries. His mouth stayed on hers, making her dizzy. When his cock pulsed one more time inside her, his tongue pushed against hers, and a burst of heat swept through her body. She arched hard, moaning with indescribable pleasure, and crazy images filled her mind.

Like spreading her arms for a swan dive but never hitting the
water, just gliding through the air. Or winding her long, leathery neck around Connor's and flicking a tail. Even better, she
imagined raising a huge muzzle to the moon and crooning with
her mate.

For one brief instant, she was a dragon. Then Connor
pulled away with a sharp gasp and muttered. "God. Sorry.
Are you okay?"

He cupped her face and pushed her hair back, calling desperately, "Jenna. Jenna..."

She let herself float a little longer before blinking and looking at him. Why did he look so worried? She'd never felt
better in her life.

"Mmm," she cooed, melting into the sheets. "That was so
good."

Connor dropped into the crook of her neck, muttering to
himself.

"Hey," she whispered, running her hands over his back.
What was wrong? Okay, they'd totally forgotten a condom,
but something told her that wasn't what worried him. "That
was great."

His mumbles were barely audible against her skin.
"Shouldn't... I shouldn't have—"

"Shouldn't what?"

He rolled to one elbow and cupped her cheek. "That heat.
The brand. You felt it, right?"

She grinned as wide as a Cheshire cat. Oh, she'd felt it,
all right. "In case it wasn't obvious, that was great." Was she
going to have to report every separate orgasm to him?

"It was a brand, Jenna."

She rolled her tongue around her mouth, savoring the taste.
It reminded her of the Flaming Bob Marley she'd once had —
not that a cocktail could give her the high Connor just had.

He looked so serious. Did that mean a brand was bad?

"What if I liked it?" She ran her leg along his. "What if I
want you to do it again?"

"It's a brand, Jenna. Do you understand what that means?
My dragon wants to claim you."

207

She took a deep breath. "What if I want to be claimed?"

His throat bobbed, and he looked down at the tangled sheets. He ran a thumb gently over her collarbone as his brow furrowed.

"Or don't you want me?" she asked. A prompt, not an accusation.

His head snapped up, and his eyes were fierce. "I want you more than anything, Jenna. I want you so much it scares me."

She stared at him for a moment then got her trembling lips to speak. "Doesn't scare me."

Which was a bit of a fib, because he was a shifter, and that was a whole different world she hadn't truly explored yet.

He looked deep into her eyes, and finally, a faint smile spread on his mouth. "Somehow, that doesn't surprise me." Then he relaxed into the mattress, tugging her back until they were comfortably spooned. He cuddled her close, nuzzling the back of her neck, making her want to purr.

"That was just a little puff," he said at last. "If I bit you and branded you deeply, we would be mated."

She covered his arms with hers, pressing them tightly against her chest.

"But you didn't bite me," she said. Or had he? She'd been flying so high, who knew?

"No." His fingers circled a spot on her neck absently.

She pressed into his hand. The idea of a vampire biting her was terrifying. But Connor biting her to make her his mate?

Hell yeah.

"So it doesn't count?" she asked, let down for the first time that night.

He kissed her shoulder. "Yes and no. It's like a mark. Like. . . saying you're mine. Keeping other guys away."

She laughed out loud. "I don't want any other guy."

He squeezed her closer, like even if she wanted, he wouldn't let her go.

A quiet minute ticked by, and when she moved, she heard a little sound of surprise.

"This is nice," he whispered, touching the tattoo on her lower back.

She grinned. "You like it?"

One coarse finger traced the blue dolphin, and he chuckled. "A mermaid with a dolphin tattoo."

She laughed back, pointing to the design that curled around his arm. "A dragon with a dragon tattoo."

That made him laugh outright, and she touched her chest, then his arm. "A mermaid... with a dragon. A real one."

He didn't reply right away, and when he did, his voice was mournful. "Yeah. A mermaid and a dragon."

Well, okay. So they weren't the world's most conventional couple. Who cared?

"Hey," she whispered, turning in his arms. She popped a kiss on his lips and smiled, ready to lighten the mood. "We don't need to figure everything out tonight." Then she tilted her head to the bonfire that still crackled away. Not quite as high as before, but the embers in the center glowed as brightly as she did inside.

When he raised his hand to touch her shoulder, the bonfire crackled, and she spotted a long, jagged scar on his upper arm. There was another scar on his ribs and a thinner line closer to his hip, but not a mark in between.

"Shifters heal fast," he whispered, catching her looking.

She touched his shoulder. "Even from this?"

He shrugged. "Wasn't too bad."

She wondered if those scars came about in human battles or shifter wars, though she didn't dare ask.

"No big deal," he said, pulling her closer.

"No big deal?" She shook her head. "Surely some things can kill a dragon."

His eyes drifted to the bonfire, and she wondered if he was picturing a near miss. When he spoke again, his eyes were darker, his voice huskier. "We're pretty tough. Maybe not so much around here..." He smiled faintly as he pressed her hand to his heart. Then he pointed to the center of his chest and went grim. "And here. Get a dragon right between the chest plates here, and, yeah. That would pretty much end it."

She gulped as he pressed her finger to his sternum, showing her the spot. She patted his chest, trying to lighten the mood.

"Plates, huh?" She used the excuse to touch his hard pecs, then teased. "Or do you mean scales?"

He huffed. "Snakes have scales. Dragons have plates of armor, like thick leather."

She grinned. For all his disdain of the dragon elitism, Connor had a pretty strong streak of dragon pride.

"And here I am, all defenseless," she murmured.

He laughed — a genuine laugh that made her grin from ear to ear. "I'd hate to be the guy who thought that."

For a minute, they grinned at each other like a couple of kids. Then she sighed, closed her eyes, and settled in against his big, bare chest. "God, this is nice."

"Better than nice," he growled, holding her close. "Good night."

She giggled and peeked up at him. "Oh, I'm not going to sleep, mister."

He stiffened. "You're not going to leave, are you?"

She snorted. "Leave?" *Never*, she almost said. But she'd told herself to keep things light, so she flashed him her best smile instead. "Hell no. Just resting up for a little more fun." She wound her leg around his, already feeling the first tingles of lust rekindling in her core. "Unless you're too tired..."

He snorted and turned her in his arms again, snuggling her close while gently cupping her breast. Hinting at more to come very, very soon.

"I'll show you too tired," he whispered, kissing her ear.

Chapter Twenty-One

Jenna woke to the sight of morning light dancing over the Pacific. In the foreground of that glorious view, Connor's hand was still clasped around hers. Her cheeks were tired as if she'd spent the whole night smiling in her sleep. Well, maybe not the whole night, because she and Connor had woken up a couple of times for a little more fun, and she hadn't smiled so much as cried his name as he came inside her again and again.

She lay still, watching the waves sparkle, wondering if she'd ever felt this good. Her body seemed aglow with more than just physical satisfaction, her mind a blur of emotions, and a little voice inside her hummed.

With one thumb, she stroked a tiny scar on Connor's forearm. It reminded her of those on his torso, which scared her, because what if something had happened to him back then? What if they had never met? She would never have known this joy, this sense of completion. This deep-in-her-bones feeling that he was the one.

We just knew, her dad had always said of meeting her mom.

Jenna stroked the fine hair of Connor's arm and closed her eyes.

Destiny, Connor had said in a choked, faraway voice.

It had to be. No other morning-after had ever made her feel as if the earth had tilted on its axis, and none ever would. She'd bet she could wake up with him for the next thirty years and still feel this incredible radiance. In fact, she didn't just *bet* — she knew. Deep down, she knew.

She smiled, wondering if someday she'd be telling her kids, *We just knew.*

Then she took a deep breath, because those seemed like pretty heavy thoughts for a girl who'd been so sure she wanted the freedom to play for a while. To be a kid the way she hadn't always been able to. Of course, that was before experiencing everything Connor had opened to her. Now, a different kind of freedom and deep-seated peace filled her.

She slid around slowly to watch Connor sleep. Responsibilities and concerns had faded from his face, giving her a hint of the man as a boy. A boy with a lot of ghosts in his closets. A man determined to make it in the world. A dragon shifter who—

Her breath hitched. A dragon shifter.

For a moment, the thought frightened her, but a second later, she found herself gently cupping his cheek. No, she wasn't crazy to want what her parents had shared. Her sister must have gone through the same thing, but she'd never been as happy as she was with Cruz. And if Jody could live with a tiger, Jenna could live with a dragon, right?

If I bit you and branded you, we'd be mated, Connor had said.

It ought to be scary, but somehow, the idea had a lot of appeal.

Then she frowned. Vampires also bit. Were they really out there, too?

She pushed the thought away and let herself melt back into the warm cocoon of Connor's arms, wishing she could stay there all day. But she needed the bathroom, so she slowly slid out of bed, careful not to disturb her sleeping dragon. She grinned, remembering the previous night.

Is that your lair?

That's the bathroom.

So she knew exactly where to go. Like the rest of the place, it was still a little provisional, with a curtain for a door and a mirror balanced on an outcrop in the natural rock wall. But the shag rug kept her feet warm, and the shower taking shape in an alcove would be spectacular when it was done. That was true of the whole place, actually. Connor's new home reflected his character perfectly — dark and edgy. Secretive, mysterious.

But it still managed to keep a straight-up, *what you see is what you get* quality. The natural beauty of the place had been left to speak for itself. It was quirky too, and as genuine as the man. So it needed some finishing touches — okay, a lot of finishing touches — and some throw pillows for sure. But on the whole? It was all too easy to picture herself living here.

She thought it over. Her dad was having a ball, being a granddad and working alongside his brother. So that feeling of responsibility was eased from her shoulders. And as for her life in California — well, she could migrate all her favorite parts to Maui in a flash. Surfing, beachcombing...

She walked out to the edge of the rocky shelf and looked out at the ocean. Sunlight glinted off the waves, promising another bright, sunny day. The swell swirled around the little bay below, and farther to the right, she could just see the tiny beach and the ancient fish pond sheltering it.

"Beautiful," she whispered.

She could see for miles — a dragon's eye view of the coast — and the ocean stretched out in bands of rich color. The higher the sun rose, the more the water sparkled. Each of those sparkles called to her like diamonds in a crown, and the whole world seemed to hum. Jenna hummed too.

The entire watery world rippled and moved in a delightfully unpredictable way. But in one spot... She squinted toward the beach. One spot shone brighter and bolder than anything else.

Jenna sheltered her eyes with a hand. Was that the same golden glint she'd seen before?

Come. Come and find out, the shine said.

She pulled her gaze away to scan the surrounding waters. The previous day, she'd nearly grasped that shimmering something, but she'd been spooked out of the water before she could. It had been terrifying at the time, but from up high and on a perfect morning like this, it was hard to believe in anything evil lurking out there. So maybe later that morning, once Connor woke up, they could meander down to the beach and take a dip together.

Why not now? The water sparkled, inviting her in.

She wanted to laugh and go back to bed, but somehow, she couldn't pull herself away. She tilted her head, listening. Was that hum in her ears, or was it coming from the sea?

If you listen really closely, you can hear the ocean sing, her dad liked to say.

She closed her eyes, listening.

Over here...

The call seemed closer now, and more distinct. She strained to understand it, finding her eyes drawn back to that one spot again and again.

Well, whatever it was, it could wait, right? She had a warm bed and a hunk of a man to make love to.

But even as she started to turn to Connor, the mystery pulled her back toward the sea, and she began to worry. What if a current rolled the object away? What if she never found out what it was?

Another ray of light bounced off that part of the water. *Come. Come and find me.*

Damn it. What was so important down there that every one of her senses pointed to it?

The more she looked, the more tempted she was to go down and find out what it was. It wasn't that far from shore, after all, and the ocean was calm as ever.

She looked back at her sleeping lover, equally pulled in that direction. She could slide back into bed beside Connor and watch him sleep. And when he woke up...

She giggled quietly. Oh, yes. She had a few ideas about how that could go.

And yet she couldn't drag herself away from the ledge, and she couldn't get that niggle out of her mind. All the other sparkles came and went, but that one spot flashed in the same way every time.

"Damn it." She didn't want to go looking for undersea treasures. She wanted to get back into bed.

Finally, she huffed and grabbed her knife, her panties, and the T-shirt Connor had left by the bed. Fine. She'd have a quick look and come right back. Connor was sound asleep anyway. She could get down to the beach and back in no time.

"Connor?" she whispered, peeking over to the bed.

He didn't stir, and she was hit by a pang of regret. All along, Connor had been the one helping her. She hadn't so much as made him a cup of coffee. She could at least do that — and while it was brewing, she could have a quick look at the beach. Even if that were just a piece of sea glass out there, she'd know.

So she kissed Connor on the forehead — still wiped out, the poor guy — and retraced her steps of the previous night. Through the lava bubble rooms, up the spiral staircase, and through the two-room building at the top. There was a coffee machine in the unfinished kitchen, and she hit the brew button on her way out. There. On her way back, she could pick up two mugs and bring Connor coffee in bed. That would make it a perfect morning, right?

She walked down the hillside with her flip-flops smacking against the soles of her feet, wondering what was drawing her on. Maybe this was one of those *We just knew* things that couldn't be explained. A feeling she just had to follow. Maybe even a mermaid thing. Who knew?

The palms lining the beach swished and swayed when she stepped out onto the sand, and the sun glinted in the same spot, more insistently than ever.

"Easy. Nothing to it. Here we go," she murmured to herself, standing at the edge of the water.

But her limbs refused to budge as she recalled what had happened the previous day.

"Don't be ridiculous," she muttered, kicking off her flip-flops.

The water was perfectly still within the shelter of the fish pond, and fairly quiet beyond, as well. She'd never been afraid of open water. Why start now? Especially with that hum sounding in her bones, leading her on.

She looked out to sea. Had there really been something out there yesterday, or had she freaked out over nothing? Connor hadn't seen a thing, and he'd flown over the entire area. Meanwhile, the glinting object was right there, so close. Begging her to take it away.

She kneeled quickly and strapped the knife to her leg, muttering to herself the whole time. Then she waded in, one quiet step after another, barely stirring the water. So slowly, it felt silly, so she finally just dove in to get it over with. Any moment now, she'd solve that damn mystery and get back to Connor. Afterward, they'd end up laughing about how silly her fears were and get back to where they'd left off last night.

She came up for a quick breath, then dove a second time, kicking hard, aiming for the bright spot. The water magnified the effect, shimmering brighter the closer she came. Up close, the source of the glow was only marble-sized, but golden light seeped out of it like a lamp. What was that?

One more kick took her close enough to snatch the smooth, pebble-like ball, and she held it in one tightly closed fist as she kicked for the surface. Connor's oversized shirt ballooned around her body as she swam, slowing her down. When she sputtered to the surface, all she had eyes for was the object in her hand.

"Gotcha," she murmured as she treaded water, looking at it.

When she opened her hand to peek, her jaw swung open. A pearl?

In the old days, pearls were harvested from the wild, the woman at the jewelry stand had said.

Her heart beat a little faster, and she swam forward until finally, her toes touched the rocky bottom. She looked down around her feet. Might there be more pearls down there?

She raised the pearl higher and rolled it over her palm, murmuring the whole time.

"Perfect."

And she really meant perfect. The pearl was round, smooth, and black with an overtone of gold. The sun shone off its unblemished surface, making it wink. She grinned, imagining what Connor would say when she showed him. When she glanced up at the ledge that sheltered his home, she broke out in a smile because there he was, standing at the edge.

"Look at what I found!" she shouted, though he wouldn't hear over the sound of the waves. The beach was calm except for the little bit of a ripple sneaking in around the collapsed edge of the fish pond, but his ledge stood above a nearby surf-washed cliff.

Connor waved back, and she half swam, half waded to shallower water, still admiring the pearl. Back at home, she'd come across the occasional discarded tire or shopping cart. But, wow — a pearl? Of course, this was Maui and not the densely populated California coast.

She marveled at her treasure, tuning in to the hum. A reassuring tune like a lullaby that came from the pearl, not the sea. She closed her eyes, listening hard. Warming inside, because it sounded like a lullaby her mother used to sing. A lullaby she'd completely forgotten until now. Which was probably a case of her mind filling in too many blanks — but still, bittersweet tears filled her eyes. She had so few memories of her mother, and to have one more emerge from the mists of her memories was a gift.

She cupped the pearl in both hands and let the tune play out in her mind. A song of love and comfort and goodness in the world, all coming from the pearl. As if that pearl were a friend — or maybe a guardian angel, or even a sign from heaven sent by her mom. When she held the pearl up to the light, it looked all gold — the color of love, life, and passion. But then something flickered, and a cloud slid in front of the sun.

When she looked up again, Connor was still waving, as excited as she was. Dragons must have incredible vision for him to have seen the pearl from so far away. Her mind fast-forwarded into rushing back to his house and showing it to him.

Coolest find ever, she'd say.

He'd ooh and ahh, and she'd make him listen for the tune, too. And that would top off the most amazing morning ever, because how often did you wake up from great sex to find a pearl in the open ocean?

The pearl shone as if it were happy too, but something itched at the back of her mind.

You found me! You found me! its bright shine seemed to cheer.

She grinned from cheek to cheek, imagining what her father would say.

She glanced up at the ledge again and, wow. Connor must have been really excited, because he kept right on waving to her. She held out the pearl, showing it to him.

"Wait a minute..."

Slowly, it dawned on her that Connor was waving with *both* arms. Gesturing. Slowly, she retracted her outstretched arm. Connor's movements weren't happy. They were frantic.

The itch swelled to a prickle, and the prickle exploded into full-blown alarm as the sixth sense dulled by her excitement kicked back on. Something was out there in the water. Something coming her way.

The peaceful tune in her mind broke off, and the lullaby became a scream.

Jenna whipped around and froze. A plume of white rushed through the water like a torpedo heading right for her.

Connor hadn't been waving. He'd been warning her.

"No!"

She gasped and lurched back toward the beach. But the water fettered her legs like chains, and she felt mired in mud. She clawed at the water with her hands — one open, the other balled, holding the pearl.

"Jenna!" Connor's bellow sounded over the splash of water and the pumping of blood in her ears.

She sprinted as an otherworldly scream filled her mind. *Watch out! It's coming! Get away!*

But moving through the water was like running in a nightmare — she barely seemed to move. Her right foot struck a jagged rock, and she staggered, nearly falling in.

Get away!

Flailing, she found her footing and rushed on. But the sound of rushing water filled her ears, and she whirled. Was that a shark coming at her? An orca?

Whatever it was, it was big. Whale-big, and nowhere near as friendly. It rushed around the open corner of the fish pond, a tsunami aimed right at her. She saw jaws — huge, white jaws. Wide, greedy eyes. The flash of a fin—

"No!" She splashed at the creature with one helpless fist.

Then she yelped as something slippery wrapped around her leg.

"No—"

Her cry broke off as the creature yanked her under water and started dragging her away.

Jenna screamed a helpless message no one could possibly hear. Water splashed everywhere, filling her mouth and nose. Bubbles exploded from her lips, but no sound emerged. She punched blindly at the mystery beast, to no avail.

No! No!

Then a voice laced with evil and greed vibrated through the water, invading her ears. *Yes, my pet. You will finally be mine.*

It was the voice of her nightmares, and her muddled mind screamed. *No! God, no!*

Come with me, my pet. Come to me.

Like hell, she was coming. She reached for the knife strapped to her calf, but it was covered by the thing clutching her leg. At first, she thought it was a tentacle, but then she caught sight of a claw.

The deep voice chuckled and pulled her deeper. *Come to me, my pet. It is time I made you mine.*

Chapter Twenty-Two

Connor ran along the edge of the ledge, hollering at the top of his lungs. One minute, Jenna had been down there in the water, beaming and waving like she'd found pirate gold, and the next...

She was gone.

"Jenna!" he yelled.

He'd slept peacefully all night — the kind of soul-deep peace he hadn't felt in years — until jolting awake with an out-of-nowhere sense of doom. Of some terrible enemy not just lurking, but rushing in to attack. And when he looked down—

"Jenna!" he screamed at the sight of a huge *something* barreling at her from the depths. It was too deep to see clearly, but the line of white trailing behind showed how fast it was.

"Get out!" he yelled. "Get out!"

God, hadn't Jenna sensed that creature coming? Hadn't she seen him waving her away?

He stared as the long line of froth zipped along, just breaking the surface, making a beeline for Jenna. A horrifying look of realization had come over her too late. Then there was a huge splash and a muffled cry he felt more than heard.

"Jenna!" he bellowed.

It came out deep and throaty, because his dragon was already struggling to emerge. But he was so rushed and frantic that his two sides tangled, and he couldn't shift.

Damn it, hurry! he ordered his dragon. That monster was dragging Jenna away.

You hurry! it shot back.

Connor's anger mounted higher and higher until he very nearly gave in to it, exactly as he'd done so many other times

221

in his life. It was only when he pictured Jenna touching his arm that the fury cooled enough to let him think.

Stop, he barked at his dragon. *Think!*

Every time he'd messed up in his life — and Lord knew there'd been plenty — it had been at a time like this, when anger or frustration led the way.

No time for that! his dragon roared back, because dragons acted. They didn't hang around thinking. Not at times like these.

A dozen competing voices filled his mind. His mother. Commanding officers he'd served under. Even his father, the few times he'd come around.

Think, boy.

Look before you leap.

You'd make a great officer if only you used your head.

What the hell were you thinking?

He closed his eyes. Precious seconds were slipping away.

Fly! We must fly! his dragon roared.

Connor shook his head and looked straight down. The swell crashed into the base of the cliff under his feet, churning and frothing.

You could dive right in from here, Jenna had said. *If you hit that spot just right. . .*

He stared. That spot between two rocks?

You mean, if you were nuts, he'd said.

Well, he was out of his mind with fear. Maybe that counted.

The old Hawaiian kings jumped off cliffs, you know. To prove themselves.

Connor stared at the water. It would be so, so easy to launch into the air and fly, but that wouldn't help Jenna. She was underwater, and with the sun glinting off the surface, he wouldn't be able to see a thing from above. Which meant. . .

He took a deep breath. He had to get down there to help her. Now. And down that cliff was the fastest way.

No, a little voice cried in his head. His own voice, but from way back when he was a little kid. *Please, no.*

The water swirled and splashed, taunting him. *Scared, are you?*

Yeah, he was scared. Coming close to drowning as a little kid could do that to you. And it wasn't just him. Most dragons hated water. They hated diving. Why struggle through the water when you could soar through the air?

Because Jenna is down there, he barked at his dragon, pushing off from the cliff at the same time.

He'd launched off that cliff dozens of times, but *launching* wasn't *diving*, because one ended in flying, while the other ended in...

Certain death, his dragon yelped.

The wind whipped his eyes, making his vision blur as he plummeted toward the rocks.

Fly, his dragon screamed.

His shoulders stretched as his wings began to emerge, too late to catch any air. He was falling too quickly, and he knew it. If he opened his wings, they'd be stretched at their widest — and most vulnerable — when he struck the surface. They'd be twisted and broken, and even rapid shifter healing wouldn't be fast enough to help.

So he clenched his jaw and folded his wings along his sides for a smooth entry, sticking with his suicidal plan. But, crap. Was he aiming at the right place?

He squinted as he dropped, keeping his nose on target. His tail stretched out behind, and he kept it ramrod straight, trying to line up for a streamlined dive.

Jenna, he wanted to scream. *Hang on.*

The surf spun and foamed beneath him like a rabid animal waiting for its prey.

Jen—

The surface of the water was a brick wall that knocked the air out of him. Everything was a white, foamy blur. Salt water filled his mouth and nose, and his eyes burned, making forgotten memories flood back in. Memories of gulping water, crying for help. Getting swept deeper no matter what he tried.

Damn it, keep it together, his dragon ordered. *Jenna needs us.*

He flicked his tail, desperate to gain some control in that muted tangle of bubbles. His tail didn't have half the effect it did in the air, but a sense of balance rushed back to his inner ear.

Swim, damn it. Swim!

The surf was pulling him toward the rocks. He had to get out into the clear.

So he kicked and beat his wings, battling the current that tugged him toward the rocks. Inch by inch, he clawed forward until he emerged into blue water instead of white.

Jenna! he roared in a muffled underwater cry. Where was she?

The ocean stretched out in front of him. An endless blue universe pierced by rays of sunshine that filtered in from above, making depth and distance impossible to judge. It was all eerily void of sound other than faint, taunting laughter.

He jerked his head left and right, growing desperate. How would he ever find Jenna this way?

Then something moved in the corner of his eye, and he saw Jenna being dragged along by her leg. She was bent at the waist, flailing and pounding at her attacker.

Jenna!

He kicked madly and beat his wings, taking off in pursuit. Discovering that childhood demons weren't so hard to overcome, at least when the woman he loved was at risk. But, shit. Dragons commanded the skies, not the oceans, and the distance to Jenna took an eternity to close. It was a miracle she was still conscious, having been under that long. How much longer could she hold out? His lungs were already burning, and it was hard to imagine Jenna hanging on much longer before blacking out.

By the time Connor swam within fire-spitting range — not that that weapon did him much good underwater — he was dizzy for lack of oxygen. His lungs screamed, and no matter how hard he clenched his teeth, he couldn't fight instinct any more. So he rushed to the surface, gulped a couple of lungfuls of air, then dove again.

The creature that was making off with Jenna was much faster than him, but she was doing a damn good job slowing it down. Which shouldn't have been possible, considering how long she'd been underwater, but hell. Her hair fanned out around her head and shone in the eerie ocean light, exactly like a mermaid's. A warrior mermaid who refused to give in.

Connor powered forward, determined to free her this time. That shark or squid or whatever it was had targeted the wrong woman, and it would pay with its life.

Inch by inch, he closed in on the beast, intent on figuring out what it was. It was too big for a shark, too small for a whale. Its movements were quick and strangely elegant. A long, pointed appendage flicked in and out of his view — a tentacle? Or was that a tail?

His frantic mind couldn't make sense of it. What kind of sea creature had a long, thin tail?

Jenna twisted in another attempt to get free, and her eyes went wide when she caught sight of him.

Connor! He could hear her cry in his head.

Hang on! He pushed the thought toward her mind, hoping she could hear him.

The creature who had her in its grip twisted around for a look, and Connor froze in recognition. That wasn't a shark, a squid, or some kind of high-tech submarine. The powerful body did taper off into a tail, but what he'd taken to be fins were wings.

Wings?

It was a dragon, yet nothing like him. The wings were stubby. The tail longer. The body armor an ugly, seaweed brown.

Mr. Hoving, it spat in disdain. The words thundered through the water and into his mind.

Draig?

The arrogant tone and haughty eyes gave the shifter away, but Connor's mind still spun. What did Draig want with Jenna?

What does every sea dragon want? Draig chuckled, reading his mind.

Sea dragon? Connor did a double take. Jesus. Did he have to learn everything the hard way?

He glared at the bearded sea dragon and flexed his claws. *What the hell do I know about what you want?* His words were part vibration, part garbled sound, but like Draig's, every word made sense to his dragon mind.

I'm an old man, the sea dragon sighed. *Ready to retire. All I need is a comfortable lair at the bottom of the sea and a nice little female to amuse myself with.*

Jenna fluttered and flailed. Connor exploded with fury and darted forward. But Draig maneuvered away with a quick flap of his stunted wings, pulling Jenna out of reach.

Oh, no. This fine prize is mine, Draig crooned. *I claimed her first, so she is mine.*

Connor snapped at him, but Draig avoided him with another lightning-fast lurch. The bastard might be centuries old, but water was his element, and it showed.

Imagine my surprise when rumors first started of a mermaid that had survived to this dreary day and age, Draig said.

A part-blood mermaid, Connor wanted to say. But, hell. She sure seemed to be able to survive underwater a long time, and thank goodness for that.

I've had my eye on her for quite some time, Draig chuckled, swaying from side to side, daring Connor to attack. Then the aging dragon's voice dripped with malice. *But she didn't accept my invitation, which left me no choice but to come after her myself.* One of his wings wrapped around Jenna. *She is lovely, isn't she? Not a redhead, but the next best thing.*

Connor felt sick. Then he nearly cheered, because Jenna wound up for a punch and landed it right on Draig's snout. The old dragon shook in surprise, letting her go.

Connor would have loved to savor the moment, but he didn't have time. He powered forward and battered Draig in the chest with the thickest part of his skull. Then he opened his jaws wide for a crushing bite and—

Connor reeled from an out-of-nowhere blow, and Draig roared in triumph.

You think you can best me, boy?

Stars filled Connor's vision, and his head spun. He'd failed to see Draig's spiked tail whipping at him and had paid the price.

You think you can best the mightiest sea dragon of the Draig clan? The sea dragon cackled. *You're a nobody, a nothing.*

Connor's nostrils flared, and his dragon snarled.

Jenna, meanwhile, kicked toward the surface, getting away.

Draig sighed and went on. *Of course, these days, many of the old bloodlines have allowed themselves to be diluted. Even the Llewellyns have claimed common brides. But I shall take the ultimate prize — a mermaid. Who better to carry the next generation of sea dragon blood?*

Connor snapped at Draig's neck, missing by a hair. Then he slashed at Draig's chest, but the armor plates were so thick, his claws raked along the surface and bounced off.

Try me, boy. Try again and again. No one can defeat me, the king of the sea. And no one shall steal my queen from me.

Suddenly, it all made sense — Draig's Neptune looks. The aquarium on his yacht. The mysterious sea creature splashing around the vessel that night.

I like the occasional swim when the water is warm enough, Draig had once said. *But sadly, these old bones are not up to flying any more...*

You bastard, Connor's dragon roared.

But Draig just went on in the same victorious tone. *I am a rich man, and now I shall have my final treasure. A mate — a very special one. She shall bear me the heir I've always wished for. Not a relative's son, like that lazy Anton. No. My queen shall bear me a son of my own flesh and blood. And he will be a mighty dragon — a sea dragon to carry on my line.*

Draig looked around for Jenna, and Connor rammed him again, landing a better blow this time. Spitting fire didn't work underwater, but his dragon tried it all the same. The water sizzled and frothed, and even Draig looked momentarily taken aback. So Connor did it again. The sea dragon's eyes glowed with fury, but he didn't spit back.

Can't spit back, Connor's dragon murmured.

He hung on to that tidbit. If sea dragons couldn't spit fire, and if he managed to lure Draig up to the surface...

Of course, the old dragon was too wily to be tricked. Connor's mind spun with ideas — vague, disjointed ideas, because his oxygen levels were dipping into the red again. He had to get to the surface, fast.

Draig's laugh followed him. *You didn't actually think yourself worthy of such a prize, did you?*

Connor gritted his teeth as he tried to take stock of the situation. Jenna had already made it to the surface and was swimming for shore. He followed, acutely aware of the danger that put Jenna in. Draig could dart up anytime and drag her under again. So Connor raced to the surface, grabbed one gulp of air, and dove just in time to slam Draig away from Jenna.

You will not have her! he roared, grappling with the sea dragon.

She is already mine, Draig thundered.

Connor had fought plenty of shifters in his time, including dragons. But a sea dragon? That was totally different. Draig didn't swoop, spit fire, or spin the way dragons did in aerial fights. He snuck in close and tried to latch on to Connor's back.

What the—

Connor twisted and roared the first time Draig did that, catching him by surprise. The sea dragon wrapped his stubby wings around Connor's like a goddamn python and dove deeper still. The pressure in Connor's ears tripled, and his vision blurred.

She's mine, Draig grunted as they whirled in circles, plunging deeper all the time.

It was just like that awful dream he'd had about hurtling through the air with Jenna, except it wasn't hurricane force winds that tugged at him, but the force of the water.

She's mine, Draig taunted.

She's mine, Connor roared back, but his voice was uneven and weak.

With a desperate swipe of his tail, he broke free and climbed toward the surface again. Once there, he snatched another all-too-brief gulp of air before diving to keep Draig safely in sight.

Back for some more fun? Draig grinned. *I'm rather enjoying this myself. Someday I will tell my heirs how I battled for their mother, and she will love me all the more.*

It made Connor sick, hearing Draig's mad plans. And it made him furious that Draig had the upper hand, not himself. He was younger. Faster. Stronger — but only in the air. No matter what he tried, he couldn't wear Draig down. On the contrary, he was the one battling fatigue — fast.

Which was when it dawned on him that this might be the first battle he couldn't win. His first and his last.

His soul screamed, not in fear of death but for Jenna. If he lost, Jenna would be abducted by Draig.

Not abducted, Draig tsked. T*aken home.*

Not happening, his dragon roared.

He hissed and clawed at his opponent, desperate for some new hope. But Draig played by a whole different rulebook — the story of Connor's life — and the ocean seemed to be on the sea dragon's side. No matter what he tried, the sea dragon countered.

Then it hit Connor that he didn't have to win. All he had to do was buy Jenna time to get away. Sooner or later, she'd make it to shore and alert the others. Kai would round up his combined shifter forces and come down on Draig, and Jenna would be safe.

His heart ached. Sacrificing himself for Jenna was fine. But, damn. They'd only just found each other. They'd only shared one night.

His thoughts skipped to Tim, Chase, and Dell. They would soldier on without him, but damn. It was hard to picture how that would go. And, crap. He'd miss them, and they'd miss him. Which sucked, because they'd already experienced far too many losses over the years. He didn't want to add another scar to their wounded soldier's hearts.

But a man did what he had to do, right?

Connor rallied the last of his strength and roared his loudest roar, putting all his frustration into it. The deck had been stacked against him from the start, but okay. He'd long since accepted that as his norm. And death, well — he'd dodged fate often enough not to argue this time. As long as Jenna lived, it was worth it.

He grinned a little madly. At least he'd die a hero. And no dragon — no matter how elitist or arrogant — could ever take that from him.

Ready? he dared his dragon.

Ready, it growled.

He spun in Draig's grip, snarled in the sea dragon's startled face, and slapped his wings over Draig's.

How dare you? Draig bellowed.

Connor laughed. He was about to write his own rulebook, and the sea dragon would have no choice but to comply.

Now what will you do, you old bastard? he snarled, smothering any motion Draig attempted. He hung on tight and straightened his tail, making them both sink deeper into the abyss.

This is my element, you fool, Draig growled, still struggling.

Well, maybe, but Connor finally had the upper hand. His wings were bigger, for one thing, and his body heavier. He was about to retort as much when an even better plan hit him. He could do better than simply delaying Draig. He could kill the sea dragon. Of course, he'd die in the process, but still. A victory was a victory. He could finish off the old bastard, save Kai the trouble, and maybe even win himself the respect he'd always craved.

That was the theory. In reality...

His lungs begged for air. Water flooded his mouth, nose, and ears. Every muscle screamed for fuel. His vision grew spotty again, and he saw two Draigs.

Agony. It was sheer agony. Still, Connor clamped his teeth together and rallied all his willpower as his world dimmed.

Jenna, he called, trying to reach her mind. *Remember me. Please. Remember me.*

Connor!

I love you, he said.

No, Connor! Don't!

Her anguished cry struck one last, desperate nerve.

Don't you dare! she screamed.

Which put him in a conundrum. To carry out his suicidal plan or obey Jenna?

The woman is always right, brah, that guy in Lahaina had joked.

Sure, that had only been a joke, but something told him to trust Jenna on this one. So he heaved Draig aside and snapped at his enemy's neck with his long dragon fangs, hoping that might end his foe. Then instinct took over, making him hurtle toward the surface, though it was the last thing he wanted to do.

For the first crazed moment of his ascent, Connor thought he'd succeeded in killing Draig. But the water below him vibrated a moment later, and his hopes sank. Draig was chasing him, gaining ground on Jenna, screaming, *Come back to me, my pet.*

New plan, his dragon grunted. *We'll lure him into the air. Burn the bastard to bits.*

Tears streamed from his eyes, both from the burn of salt water and the emotions roiling inside.

Concentrate, he barked at himself, trying to pull together a Plan A and B. One of them involved roasting Draig in the open air, and the other called for drowning the bastard. But his mind was dull and foggy, and everything kept getting mixed up.

So close, Draig hummed, seeing Jenna churn the water above.

Connor was rocketing toward the surface in desperation, but the sea dragon undulated smoothly, rapidly catching up. The sun shone, growing brighter all the time.

Connor gritted his teeth. This was it. His last chance. Possibly his only chance, because failure only left the suicidal option of drowning along with Draig.

Hero, he reminded himself.

Dead hero, his dragon grumbled.

Connor clenched his teeth and rushed to the left, willing Draig to follow. This was it. His final test.

I shall return to you shortly, my pet, Draig cackled, nipping at his heels.

Over my dead body, Connor bellowed.

But Draig just laughed. *Just what I had in mind, boy. Just what I had in mind.*

Chapter Twenty-Three

Jenna broke through the surface — really broke through it like a pane of glass, sending water flying in all directions. Without a pause, she paddled frantically for shore. Her leg burned where she'd been touched, and her heart hammered away.

Holy shit. A dragon. Worse — a sea dragon.

All along, she'd been worried about vampires, but man, had she been wrong. Her stalker was an ocean dweller who wanted her as his concubine.

All I need is a comfortable lair and a nice little female to amuse myself with.

Connor and Draig had communicated through a series of bellows and roars, yet she'd understood every terrifying word. A vestige of her mermaid blood, perhaps? At the same time, she couldn't comprehend a thing, because it was just as Connor said. Dragons lived in an archaic world of their own, playing by a whole different set of rules.

Well, not with her. She was getting the hell away from that dragon fight, and fast.

Draig had dragged her a good mile out, making the familiar landscape look like a foreign shore. The mountains looked taller and mistier, the coastline rockier and less hospitable. The calm of daybreak was slowly giving way to the first small waves, and they splashed her face. She sputtered and swam on. But a second later, she paused and treaded water, listening to her own panting breaths.

Breath... panting... water... She looked down past her feet.

Whoa. Wait a minute. How long had she been underwater?

A few minutes, at least. That whole time, her sole focus was escaping Draig. The need to breathe hadn't registered in the least. How was that possible? She was good at holding her breath — but not that good. By all rights, she should have drowned.

So maybe Connor had been right about not knocking only having a little mermaid blood. Maybe it was enough.

Or was it?

Her left hand was still clutched around the pearl, and she loosened her grip just enough to peek at it. What had that woman in Lahaina said?

Precious pearls. Magical pearls. Pearls that could. . . could. . .

The pearl shone brighter, gold beating out black as if it were soaking up sunlight and stocking up its power.

. . . could. . .

Could what? Jenna wanted to yell.

You should read the stories, honey, was all the saleswoman had said.

Jenna grimaced. Yeah, sure. She'd do that just as soon as she escaped the sea dragon nipping at her heels.

As if on cue, the water behind her erupted, and two massive dragons rocketed into the air, sending a huge wave her way. It lifted and propelled her as roars echoed in her ears and water rained down from above.

One of the dragons bellowed furiously. *Go, Jenna! Get out of here!*

Her heart squeezed. That was Connor, fighting for her.

No! Wait for me, my pet, Draig called in a spooky, hypnotic voice.

How her mind translated their throaty growls into words, she had no clue. It took a while for her mind to process, though, and all she could do for one breathless moment was watch the dragons fight. The massive beasts grappled wildly, rising thirty feet above the water before plunging down in a relentless fight that unfolded above and below the waterline.

Go! Get out of here! Connor urged as he unleashed a long plume of fire.

Jenna ducked underwater in a rush. Then she surfaced, snapped her hand shut around the pearl, and started racing toward shore. It didn't matter whether the pearl or her mermaid ancestry had helped her survive underwater for that long. Neither had helped her escape Draig, so her best bet was to get the hell away. But when a pained groan sounded, she couldn't help but spin around to look.

The darker, more compact dragon — Draig — gave a mighty heave and flopped sideways, dragging Connor under.

"Connor!"

The water roiled as they disappeared, and the surface gradually quieted, erasing every trace of her lover.

"Connor!" she screamed, looking down. Sheer panic seized her, and she'd never felt so alone. There was no one to yell to for help, no emergency number to call. There was only her.

"Connor," she whimpered, completely lost as to what to do.

She wished for her dad. Her sister. Connor's brothers. Anyone! How could she possibly help him on her own?

Her hand grazed her chest in a frantic movement, and a memory zipped through her mind.

If you get a dragon right between the plates...

She forced herself to slow down and trace the pattern of her own sternum. If dragons were vulnerable there, as Connor had said...

She took a deep breath and reached down, checking that her knife was still strapped to her leg. Her spelled-against-vampires knife. Would it work against a dragon too?

Smacking the water in frustration, she cried out. Who the hell knew? No one had taken the time to explain it all to her. Maybe no one person knew how the crazy shifter world worked.

It's not fair, she wanted to scream.

But her dad had taught her better than that, so she forced the thought out of her mind. Lots of things in life weren't fair, but Monroes didn't moan. They looked for love and sunshine and soldiered on.

Jenna closed her eyes, looking for some thread of hope, figuring it would be hard at a moment like this. But *love* instantly brought her to *Connor*, and *sunshine* immediately conjured up an image of him holding her close.

She took a deep breath. Okay. Love — check. Sunshine — check. What else did she have?

The muscles of her right arm twitched, replaying a move Connor had taught her with a knife. The round lump of the pearl warmed her hand at the same time, adding another item to her list.

Knife. Pearl. Love. The only other thing she needed was courage, right?

She stalled out there. Courage was the hard part.

The scent of coconut and ginger tickled her nose, urging her to swim for shore. But angry little wavelets slapped at her face, ordering her to get her shit together. Was she really going to let Connor fight while she fled to safety, leaving him alone?

"Damn it," she muttered, disgusted with herself. She could damn well muster up some courage too.

Before she could talk herself out of it, she sucked in a quick breath and dove.

I am not a wimp. I am not a wimp, she mumbled as she kicked down. Deeper and deeper, until the water temperature dropped and sunlight split into ever-thinner shafts. Alarms clanged in her mind, telling her she would die. But a tiny little partitioned corner of her mind pushed her onward.

Just a little farther. They're right over there.

The air pressure built in her ears, and her eyes narrowed to slits, but she spotted the dragons another thirty feet down. The depth washed out most color, but the glow of their eyes stood out like submarine lights, flashing and strobing as they twisted and turned. Draig had to be the darker one with stumpy wings and a thicker tail. Connor was the big green one — but, shit. The trail of bubbles streaming from his mouth was getting thinner all the time.

She turned on the most determined dolphin kick of her life, keeping her hands at her sides. In a pool, she could only keep that stroke up for a length or two, but out here in the open ocean, she seemed to zoom along. So, yeah. Either she was halfway to death and hallucinating, or the mermaid thing wasn't bullshit, after all.

No... Jenna... Connor called in a grim, weak tone.

My pet, Draig crooned, sounding fresh and triumphant. *I knew you would return.*

Jenna made a face. She'd show him what kind of pet she'd make.

And you've brought me a special gift. I can feel its power. Where are you keeping it, my dear?

Jenna kept her hand closed tightly. Shit — Draig knew about the pearl? She wondered if he knew exactly what its power was. She couldn't tell — only that some kind of force seemed to quietly pulse from it, helping her. Would it help anyone?

Connor lashed at Draig with his tail, but the sea dragon spun deftly sideways and raked two massive claws across his back.

Stop, she yelled, using a bubbly voice and the force of her mind to get the message across.

They did no such thing, and she huffed. Men!

Connor wrestled Draig sideways, and for a second, a gap opened between their struggling bodies. Jenna gulped, forcing herself to observe. Somehow, she had to squeeze between them and strike Draig deep in the chest. Was that even possible without being crushed?

Reason told her to forget it, but the pearl in her hand stayed warm, giving her hope.

Connor, she cried, willing her voice into his head. *Do that again.* She had no idea what that kind of side-twist wrestling move was called, but she pictured it and pushed the image out with her words.

Just go, Jenna. Go!

Not going anywhere, she shot back.

Soon, my dear, Draig crooned.

Jenna scowled. Right, like she was eagerly waiting to elope with him.

Come on, Connor. Do it again, she begged, swimming to within an arm's length of their flailing wings. It was as terrifying as edging up to an out-of-control buzz saw, but she forced herself to watch and wait.

Please, Connor. Please.

A tail whipped right in front of her face, and she ducked. Connor grunted, and both dragons lurched sideways.

Now! Now! a voice screamed in her mind as a tiny gap opened between their chests. Connor was giving her the opening she needed.

Jenna kicked forward then scuttled away as the dragons crashed together again. Her heart hammered in fear and dejection. It wasn't possible. It just wasn't possible.

She thumped her own thigh. It had to be possible, damn it. She had to find a way.

One more time, Connor. You can do it.

I can do it, she added to herself.

The minute I rid myself of this troublesome half-breed, Draig grunted between breaths, *you shall have the mate you deserve.*

That would be Connor, she nearly yelled. But she kept the thought to herself, because she had to get close to Draig to execute her plan.

She grinned wildly at her own thought. *Execute.* Now *that,* she liked.

The dragons flipped around, locked in mortal combat, and Connor's eyes flashed. Still glowing, but growing dimmer. He looked about as convinced of himself as she felt about her own chance of pulling off this crazy stunt.

Jenna, he murmured, sounding frighteningly apologetic.

She shook her head, steeling herself to be tough enough for both of them. *Are you saying you're ready to give up?*

Connor's eyes glittered with recognition. *Hell no,* he said through clenched teeth.

Good, she grunted, yanking the knife from its scabbard.

Was that pride in his eyes? Love? Jenna swore she'd find out someday. But at that moment, Draig rolled, dragging Connor around, breaking their eye contact. Fury rose within her, and she pushed the pearl deep into the scabbard at her calf to free both hands. Then she dove under the grappling dragons, more determined than ever.

This fool thinks he deserves you, Draig gloated. *But I shall protect you. I shall give you the future you deserve.*

Jenna pushed the horror of that suggestion aside and concentrated on the fight. The dragons rolled into exactly the angle she needed to slip in between them, so—

Now, Connor! she barked. *One more time.*

His green eyes glassed over with pain. A bubbly grunt sounded as he heaved Draig around with the last of his strength, lifting and twisting at the same time. Their bodies parted, and—

Jenna darted between their wings with the knife clutched in one hand. Thanks to all her practice with Connor, the knife felt comfortable in her grip, and the handle warmed. Was the spell stirring, ready to work even if the enemy wasn't a vampire?

Connor's words echoed in her mind.

Get a dragon right between the plates here. . .

He'd showed her *here*, and she forced herself to shimmy up Draig's chest to find the same spot, keeping the knife at her side.

Draig laughed — the kind of deep rumble that vibrated through the ocean and made entire schools of fish flee for their lives. Jenna wanted to join them. Venturing this close made it all too easy to picture the horrors Draig had in store for her if he won.

Isn't she lovely, he cooed, as if she'd had a change of heart and had sidled up to fondle him or something. *My pet already recognizes her master.*

Master? She snorted. Then she focused entirely on concealing the knife and finding that vulnerable spot.

Draig's chest was covered with wide, interlocking plates. The top plates were divided into two sections, corresponding to the pectoral muscles, she supposed. And between there, exactly as Connor had said, was a notch. But water swirled all around her, and the pressure changed, telling her she was about to be crushed.

Jenna! Connor yelled, straining hard.

Don't get hurt, my pretty pet, Draig murmured, starting to twist to one side.

Jenna flicked the knife around exactly as Connor had taught her. *Index finger, flip, grab.*

Not your goddamn pet, she barked, stabbing the knife deep.

She'd imagined the blade sliding smoothly in, but it entered in jerks, and it took all her might to drive it in. Every time she thought she couldn't drive it an inch deeper, the pearl at her calf heated, and she was able to give it one more shove until the weapon was lodged in to the hilt.

That's what you get for trying to separate a mermaid from her mate, she spat into his mind.

Draig's eyes went wide, and his whole body shuddered. His wings flailed as blood poured from his chest in strangely mesmerizing swirls. Jenna hung on with everything she had, determined to keep the blade in place.

But... But... Draig protested, still not getting it. Then his eyes narrowed, and he growled. *Bitch!*

Jenna gave herself an inner nod. Yeah, when she had to be.

Fine, then. Die with your no-good lover, Draig spat.

His tail whacked around, and pain flared through her legs. A claw big enough to skewer her raked the water beside her ear. Jenna squeezed aside, barely avoiding it. The only thing keeping her alive was how close she was sandwiched against Draig, much as that disgusted her. The next slicing blow, though, would be harder to avoid. That and the crushing power of two dragon bodies about to smack together again. The water pressure rose, making her ears pop, and she screamed.

Connor!

But not even Connor could prevent the inevitable as momentum brought the two dragons together in the massive collision she could sense coming. Their wings were all tangled, and the pendulum of forces was about to swing the other way. Tears streamed from Jenna's cheeks, because this was the end. To kill Draig, she had to keep the knife in place. That meant holding on, no matter what came.

Release me, Draig yelled, thrashing about. But nothing was going to loosen Jenna's hold on that knife. Nothing.

Connor, she murmured, wishing they could have had a happier end. More time. More words. More everything.

The water whirled around her, thrust aside by the truck-sized bodies about to collide. Jenna pushed words like *thank you* and *I love you* into Connor's mind. If she was going to die, she'd make it clear what he meant to her first.

Then, *boom!* What felt like a brick wall smashed into her back, propelling her into the left side of Draig's chest, just beside the protruding knife handle. The slam drove the weapon even deeper, and Draig groaned. Which was good, but Jenna was being crushed. The force squeezed her lungs, hammered her ribs, and cut off her yelp.

She briefly wondered if there was a heaven. Would she meet her mother there? Would she ever see her loved ones again?

Her father. Her sisters. Her niece. Connor...

Then she didn't think at all, because a roar filled her ears, and her whole body lit up in pain. Then a switch flipped in her, and everything went black.

Chapter Twenty-Four

Jenna!

Connor roared with more than just his voice. His whole body screamed, *No, no, no!*

Jenna wasn't supposed to come back to help him. He was the one trying to save her, not the other way around.

But his body was slamming into Draig's, and Jenna was in between. And no amount of flailing his wings, churning his tail, or clawing at the water would prevent the inevitable. He'd wrestled Draig to one side as Jenna had ordered, but now, their interlocked bodies were swinging back into place. And once that much tonnage got moving, it didn't stop, not even underwater where everything moved slowly, giving him all too much time to imagine the result.

On paper, it all came down to a nice, neat formula Newton had come up with. The one about equal and opposite reactions. In real life, every nerve in his body screamed, because Jenna was going to die.

Fuck Newton, his dragon roared. *She can't die!*

Yes, she can. Draig rasped with one last, vengeful breath that said, *If I go, she goes too.*

No, Connor bellowed, desperate for some way to prevent a crushing blow.

Water rushed over his wings, twisting them painfully. Instinct had made him tuck them in close to protect the thin spans, but then a new realization hit him. Any amount of resistance he created would help soften the blow. So with one abrupt, bone-tearing jolt, he flipped his left wing open. The rushing water twisted his wing backward, and bolts of pain tore through his body as bones snapped and ligaments ripped.

243

He howled in pain but forced his long neck aside, further redirecting the motion of their bodies.

And, *slam!* The air was knocked out of him as he collided with Draig.

Jenna! he cried, straining every muscle to pull back as far as he could. He'd managed to twist enough to avoid a chest-to-chest collision that would have instantly crushed the life out of Jenna, but was that enough?

With his good wing, he shifted backward to clear some space. His left wing dangled, a twisted wreck.

No. . . Draig protested one last time. The glow in his eyes intensified then dimmed and finally extinguished. His limbs and tail went limp. Jenna floated between them, motionless. Her hair fanned like a mermaid's, hiding her face.

Jenna?

Connor swam forward and scooped her closer with his good wing. Tucking her carefully against his chest, he kicked for the surface. The sun glowed brighter with every foot of his ascent, but a terrible sense of doom pressed on his heart.

No. . . no. . . His dragon fretted every inch of the way, terrified that Jenna was dead.

His lungs burned. His eyes stung. The pain in his wing was agony. But he thrust all that aside, focusing on Jenna.

Please. . . Please. . .

He burst through the surface and into clear air that seared his lungs. Something in his chest gurgled — all the water he'd gulped, no doubt. He slapped at the water, racked by an uncontrollable coughing fit that made his ribs ache. Throughout it all, he forced his right wing up, keeping Jenna on the surface.

Jenna, he called, hunching over her.

Her eyes were closed, her expression peaceful. Terrifyingly peaceful.

She was laid out on his right wing the way a person might lie on a floating beach mat. Slowly, carefully, he combed a strand of hair away from her face with the point of one claw. If Jenna woke, she'd probably scream at the sight. He wouldn't mind scaring her to death if it meant she'd survived the worst. But had she?

He churned the water with his tail, keeping her above the waves.

Jenna... Jenna... He tried calling to her. Not just in rumbly dragon-talk but in carefully forced sounds more familiar to human ears.

"Jenna?" he whispered, holding his breath.

She didn't stir, and his mind went to Plan B — holding her tight against his chest and letting himself sink to the bottom of the sea. Drowning himself shouldn't be too hard with a busted wing and a shattered heart. But just as he was about to exhale and sink, Jenna's hand flexed into a fist.

He stared.

Her lips twitched, and a second later, she rolled sideways and convulsed. Then she broke into a coughing fit, wincing and moaning at the same. And even though her pain was obvious, his heart leaped. She was alive!

"Connor?" she whispered, blinking in the light.

"I'm right here," he managed, keeping her propped up. "I'm right here."

∞∞∞∞

He stayed *right there* for the next four days, refusing to budge from Jenna's side. Not long after Jenna had come to, a roar had sounded over his head, making him fear the worst. That Draig's lackeys were rushing in to finish the job, perhaps, or that the sea dragon had a furious widow out for revenge.

And it had been a furious widow, as it turned out. But not anyone related to Draig.

Cynthia? he'd called, squinting at the gold-toned dragon that swooped overhead.

Cynthia was just about the last person he wanted to fish his battered ass out of the sea. He couldn't afford to show weakness, especially not to her.

Mr. Hoving, she had tsked, circling overhead. *May I assist?*

Her body was gold, the rarest dragon color, with a crown of solid black, like her hair. Definitely some kind of dragon royalty, one blurry part of his mind noted.

A lot of the aftermath of the fight with Draig was fuzzy in Connor's mind but not that part. He'd flopped back in the water and exhaled hard, considering briefly. A true alpha would never accept help from the very person pitted against him in a struggle for clan dominance but, hell. What did pride matter as long as Jenna was safe?

So he'd croaked a *Yes, please,* and Cynthia had helped him get Jenna back to shore. Tim had rushed them both to the hospital. Dell made sure Connor didn't kill any of the medical staff who tried to pry him from Jenna's side, and Chase had guarded the door of her room in case any of Draig's men turned up. They didn't, thanks to Kai, who'd made a beeline for Draig's yacht as soon as he heard the news. Apparently, there hadn't been much resistance from the staff once their boss was dead, and within hours, Kai had escorted the yacht out of Hawaiian waters, eliminating another potential threat.

Jody was a teary mess when she got to the hospital, but Jenna was a trooper, insisting she was all right.

"Just a little bruised," she kept saying, even though her lips were drawn into a thin line.

According to the doctors, Jenna was badly bruised inside and out, but she'd escaped more serious harm.

"Now you know never to try to snorkel close to whales during breeding season," a stern nurse had said, shaking a finger at Jenna.

Connor had nearly snorted before ushering the woman out. Whales. Breeding season. Right. Cynthia had concocted that cover story, but he had to admit it worked. Other than a couple of mentions in the back pages of local newspapers, the media interest they had feared never materialized.

"Definitely learned my lesson," Jenna had said with a wink. Then she'd patted the space on the bed next to her and grinned weakly. "Now I need the kind of nursing that counts."

Connor's arm was in a sling at that point, but he managed to maneuver into the tiny space beside Jenna and cuddle close. Before long, his eyes were drooping and his mind blissfully blank. He had a million things to worry about — starting with Kai's reaction to all the rules he had broken. A hell of a lot of rules, all the way from *Don't mess with Jody's sister* to *Don't draw attention to Koa Point* and down to *Keep a close eye on Draig.* But Connor didn't care any more. All that mattered was that Jenna was safe.

He watched over her like a hawk, night and day. Worrying every time she drifted off to sleep, celebrating every time she woke up. Grinning as she yawned, because it was just like the first time he'd met her back on the plane. Her nose would wiggle a little, and she would blink like a sleepy kitten. Then she stretched and smiled right at him.

Mate, his dragon hummed again and again.

Jenna's biggest worry was that she'd lost the knife but, damn. Who cared about that? Certainly not Jody, who'd given it to her.

"God, Jenna. You're alive. Who cares about a knife?"

Not Connor. But Jenna seemed awfully attached to the scabbard, for reasons he couldn't understand. She'd made him hold on to it for her, insisting he keep it safe.

"I'll explain later," she'd whispered before falling asleep with an enigmatic smile.

The doctors had kept her in the hospital for three nights, but the second they cleared her...

"Wait a minute," Jody had said when Jenna pointed to be dropped off at Connor's place after the drive home.

"The doctors said I could go home, and that's where I'm going," Jenna had declared.

Connor had just about floated on cloud nine at that point, and the second he got Jenna tucked into his bed, he fell in beside her and carefully held her close. From then on, it was Jenna reassuring him.

"I'm right here," she whispered over and over through the next few days.

Sometimes, her words were sleepy. Other times, they came out in a joyous giggle. And on the fourth day, as the sun set, illuminating the entire open ledge of his dwelling with a brilliant red light, her voice took on a sultry tone.

"I'm right here, dragon," she murmured, kissing his ear. "Right here and a little hungry, if you know what I mean."

Hell yeah, he knew what she meant. His dragon had been going crazy with the need to permanently mark her as his, but he'd been fighting off the instinct. He was out of his sling by then, only feeling a little sore. But shifter healing didn't work for Jenna, so he'd been careful to keep his touches limited to the nursing-back-to-health kind. But when she ran her hand up his chest then down his abs, lower and lower, he growled in need.

"Are you sure you're ready?" he managed to ask, halting the progress of her touch before he exploded with need.

She grinned and wound her leg around his. "How sure do I seem?"

Oh, she seemed sure, all right. But she was talking about sex while he was thinking about mating, and they hadn't talked that over yet.

"I mean being sure about me," he said, straining not to give in to the urge to mate. "I'm not sure I can do this without... without..."

His cheeks heated as he searched for a nice way to say *without plunging my dragon fangs into your neck and following that up with a burst of fire that will permanently bond you to me.*

"Without biting me?" she whispered, looking him right in the eye.

For the thousandth time in the past week, he thanked destiny for sending him a woman who didn't shy away from... well, anything.

He nodded. "Mating is forever, Jenna. You need to be sure."

She cupped his face in both hands and circled her thumbs over both cheeks — a motion that made his inner dragon hum. "Let's see. I love you. You love me. You saved me from the worst possible fate—"

He cut her off, kissing her knuckles. "You saved me."

She'd saved him in more ways than one, really, but he hadn't found a way to put that into words yet. Someday, he swore he would.

She shrugged — just shrugged, like it was perfectly normal for nice girls who worked in their dad's surf shops to slay sea dragons in their spare time — and shook her head.

"What other proof do I need? I'd do anything for you, and I know you'll do anything for me. Of course, we can wait for a couple of years, but what would that change?"

His brow pinched, because he was pretty sure he couldn't wait a week, let alone a couple of years.

"Some people need time to be sure," she went on. "But I don't. Believe me, I don't. I just know." She smiled a little secretly and looked out at the first of the stars like someone out there was winking at her. Then her eyes wandered back to his and warmed. "Do you need more time to be sure?"

He shook his head vehemently. "Of course I'm sure."

She grinned and settled back on the mattress, inviting him in. "Then what are you waiting for, my mate?"

Chapter Twenty-Five

Jenna wrapped her arms around Connor's neck and drew him in for a kiss. If he asked her one more time if she was sure, she'd scream. She'd never been more sure of anything in her life. Didn't he know that?

She cast a sideways glance at the pearl lying in a shell on the bedside table. The light of the setting sun gave it a golden sheen — a little like her own skin. It had been good to rest over the last few days, but she'd woken up from her last nap in a totally different state. As if her body had flipped the switch from *recovery* to *restless* in every sense of the word. Restless to claim her mate and to step into a new future. To scratch the relentless sensual itch that told her Connor was the one.

"What are you waiting for?" she whispered again.

"Not waiting any more," he growled, sliding over her body.

His eyes roved over her face, glowing like a traffic light that had just switched from red to green. When his lips touched down on hers, she moaned. He swept his tongue over her lips, asking to be let in. At the same time, he slid a knee between her legs. But a minute later, his movements were still slow and careful.

"No," she muttered.

He pulled back, staring at her. "No?"

"Too slow. Too careful. Too..."

He arched an eyebrow. "Too what?"

She stirred a hand in the air, searching for the right word. "Pedestrian. If I'm going to mate with a dragon, I want dragon love, buster."

He broke into a deliciously dangerous smile, and the glow in his eyes grew.

She coaxed him closer with one finger, speaking directly to his dragon side. "Come to me, my mate."

Connor's eyes glassed over, and he lowered his head, sniffing her neck.

She turned, giving him space, whispering, "Take me."

It was like a car race she'd once seen on TV — all the vehicles lined up at the start, revving madly without going anywhere, waiting for the start signal to fire. Connor inhaled sharply. His body was stiff and steely, the bulge in his pants hard against her hips.

Impatient, she crossed her arms over her chest and pulled her own shirt off, leaving her naked but for her panties. After that, she settled back and stretched her arms overhead, giving him a wicked grin. There were times when she liked to show a guy she was no pushover, but right now, all she wanted was to lie back and be ravished. And they were definitely headed that way, judging by how quickly the pulse in Connor's neck beat.

"Make me yours, Connor," she whispered. "Please."

He drew back to look at her, his gaze firmly on her lips. His chest heaved like they'd already gone a few rounds, and the lines on his brow deepened in concentration.

"Please," she whispered one more time.

One second, he was looking her over with those intently glowing eyes. The next—

She moaned as his mouth slammed over hers, claiming her with his plundering tongue. His hands threaded through her hair, gripping her like the world's most carefully tightened vise. She couldn't move, but she didn't want to move, not unless it was to buck beneath his weight.

But his hips pinned her down, so all she could do was moan. Faint rumblings like distant thunder echoed in her mind. Growls. A male voice, whispering something about how beautiful she was.

Her eyes flew open. Were Connor's thoughts — and his dragon's — reaching her mind?

In the past few days, she'd spent some time with her sister, who'd explained that and more. How closely bonded shifters could hear and feel each other's emotions, for one thing, and how indescribably satisfying mating was — not just the act, but the state of being.

"Yes..." Jenna whispered — to all those things. Yes to being his mate. Yes to the nudge of his leg between hers. Yes to him opening himself to her as completely as she revealed herself to him.

The rumble increased as Connor swept one big hand down her body. Stroking her everywhere that counted, making her gasp and arch. She was still a little sore from her injuries, but somehow, that just heightened her awareness of how alive she was.

"Beautiful..." Connor rasped, dragging his chin down her chest until his mouth was at her breast.

Jenna hung on to the rungs of the headboard and arched into him as he nipped and sucked the soft flesh. The sun dipped toward the horizon, sending slants of red light over Connor's back, giving him a golden-red glow. Surf crashed into the cliff beneath their rocky ledge, and she pictured Connor slamming into her the same way.

The images in her mind heated, and he whisked a hand to her core, stroking her there. Mumbling something she didn't catch for the blood rushing in her ears. Something like *perfect*?

Well, if so, he was the perfect one. Touching her like he'd memorized the Jenna Monroe manual, whispering like a Cyrano whose dragon provided every poetic line.

He pushed the fabric of her panties aside to touch her, but then he grumbled and ripped them off in one quick motion that made her hips jerk.

"Sorry," he muttered.

"You are so not sorry." She chuckled. Then she howled and surged under his hand, because he'd touched her *there*, igniting a whole new set of nerves.

There was nothing like the sight of Connor lying over her. And although her head was tipped too far back to watch, her mind filled in the details. His broad, dragon shifter shoulders, rippling with muscle. The sweat making his skin glint under the sun. His hips, smothering hers.

She wished she could do the whole rip-clothes-off trick with his shorts, but she couldn't reach that far. Of course, they did add a certain amount of friction to the equation.

"So good..." she moaned as Connor rolled his fingers, spreading her wetness, probing inside.

Then he clamped his hand along her inner thigh and shifted her body on the bed before rearing up over her with an intent expression, like this was the most important thing he'd ever done.

And, she supposed, it was, if he really was going to bite her neck and send a puff of fire through her veins.

She shivered — more from arousal than fear — and watched him yank off the rest of his clothes. His cock jutted high, his firm ass muscles bunched. A vein throbbed in his neck.

Oh, yes. This was going to be good.

"Connor," she whispered, putting her hands on his shoulders. There was no fabric there to haul him over by, but she managed to guide him closer, bringing his face to within a few inches of hers. Had she ever wanted anything as much as she wanted a life with him?

He paused long enough to smooth her hair back and run his hands over her cheeks with a look of sheer wonder on his face. Then his eyes flickered, and he dropped into another of those antigravity kisses that seemed to lift her off the mattress instead of pressing her into it.

She wrapped her legs around him, desperate for more. His cock bumped her belly, hip, and thigh before they lined up just so, and he powered inside.

"Oh," she cried, sliding up the mattress with his thrust.

Connor held her pinned there for a few hard breaths, then drew back. A heartbeat later, he rocked back in. He did that over and over, using long, deliberate strokes. Watching her come undone from an inch away, his face a mask of concentration. She wanted to chuckle, because even if he'd managed to make a few mistakes in life, there was no way he was going to mess this up. But chuckling was out of the question, because she was tripping so high on desire.

"So good," she moaned, pumping her hips against his.

His breath hitched, and he paused long enough to pull her left leg higher along his side. "That okay?"

She let out an out-of-control cackle. "*Okay* does not begin to describe—" She cut off into a moan when he thrust in even deeper. Deeper *and* faster until she was writhing and calling his name.

Her breaths were wild pants, her grip so tight around the rungs of the headboard she feared one would snap. All her focus went to Connor's long, searing thrusts and to timing her inner muscles to squeeze at exactly the right time. Her mind exploded with the echoes of Connor's pleasure as he closed his eyes.

"Yes..." she murmured, urging him on.

Connor touched her neck, making her tingle all over. He wasn't just making contact. He was seeking out the spot. Getting ready to bite her.

"Yes..." She tipped her head farther back, giving him space.

His breath warmed her skin. His body pressed over hers, and his teeth scraped her neck.

"Please," she murmured, tightening her legs, feeling the moment approach.

Connor ducked, concentrating on thrusting for a few last strokes. Every sharp push made her blood heat. Pleasure lifted her higher and higher like the world's most perfect wave. Then it rose even higher, making her drunk with ecstasy.

"Connor!" she cried.

Bright white light flooded her mind, and her body convulsed. Connor came, too, pushing her off on a wild ride. The rush of images in her head all hit pause at the same time, giving her just enough time to pull in a deep breath before Connor—

"Oh!" she cried when his teeth punctured her flesh.

She arched, mindless with pleasure. Her voice rattled as she released a long, keening cry. The bite burned without hurting — unless she counted the near-pain of intense pleasure. His teeth were razor-sharp, yet all she felt was their firm hold.

Ecstasy. Now she knew what the word meant.

Mine, Connor's dragon voice rumbled. The images in her mind became an inferno.

She clutched the headboard tighter, knowing what was about to come. The brand. The puff of fire that completed the dragon mating bite.

Connor held her tightly, stiffening all over. On the outside, his only movement was a tiny push of his lips. But on the inside—

Jenna rocked as the flames licking around her mind all turned at the same time and shot down a long, dark tunnel.

Not a tunnel, she realized. That was the brand traveling through her veins.

Mine, Connor's deep, rumbly voice crowed. *Mine.*

Heat rushed through her body, and she pictured tiny flaming arrows — thousands of them — zipping through her veins, marking every corner of her body as his. Searing her from the inside in the best possible way.

Wow. No wonder mating was forever.

Her blissed-out mind hung on to the word. *Forever* had never felt closer than just then.

"Connor," she whispered, trembling.

For another long minute, she lay still, unable to do anything but feel good. Connor was equally lost in pleasure, clutching her close, not moving a muscle.

The fire crackled and sang inside her, gradually going from all-out blaze to embers she knew would glow for a long, long time. Connor's fangs receded, leaving just his lips covering the tingling spot on her neck. When he finally pulled away, he did so slowly, checking that she was okay. Only then did his muscles relax and his weight press down over her.

"So good," she mumbled, touching his shoulders. Her legs were still snug around his waist, her chest rising and falling with heavy breaths.

"So good," Connor whispered.

His eyes remained tightly shut, as if he couldn't believe his luck, so she cupped his cheek and tapped with one soft finger. When he opened his eyes, her breath caught, and she couldn't help murmuring, "Wow."

She'd seen his eyes glowing before, but this deep and intense green was different. Bolder. More powerful. More settled, somehow. As if the last of the young rebel had given way to a steadier, quieter man. The kind of man who'd been through hell and come out the other side.

His lips wobbled as he stared into her eyes. Were they glowing too?

"Wow back to you," he whispered.

She peeked over his shoulder. The horizon was dark, the sun off visiting other lovers on distant shores.

"So... Now we're mates?"

The second she spoke the words, they felt unnecessary, because she could sense it in her bones. She and Connor were one. Bonded for life.

Connor rolled to his side and hugged her from behind. "Sure are. Hope you're not getting second thoughts."

She snorted. "No way, buster." She rolled slowly, facing him. "I'm just wondering where we take it from here."

He considered that for a while. "Where do you want to take it from here?"

She kissed his chest. That Connor was a good man, she already knew. But the contrast to Draig, who felt entitled to drag her away without asking, made her appreciate her mate even more.

"Truthfully?" she whispered.

He nodded, drawing a finger along her arm. Slowly. Patiently. Waiting to hear her out.

Jenna closed her eyes and thanked destiny for giving her the world's most amazing man. Then she looked around Connor's home.

"Honestly, I don't want to take this anywhere." Then she sputtered and corrected herself, because that came out all wrong. "I mean, I don't want to go anywhere, as in move. I'd like to stay here if I can. With you."

His eyes flared in satisfaction, and his hands tightened around hers. "I want you to stay here. More than anything." Then his face fell. "But I'm not sure I'll be allowed to stay."

She cupped his face. Back in the hospital, she'd picked up on his fears about that. But surely, the shifters of Koa Point wouldn't send him packing for killing a jerk like Draig?

"I can't imagine Kai has a problem with what happened. Who knows what other trouble Draig has caused or how many victims he claimed?"

Connor tensed as she did, recalling how close it had been.

"Let's just play it out. Suppose we get to stay here," she continued, trying to dismiss his doubts. "You keep working your job..."

He nodded slowly, hopefully.

"And I keep working at the surf shop."

He perked up at that. "You can stay?"

She grinned. "Big news. Jody told me in the hospital. Can you keep a secret?"

He nodded eagerly.

"When Jody first got her job at Teddy Akoa's surf shop, we were all thrilled. Teddy is a legend. And getting to help out there has been a great opportunity for me. But that's not all."

Connor waited breathlessly, so she rushed on.

"Teddy is awesome, and he likes us." She beamed. "He says we're the daughters he never had."

Connor grinned. "As long as he thinks of you as a daughter, I'm okay with that. But if he gets any other ideas..."

She laughed and play-smacked him. "Teddy's not like that. He's awesome. Very laid-back. The thing is, his boards are so good, he gets more orders than he can fill, so he offered to turn over some of the new customers to Jody."

Connor's eyes shone. "Great chance for her."

Jenna grinned. "For me too. We've always talked about going into business together, she and I. And now..." She got goose bumps just thinking about it. "Now we have our chance. Helping my dad was great, but even he said it's time to spread our wings. My uncle is helping him in the shop now, so really, I could stay here."

"You could?"

She'd never heard a man sound as hopeful and eager as that.

"I could. And it gets better. Teddy got an offer he didn't have time for, but it's perfect for us. Some Hollywood producer wants eight boards for an upcoming movie — eye-catching boards for the female stars to 'capture the 18-25 female demographic,' as he put it. So the contract is ours for the taking. Just think."

Connor looked as excited as she was. "People see the movie. They want your boards..."

She nodded a hundred times a minute. She and Jody had already reached the same conclusion. "It would be a great way to kick off our business. And we can make our dad the sole distributor of our boards, so it would all stay in the family."

"Wild Side Surf Shop meets Surf Chique," he murmured.

She gaped. Connor remembered? Not just the name of her dad's shop, but the name of the business she'd dreamed of. Some guys didn't bother to remember what a girl said or liked. But Connor had listened and stored it all away.

She kissed him. Once. Twice. Trying to calm herself down. Her heart was still racing from the physical high she'd just hit, and combining that with so many hopes and dreams made her stomach do flips.

"Anyway, that's the idea. There are still a lot of details to work out, but I think it could work. Heck, even if we failed, we want to try."

He held her hands tightly. "You have to try if it's your dream."

She held his gaze. "What if you're my dream, Connor Hoving?"

He pulled her into a hug. "I want you to have *all* your dreams. But yeah, especially that one."

She burrowed against his chest and held on to him for a long time. So much was undecided, yet the future had never seemed so promising.

When she rolled in his arms, spooning up again, her gaze landed on the pearl beside the bed. It looked just like an ordinary pearl — okay, a gorgeous gold-black pearl — yet there was something about it that suggested a slumbering, secret power.

Connor hugged her to his chest and looked too. "I guess destiny was on our side all along."

His jaw had just about dropped when she'd first shown him the pearl, and then he'd looked up at the sky and whispered, *Thank you.*

To who? she'd asked.

To destiny. For bringing us together, and for keeping you safe.

Now, his eyes were bright and trusting as he gazed at the pearl and whispered, "Still wondering about it?"

She nodded, slowly reaching for it. "I guess I'm wondering about a lot of things."

They studied it in silence. Was it glowing slightly, or was that just the shiny surface?

"It's warm," she whispered, bringing it closer.

Connor cupped her hand, and they both stared at it for a time.

"It's amazing," she whispered.

Connor snorted. "You're the amazing one."

She grinned for a while then went back to thinking about the pearl. "I definitely need to chase down that saleslady. The one who knew about the old legends. Maybe she can tell me more."

"Maybe."

She rolled in his arms, wondering why he didn't seem more interested. "Hey. I thought dragons were all into treasure."

A little smile played over his lips as he stroked her cheek with his thumb. "Like I said. Got all the treasure I need."

Then he kissed her, making her body heat all over again.

Chapter Twenty-Six

Connor never wanted to get out of bed, but even a freshly mated dragon had duties to attend to. Starting with the meeting Kai had called.

So after a long, frisky night — and most of the following day — that had Jenna and him fluctuating between utter exhaustion and insatiable lust, they had finally risen and showered. But they'd made the mistake of showering together and ended up wrapped around each other again.

"Okay. This time, I'll shower alone," Jenna had laughed, pushing him back gently as she went in for the second time.

So she'd showered alone, followed by him. By the time he finished, she was dressed and standing at the ledge, looking out at the sea. The sun was setting, outlining her silhouette in orange and red. Was she dreaming of shifting into dragon form and flying toward the burning point of light on the horizon or — shit — was she having second thoughts about the whole thing?

But then Jenna turned to follow the flight of a bird, and the smile was clear on her face.

He leaned against a wall and watched her. There'd been so many times he and the guys had joked about one or the other of them getting hitched, and the prospect hadn't sounded particularly appealing at the time. Why would he want someone else messing with his stuff or changing things around in his place?

But suddenly, that was all he wanted, and his imagination ran away with images of him and Jenna finishing the place together, deciding on the details, making it their own. Maybe even filling it with a couple of little dragons someday.

Then he frowned. He wanted that more than anything, but he would have to make sure he still had a job. Would there be repercussions in the dragon world from the fact that he'd help kill an established powerhouse like Draig? What if Kai decided Connor had acted rashly? Kai had avoided the subject while Jenna was recovering, but he was sure to address Connor's handling of the crisis at the meeting today. Then there was the question of Connor mating with Jenna. He was supposed to keep his hands off her, not mark her permanently as his.

But all that fled his mind when Jenna turned and beamed. "It's amazing." She spread her arms as wide as wings.

He stepped over to hug her while his dragon puffed happy little swirling flames inside.

Do we get to teach her to fly now?

Well, maybe not just yet. The Change could take several weeks, and they sure wouldn't start at the top of this tall a cliff. But someday. . .

He tucked his chin over Jenna's shoulder, sniffing her scent, watching the sun sink lower. He didn't need to fast-forward to *someday*. Right now was just as good.

He kissed her near the tiny scar of his mating bite, delighting in the lusty shiver it sent down her spine.

"Mmm," she cooed, bumping back against him.

He could kiss her — just kiss her — for hours. But they didn't have hours, not with everyone waiting.

He grinned to himself. Actually, they had a lifetime. But they did have to get to that meeting. So he broke off his next kiss and took her hand.

"Ready to go?"

"Ready." She said it in a firm, *ready for forever* kind of way that kept his step light and bouncy all the way across the grounds to the big plantation house.

The closer they drew, the more he wondered what his fate would be, much as he had when he'd arrived on Maui and met Tim at the airport. So much had happened since then. Surely destiny wouldn't have brought him to his true love, only to have him thrown off the island, out of work and out of luck yet again?

Jenna squeezed his hand, and he stood straighter. She helped his mind stay in the right place. His incredible, dragon-slaying mate. He kissed her knuckles then made the last turn for the house — and stopped abruptly in his tracks.

"Whoa," Jenna breathed. "What's that for?"

Two long rows of tiki torches were stuck into the ground along the path that led to the plantation house. A living, dancing lane of fire. Up on the porch, everyone was waiting. His brothers, Dell, Cynthia, and little Joey. Kai was up there too.

Connor's voice stuck in his throat. He tried explaining, but the words wouldn't come out.

"Connor?" Jenna asked, touching his shoulder. "What does that mean?"

He took a deep breath. Those torches meant everything was all right. He wasn't in trouble — well, not big trouble anyway.

"Shifters do that... sometimes, to welcome someone important, like the big boss," he managed to explain at last. "Other times, they do it for... for..." His tongue tangled with a word he'd never used for himself before. "Heroes."

She grinned like she'd known that all along. "You."

He looked at her. "You. Both of us, I guess."

She laughed. "Well, let's go find out."

Only Jenna could stride that casually into a hero's welcome. Nothing went to her head, and nothing scared her. Which was a damn good thing, because danger was part of the shifter world. He wished he could pretend otherwise, but that was the way it was. Still, they could handle anything together, right?

Right, his dragon growled, leaning closer to her.

He fell into step beside Jenna, expecting to climb the porch steps and get the meeting started. But then another thing happened that blew him away. Kai left his spot at the top of the stairs and descended to meet them at ground level with a firm handshake.

"Connor. Jenna. Good to see you both on your feet again."

The words weren't much in themselves, but the gesture meant everything. Shifters were big on hierarchy, and Kai had every right to remain on the top step while Connor came to him. Coming down was the ultimate sign of respect. Connor didn't know much about dragon society's rules, but he knew that much.

"Thanks," he murmured. Another woefully inadequate word.

Kai kissed Jenna on both cheeks and winked. "So, you sure about this guy, huh?"

Jenna didn't so much as blush. She just looped her arm around Connor's waist and grinned. "You bet I am."

Connor could have kissed her right there — but if he started, he wouldn't be able to stop. So he settled for throwing his arm over Jenna's shoulders and tugging her closer.

"Well, let's get started," Kai said. "We have a lot to talk about."

"That, we do," Cynthia said, coming halfway down the stairs.

Connor hid a smile. Halfway was a message too. Cynthia was ready to acknowledge what he and Jenna had accomplished — but she wasn't about to roll over and let him take the alpha position without a fight.

Which ought to have riled him, but Connor didn't care anymore. If he was appointed alpha of Koakea, great. He'd be glad to take the job. But if Cynthia got the job — well, okay. Serving his clan would always be his top priority, whatever role he filled.

He chuckled inside. *Perspective.* Now that he had a mate, he knew what that meant.

Tessa, Kai's partner, greeted Connor with a warm smile and one of those two-cheek kisses that made him feel ridiculously proud, like he'd arrived in society or something. But Tim, Chase, and Dell made sure he stayed grounded as they all met him with extra-hard smacks on the back. They'd seen each other over the past couple of days, but not since Connor and Jenna had bonded. Jody and Cruz were also there — Jody beaming like a mom at the sight of her firstborn all grown-up, and Cruz with that guarded expression that fell somewhere between *Don't make me kill you* and *Life is great when you have the woman you love.*

"Hey," Tim said, all gruff and tough. "Congratulations."

Connor tried putting everything into one handshake, but it was hard. He'd put a lot at risk for his brothers as well as himself, and yet Tim had stood by him. Tim, who was right up there with Dell when it came to resisting the idea of a mate, if only because his logical bear mind couldn't quite grasp the concept of loving someone other than immediate family. Connor used to think along the same lines, but now...

Jenna and Jody hugged while Connor studied Tim. Wait — was there a hint of sadness in his smile? The wish for a mate of his own?

Connor made a mental note to pay his brother back somehow. Surely there was a nice woman out there waiting to find a good guy like him.

"Thanks for the torches. Your idea, Tim?"

Tim tilted his head toward Cynthia. "Hers. She said you deserved it."

Connor's jaw just about hit the floor. *You're kidding me, right?*

His brother waggled his thick eyebrows. *Not kidding. It really was her idea.*

Like I said, Dell added. *She might be all fire and thorns on the outside, but inside, she's a kitten.*

Kitten might have been an exaggeration, but Connor had to agree with the rest.

"Yes, well. Tradition, you know," Cynthia said, casually downplaying the gesture.

Connor stared for a second longer. Wow. Cynthia definitely got the *good sport* award.

Then Dell smacked him on the shoulder and grinned broadly. "Anyway, congratulations. Took you long enough to figure out love."

Connor snorted. "Like you have it all figured out?"

"Yep. I know to keep clear." Dell laughed then turned to Jenna. "Poor thing. You're stuck with him now. And even worse, you're stuck with all of us by extension. Clan is clan, you know."

Jenna didn't miss a beat. "Being stuck with Connor? Yes, please. Being stuck hanging around with you guys..." Her eyes twinkled in friendly jest. "We'll see how bad that turns out to be."

Chase shook Connor's hand, flashing a genuine smile. Typical Chase — all action, no words except for a quiet, heartfelt, "Congratulations."

Connor didn't have time to reply, what with Dell reaching over and lifting Joey onto the armrest of the couch so he could join the receiving line like a real grown-up.

"Joey, sweetie. It's not nice to stand on furniture," Cynthia protested.

"It's a special occasion," Dell said, ignoring her hard look. "A man has to be able to look another man in the eye, right?"

Joey stuck out his hand and shook solemnly with Connor. "Congratulations."

At first, Connor figured that was for finding the love of his life, but of course, Joey's mind was on other things.

"Did you really kill that bad sea dragon?" the boy asked with wide, hero-worshiping eyes. "Will you tell me about it? Will you? Please?"

Before Connor could answer, Cynthia cut in with another strict frown. "Killing is a bad thing, sweetie."

Connor held back from sharing his two cents. Cynthia was right. But, hell. He'd been that curious kid once upon a time. He knew how important it was to get answers — and how frustrating it could be not to find out.

"She's right, you know," he said. When Cynthia turned away with a satisfied nod, he leaned closer to Joey and whispered, "So how about I tell you about it some other time?"

Joey beamed and winked. Well, he tried, though it came out as a two-eyed squint.

Connor tousled Joey's hair and made another mental note to himself. *Help that boy not be the frustrated kid I used to be.*

He shook with Cruz next, who didn't even squeeze his hand too hard. His eyes did hold a veiled warning, though. *Be good to Jenna, or else.*

Oh, he'd be good, all right. Every day to the end of his life.

"Oh my gosh, that looks so good," Jenna said of the hors d'oeuvres set out on the table. "Could I take one?"

Kai waved a hand. "Help yourself. Tessa's treat."

"I've kind of taken over the kitchen for tonight," Tessa said. "I hope you don't mind."

"You can take over the kitchen any night," Dell called. "Especially on Tim's nights to cook."

Jenna took three sushi rolls and wolfed them down with an apologetic look. "I'm a little hungry. Sorry."

Dell chuckled. "It's all that — ahem — *recovering* you've been doing."

Connor growled under his breath until Dell cast his eyes down in a sign of respect. But Dell was Dell, and nothing would wipe that knowing smile off his face.

Just think of the payback you could get someday, Tim said, shooting his thoughts into Connor's mind.

What do you mean?

Tim grinned. *Imagine Dell finally settling down with someone. Imagine all the ammunition we'd have to tease him with.*

Connor cracked into a smile. That *would* be fun. But Dell settling down was about as likely as an iceberg hitting their little strip of beach. Plus, Connor had more important things to do these days, like protecting his mate and his clan.

"So, to business," Kai said as if he'd read Connor's mind.

Everyone took a seat — including Joey, who slid into his mother's lap. Chase was the only one who remained standing. He prowled around the perimeter silently, taking in everything, saying nothing.

Connor made another mental note. Find a good woman for Chase. Someone to anchor his brother the way Jenna anchored him.

"First of all, Draig," Kai started with a deep scowl. "One of the last of a long, respected line of dragon shifters."

Connor refused to look down. Even if Kai lectured him on all the trouble he and Jenna had brought down by killing the old coot, he had no regrets.

Kai looked around with a weary expression then locked eyes with Tessa. "The Draigs are one of the oldest, richest dragon clans. Old and established enough to have fooled me."

Connor held his breath, wondering what Kai would say next.

Kai let a long, torturous pause go by until he frowned and continued. "I had no idea he was a sea dragon."

"Nobody did," Cynthia said. "It's a rare, recessive gene that only comes out every few generations or so. Like red hair." She grinned, running her fingers over her son's head. "But red hair is beautiful, while that sea dragon..." Her smile turned into a scowl. "Well, he guarded his secret carefully."

"Are all sea dragons bad, Mommy?" Joey asked.

"No, sweetie. There were some famous sea dragons who did good deeds, too. Berwyn Reese, Elfion Rhydderick..."

"There was even a great sea dragoness in my family tree somewhere," Kai added.

Cynthia nodded. "Manon Llewellyn, who died in 1793."

Connor stared. Did dragon clans go around memorizing family lines? Well, he wasn't surprised. But the fact that Cynthia knew them even better than Kai confirmed his hunch that *Brown* was an alias of some kind. Who was Cynthia, really? What was she hiding from?

Tessa winked at Jenna. "Oh, I like the idea of that. A kick-ass she-dragon who can fly *and* swim."

Cynthia crinkled her nose. "I'm not sure *kick-ass* is the term the history books used but, yes. Manon was a force to be reckoned with."

Connor looked at Jenna. She already was a force to be reckoned with. And when she learned to shift... His heart thumped a little faster at the thought of Jenna adding flying to her long list of skills.

"In any case, I underestimated him," Kai admitted as Tessa placed her hand over his. "When I interrogated the members of his crew, they said Draig had developed an interest in Jenna weeks ago, ever since her picture made the newspaper with that *mermaid* caption."

"Stupid LA Times," Jenna muttered.

Jody gave a tiny smile. "Maybe not so stupid, because the mermaid part was true."

Kai nodded. "Somehow, Draig figured that out and decided Jenna would make a perfect mate."

Jenna snorted, and Connor growled out loud, bristling at the thought of any man lusting after a woman who wasn't interested — especially *his* woman.

Kai nodded. "I know how you feel. Apparently, he was interested in Tessa too."

Tessa made a face. "He definitely had a thing for redheads."

Connor nodded, remembering the female crewmembers aboard the yacht. Hopefully, they would find a better boss in their next job.

Kai squeezed Tessa's hand. "That too. But you being a fire maiden also must have fit that bastard's bill. I guess he figured Jenna was the softer target, though."

Jody snorted. "Ha. Soft target. I guess Draig's the one who underestimated her."

He sure did, Connor's dragon hissed.

"Well, Draig paid the price," Jenna said, totally matter-of-fact, as if she were commenting on the tenth or twentieth dragon-slaying in a long, illustrious career.

"So you're okay with that?" Connor asked, looking at Kai. Waiting for the other shoe to drop. Surely there were repercussions to deal with.

Kai nodded firmly. "No way will we tolerate an enemy shifter on our turf, targeting one of our own. Silas and I agree one hundred percent, and the couple of old-timers who started raging about their old buddy being killed have already been set straight. I've met with a few, and Silas called meetings in London and New York to make that perfectly clear."

Connor exhaled slowly. "Eliminating him doesn't bring trouble here?"

Kai snorted. "In a way, it's done the opposite. The more shifters who know we are not to be fucked with, the better."

Tessa elbowed him as Cynthia covered Joey's ears.

"Sorry, kiddo," Kai said quickly. "But I mean it. Would I be happier if Draig had never turned up on Maui? Of course. But what's done is done, and Draig is the one who instigated the fight. Draig is the one who acted without honor, and he got what he deserved. And as for you two..."

Connor held perfectly still, gripping Jenna's hand under the table. Now what?

"There is the matter of Draig's wealth. To the victor go the spoils, you know," Kai said.

Connor tilted his head. What exactly was Kai saying?

"Spoils?" Jenna asked.

Kai laughed aloud, looking at Connor. "You didn't know? It's tradition."

"Tradition," Connor sighed. No, he didn't have a clue. What exactly was Kai getting at?

"The winner of a fair fight gets the loser's holdings. In Draig's case, that means—"

Dell's eyebrows shot up. "Holy shit. The yacht? Connor and Jenna get a yacht?"

"The yacht, the properties, and whatever loot Draig has in his lairs," Kai said.

Connor would have tipped off his chair if Jenna hadn't been holding his arm. Rich? Him? "Wait. What about that idiot nephew of his — Anton? Or some other relatives?"

Kai laughed so loud, a pair of birds took flight from the roof of the porch. "That's the best part. Draig was such a selfish bastard, he wrote everyone out of his will. His dragon will, I mean. The one that really counts, because it includes everything humans don't know about — the hidden treasure troves, the centuries-old deeds. Anton might get the scraps on the surface, but the rest is all yours."

Jenna's jaw dropped. "Ours?"

Connor knew he was supposed to be excited about that, but it felt wrong somehow. "That would be dirty money, right?"

Kai tilted his head in a way that said, *maybe yes, maybe no.* "A lot of Draig's wealth dates back hundreds of years. So I guess it would be hard to say."

Connor had always considered all wealth dirty, in a way. And right now, it was definitely too much to process. He'd never had much money, and never felt the need for more than enough to get by.

He looked at Jenna, and she nodded back, already reading his mind. "Not sure we want it, either way."

Connor cut in. "Well, maybe apart from enough to get Jenna and Jody's business off the ground."

Jenna grinned, and Jody gave her a high five. "I'd call that a fair way to spend the — what did you call them? — spoils."

"Hell, if you don't want the rest, I'll take it. Starting with that yacht." Dell grinned.

Connor's mind spun. That kind of money could help Tim build the construction company he'd always talked about, too, and it would make sprucing up the house easier. Hell, everyone could spruce up their houses. Maybe even buy halfway decent cars. . .

But the train of thought petered out quickly, and all he felt was annoyed. He didn't want any of that stuff. He just wanted Jenna.

When he glanced at Jenna, her eyes shone with pride, not dollar signs. So, whew. They really were cut from the same cloth, him and her.

"Well, I'll believe it when I see it," he decided.

Kai nodded. "It will take ages to sort out Draig's assets. Silas can help decide what to do with it. But let's move on. It's time to establish a leader here."

Everyone went very quiet. Cynthia stared at Connor, and Connor stared back.

"According to tradition, the choice of alpha is made by a council of elders," Kai began.

Connor nearly rolled his eyes, but Kai wasn't done yet.

"However, we have our own way of doing things. A little more in tune with modern times, you might say. A clan should appoint their own leader. We at Koa Point agreed on Silas a long time ago, and the guys named me as second-in-command. So, here on Koakea. . ."

A weighty silence settled over the group. Candlelight flickered over serious faces, though Connor kept his focus on Jenna, trying not to pressure his brothers. It was time to let them speak and for him to listen. To respect whatever decision was reached and to trust fate a little bit. That much, he'd learned.

Jenna wound her fingers through his, quietly backing him up.

Mate, his dragon sighed.

The word had so many more meanings than he'd been aware of before. Jenna wasn't just his lover. She was his partner. His anchor, his cheering squad, and his compass at the same time.

Tim shifted uncomfortably in his chair, and a floorboard creaked under Chase's uneasy step. For a few too-quiet minutes, the only other sound was that of waves rolling onto the shore a quarter of a mile away.

It was Joey who finally broke the silence. "Can I vote for Mommy *and* for Connor?"

Cynthia rushed to shush him, but Dell laughed hard enough to break the tension everyone felt.

"Sweetie, there can only be one alpha," Cynthia said. *And I want it to be me,* her unwavering eyes said.

Connor could understand that. She'd worked as hard as anyone and proved her capabilities. In a way, he was glad not to have a vote. Who would he choose if he were in the other guys' shoes?

"You know, I think Joey might be on to something there," Dell said, giving the boy a thumbs-up. "If he's thinking what I'm thinking."

"And you're thinking... What, exactly?" Tim asked.

Connor half expected Dell to make an inappropriate wisecrack, but the lion shifter went serious.

"Well, it's clearly between Cynthia and Connor. I mean, given that I've decided to graciously step aside and let these inferior dragons take the stress of leadership," Dell joked.

Tim snorted. "Right. Dell as alpha. Every day would be a day off."

Dell sighed. "And what a life that would be. But sadly, I don't think you guys deserve me. Which leaves us Connor and

Cynthia, right? I mean, until Joey is old enough to be alpha."
He winked.

Joey beamed and sat straighter in his mother's lap.

"Right," Tim agreed.

"So let's see." Dell waved between them. "Cynthia definitely wins in the graphics department." He motioned at the whiteboard with the neatly penned duty roster. "And at coordinating manpower — er, man and woman power," he added quickly. "Just look at how quickly we've gotten this place in shape."

Connor let his eyes drift around the porch and beyond. When he'd first arrived, the plantation house was practically rotting on its foundations, and the grounds were a mess. But under Cynthia's direction, the place had been restored to its former glory. Well, the house, at least. The grounds were coming along, and everyone had made a start on their own places. He had to hand it to Cynthia. She knew how to get work done.

Cynthia didn't say a word. She just sat there, waiting for the others to decide, not showing the slightest bit of emotion.

We need to get her a mate, Tim whispered into Connor's mind.

Connor nearly broke out laughing. It would take a brave man to break through all that ice. But, hell yeah. If they ever found the right guy, Cynthia might finally relax a bit.

"Of course, Connor has a few qualities too," Dell continued.

Connor went perfectly still, more self-conscious than he'd ever been.

"He's pretty good at roofing, not too bad at cooking..."

Tim chuckled. "Everything we need in an alpha."

"...and he's actually learned a little diplomacy lately. Oh, and he did slay a sea dragon. Or was that Jenna?"

Connor pointed at Jenna. She pointed at him, and they both spoke at exactly the same time.

"Her."

"Him."

Connor poked her. "You're the one who knifed the bastard."

Cynthia made a face and tilted her head toward Joey, but Connor ignored her. It wouldn't kill the kid to hear the plain and simple truth.

"You're the one who got Draig to expose his chest," Jenna insisted.

Dell scissored his hands. "Whatever. The point is, Connor is the one who reacted in time to take decisive action to stop Draig. Connor is the one who has been organizing patrols, tailing Draig, and working here at the same time. Connor is the glue that holds us together, and we all know it."

Connor stared at Dell. Wow. When was the last time the lion shifter spoke from the heart like that?

"So what are you saying?" Kai asked.

Dell shrugged. "I'm saying they both have their strengths. Cynthia is wicked smart and ridiculously organized."

"Ridiculously?" she protested.

Dell nodded. "Sorry, Cynth. But, yeah — she runs a tight ship. And Connor — well, the Special Forces experience shows. He has a nose for trouble." Dell grinned. "For getting in and out of it. So why compromise? Why not do like Joey says and put them both in charge?"

Kai scratched his head. "How would that work?"

Yeah, Connor wanted to ask. *How?*

"Just like we initially set things up," Dell said. "Cynthia runs the grounds. Connor runs security. They work together on the parts that overlap, like assigning workloads."

"That was a temporary solution," Kai said.

Dell shrugged. "If it ain't broke, why fix it?" He looked around. "What do you guys think?"

Connor blinked a few times. He'd always figured it was all or nothing, but Dell did have a point. Cynthia was better at some things than he was, and he was stronger than her on others. The question was, could he handle working with her in an equal-alphas partnership?

He glanced over and found Cynthia eyeing him, probably asking herself the same thing.

Tim nodded. "I'm good with that. What about you, Chase?"

Chase nodded simply. "Yep. All good."

"That's a bit...unconventional." Kai frowned.

Cynthia frowned too. "Untraditional."

Connor grinned. "I think that's what I like about it."

He looked at Jenna, because she was part of this decision too. Her eyes sparkled with pride and confidence, telling him everything he had to know.

He stretched a hand toward Cynthia. "What do you say, Ms. Brown?"

She gave him that *I know you know that's not my name, but I still refuse to tell you* look. Her eyes were stern and hard, but for a split second, he thought he glimpsed something like relief. Running a shifter clan — even a small one like this — was a huge responsibility. And, hell. The more he thought about it, the more he liked the idea of sharing the load. Did she, too?

Joey looked up at Cynthia, and she looked down at him, reminding Connor she had as much at stake in the future of their clan as him. She broke into a smile and stroked Joey's red hair, revealing the sensitive, caring mom within for the briefest of moments. Then she nodded firmly and clasped Connor's hand in a firm shake.

"Mr. Hoving, I agree."

Connor laughed. Cynthia could be as formal as she wanted. He wouldn't be. The second he finished shaking hands, he turned to Jenna and scooped her into a huge hug. Was it really possible to have so many good things happen at once? Or was this payback for all the times he'd experienced the opposite?

And just like that, the weight of it hit him. He'd done it. He'd finally overcome. Not just one hurdle but a whole obstacle course he'd been navigating for the past years.

He squeezed his eyes shut and held Jenna close. Never mind that the others were there watching. He would never have gotten here if it weren't for Jenna, and there wasn't a single part of his future she wouldn't be a part of. So the guys had better well get used to seeing his love for her, damn it.

The funny thing was, when he finally let Jenna go and refocused on the others, they were all grinning and patting each other on the back like they'd accomplished something too.

Dell whooped. Tim smacked him on the back. Chase looked like he was tempted to howl his happiness to the moon. Cynthia kissed Joey, and the other two men hugged their mates.

They had all accomplished something, Connor realized. All of them. They'd gone from being unsure about just about everything — the work, the place, the division of labor — to having carved out a place in the world for themselves. Dell, Tim, Chase — and Cynthia too. They'd gotten to know each other and their new home. Of course, they still had a long road ahead, but they'd made their start, and a solid one, at that.

"Dell, man," Connor said, clapping the lion shifter on the shoulder. "Who knew you had that in you?"

Dell gave a theatrical sigh. "One of these days, you guys will appreciate my genius and stop underestimating me."

Maybe someday, he'll stop underestimating himself, Connor's dragon murmured.

He kept that part to himself. Dell had a knack for picking exactly the right moment to shine. He'd done it before, and he'd do it again. And maybe someday, he would make it enough of a habit to keep up all the time.

Down in the yard, the tiki torches crackled, throwing playful shadows about. Excited voices bubbled and rose as everyone talked at the same time. A sea breeze wafted over the porch, carrying the scent of tropical flowers.

"It's beautiful," Jenna whispered, catching Connor in another hug. The kind that made him think of wrapping up business and getting back to bed.

"It's perfect," he rumbled back, sniffing his mate's scent.

"There's just one thing," Kai said in a grim tone that silenced everyone. "The pearl."

His voice was a low tone of warning, and everyone waited for him to explain.

Chapter Twenty-Seven

"The pearl," Kai said with gravity, looking at Jenna. "Do you have it?"

Connor looked on as Jenna pulled it from her pocket and laid it on the white tablecloth. Everyone leaned in. Even in the pale moonlight, the pearl shone in its unique way, with the gold hues coming to the forefront, and the black fading away. It looked a little different every time he saw it. Was that part of its magic?

"I still can't figure it out," Jenna said, gesturing toward it. "Did the pearl help me stay underwater that long or was it my mermaid blood?"

"A little of both, I think," Kai said, studying the pearl.

Then he cleared a space on the table and nodded to Tessa, who pulled out a huge leather-bound book. Connor sniffed deeply. It smelled of dried leaves. Of cobwebs. Of mystery.

"We did some research," Kai said in a weary voice that spoke of many hours hunting down that volume.

Tessa opened the book, carefully flipped a few pages, and finally turned it around for everyone to see. Connor squinted at the ornately designed page.

The top of the page was covered in swirling, calligraphic script. The middle was full of text, and the bottom decorated with a hand-illustrated scene. The latter showed the kind of rugged, green mountains found throughout Hawaii, all drawn in a style that had to be a century or two old. A woman stood waist-deep in the ocean, cupping something in her hands while a shark fin circled around her. She seemed more sad than panicked, though. Behind her, the background was filled with details like lush slopes, waterfalls, and a thatched hut.

"Maui?" Tim murmured.

Jenna leaned over the looping calligraphy at the top. It didn't even look like English to Connor until Jenna managed to sound it out. "Pearls of desire?" She touched the binding. "What book is this?"

Tessa gave them a peek at the cover then laid it open to that page again. *"Mates, Myths, and Legends.* It was written by one of the first shifters to visit Maui, way back at the end of missionary times."

Jenna ran her finger along the text. *"Nanalani, daughter of Kamohoalii, the shark king. She could only love from afar for fear of her shark side coming out. Terrified of wreaking death and destruction upon her friends the way her brother had done when he took human form, Nanalani kept herself sequestered in a cave for years. Finally, in her loneliness and sorrow, she called forth the spirit of the sea..."* Jenna's voice rose in excitement. "That's the legend the lady at the store mentioned."

Tessa pointed to the woman in the illustration — an island beauty with long black hair and dark eyes. "That has to be Nanalani. And look there." She pointed.

"Pearls," Jenna breathed.

Connor peered closer. The woman in the picture was holding a seashell filled with pearls. White pearls. Gold pearls. Black, pink, and blue, too.

Jenna read on. *"Nanalani called forth the spirit of the sea and put a spell on her pearls — the pearls of desire. Her treasures allowed her to go safely forth as a woman and love a man she had admired from afar. Over the years, Nanalani had many lovers, though she never found her mate. As time went on and her lovers passed away, Nanalani threw her pearls back into the sea, one by one. 'Now I am alone again,' she sighed to the god of the sea. 'I give you my pearls, not to keep, but to safeguard for another worthy lover who needs their power someday.'"*

Jenna's finger trembled as she moved it over the flowery script. She stopped for a deep breath, and her eyes locked with Connor's. He gulped a little. Jenna might be worthy. But was he?

She read on. *"And so it was that the pearls of desire — one for every kind of desire known to mankind — were lost, though legend claims they remain slumbering under the surface, waiting to be reawakened to inspire great acts of love again."*

Jenna's cheeks turned pink when she finished with a solemn, "Wow."

Dell whistled. "Pearls of desire? Yeah, I'll take one."

Tim beat Connor to elbowing the lion in the ribs.

"Mommy, what's desire?" Joey piped up.

Cynthia turned pink. It was kind of cute, seeing her flustered for a change. "It's like love. When you really, really love someone and want to kiss them all the time."

Connor traded not-so-secret smiles with Jenna. Oh, they knew about desire, all right.

"Oh," Joey muttered, utterly disappointed. "Yuck." He went back to unrolling the maki on his plate.

"Wait a minute," Tim said. "Remember the aquarium Draig had on the yacht? There were pearls in there."

Connor frowned. God, he'd been so — er, distracted — lately, that he hadn't thought of that.

Apparently, Kai had, because he nodded right away. "I checked them out. They look — and feel — like regular old pearls, but I sent them to a contact of Silas's to make sure. I didn't pick up on any hint of energy or power, though. Not the way I do with Jenna's pearl."

"Precious pearls. Magical pearls. That's what the woman in the shop said," Jenna recalled. "But, wow. Enough magic to help me stay underwater that long?"

Kai nodded. "Absolutely, especially when combined with your mermaid ancestry."

"The Spirit Stones are like that," Tessa added, fingering the emerald around her neck. "Mine made me immune to dragon fire, but only because it amplified an ability I already had thanks to my fire maiden blood. You have to have it in you in the first place."

"Did Draig know about the pearls?" Tim asked, stroking his chin.

"He knew something," Jenna said with a deep frown. "He said he could feel its power, but then again, so could I. I just don't know exactly how it works."

Cynthia wore a wistful smile. "Maybe it's like love. The kind of power that's hard to define."

Connor blinked at her rare hint of emotion, then cleared his throat. "Anton said something about looking for pearls that night out by Molokai."

Jenna sighed and picked up the pearl. She studied it, then the book. "Do you have any more books about pearls — or mermaids? I have the feeling I need a crash course on all this."

Connor took her hand. He might not be the most well versed in shifter lore, but he'd be with her every step of the way.

Kai motioned over toward Koa Point. "We have thousands of books, so I'd say we have our research cut out for us. But the library's open to you anytime."

"Yours must be a Tahitian pearl," Cynthia said, fingering her own string of white pearls. "Very rare, if it's natural, and I'm sure it is. A symbol of wealth and prosperity."

Connor stared. Now where did Cynthia learn that?

But Jenna just shrugged and squeezed his hand. "The only wealth that really counts is love, and I've got all I need."

It was one of those *I want to hug you and never let go* moments, and Connor very nearly did. But Dell waved frantically, dragging his attention away.

"No, no. None of that, kids." Dell laughed. "Can you try to get through one dinner without falling into each other's arms? The goo-goo eyes are bad enough."

Connor slid a hand across Jenna's shoulders, compromising a little. If he wanted to show his mate how lucky he felt, he would, damn it. But there was a tiny note of jealousy in Dell's voice, just a minuscule hint the lion shifter probably wasn't even aware of. There was no need to rub in what he had and the others didn't — especially when it came to Cynthia, who'd lost her mate. Just the thought of such a blow made him tug Jenna closer to his side.

Tim squinted at the text. "What's this part about every kind of desire?"

Tessa tapped her lips. "I don't know. Lust?"

Connor scowled, thinking of Draig. "Greed."

"True love," Cynthia said in a faraway voice. "Passion."

"Yearning," Chase whispered, looking out over the shadowy landscape.

"Carnal desire," Dell said in his lustiest voice.

Cynthia made a face and clapped her hands over Joey's ears. The boy had clearly stopped listening by then, though.

Dell grinned. "Okay, seriously. You want to know about desire? Buddhists say there are three types: *kama tanha, bhava tanha,* and *vibhava tanha.* Wanting something that feels good, wanting to become something, and wanting to get rid of something." Everyone stared at him, but he just sighed. "I told you, everyone underestimates my brilliance."

"Did you study Buddhism?" Jenna asked with wide eyes.

He gave an apologetic shrug. "No, but I had this girlfriend once..."

Tim rolled his eyes. "Dell has had a lot of girlfriends — once."

Dell just gave a smug smile, and Connor shook his head. The poor guy had no idea what he was missing. Hell, before meeting Jenna, *he'd* had no idea what he was missing.

Kai rubbed his chin. "It's possible the pearl — or pearls, because it sounds like there are more — can embody all types of desire. Like the Spirit Stones — it could depend on the bearer. A pearl that heightens the greed in one person could empower the passion in another."

Jenna nodded slowly. "Maybe like this pearl. Gold and black. Opposites, but all wrapped together."

Connor smiled faintly. He and Jenna were opposites in some ways but, yeah. They made a good pair.

"What was that last one again?" Jenna asked Dell.

"*Vibhava tanha.* The desire to get rid of something, like a sickness."

"Well, I did want to get rid of Draig," Jenna said, rolling the pearl in her hands. Then her gaze wandered to Connor, and her eyes sparkled. "And I wanted... some other things."

He grinned. Yeah, he wanted some other things too. They'd have to move along to someplace private very soon.

"But I swear the pearl was calling to me for days before," Jenna added, growing pensive again. "Like it wanted to be found."

Kai nodded gravely. "That's what concerns me. And if there are more..."

"What's wrong with spreading the love?" Dell joked.

Connor followed Kai's gaze as he looked across the long plantation lawn toward the ocean. Moonlight sparkled silver and white over the waves, and a frigate bird swooped over the surface, holding out its forked tail.

"Nothing wrong with some forms of desire, like love. But if the remaining pearls call to other shifters for the wrong reasons..." Kai trailed off.

Connor waited for more. What did he mean?

Kai fingered a crease in the tablecloth. "Where there's power, there's greed. And where there's greed, there's..."

He trailed off, but Tessa filled the rest in. "Moira."

Connor took a deep breath and held Jenna's hand tighter. He didn't know much about Moira, but he knew she meant trouble. Apparently, Cynthia knew too, because her face fell at the mention of the name.

"You mean the same Moira who..." Jenna started, then stopped when she spotted Cynthia's expression.

Connor tried not to stare at Cynthia. He'd seen her look strict, serious, and unamused. But he'd never seen her like *this*. Her fingers scratched — no, clawed — the edge of the tablecloth, and her lips drew tight. Her eyes took on a ferocious glow as she gave Kai a curt shake of the head that ended with a tilt toward Joey.

No one spoke for a moment, and Jenna looked around, confused. A feeling Connor knew all too well — that *everyone is in on a secret except me* sensation that made his dragon want to snort flames.

He stood quickly. Obviously, the subject was touchy enough that Cynthia didn't want Joey to hear, and he respected that. But Jenna was an adult, and she had to be warned about Moira, the vengeful she-dragon who had targeted the shifters of Koa Point again and again.

"Hey, Joey," he said, standing quickly. "I almost forgot. I have a present for you."

"For me?" The boy's eyes went wide.

"Yep. Hang on a second." Connor walked to the far end of the porch where he'd stashed it earlier. Throughout the time Jenna was in the hospital, she'd forced him to go for short walks — to relax and clear his mind, as if he had any chance of that with Jenna in such rough shape. But she'd insisted, so he'd gone. And one day, he'd passed a store, looked in the window, and—

"A kite? Wow, a kite!" Joey exclaimed, taking the package.

"Not just any kite. A dragon kite. Look." Connor pointed at the diagram.

Joey scrunched up his eyes and examined it carefully. "Like a Lusitanian dragon, right?" He looked to Cynthia. "We learned about it in our dragon book."

Connor had no idea what that was, but Cynthia nodded. Well, whatever. A kite was a kite.

"So come on. Let's try it out."

"Now?" Joey jumped up. "At night?"

"Best time to fly," Connor winked, waving him down the stairs.

"Fly?" Cynthia yelped.

"The kite," Connor said quickly. "Just the kite." The second he and Joey got to the bottom of the stairs, he leaned in toward Joey and whispered, "Can you keep a secret?"

Joey gave him a solemn nod.

"Kite flying teaches you all about wind patterns. Gliding. Finding thermals. So when you're old enough to shift into dragon form..."

Joey's eyes shone. "Then I'll really be ready."

"Exactly. You'll be a pro. Now let's get this thing set up."

He moved just far enough from the porch for the others to be able to huddle and talk — and close enough for Cynthia to be able to keep an eye on Joey. Kai, he figured, would take the lead in telling Jenna about Moira. *She was betrothed to my cousin Silas a long time ago,* he'd probably start with, and Connor could imagine how the rest would go. Moira had broken Silas's heart by leaving him for the powerful dragon lord, Drax, and the ruthless couple had wreaked havoc on Silas's shifter clan several times in recent years. Silas had finally vanquished Drax in a recent showdown among the volcanoes of the Big Island, but Moira had escaped.

What Connor didn't know was how Cynthia had tangled with Moira. He would love to listen in, but right now, he'd give Jenna a chance to learn.

He looked up and got lost for a second in the universe above. So many stars, winking their greetings to him — even Draco, the constellation he'd never counted on for much guidance. It curled around the Little Dipper, glaring at Hercules, and beyond that, to the lurking Serpent.

Connor looked around. So much beauty in the world, but so much danger too. He put a hand on Joey's shoulder, vowing to protect the child no matter what it took. But tonight, thank goodness, was a kinder, more peaceful night than most.

"Okay," he said. "Tell me which way the wind is coming from."

Joey looked around and pointed north. "There?"

Connor gave him a big thumbs-up. "Perfect. So to launch, we have to start..."

"That way!" Joey exclaimed, hopping up and down.

It was kind of cute, watching Joey run across the lawn, pulling the kite. The kind of simple fun Connor hadn't experienced in a long time. Soon, the kite was up and flying, its long tail fluttering in the breeze. Joey bounced from foot to foot in glee. Connor stood behind him, helping control the strings.

"The wind gets funneled up the hill, with a little more coming from the right. You feel that?"

Joey nodded earnestly.

"So keep a little more tension on that side. And to turn..."

Connor had never flown a kite in the dark. He'd never flown a kite with a kid either. But it was nice. Really nice. And Joey was beside himself, laughing and beaming like he did with Dell.

"Look, Mommy! My dragon is flying!"

"That's great, sweetheart."

Connor watched the kite dip and sway. The tail streamed out, and though the rainbow colors of the design were hard to make out in the dark, the yellow eyes showed.

"Fly, dragon. Fly!" Joey sang out.

Connor pictured two dragons up there instead of one, and his heart sang too. Someday, he'd be able to take to the air with Jenna. And between the two of them and the others, they'd keep their home safe. For themselves, for Joey. Maybe even for their own kids someday.

He looked out over the plantation grounds, all the way out to the glittering ocean. What a view. And he was actually enjoying it for a change. He smiled and looked back at the kite, whispering into the wind.

"Fly, dragon. Fly."

He lost sense of time and place for a while, and his mind wandered. To his father, who'd never taught him anything useful, unless it was what *not* to do. He thought of all the times he'd yearned for acceptance. Years of wishing to find his place on this earth.

And, wow. Now he had all that. A home. A mate. A clan.

Jenna came up behind him and slipped her arms around his waist. Apparently, the talk about Moira was over. Jenna tipped her head back and looked up at the kite against the background of that incredibly starry night.

Her chest rose and fell with a sigh. "So beautiful."

Connor closed his eyes and covered her arms with his.

"Beautiful," he whispered.

Epilogue

Six weeks later...

Jenna took a deep breath and looked down at the swirling surf from the edge of the cliff. The prospect of jumping off it was pretty terrifying, and all of Maui seemed to hold its breath — either in anticipation of the sunrise or for the feat Jenna was contemplating.

I can do this. I can do this... she mumbled to herself.

"You ready?" Connor murmured from her side.

She gulped and nodded in a jerky way. Was she really ready? Maybe today wasn't the day. And it was still dark. Really dark. Plus, the wind wasn't right, and the distance seemed twice as high as usual. Then there were all those rocks to crash into if she messed up...

Of course I'm ready, a deep voice rumbled inside her.

According to Connor, every human had an animal side, and turning into a shifter simply woke it from its slumber. But, wow. Her dragon had come charging out of nowhere a few days after Connor had given her the mating bite. A dragon just as adventurous and unconcerned as she had always been with things like surfing — but, damn. This was flying, not riding a wave.

"No need to rush if you don't want to," Connor whispered after a few more agonizing seconds ticked by.

"I want to," she said quickly, though she didn't budge.

Definitely want to, her dragon growled.

She pushed the beast a little bit further back in her mind. Connor had taught her the importance of controlling her second side lest it begin to control her, but it still took an effort sometimes. Like now.

Way back when, she'd made a flippant remark about diving off the open ledge of her new home — a feat Connor had actually pulled off the day he'd saved her from Draig. But now that she faced it herself...

Not diving. Just launching into the air, her dragon said. *Easy.*

Right. Launching. At night. From this cliff. She gulped.

Her dragon snorted. *The sun is about to rise, and the wind is just right.*

Really, she had no reason to be nervous because she'd already been out flying a few times. Connor had helped her learn after her first shift, starting with little hop-glides down at the beach. Those were pretty short at first, but like the Wright Brothers at Kitty Hawk, she quickly progressed to longer and longer flights. Then she'd tackled taking off from modest heights, and that had gone well too. But somehow, this looming cliff seemed harder.

Pink light tinged the Pacific as another slow minute ticked by.

It's easier from up here, her dragon said. *More space and time for our wings to catch the wind. Nothing to it.*

Jenna twirled the end of her hair with a finger, buying time. Nothing to it?

Come on, already, her dragon insisted. *We're running out of time.*

"Listen, we can—" Connor started, ready to give her an easy way out.

"I'm ready," she cut in, trying to act and not think. "Totally ready."

Well, that was an exaggeration, but she did have to get herself into gear. She and Connor couldn't risk flying in broad daylight, especially with her not yet completely in control, so it was now or never.

"Totally ready," she muttered as she turned back to the bedroom area where she slipped off her clothes and removed the bangles from her wrists. She laid them beside the pearl on the bedside table, wondering what her mother would say about all this.

Then she smiled. Her mother would probably say, *Go for it!*

So she strode back out to the edge and raised her arms, releasing her inner dragon.

Shifting, she'd learned, was a lot like pulling on a wetsuit, what with the contortions and stretchy feeling that reminded her of the way the neoprene clung to her body while she tugged. Her skin stretched, growing dry and leathery, and her shoulder blades pulled back. But the changes in her senses always stole the focus from the strain in her limbs. Her vision narrowed slightly due to the protruding brows that protected her dragon eyes. At the same time, her eyesight was keener and the colors more intense, which meant the lush palette of Maui became even richer, like a magical wonderland. Her ears differentiated between many more sounds, just like her nose analyzed many more scents. The calls of a half-dozen birds, all greeting dawn with their own distinctive songs. The first whiff of ginger, and the waning scent of the night-blooming flower.

"You want me to go first?" Connor asked.

She nodded through the last of her shift then opened and closed her wings a few times. The first time she'd shifted, she'd nearly knocked a table over, but she'd learned to judge things better since then. She flicked her tail left and right, trying to form a mental picture of a graceful turn in the air. But mainly, all she imagined was the massive splash that would mark an epic fail.

Connor shifted smoothly and stood on her right side. Even in her bigger, mightier dragon form, he still seemed massive. Not so much from his greater stature, as from the alpha power that throbbed off him in waves. He kept that power semiveiled when in human form, but in dragon form, it was impossible to miss.

She grinned. Her man was one badass dragon. Of course, she'd known that all along, but it was nice to get a reminder of just how powerful he was.

And, damn. They made a pretty imposing couple — Connor with his gorgeous greenish-brown hide, her a creamy color, much like her hair. Him big and towering, her a little more petite — a perfect match, at least in her eyes.

Plus, we have matching mating scars, her dragon added with a sultry undertone.

That was true, too. Connor had explained that she could give him her own mating bite whenever she was ready, but the notion of biting him was so scary, she'd shelved it all the way at the back of her mind. But one night, in the throes of passion, she found herself leaning over in her cowgirl straddle of her man and baring her teeth.

Jenna, Connor had rasped, begging for her bite.

Instinct told her just how to do it, and wow. She'd never experienced a sexual high that long or that intense. Connor had thrown his head back and cried out too, assuring her it was just as good for him.

See? her dragon said. *Just trust me.*

She snapped her eyes open again, going from steamy memories to wobbling at the edge of the cliff.

Connor's low, smoky dragon voice sounded in her head, repeating the coaching points they'd gone over dozens of times. *So, here we go. Open your wings, get a feel for the wind, and hop.*

Jenna shuffled forward, raking her claws over bare rock. Opening her wings and getting a feel for the wind were easy. But *hop* was the understatement of the year. She stared over the lip of the cliff into the crashing surf.

Connor, of course, made it look like child's play. One little step and he was gliding gracefully away.

It is easy, her dragon insisted.

Jenna closed her eyes, concentrating on the flow of wind over her outstretched wings. The sensation made sense to her rewired mind, but when she overthought things...

She froze like a diver who'd ventured to the edge of a too-high board.

You got this, Jenna, Connor called.

I can do this. I can do this... she tried.

Just go, already, her dragon barked. *Hop.*

The beast must have pulled a sneaky move, shifting her weight just enough to make her lose her balance because a moment later—

"Oh!" she yelped, toppling over the cliff.

Ugly images flashed through her mind as she spiraled toward the rocks. Her father, who'd be so sad to hear of her senseless death. Her niece, whom she'd never see grow up. Connor, kneeling beside her grave, weeping into his hands, and a gravestone that said, *She failed.*

Oh, for goodness' sake, her dragon muttered. *Open your eyes.*

Jenna snapped them open, prepared to see a blur before blacking out into death. But her field of vision was solid blue, like the ocean she was soaring over.

She blinked a few times. Soaring? As in, gracefully?

Gracefully, her dragon huffed. *Just leave it to me.*

She stared. She was flying a good sixty feet above sea level, gliding smoothly down toward the surface, then leveling out. Staying under the radar, so to speak, by flying a few feet above the tiny morning waves. The trade winds had been napping all night, so the Pacific was quiet, barely moving except for the light swell.

Perfect! Connor cheered, swooping over to glide off her right wing.

I did it! she squealed.

The wind rushed under her wings and along her tail, cooling and lifting at the same time. Her feet tucked tightly against her body, and her neck stretched long, keeping her streamlined the way she did when surfing out of the barrel of a long, rolling wave. Silver sparkles bounced off the ocean, showing her the way.

Woo-hoo, she cheered, swiveling around to dip one wingtip then the other. *Look at me!*

Connor laughed. *Where else would I look, my mate?*

Her dragon preened at that and started showing off with subtle little moves Jenna observed rather than controlled.

Watch this, her dragon murmured, sweeping into a barrel roll. Her snout pointed forward, but her whole body swiveled around it, doing a complete turn. And she didn't stop there, rolling another quarter turn until she was sideways to Connor.

Oh, I like that, his dragon rumbled, turning at the same time.

They flew on in an erotic, belly-to-belly aerial move that made her dragon hum with pleasure. Blurry images of rolling in bed with Connor rushed through her mind, and Jenna had to take a deep breath to put them on pause. She could act on those urges when she got her man back on land. For now, she had to concentrate on flying.

When they broke apart, Connor swooped over, around, and under her. *My mate,* the gesture announced to the world. *No one comes close. No one touches her but me.*

My mate, Jenna crooned, wishing she could trumpet that message all over the state.

When Connor rose, she followed, feeling ever more peaceful. The human world and all its troubles seemed further and further away, and the dangers of the shifter world even more remote — especially with Draig's yacht gone from the anchorage in the distance. A yacht she never wanted to see again, even if she and Connor ever did cash in on any part of Draig's vast holdings.

Good riddance, her dragon snorted and sidled closer to Connor's side.

They'd started out on a beeline toward the low pyramid of Lanai, then curved gradually toward the hulk of Molokai.

Someday, when you're ready, we'll fly over the islands together, Connor said. *The cliffs and waterfalls of Molokai are amazing at night.*

She couldn't even formulate an answer except for thinking what a privilege that would be. Tourists with cash to burn might buzz over the neighboring islands on helicopter tours, but to glide over those sights in the sheer silence of night, and on her own wings...

Wow, she whispered, picturing it. *That would be great.* Then she laughed and added, *Wait a minute. This is already great.*

Connor chuckled. *It is pretty great.*

Slowly, they curved through every point of the compass until they were headed back to Maui. The rising sun was hidden behind the island's tall peaks, but its light was streaming through the Central Valley in thick, golden rays. All too soon, she and Connor would have to land and hide from prying human eyes. Of course, that meant they could go back to bed and work off the thrill of flying in other fun ways. Then they could nap, eat, and be ready to set out on their next flying adventure the second it grew dark.

Connor laughed, reading her mind. *Good thing we have the whole day off, huh?*

A damn good thing. When she and Connor had just bonded, the others had reworked their schedules to treat them to a week off — a honeymoon, so to speak. After that, they'd both dived back into work — Connor as co-alpha of the Koakea clan, and she in her new surfboard-shaping partnership with her sister, Surf Chique. She'd been working six days a week to make up for lost time, but today was a day off. And that meant...

We have all day, she hummed as they flew along.

Life didn't get better than that. Connor had won his place in his clan, and she had the fresh new start she needed, too.

The higher the sun rose, the lower they kept to the wave tops. Little splashes kicked up from time to time, spraying her wingtips.

Feels good, her dragon sighed.

It did feel good. Good enough for a dip.

The idea flitted through her mind, quick as a sparrow. She looked down into the ocean. A dip would feel great.

Yes, her dragon agreed. *Just a little swim.*

She looked at the horizon. They had a few minutes left. Why not give it a try? Draig was dead and gone, and turning into a shifter had definitely stirred something in her mermaid blood. She'd been swimming, diving, and surfing every day.

She thought it over, trying to calculate out the mechanics of diving from mid-flight.

Trust me, her dragon rumbled in a dangerously determined voice. *Trust me.*

After one more minute of deliberating, she finally gave in and called to her mate.

Hey, Connor.

He craned his long, dragon neck around and shot her a toothy dragon grin. *Yeah?*

Watch this.

A second later, Connor yelled, and she nearly did too. But hers was more a yelp of glee, because her dragon knew exactly what to do. She folded her wings tightly against her sides, threw her head forward, and dove.

Whee! her dragon hollered as she plunged into the sea.

A stream of bubbles followed her under, making her feel rocket-fast. And even when the momentum of the dive ended, the bubbles continued, because she knew instinctively how to kick, flap her wings, and churn her tail for maximum effect. She slipped through the water, as sleek and streamlined as a dolphin. As agile as a fish. As at home in the water as... as...

A sea dragon, that inner voice crowed.

She jerked to a stop, making the water roll and foam. She held up a wing. It wasn't stumpy like Draig's, but it was thicker than Connor's, now that she looked. And her tail was longer, too.

Cool. I'm a sea dragon. She grinned.

Then it hit her. Sea dragons were bad, like Draig. Why would she want to be like him?

Not like Draig. Like me, her dragon insisted, zooming away again and showing off another impossibly tight turn.

Then she remembered what Cynthia had said. *There were some famous sea dragons who did good deeds. Even a great sea dragoness.*

Oh, I like that, Tessa had said. *A kick-ass she-dragon who can fly and swim.*

Jenna let out a shocked cough of bubbles. Could *she* be a kick-ass she-dragon who could fly and swim?

Ha. Watch.

Her dragon shot forward and turned in a spiral until she was dizzy. Then, with a sharp contortion of her core muscles, she twisted and zoomed off the other way. A short distance later, she spun around and torpedoed into the depths before snapping around and speeding for the surface.

Watch this, her dragon taunted.

She exploded out of the water, curved gracefully through the air, and dove back in with nary a splash. All in all, she was airborne just long enough to hear Connor's frantic yell.

Jenna?

She splashed to the surface, chagrined. Poor Connor. For all he knew, she'd been attacked again.

Sorry! I'm fine.

What the hell are you doing? he boomed, hovering over her.

She paused, not quite sure what to say. Luckily, Connor spoke first.

"Wait a second. Do that again."

Before she could even think about it, her dragon dove, eager to show off her tricks. She spiraled, turned, and breached out of the water, rising high enough to clear Connor before splashing down again.

A long-forgotten memory welled up out of nowhere, one of her father — or was that her mother? — holding her over the incoming surf at Seal Beach, back when she was tiny. She'd kicked at the waves with her tiny feet and squealed with glee. The kind of unbridled, unfiltered joy that grew rarer and rarer as she'd grown up. As a dragon, though, she felt it all over again.

Sea dragon, Connor breathed.

Her joy fled, replaced by fear. What if Connor hated that about her? What if she repulsed him?

But a second later, he broke out into a huge grin. *A sea dragon. Holy shit, Jenna. I knew you were amazing, but... Wow. Is there anything you can't do?*

Live without you, she said without thinking. Then she looked around. *Also, I'm not sure I can take off from the surface.*

Connor laughed so hard, he nearly fell in.

Of course, I can take off from here, her dragon sniffed.

She pictured herself splashing and kicking like an albatross and decided to quit while she was ahead.

Hang on, she told Connor. Then she dove once more, built up some speed, and sped back up into the air with enough momentum to stay airborne.

Sorry, she said, shaking the water from her wings.

Connor fell into formation off her left wing, muttering *Amazing* again and again.

Jenna grinned and bumped him gently in mid-flight. *You know who else is amazing?*

He looked at her. *Who?*

You.

They laughed, free as a couple of kids, all the way back home. Jenna was still laughing when they landed on the ledge and shifted back to human form.

"So how about we—" she started, then froze in her tracks.

"How about we what?" Connor asked in a way that made it perfectly clear what he had in mind. He was in human form again, all man — and hungry for his woman, judging by the heat emanating from his body. His touch made her tingle, and her body yearned for his.

But part of her was still replaying what she'd just done. She about-faced right into Connor's chest, then peered around him toward the ledge.

"Holy crap. Did I just land here?"

He chuckled. "Sure did."

All her landings so far had been in wide, open spaces where she had plenty of room. To land on that shallow an area seemed impossible.

Maybe impossible to you, her dragon sniffed.

"Wow," she whispered, still staring at the cliff.

"Told you you're amazing." Connor laughed, hugging her from behind.

She covered his arms with hers and settled back against his chest, humming as his touches ventured away from her belly. Slowly, sensually, he explored her human body.

She closed her eyes, swaying in time to Connor's movements, playing different options out in her head. Did she want to lead him to the bed and wrap her legs around him there? Or should she turn, kneel, and reward her man with a few tricks of her own? The other day, she'd drawn him over to the rug, gotten down on all fours, and let him rock her from behind, and she sure wouldn't mind trying that position again.

How about all three? her dragon growled.

Connor laughed, reading her mind. "No need to rush. We're bonded forever, you know."

Forever had a new ring to it these days, like a synonym for *free.* Which, she supposed, was the power of love.

The power of destiny, her dragon whispered.

She tipped her head back and let her mind blur as Connor fluttered kisses over her neck and collarbone. Finally, she let out a lazy laugh. "Wow. It's morning, but it already feels like a whole day has gone by. Flying, swimming..."

Connor chuckled and spoke in that low, dangerous rumble that never failed to turn her on. "We're just getting started, my love."

Her body heated, and she broke into a huge smile. That was true in more ways than one.

Connor scooped her up effortlessly and carried her toward the bed. "Just getting started," he murmured once again.

Books by Anna Lowe

Aloha Shifters - Pearls of Desire

Rebel Dragon (Book 1)

Rebel Bear (Book 2)

Rebel Lion (Book 3)

Rebel Wolf (Book 4)

Rebel Alpha (Book 5)

Aloha Shifters - Jewels of the Heart

Lure of the Dragon (Book 1)

Lure of the Wolf (Book 2)

Lure of the Bear (Book 3)

Lure of the Tiger (Book 4)

Love of the Dragon (Book 5)

Lure of the Fox (Book 6)

The Wolves of Twin Moon Ranch

Desert Hunt (the Prequel)

Desert Moon (Book 1)

Desert Wolf: Complete Collection (Four short stories)

Desert Blood (Book 2)

Desert Fate (Book 3)

Desert Heart (Book 4)

Desert Yule (a short story)

Desert Rose (Book 5)

Desert Roots (Book 6)

Sasquatch Surprise (a Twin Moon spin-off story)

Blue Moon Saloon

Perfection (a short story prequel)

Damnation (Book 1)

Temptation (Book 2)

Redemption (Book 3)

Salvation (Book 4)

Deception (Book 5)

Celebration (a holiday treat)

Shifters in Vegas

Paranormal romance with a zany twist

Gambling on Trouble

Gambling on Her Dragon

Gambling on Her Bear

Serendipity Adventure Romance

Off the Charts

Uncharted

Entangled

Windswept

Adrift

Travel Romance

Veiled Fantasies

Island Fantasies

visit www.annalowebooks.com

About the Author

USA Today and Amazon bestselling author Anna Lowe loves putting the "hero" back into heroine and letting location ignite a passionate romance. She likes a heroine who is independent, intelligent, and imperfect – a woman who is doing just fine on her own. But give the heroine a good man – not to mention a chance to overcome her own inhibitions – and she'll never turn down the chance for adventure, nor shy away from danger.

Anna loves dogs, sports, and travel – and letting those inspire her fiction. On any given weekend, you might find her hiking in the mountains or hunched over her laptop, working on her latest story. Either way, the day will end with a chunk of dark chocolate and a good read.

Visit AnnaLoweBooks.com